"I've seen nothing like *Dreaming Down-Under* before, probably the biggest, boldest, most controversial collection of original fiction ever published in Australia. It defines and concentrates and refines the 'wild side' of Australian fiction: magical realism, fantasy, science fiction, horror. Heady stuff. A word of caution: don't peer into the voids revealed to you by Dann and Webb before sleep — you may find yourself falling ... and falling ... "

— Peter Goldsworthy

"*Dreaming Down-Under* is a book on the edge. More importantly, it is a book that is on time. Speculative fiction in Australia is experiencing unprecedented growth and vitality, producing exciting and talented writers, who rank amongst the very best in the world today. *Dreaming Down-Under* is the single most coherent expression of this time, gathering together a staggering array of writers in the largest, and most comprehensive, anthology of Australian speculative fiction ever assembled.

As a book, *Dreaming Down-Under* manages to both survey the phenomenon of speculative fiction in Australia at the end of the 20th Century, and to define it. It may be the most important anthology of Australian speculative fiction ever published."

— Jonathan Strahan, co-editor of *The Year's Best Australian Science Fiction and Fantasy* and publisher of *Eidolon*

DREAMING DOWN-UNDER

BOOK ONE

DREAMING DOWN-UNDER

BOOK ONE

EDITED BY
JACK DANN AND JANEEN WEBB

HarperCollinsPublishers

Voyager
An imprint of HarperCollins*Publishers*, Australia

HarperCollins*Publishers*
First published in 1999
by HarperCollins*Publishers* Pty Limited
ACN 009 913 517
A member of the HarperCollins*Publishers* (Australia) Pty Limited Group
http://www.harpercollins.com.au

HarperCollins*Publishers*
25 Ryde Road, Pymble, Sydney, NSW 2073, Australia
31 View Road, Glenfield, Auckland 10, New Zealand
77–85 Fulham Palace Road, London, W6 8JB, United Kingdom
Hazelton Lanes, 55 Avenue Road, Suite 2900, Toronto, Ontario M5R 3L2
and 1995 Markham Road, Scarborough, Ontario M1B 5M8, Canada
10 East 53rd Street, New York NY 10022, USA

National Library of Australia Cataloguing-in-Publication data:

Dreaming down-under
    ISBN 0 7322 6404 9   (bk. 1)
    1. Short stories, Australian – 20th century. I. Dann, Jack. II. Webb, Janeen S.

A823.0108

Cover illustration by Nick Stathopoulos
Printed in Australia by Griffin Press Pty Ltd on 50gsm Ensobulky

9 8 7 6 5 4 3 2 1   99 00 01 02

In Memory of George Turner

ACKNOWLEDGMENTS

The editors would like to thank the following people for their help and support:

Justin Ackroyd of *Slow Glass Books*, Theresa Anns, Denise Barnes, Maurice Baker, Jeremy Byrne, Sean Cotcher, Edith Dann, Lorne Dann, Ellen Datlow, Jim Demetriou, Helen Doherty, Brian Douglas, Terry Dowling, Melanie and Lewis Downey, Sue Drakeford, Harlan and Susan Ellison, Andrew Enstice, Christine Farmer, Russell Farr, Keith Ferrell, Deonie Fiford, Laura Harris, Louise and Ron Harris, Merrilee Heifetz, Barrie Hitchon, Phil Klink, Belinda Lee, Angelo Loukakis, Anna McFarlane, Sean McMullen, Peter McNamara, Paul Montaut, Rod Morrison, Nicola O'Shea, Sue Page, Steve Paulsen, Robert and Opal Pemberton, Tracey Schatvet, Nick Stathopoulos, Jonathan Strahan, Dena Taylor, Kate Thomas, Louise Thurtell, Norman Tilley, John Wilkinson, and Kaye Wright.

CONTENTS

WHAT PASSES FOR A PREFACE

HARLAN ELLISON

How do you do? Or, if I were trying to ingratiate myself as some overcompensating tourists do, I'd say, "G'day". But since it is not my intention to hold you long, here at the beginning of this most excellent book, I will merely state that which is never nakedly spoken: I am an intruder here, and this book is the least book that ever needed preface.

I am a Person from Porlock, an interloper, a figurehead and "loss leader" whose brief ramblings have been solicited, and are tolerated, only because I have known Jack Dann for more than thirty years, because we are close friends, because I was lucky enough to have been at the right spot at the right time in the late sixties when editing a book like *Dangerous Visions* made me appear to be some sort of firebrand, cutting-edge champion of the Bold New Word. Well, that was then, and as the saying goes, this is now ... and my pal Jack has found himself at the right spot, at the right moment; and I am the resonating shadow that serves the purpose of foreshadowing echo.

But, in absolute truth, this book needs a preface from me — or anyone — about as much as a fish needs a bicycle. As much as the ghost of Himmler needs forgiveness. As much as a cyclotron needs a sphincter. I love metaphors. I could go on for days. As much as the Sphinx needs a new pair of Nikes.

In June of 1983 I visited Australia for the first time. To say that I fell in love with the very scent and sight of the down-under would be to diminish to the point of disrespect what I found there. Not the least of which was my poor benighted tourist moment when, somewhere above Arkaroo Rock, all alone, I fell willing supplicant to the Dreamtime and would likely have died out there had not Terry Dowling and Kerrie Hanlon found me and led me back to my life and the prescient world.

Most of all, I found a new world of literature in Australia. I had been a great admirer and friend of A. Bertram Chandler, the towering forefather of all the young growlers you'll find in this book, and I was one of the first Americans to recognise that Peter Carey was probably going to be the next Aussie (after Patrick White) to win the Nobel Prize for Literature; but until I met Damien Broderick, Terry Dowling and Stephen Dedman and the late, more than wonderful George Turner ... I had no idea of the depth of richness that existed in the pool of Australian fantasists.

I wanted desperately to connect with all that, to be the one — as I had been in the '60s — to let the light of all that talent shine here in the States and in England, where the arrogant imperialism of the New York/London *apparat* breathed heavily with its own certain wisdom that nowhere else was magic realism written at their level. I wanted to be the one to amass those talents who created great dreams while bowing their heads in a ridiculous cultural cringe to the titans of Anglo-American sf; I wanted to gather them and house them in an exhaustive anthology, and smack the New York publishing smirk across its mouth with a book that would convince them the New Wave was the *tsunami* from down-under. I got a contract, and I started soliciting stories, and I found Lucy Sussex, Norman Talbot, Sean McMullen and others, and ...

Well, I stumbled. The book never happened. *Down Deep* it was called. And it never happened. I couldn't keep my promise to the excellent writers I had met and bought and marvelled at.

I have led a productive, terrific life, filled with great happenings and splendid deeds. There are few things I regret not having accomplished. Do I need to write the next sentence?

And now, it is a decade and a half later; and the promise that trembled in the work I read in Perth, Brisbane, Sydney and Adelaide has exceeded even the most scintillant of my expectations. Dowling, Egan, McMullen and all the ones who have come rushing in after them, have created a superimposed pre-continuum of excellence that makes the weary, inbred, commercially-bloated output of most of what passes for modern American science-fantasy read like the drivel found on the backs of cereal boxes.

Jack and Janeen have found themselves at the right spot, at the right moment; and the result is this huge testament to the new order of things literary in this genre. They have edited the book I wanted to do.

And they seem to think that allowing me to jingle my cap and bells here in this corner is a fitting tribute to *Dangerous Visions*, to June of 1983 and January of 1996 when I came back to the aborted vision that would have been *Down Deep*. They think they honour me.

I hate them for it. I envy them more that I can say, I burn with shame at my failure, I grit my teeth in frustration at how powerful a collection they have put together, and the only thing that keeps me from killing the pair of them is that they are my long-term friends and I love them. But oh! how this hurts; and oh! how unnecessary is a preface, by me or anyone else.

Because the work, all this work, all this fresh, tough and brilliant work, all these stories, they need no California fantasist to shill for them. They speak for themselves. They have voices. Now, go away; and listen to them.

Harlan Ellison
Los Angeles
9 September 1998

INTRODUCTION

BY JACK DANN AND JANEEN WEBB

Sometimes history repeats itself . . .

In 1967 the American author and editor Harlan Ellison wrote: "What you hold in your hands is more than a book. If we are lucky, it is a revolution.

"This book . . . the largest anthology of speculative fiction ever published of *all* original stories, and easily one of the largest of *any* kind, was constructed along specific lines of revolution. It was intended to shake things up. It was conceived out of a need for new horizons, new forms, new styles, new challenges in the literature of our times."

That book was *Dangerous Visions*.

It was a lightning rod for the "New Wave" literary movement that was taking place in England and the United States in the late '60s. The "New Wave" was a movement toward literary experimentation in science fiction. Authors such as J.G. Ballard, Brian Aldiss, Thomas N. Disch, R.A. Lafferty, Samuel Delany, Sonya Dorman, Carol Emshwiller, Ursula K. Le Guin, Pamela Zoline, Roger Zelazny, Kate Wilhelm, Joanna Russ, Robert Silverberg, M. John Harrison, James Tiptree Jr, Josephine Saxton, Norman Spinrad, Michael Moorcock, and Harlan Ellison himself, opened up the genre to the literary tropes of "mainstream" literature, broke down the boundaries between science fiction and other forms of fiction and, perhaps most importantly, produced some of the finest work in the history of the genre.

It was a heady, exciting time. It was the new zeitgeist, and science fiction would never be the same after that.

Fast forward to January 1996 ...

Your editors were the guests of a conference in Sydney, sponsored by Qantas Airlines and the Powerhouse Museum. Harlan Ellison was the featured guest. We were on a panel called "The Australian Renaissance". The auditorium was packed with science fiction readers ... *and* with some of Australia's most important writers — from multiple award winners such as Terry Dowling and Sean McMullen to hot "new" writers such as Sean Williams. At one point in the panel discussion Harlan leaned over the speakers' table, pointed at the audience, and said, "Do you guys *understand* that this is the Golden Age of Australian science fiction? Do you realise that you're living it right now? This is it. And I'll be damned if I don't envy you!"

The effect was electric. We all felt that we were indeed participating in something new and exciting ... something that was filled with possibility.

And Harlan was right. We *are* in a Golden Age.

Or it damn well feels that way.

*　*　*

There is a bit of history echoing in Harlan's words, a reference to a period in American science fiction that we fondly call ... the Golden Age. It began when the late John W. Campbell took over the editorship of *Astounding Stories* in 1937. Campbell wanted rigorously extrapolative and *literate* science fiction stories (not the stereotypical super-hero space opera that dominated the "pulps" of the '30s), and he developed new writers to write them, writers such as Isaac Asimov, A.E. van Vogt, Robert Heinlein, Lester del Rey, Eric Frank Russell, Alfred Bester, Frederic Brown, Arthur C. Clarke — and the list goes on and on. This "Golden Age" continued right through the '40s, and what a time it was — the tropes and devices and conceptual "furniture" of modern science fiction were being created in the magazines; and the best stories contained "real" science, they were well plotted and well-written, and they were intellectually and emotionally thrilling.

They instilled the proverbial sense of wonder in the readers.

The stories in Harlan's anthology instilled that same sense of wonder for a new generation ... but many of those who had grown up with and loved the old *Astounding* stories scratched their heads in bemusement at what they considered the dangerous literary experimentation in *Dangerous Visions*. But *Dangerous Visions* wasn't just about literary experimentation; it was about showcasing the finest stories by the finest writers. It became the book to point to when someone asked you, "What is this New Wave business all about?"

Which brings us to the anthology you're holding in your hands ... and what's really going on in Australia.

*　*　*

There's a long history that connects Australia with speculative fiction of one sort and another. Way back in 1726 Jonathan Swift extrapolated the geography of

Gulliver's Travels from pirate captain William Dampier's 1697 bestseller, *A New Voyage Around the World*. Swift set the land of Lilliput in what we now call South Australia.

When the white settlers eventually came to what was, from their perspective, the most alien of continents, the idea of the lost race, the undiscovered civilization that surely *must* be out there somewhere, held a peculiar fascination. Australian authors populated the mysterious interior of the continent with everything from the lost tribes of Israel to the last of the Lemurians.

Once Darwin's *Origin of Species* was published in 1859, the lost race stories amalgamated with new scientific romances, and Australia found itself host to any number of missing link stories such as the anonymous *An Account of a Race of Human Beings with Tails* (1873) and Austyn Granville's *The Fallen Race* (1892).

As scientific romances grew in popularity around the world, Australian writers added their voices to the growing genre, and some of the internationally common themes emerged here. A case in point is Robert Potter's 1892 Melbourne novel, *The Germ Growers*, which has the doubly dubious distinction of being the first story about "alien invasion", and also the prototype story of "germ warfare".

Less pessimistic Utopian models were also popular in early Australian works such as Joseph Fraser's *Melbourne and Mars: My Mysterious Life on Two Planets* (1889) and G. McIvor's *Neuroomia* (1894). Feminist speculations were also with us early on, with works such as Catherine Helen Spence's *Handfasted*

(1879), Millie Finkelstein's *The Newest Woman: The Destined Monarch of the World* (1895), and Mary Anne Moore-Bentley's *A Woman of Mars, or Australia's Enfranchised Woman* (1901) leading the way to future worlds where women hold positions of power.

Mid-nineteenth century gold-rush Australia also began producing darker speculative writing in racist and xenophobic fictions that played on popular fears of "Asian invasion", in works such as the anonymous *The Battle of Mordialloc, or How We Lost Australia* (1888), "Sketcher" (William Lane)'s *White or Yellow? A Story of the Race War of A.D. 1908*, Kenneth Mackay's *The Yellow Wave: A Romance of the Asiatic Invasion of Australia* (1895), "Rata" (Thomas Roydhouse)'s *The Coloured Conquest*, and C.H. Kirmess's *The Australian Crisis* (1909). This is a theme that spilled over into the twentieth century, in works such as A.J. Pullar's *Celestalia: A Fantasy A.D. 1975* (1933), Erle Cox's *Fool's Harvest* (1939), and John Hay's *The Invasion* (1968). Erle Cox further explored the vexed question of white racial dominance in his famous 1919/1925 novel, *Out of the Silence*.

There were also tough minded visions that depicted Australia as the future centre of the world, its young civilization surviving the inevitable collapse of the old Europe. Works such as Henry Crocker Marriot-Watson's *The Decline and Fall of the British Empire, or The Witch's Cavern* (1890) explore this post-disaster theme, a theme that was to continue later this century in post-apocalyptic novels such as Nevil Shute's *On The Beach* (1957) — which became the first science fiction movie to be written, set and filmed in Australia.

Like any genre, speculative writing in Australia has had its ups and downs. The 1930s and 1940s were lean times, though we should not overlook works such as J.M. Walsh's *Vandals of the Void* (1931) or M. Barnard Eldershaw's important *Tomorrow and Tomorrow and Tomorrow* (1947), which was cut by the censor and not restored to full text until 1983. The 1950s saw renewed interest, with magazines like *Thrills Incorporated* (1950–52), *Future Science Fiction* and *Popular Science Fiction* (1953–55) and *Science-Fiction Monthly* (1955–56) publishing local authors: Anglo-Australian Norma Hemming for one. Australian authors like A. Bertram Chandler and Wynne Whiteford were now making it in the USA and UK magazines, and were joined in the 1960s by writers such as John Baxter, Damien Broderick, Lee Harding and Jack Wodhams. Yet the local market remained tiny, and the sense that overseas publication was essential to any serious career loomed large for Australian writers.

The 1970s saw the arrival of Paul Collins' *Void* magazine, which published local writers, and the emergence of more new science fiction writers, especially George Turner, who already had an established mainstream literary career. The growth accelerated through the 1980s, with the emergence of Terry Dowling and Greg Egan (who have both won major international awards), and into the 1990s with its impressive crop of new writers.

*　*　*

After all this, why are we talking *now* about a Golden Age?

In the last few years there has been a yeasty literary foment going on in the science fiction, fantasy, and horror genres. A recognition of the sales potential of genre fiction by major publishers in Australia — and the introduction here of science fiction imprints such as HarperCollins' Voyager; the healthy vitality and competition of Australia's two major science fiction and fantasy magazines, *Eidolon* and *Aurealis*; the annual *Year's Best* edited by Jonathan Strahan and Jeremy Byrne; new professional awards such as the Aurealis Award and the Turner Award, as well as the well-established Ditmar Award (which is voted on by readers), have all combined to produce this foment. There are new and vigorous small presses right around the country: *Eidolon* and *Ticonderoga* in Perth, *Aphelion* in Adelaide, *MirrorDanse* and *Five Islands Press* in Sydney, *Sybylla Feminist Press* in Melbourne, *Desdichado* in Hobart, all are pushing the boundaries, adding to the mix by publishing a vast quirky range of speculative titles.

But even all of the above wouldn't be enough. We needed to smash the idea that we were isolated, too far away from the cultural meccas where the action was.

We needed to be "in the loop"; and thanks to the information revolution — that combination of the internet, e-mail, fax and phone — the distance has all but been eliminated. Many of the writers in this anthology now have US agents and publish regularly in the US, the UK, and Europe. Australian science fiction is appearing regularly in American "Best of the Year" collections and receiving serious international critical attention; it is being perceived as vital and interesting . . . and more importantly, *we've* discovered that the "action" isn't always somewhere else. It's right here.

Although Australia's much discussed "cultural cringe" — the idea that the real culture, the real action, the "party" always has to be somewhere else — is still around, it's getting harder to find it in the genre. Australian writers have gone beyond the limiting notion that being "international" somehow meant not admitting to an Australian accent. They are e-mailing each other, discussing new ideas among themselves and with writers and critics in England and Europe and America, travelling to see each other, workshopping stories, going to conventions, collaborating, criticising, encouraging new writers, and revelling in the idea of being part of an exciting, expanding, extended literary community. And they are producing world class works whose Australian identity is neither parochial nor sentimental.

However the pundits try to describe it, everyone involved in this process can sense its energy. It *feels* like a revolution. There's *something* new and vibrant and exciting going on. Maybe it's a renaissance. Maybe it's just a confluence of talent in this English-speaking region of the world. Or maybe, as one editor said when Asimov and Clark and Pohl suddenly started producing some of their most vital and interesting work late in their careers ... maybe it's sunspots!

* * *

Dreaming Down-Under was conceived to shake up the established thinking about the "shape" of contemporary writing in Australia: to open up — and redefine — the literary canon to include the non-mimetic side of our literature. Author and critic John Gardner was fond of reminding students that fiction is a "waking dream"; and this conception of the term "dreaming" has a special resonance for contemporary Australian writers, writers who share a landscape rich in tradition, rich in possibility. Writers who are exploring their landscapes of the mind in works that are imaginative, visionary, fanciful, extrapolative, extravagant, quixotic.

There has never been a collection of speculative fiction in Australia quite like this. This is a showcase of the very best contemporary "wild-side fiction" (those stories that have an edge of horror or fantasy, or could be categorised as magical realism) and the very best genre fiction — science fiction, fantasy, and horror. This book contains over 100,000 words of original fiction and another 10,000 words of notes by your editors and thoughts by the writers on their stories. And even with 110,000 words, there are *still* so many wonderful writers who for one reason or another are absent from these pages, writers such as Peter Goldsworthy, Greg Egan, Yvonne Rousseau, Richard Harland, Penelope Love, Sue Woolfe, Leanne Frahm, and the list could go on and on.

Dreaming Down-Under raised the bar for writers in Australia. We asked the best authors working in the field to write the story they wanted to be remembered for. We weren't willing to compromise ... to accept mediocre work from big name authors. In fact, three "name" authors actually rejected stories they had already sent to us — they didn't think the stories were quite good enough, and so they sent us new stories, which we bought!

Our only criterion was quality.

So this is it — a showcase of some of the very best work being done in Australia, a compendium of stories intended to produce in you that unique intellectual and visceral thrill we have always identified as "sense of wonder"; and if we're lucky, this book will become the lightning rod for Australia's Golden Age ... or renaissance ... or revolution ... or zeitgeist.

Or perhaps it will just show off the sunspots!

As Harlan said about his volume some thirty years ago, "If it was done properly, it will provide these new horizons and styles and forms and challenges. If not, it is still one helluva good book full of entertaining stories."

Lastly, this book is dedicated to the late George Turner, one of Australia's finest authors, who thoroughly enjoyed being at the cutting edge of Australian writing, enjoyed the most rigorous of debates, enjoyed turning convention on its head.

George, this one's for you!

SEAN WILLIAMS

Sean Williams is the author of *Metal Fatigue*, which won the Aurealis Award for Best Science Fiction Novel of 1996; *Doorway to Eternity*, a collection of three novelettes; and *The Resurrected Man*. He has also written *The Unknown Soldier* (with Shane Dix) — this novel has been reworked into the first book of a new trilogy and will see print simultaneously in the US and Australia.

Since 1991, he has sold almost fifty short stories and novellas to magazines and anthologies in Australia and overseas. His story "Passing the Bone" won the Aurealis Award for Best Horror Short Story of 1996. He is also a past prize-winner of the international Writers of the Future Contest.

Sean lives in Adelaide, works in a CD shop, (cooks a mean curry), reviews for *Eidolon*, was a judge for the Aurealis Awards in 1995, and he is also one of the hottest "new" writers in Australia. The science fiction newsmagazine *Locus* wrote that "it's a safe bet that Williams will turn into another of Australia's impressive sequence of major science fiction discoveries."

In the story that follows, he brings to life the beauty, decadence, and dangers that are only to be found in the privileged world of the living dead.

ENTRE LES BEAUX MORTS EN VIE (AMONG THE BEAUTIFUL LIVING DEAD)

SEAN WILLIAMS

Le Chateau de la Mort Dorée — known as Fool's-Death House in the vernacular — was situated halfway up the vertical flank of a mountain not ten minute's powered flight from Jungfrau, in the region that had once been called Switzerland. Sandwiched between stone and air, the sprawling, rococo structure with its four hundred luxury rooms and five banquet halls looked like a pimple on a granite giant's cheek. Tunnels, elevators and airships provided the usual means of gaining access. Only a few people dared to climb in person. The view from the Chateau's tiered terraces was spectacular enough to negate the need for such foolhardy, if courageous, gestures.

Yet some people still made the effort. Ordinary people, of course; never the reves themselves, although this was one of their favourite sites. Of anyone on Earth and off, the reves knew best how fragile life could be. Yet how resilient.

All this passed through Martin Winterford's mind as he stepped off the airship and onto the Chateau's wide receiving platform. Buffeted by the crisp, mountain wind, and with the setting sun hidden behind a mile of solid rock, he experienced a moment of near-*satori*. This, the first time he had visited the Chateau, would possibly be the last — in his lifetime. Although he would no doubt return many times, if he chose to accept his uncle's ultimatum, it would be as a reve, and he would no longer be, by ancient definition, alive.

He tried to reassure himself that, living or dead, by whatever definition, it made no difference to *him* — but the doubt still nagged two hours later, as *La Célébration Annuelle* began.

*　　*　　*

"*Je vois que vous êtes en souffrance le changement,*" said a melodic voice. "*Apprendez-vous déjà le français?*"

Martin turned. A tall woman in a white silk ball-gown, complete with gloves, fan and blonde coiffure, had come up behind him. The skin of her shoulders and throat was bare and very pale, flawless. Her eyes were the deepest brown he had ever seen, her lips the richest red.

"I'm sorry, but I don't speak Old French," he said, raising his champagne flute to cover his uneasiness. Make-up couldn't hide the truth, not from so close. Not that she wanted to, either, or else she wouldn't have left her shoulders and throat exposed. The woman was a reve.

"*Pas mal,*" continued the woman. "*Vous aurai beaucoup du temps à combler son retard.*"

He shook his head, nervousness becoming irritation at her persistence. If she wanted to be fashionable, why didn't she find someone else to do it with?

With an amused smile — perhaps at his expense, he couldn't tell — she raised her fan and indicated that he should follow her into the next room. Martin hesitated for a moment, then obeyed. He had nothing better to do. The party, for all its glamour and opulence, had proved to be slightly dull. Its many cliques left him wandering alone, wary of intruding.

"You'll have to pardon me," said the woman over her shoulder as she led him through the crowd, past two tables piled high with exotic hors d'oeuvres and wines, mostly untouched. He caught a hint of delicate perfume in her wake. "We like to have our little games. Someone must educate the newcomers, put them through a rite of passage. That is our purpose here at the Chateau — unofficially, at least. It's important, *n'est-ce pas*?"

Martin simply nodded at first. The woman's perfect English, with its qualifiers and clauses, threw him so off-balance that what she actually said didn't register until they were half-way across the room.

"You *know*?" he exclaimed, wondering what had given him away. He had chosen his outfit carefully: a black suit with ruffs at neck and collars, leather shoes and skull-cap. He had hoped to remain anonymous.

"Of course," said the woman. "I am observant. There are three hundred and twenty-seven guests attending this *soirée*, of which seventy-nine are revenants. Two hundred and forty-five are government officials: doctors, diplomats and examiners, mainly, all known to me either personally or by reputation. That leaves three." Her eyes twinkled. "You are clearly not a waiter, for you cannot speak French. Besides, your age seems about right."

Martin didn't bother denying the truth. If games were her *métier*, then he would acknowledge defeat early. Either that, or risk arousing a deeper interest that he could not afford to indulge.

"Where are you taking me?" he asked, more curious than concerned for the moment.

"Does it matter?" She fluttered her fake eyelashes and pouted like a teenager. "Our table is boring, boring, boring. It lacks interesting conversation — or interesting people to make conversation, perhaps I should say. I was in the process of looking for someone to liven up the evening when I spotted you." Her smile returned as they weaved past a cluster of potted palms and through an arched entrance-way. "Would you care to join us?"

Martin side-stepped a waiter carrying a tray of garishly coloured drinks. The banquet hall looked like something plucked from Eighteenth Century Europe, with gilded walls, a string quartet playing in one corner and crystal chandeliers suspended from a high, domed ceiling. He raised his voice to be heard over a melange of music and speech filling the room.

"Do I have a choice?"

"Of course. Don't be obtuse, my dear. You have a choice in everything."

Again the coquettish flutter that did nothing to ease his disquiet. The echo of his uncle's words was uncanny. But before he could answer, the woman brought him to a halt with a hand on his chest.

"Ah," she said, "here we are. Why don't you take a seat ... I'm sorry? I didn't catch your name."

Martin faltered. The table before them held six "people". He stared at them dumbly until he realised that they were all staring back at him just as hard.

He turned to face the woman who had led him to the table. Only then did he realise that her words had been a question. He almost blurted out his full name before natural caution caught up.

"My name is Martin," he managed. "And —?"

"Allow me to introduce you." The woman gestured around the table with a flourish of her fan. A fat man in purple robes was Professor Algiers Munton of the Revenation Institute in New York. M. Elaine Bennett, a narrow-faced, female reve dressed in simple grey peasant attire, hailed from Port Moresby. The sexless mod with orange veins glowing under its ceremonial skin and the AI node sporting the usual black suit preferred by the AI conglomerates for formal occasions were Alkis and PERIPETY-WEYN, both from the Moon's Armstrong Base. An android rem from Attar, judging by its coat of arms, was being ridden by someone called "*Le Comptable Froid*", or "Count" to his friends, who had been unable to make the physical journey from that remote moonlet to Earth in time for the Celebration. All indicated their pleasure at meeting him with nods, smiles or brief but sincere hellos.

Only the last member of the small party, a bald young man wearing a blue period suit, remained silent when introduced as "Spyro Xenophou", and went otherwise — almost pointedly — unexplained.

Martin swallowed, his mouth dry, after greeting them all in return. What had his uncle said when news of his application had arrived? No true aliens, but plenty that *seem* alien ...? As a summary of his current situation, that would do as well as any other.

"Sit, sit." The woman — *reve*, he reminded himself, although the distinction seemed like splitting hairs in such a crowd — ushered Martin towards a chair. "Or leave. If you're going to make a fool of me by declining my invitation, then at least do so quickly. Don't allow me to waste any further breath. Air is rarefied so high in the mountains, you know."

"I beg to disagree," broke in the Count via his rem, its artificial voice smooth but eerily inhuman. The lag between Earth and Attar was much smaller than Martin would have credited, so-called instantaneous transmissions still usually taking a second or two. "Had I access to atmosphere as 'rarefied' as yours," the Count said, "I could increase my profit by four hundred percent."

"Don't be such a wet blanket," chided the woman with fleeting *moue*. "And don't interrupt. I haven't finished introductions yet."

Martin lowered himself with a sigh of relief into the only available seat, either a genuine antique or a very good copy of a Louis XIV. "Please," he said. "I'd be grateful."

"Of course. I, dear Martin, am the Reve Guillard — although you can call me Marianne if you prefer. I am most pleased to make your acquaintance."

Without the slightest self-consciousness, the immortal woman extended her hand to be kissed.

The only other reve at the table, Elaine Bennett, smiled at the expression on Martin's face as he reached out to clasp the cold, perfect fingers. The Reve Guillard had been a contemporary of Paul Merrick — the world's first reve and founder of the Plutocracy. Her age was therefore somewhere between four hundred and eighty and five hundred years. Martin felt like he was touching a precious work of art, or a shrine. His lips tingled when she withdrew her hand, as though some of her had rubbed off on him.

"I am honoured, M. Guillard," he said.

The woman waved her fan; in another age, another body, she might have blushed. "*C'est peu de*," she said. "And please do call me Marianne. I'd hate to have to insist."

"Thank you." He felt dizzy; the rush of blood to his face threatened to overwhelm his brain. As he tried to regain his composure, he was acutely aware of the silent young man watching him closely, almost resentfully. It bothered him, but he couldn't afford to let it distract him.

Perhaps sensing the new arrival's discomfort, the AI node stepped in to fill the silence. "We were discussing the latest trend," PERIPETY-WEYN said. "*Le mode du temps*, as it were. M. Bennett noted some interesting parallels between it and the French Revolution."

"Naturally she would," M. Guillard said, assuming control of the conversation with confident ease. "And she is correct: there *are* superficial parallels. The term 'plutocracy' was not chosen lightly, you know."

"And not without a sense of humour," said the mod, Alkis.

"Yes." M. Guillard cast the cyborg an ambiguous look. "Paul always liked puns. But the similarities run no deeper than that. The trend for things Old French is deliberate, not symbolic of some deeper human conflict. How could there be a French Revolution today when the members of the ruling class, no matter how wealthy they might be, are already dead? Besides, next year it might be Twenty-First Century America that takes our fancy, or White Russia."

"Each with its own revolution," the mod observed.

"Yes, yes, Alkis. That too is deliberate. We gravitate towards potent times in order to stave off boredom —"

"Or to allay subconscious guilt," interrupted M. Bennett with a grimace. "Or fear."

"Nonsense. You imagine cause in a world of effects."

"I feel it." M. Bennett met the Reve Guillard's stare unflinchingly. "In my youth, I felt it too."

"*Naturellement, ma chère.* And that is why you are here: because you are something of a radical. We require diversity and dissent if we are to remain vital." M. Guillard flapped once with her fan, and sighed theatrically. "Do you see what I mean now, Martin?" she asked, pinning him with her wide, brown eyes. "These are old arguments, centuries-worn and boring, boring, boring! Why don't you tell us about yourself instead? Who invited you here this evening?"

Martin leaned forward and chose his words with care. "My sponsor, ah, Gerome Packard, thought it might be a good idea."

"Did he, now? That sounds like uncommonly good sense from dear Gerome."

"He said it would help me acclimatise."

"Socially, yes. Physically, probably not. No-one can predict with certainty the effects of revenation on a given individual."

"I take it, then," put in the mod, "that you are aspiring to the Change?"

Martin felt sweat bead on the back of his neck. *Maybe one day, I'll be like her — the Reve Guillard.* "My application was approved five weeks ago," he said to avoid a direct answer.

"Interesting." The mod folded its glowing hands on the table. "Of all the alternatives presently available, revenation remains the only proven means of achieving extreme human longevity. I envy you the opportunity."

"Thank you, Sir." Coming from a mod, that was candour indeed. "Sometimes I wonder whether it's really going to happen."

"No doubt. You must be nervous," said Professor Munton. "I would be, in your shoes."

Seeking a distraction, Martin hailed a waiter. One appeared instantly at his shoulder. He offered to pay the round, but only Professor Munton joined him in ordering a drink. None of the others required fluid intake, being either self-sufficient within themselves or partial to other means of gaining nutrients.

"How long until your birthday?" asked the AI node when the waiter had departed.

"One month," Martin answered, realising that the topic would not be so easily evaded.

"I presume you are cognisant of the risks, then?"

"Yes." That Martin could answer with certainty. His Uncle Arthur had more frequent dealings with the Plutocracy than most people; he had made sure that Martin knew what was at stake. "Of every ten thousand inductees, one will never wake from the death-sleep."

"And a dozen others will experience difficult transitions," added M. Bennett, glancing at the bald young man. "Even today, after hundreds of years of research, a sound awakening alone is no guarantee of success."

With a jolt, Martin suddenly realised what Spyro Xenophou was. Braving the young man's dark stare, he asked him directly: "When was *your* birthday?"

"In June," M. Guillard answered for him. "You'll have to forgive my ward, Martin. He woke six weeks ago and hasn't spoken since. Part of him resists; the fear of death is strong in him still." She shrugged. "It is often that way with the more established families, although that seems paradoxical."

"Not really," said the AI node. "Social evolution, albeit relatively rapid in the last five hundred years, still has a long way to go before it eradicates the base impulses present in every human. The concept of passing through death is still paralysing, I am told, even among those for whom revenation is a common occurrence."

"That would not be the case if it were available to all who wanted it," said M. Bennett. "By restricting the process, we perpetuate a class system that is both prejudicial and morally abhorrent."

"The system of Houses makes perfect sense, and you know it," M. Guillard insisted. "Otherwise there would be chaos. Even with the present ratio of one reve for every four thousand natural humans, there are problems."

"I must concur," said the android. "By removing the tools of government from the hands of the short-lived, Earth and the rest of the System has achieved the kind of long-term stability only dreamed about in pre-history."

"But at what cost?" M. Bennett accentuated her point with one finger on the table-top. "The Plutocracy is in-bred and constantly at risk of stagnation."

"Hence the revolutionary trends," said the mod. "Balance, feedback, homeostasis."

"*Desperation*," retaliated M. Bennett. "We may reach for the stars, but inside we are all still frightened children in need of reassurance."

Martin sank back into his seat, glad that the spotlight had drifted from him. Both his sponsor and uncle had warned him to steer clear of such debates, to be wary of associating with any one camp among the reves. There would plenty of time for that after his induction. If things went as planned, he would have centuries in which to grapple with the arguments for and against — although he believed that he already understood it well enough to reach his own conclusion. The problem was that it kept changing.

Revenation was an expensive process, restricted by necessity to the few. Applicants had not only to demonstrate fitness but ability to pay their way through the process and out the other side. A single immortal life would be an expensive burden upon the welfare system if that person proved to be unproductive. As result, only wealthy families could afford to raise a member to reve status. And the wealthiest families already contained significantly large numbers of reves; some had even brought their line to an end in order to spare a single member from death, although this practice had waned over the years.

Hence the appearance — illusory or not — of in-breeding, and of decadence.

Watching M. Guillard speak, with her many gestures and flourishes, the often direct way she manipulated conversation to suit her own agenda, Martin was reminded of his school-years, and the rumours that had circulated among his fellow students. The reves were vampires, he had been told once: un-dead and un-living creatures frozen forever in a state of inanimate animation. Infrequent glimpses had confirmed this impression: of pallid, beautiful people riding past in patient comfort; aloof and isolated, even dismissive at times. Although information was wide-spread about the truth, it had only added to their mysteriousness: cut a reve and it failed to bleed; bury another, and it could be exhumed without damage a month or a century later; expose a third to deadly viruses and its pseudo-animate cells would be completely unaffected.

Yet inflict upon any reve a magnetic field of more than a few thousand Tesla and he or she would experience spasms, even unconsciousness. Or put it to the flame and watch it burn like summer kindling to nothing, as though its life had vanished in a single, sudden flash.

Reves were potentially immortal, and some — such as M. Bennett, a reve herself — would add *immoral* to the charge. In his younger years, Martin had hated and feared them. But now he was among them, potentially about to become one of them. He found the thought wildly disorienting.

The string quartet playing in the background had acquired a singer. To the tune of an ancient folk-song, she began to recite:

On the golden hill where the sun once stood,
and the blood-red man with hearts for eyes
sold words that sung of forever, forever,
Paul Merrick found his first love, and died.

Martin wondered to himself whether the man who had given immortality to the world had felt the same confusion when choosing life over mortal passion. Perhaps he was still feeling it today. Sadly, Martin was unable to question him directly, since the reve had departed for Capella two hundred years ago. And in the end, he supposed, there could only be one answer.

Humanity's ambassador to the stars was only nominally human. That fact alone spoke volumes.

Survival of the fittest ...

"To which Familial Affiliate do you belong, Martin?" asked Professor Munton, startling him out of his reverie.

Martin inwardly cursed himself for not paying attention. The question, easily anticipated once the subject had been brought up, was one he had nonetheless hoped to avoid. Confronted with it, he mentally tossed a coin, and honesty won. In the back of his mind, he heard his uncle curse in turn.

"None," he replied to the fat man's question.

"Impossible," stated M. Bennett. "There hasn't been a foundling House for three hundred years."

"That's correct," said M. Guillard. "Unless — wait! Martin, you wouldn't be the son of that engineer we've been hearing about, would you? Alex Winterford, wasn't that his name?"

He shrugged. There was no use denying it. "At your service."

"Oh, tremendous!" The fat scholar clapped once. "Marianne, what a coup! The founding father of the House Winterford, right here at our table! You couldn't have brought anybody more interesting to talk to had it been Paul Merrick himself! Tell me, Martin —"

"*Attends*, Algiers." M. Guillard raised a finger to her lips. "Don't jinx the poor boy before his time. Let him tell his own story at his own pace."

"Do I have to?" Although Martin didn't want to sound churlish, he couldn't help it.

"Of course not, as I said before." M. Guillard winked. "You can leave if you'd rather not talk."

"I'd rather not do either, to be honest."

"Tish. What do you fear? That we will embarrass you, or judge you? If the latter, please bear in mind the diverse natures arrayed at this table. Surely you realise that our opinions will be firmly divided?"

"Too true." The mod's skin rippled a pale green.

"And you shouldn't be afraid of your innocence, if that's the case," said M. Bennett, regarding Martin with intense eyes. "It is your very naivety we crave. So much time has passed since someone new joined our ranks that any uncorrupted viewpoint is welcome."

"'Uncorrupted', Elaine?" asked M. Guillard. "By what, exactly?"

"By *reves*, of course, Marianne." M. Bennett scowled across the table at the older woman. "Or '*tous les beaux morts en vie*', if you prefer. There are none in his immediate family. The only one he's ever met in person, prior to now, would be his sponsor — and then only after his application was approved. His viewpoint will be quite external to our affairs, and all the more valuable for it."

"Is that true, Martin?" asked the rem. "You came this far without a patron ward, or even a beneficiary?"

Martin studied the faces watching him expectantly, and realised just how expertly he had been trapped. To refuse an answer now would be insulting, and to answer incompletely would only encourage more questions. Still, just because he had been backed into a cul-de-sac didn't mean he had to abandon common sense. He would be better off revealing a measure of the truth before all of it was pried out of him, hoping all the while that they would grow tired of him sooner rather than later.

"Yes," he said. "A paternal great-uncle ran a water mine on Titan for a while, I think, and my grandmother helped design a starship, but none of my blood ancestors came close to meeting the fiscal requirements."

"What changed?" prompted the mod.

"My Uncle Arthur and Aunt Sue both forewent their reproductive rights to further their careers," he explained with deliberate paucity of detail. "At the same time, my father followed my grandmother into aerospace design and patented an improvement on the Komalchi drive. These three incomes combined were enough to guarantee either myself or my sister a hearing from the Applications Board."

M. Bennett frowned at that. "I've heard of whole families pooling their resources — large families, too — and not coming close."

"Didn't you catch the names, Elaine?" asked M. Guillard, her smile as cutting as a shark's. "Arthur Winterford, despite his short-lived status, is Chief Executive Officer of the American Multi-Immersal

Conglomerate, which currently controls twenty-seven percent of the System's broadcast media. And Martin's mother's sister, Susan Firth, prefers to operate under the *nom de plume* 'Jenny Martinez' in order to avoid accusations of nepotism."

Among the raised eyebrows, where allowed by physique, and the silent surprise evident in every stare, only one voice stood out:

"Jenny who?"

M. Guillard pursed her lips in annoyance. "Really, Count. You can't be that isolated, can you? M. Martinez is the author credited with the resurgence of the novel — the planet's first best-seller in four hundred years."

"News to me, I'm afraid." The rem turned to face Martin. "The AMIC and Komalchi connections both make sense, though. Your grandmother must be proud to have such successful children."

"She would have been, I'm sure. She died when I was fifteen, just before I made my primary application."

"I'm sorry. Is there a connection between the two events?"

"Obviously there is," said the AI node before Martin could answer: "*Mortality*."

Martin confirmed this with a nod, unwilling to elaborate how close to the mark the AI node's guess was. His uncle's grief had been profound at the death of his mother. Restricted by breeding laws to families no larger than four, with only one child inheriting that generation's right to reproduce in turn, mortal humanity had become well-used to uncles and aunts leaving their estates to siblings' progeny. In Martin's case, and his sister's, that had amounted to a fortune almost too vast to comprehend. When his uncle had first suggested that they should use this capital to advance one family member to reve status — thereby removing him or her forever from the threat of age and natural death — he had in part been motivated by that grief, and fear that another loved-one would succumb before he did. At least this way, one child would have a chance of avoiding the fate awaiting the remainder of his family.

In part, anyway. The rest Martin had no intention of even thinking in such company.

"You mentioned a sister," said M. Bennett. "You were chosen above her, is that correct?"

"No. I'm older and therefore theoretically first in line, yes, but that wasn't really an issue. She wants to have children, you see."

"And you don't?" The question was playfully put by M. Guillard.

Don't I? Martin asked himself, although he knew the only answer he could give: "Whether I failed the examination, or fail at the Change, or not, is irrelevant. I was sterilised at thirteen, and have always expected to be childless. Perhaps a niece or nephew will follow me, one day, if I succeed."

"Nobly put." The ancient reve touched his arm lightly. "Indeed, once a family is established, subsequent revenations from that line become more likely with time. The chances are you will have blood relations to keep you company before long."

"I hope so."

"*Certainement.*" M. Guillard pulled away. "But look, Martin, your glass is empty. Spyro will top you up while you tell us about your plans for the future, if you have any."

"I haven't really thought that far ahead," he lied, handing his glass over. The bald reve took it from him without comment and collected the scholar's as well before heading off through the crowd.

"No?" M. Guillard expressed her disappointment with a sniff, then brightened. "I know what we'll do, then. We'll advise you now. What do you think, Elaine? Plutocrat or star-voyager? How best should Martin while away eternity?"

M. Bennett shrugged noncommittally before suggesting the former. PERIPETY-WEYN, the AI node, immediately disagreed, and went on at length to explain that, in his opinion, the System government was stable, and would be for a very long time; what was needed was not more politicians, but explorers with courage enough to venture into the dark.

"Courage is for the young," said M. Bennett, with which M. Guillard solemnly agreed.

✳   ✳   ✳

Martin settled back into his chair to listen while his future was dissected; when pressed for an opinion, he hinted at the possibility of becoming an artist. That was a vocation he had considered as a child, before the death of his grandmother, when life had seemed so much simpler.

Until he made his decision, all he really had to do was watch, and learn. After that, his uncle and fate could toss coins to see what happened next. At least for the moment, he had managed to avoid M. Guillard's probing curiosity.

When the time came, four gruelling hours later, to announce that he had decided to retire for the night, he declined the offer of stimulants from the bar. Although he had enjoyed the company of M. Guillard's friends, he was no match for them — intellectually or physically. He had heard that reves could party for days on end; certainly they could discuss a single topic for hours without losing interest. When one's life was measured in centuries, he supposed, the everyday passage of time became somewhat trivial.

He wasn't yet at that stage, and Professor Munton never would be. The fat scholar had left an hour ago, wishing Martin the very best of futures and expressing sincere hope that they would meet again another day.

As Martin bade his own farewells around the table, shaking hands with all but the mod, who deferred physical contact for a simple bow, M. Guillard saved herself and the enigmatic mute deliberately until last.

"It has been a pleasure, Martin," she said when it was her turn, curtsying expertly.

"The honour was mine," he replied, although he hadn't failed to notice the way she had deflected conversation from her own affairs. He knew as little about her now as he had before: that she was a multi-faceted enigma twisting like a bauble in one of the chandeliers above their heads, casting brilliant reflections wherever she pleased.

"*Mais oui*," she purred, gracefully kissing him on both cheeks. "The Celebration will last another three days. Maybe we will meet again before it ends."

"I doubt it," he said. "I leave on the first flight tomorrow morning."

"Well, it was a nice thought." She turned to her companion. "Spyro will walk you to your rooms. I hope you have a pleasant night."

Before Martin could protest that he could find his own way, M. Guillard had whispered something into the ear of the mute reve and glided swiftly away, leaving the two men awkwardly facing each other.

"You don't have to," Martin said, hoping against hope that he would be allowed to leave alone. Whatever had happened to Xenophou before or after the Change, he didn't want to know. The thought was heavy in his mind that *he* might be like this in a month's time — that he too could come out the other side disadvantaged or, worse still, truly dead.

Xenophou shrugged, the only form of communication he had made the entire night, and indicated the exit.

Martin gave in. Xenophou followed him through the crowd, then came abreast as they entered the empty corridor beyond the banquet hall. Martin's suite lay on the windowless second floor, well-appointed for someone yet to undergo revenation, but not immodest. Most of the rooms on that level were unoccupied, as testified by the silence around them. Their footsteps were muffled by the thick carpet, smothered in the rich crimson impregnating the weave.

At the door to his rooms, Martin fumbled for the key in his pocket and turned to face his silent companion.

"Thanks, Spyro. I know you probably didn't want to do this, but ... she is hard to resist, I realise, and I appreciate the gesture anyway. So thanks. I hope things work out for you in the end."

Martin turned to open the door. The air inside the suite was clean and smelled of flowers. The lights were already on, and the bed, glimpsed through the opposite doorway, had been turned back in anticipation of his arrival.

Xenophou nodded, but didn't leave. When Martin took a step forward, he followed.

"You want to come in?" Martin asked.

The bald reve shrugged again.

"I guess that means yes." Martin sighed, resigning himself to the situation. "Come on, then. Take a seat, make yourself comfortable. I'm going to slip out of my shoes and jacket, if you'll excuse me for a moment."

Martin strode through to the bedroom while his guest moved towards the sofa. He shrugged out of his jacket and rolled up his shirt-sleeves, then tugged off his tight leather shoes. Relishing the feel of air on the soles of his feet, he took a moment to reflect upon the situation.

His overnight valise lay in one corner, ready to be repacked before he went to bed. The trip had been fleeting but productive. He already had two names for his uncle: Elaine Bennett and *Le Comptable Froid*, the latter being, he was almost certain, another reve. Both had demonstrated themselves to be removed from the core politics of the Plutocracy, the sort to entertain innovative thought rather than to blindly follow the current trend. Whether they would prove to be allies depended on what happened in the future, and whether Martin met his side of the bargain or not.

He stared grimly at the reflection in the mirror. Revenation, except in highly unusual circumstances, always occurred at twenty-one years of age, and his birthday was only a month away. If he chose to proceed, his tanned skin would become pale; his hair would fall out and not grow back anywhere on his body; his eyes would dull and crystallise unless he used eye-drops or had artificial tear ducts installed. He would cease to be human, and become something altogether different.

A reve.

Sudden tightness in his stomach caught his breath. Silently, he mouthed the most offensive word anyone could utter in an immortal's presence:

Zombie ...

"I don't really have anything you might want," he called through the doorway, remembering his guest, "but help yourself anyway. Perhaps we can talk. If you *can* talk, that is."

Only silence answered him. Whatever Xenophou wanted, it obviously wasn't conversation. Slipping his skull-cap off and putting it on the dresser, Martin stepped out of the bedroom and into the lounge, half-hoping to find that Xenophou had departed.

Instead he came face to face with two women he had never before seen in his life.

"Hello," said one, a brunette with short hair and a slender figure, wearing a sheer, silk dress. "Are you Martin Winterford?"

Martin glanced past the women to the door. It was open. *Fool*, he chided himself. Xenophou's presence had disturbed his usually impeccable sense of security.

"Yes," he said, wary of sudden moves. The other woman moved closer, her long blonde hair swaying with the movement. He didn't recall seeing her at the party; he would have remembered if he had.

Xenophou stood between them, frozen but attentive, as tense as an animal about to bolt.

"I'm Martin Winterford," he reaffirmed more loudly, trying to bluff his way out of whatever situation he had blundered into. "How can I help you?"

"You've got it the other way around," said the blonde, smiling and keeping her eyes fixed on his. Her skin was refreshingly pink, and patently human.

"We're here for you," said the brunette. To Xenophou, she added: "Both of you, if you like."

"I'm not sure I understand," he protested, backing awkwardly into the wall as the blonde approached him.

"Sssh." One finger touched his mouth, followed shortly afterwards by her lips. Too stunned for the moment by the boldness of her advance, he was unable to resist. It wasn't until the lock snicked shut in the doorway that he finally forced his hands to push the blonde away.

"Wait," he gasped, reeling. "What's going on?"

The blonde shifted a shoulder. "We're yours for the night, if you want us. We can't force you to do anything."

"No, no — of course not." Martin glanced at the mute reve, who silently echoed his own puzzlement. Not a conspirator, he decided; caught in the cross-fire. "Who sent you, then? Can you tell us that?"

"No," replied the blonde. "But they said you've earned a reward. And we are it." She slid a hand across Martin's shoulder. "Well? Do you want us to stay?"

Martin found it hard to think through the alcohol in his system. But part of him rebelled, discomforted by Xenophou's presence.

Sensing his awkwardness, the blonde's hand tightened. "Come on," she said. "Let's go into the other room. At least I can give you a massage. You look very tense."

He did as she suggested and, despite the cliché, was grateful for the reprieve. She guided him to the bed, and indicated that he was to lie face down upon it. He did so nervously at first, ready for any unexpected moves. He didn't anticipate an actual attack — not in the high security of the Chateau, where weapons were confiscated immediately upon arrival — but he found it hard to let his guard down. The simple act of being there made him feel guilty and vulnerable.

Gradually, however, he relaxed. He let her strong fingers worry at the knots in his back and shoulders while her voice whispered soothingly in his ear. Her smell was tantalising, part perfume and part natural female. Whoever had sent the women had certainly paid for quality.

That in itself helped convince him. If she wasn't a professional sex worker, then she was maintaining a skilful performance. Which only made her all the more difficult to resist.

In that day and age, prostitution was both legal and perfectly safe, and he wasn't a prude by choice. Although young and fair-looking, he had avoided serious relationships ever since his primary application had been accepted — at the age of sixteen — for fear of heartbreak when and if the final approval was granted. One night stands had been few and far between since then, however. The offer was therefore extremely tempting.

And, if the truth were told, he really didn't want to think about it at all. He had no enemies yet, that he was aware of. What did he have to fear, except, as they said, death itself?

When she asked him to remove his shirt, he didn't resist. He rolled over and she straddled him to work on his chest, temples and throat. Her thighs were warm, and growing warmer as she worked. His own hands began to move, stroking her calves in return, revelling in the feel of warm skin beneath his fingertips. With every stroke, her hips swayed, ground languidly against him.

Then she was undoing his trousers, and he had forgotten all thoughts of resistance. He helped remove her dress. They coupled smoothly, he revelling in the wetness and practised muscles of her vagina. Her breasts swayed before his face, and he reached upwards to cup them, brought one nipple down to his mouth. She shuddered and began to move more urgently. If it was an act, it was a good one. His hands wandered to her buttocks. With one in each palm, kneading gently with every thrust, he felt the passion build. And when it erupted, his mind went blank ...

Afterwards, they played less seriously; teasing coyly, arousing sated flesh, exploring. For her, he was sure now, he was just another client, but for him she was something special. A time to be enjoyed, a celebration of life — of *le petit mort*, the little death — however he had earned it.

For an hour they did nothing else. They might have for longer had it not been for the noises coming from the other room.

"Let's go see," the blonde eventually whispered.

He, both relaxed and emboldened by then, agreed that they should.

The lounge looked as though a small but effective storm had ripped through it. Clothes lay everywhere, and cushions had been scattered across the floor. Clearing a seat on the sofa, where they spooned together with legs entwined, Martin and the blonde settled back to watch the show.

Xenophou was naked but for his unbuttoned shirt; his pale, hairless skin shone a pearly white, marred by shadows when his muscles flexed. The brunette was covered only with sweat, glistening on her buttocks and back. The bald reve had penetrated her from behind and was maintaining a steady, firm stroke, neither speeding up nor slowing down unless his partner requested it. With every thrust, the woman gasped for breath, in time to the movement of her own fingers on her clitoris.

Both seemed oblivious to the spectators on the couch. They looked, the blonde whispered into Martin's ear, as though they had been fucking for hours. The sight clearly aroused more than an academic interest.

Martin watched less pruriently. He knew that reves were unable to sire or bear children, but this was the first hint he had received that they might still enjoy sexual congress. Certainly the activity of the couple was as vigorous as and even more prolonged than that between fully mortal partners.

Xenophou's mien, however, was one of intense concentration, not enjoyment, as the brunette's hands guided his to her breasts. Her mouth opened in ecstasy, and she arched her back. Her heels clasped Xenophou's tightly, rocking her hips with every thrust. Riding high on a wave of constant stimulation — and perhaps with the help of drugs — she looked as though she was about to achieve orgasm — the latest of many, if the sounds she made were anything to go by. The only sound Xenophou made was his breathing, fast and heavy.

Then the blonde woman's hand found Martin's stiffening penis behind her, encouraged it, guided it home. For the next few minutes, he completely forgot about Xenophou and the brunette. His second orgasm of the evening took longer to achieve, but was even more intense than the first. It seemed to last forever.

When he was spent, he sagged back onto the couch and stroked the sweat-sheened skin of the blonde's hips and stomach, filled with a sense of satisfied peace. The room was silent, the stillness after a storm, and he felt like sleeping.

A moment passed before he realised what was missing: the brunette's gasping had ceased.

He belatedly turned to see. Xenophou and the woman had stopped moving, although they were still coupled. As Martin watched, the reve levered himself backwards and slid his erect penis from the woman's pouting vagina. The brunette made a small noise deep in her throat, and, breathing heavily, sank back onto her haunches. Xenophou stood just as wearily, his legs shaking. By the time he was upright, his erection had completely vanished.

Looking around the room — at the brunette, at Martin and the blonde, still entwined — the reve blinked his dark eyes once and shook his head.

"Enough," Xenophou said, his voice soft and filled with what might have been sadness.

Martin stared up at him, remembering what the Reve Guillard had told him. This was the first word the new reve had spoken in weeks.

Before Martin could think of anything to say in response, Xenophou had gathered his clothes in a bundle and moved for the door. Hastily disentangling himself from the blonde, Martin leapt to grab his arm. The reve's flesh was uncannily dry and cold. Xenophou looked down at his hand, and Martin removed it.

Without another word, the reve opened the door and left the room.

Martin made sure the door was locked before turning around. Behind him, the brunette had taken his seat on the sofa. Stretching her limbs, ignorant of the significance of what had just happened, she whispered softly to the blonde: business talk. Martin caught a few fragments of the conversation as he walked to the bedroom to regain his composure.

The brunette was exhausted, as was only to be expected. The reve's performance had been far more than she had anticipated; nothing had prepared her for this, although she had heard occasional rumours. The blonde sounded almost jealous, until one item of gossip caught her attention.

"Not once?" she asked, obviously disbelieving her ears. "After all that?"

"Not even a trickle." The brunette sounded deeply puzzled. "And you know, I don't think he ever would have."

Martin nodded silent understanding to his reflection in the bedroom mirror. No sweat, he thought. No fluids of any kind. Even if they had continued for an hour longer, neither the brunette nor Xenophou could have coaxed so much as a drop from his desiccated, dry flesh.

Even if he'd wanted to.

Enough . . .?

Martin went back into the other room to ask the women if they wanted to leave. When the blonde smiled up at him and said no, the brunette agreed. They had been paid for the night and, whether anything else happened or not, his bed was more comfortable than either of theirs. Martin, although his mind was torn between conflicting impulses, didn't doubt that something *would* happen, if he was up to it. It wasn't every day he had the chance to spend the night with two beautiful women. Besides, sleep would be a long time coming, and he wanted to be spared the involuntary wakefulness.

Finally, with the brunette beneath him and the blonde stroking his stomach from behind, he managed to forget about Xenophou and remember himself again — hairy, sweating and above all alive . . .

And when sleep did come, it was black and empty, like death.

* * *

Sudden movement woke him an hour before his alarm was due to go off. Rolling over with a grunt, he realised that the lights were on and the bed was empty.

"I'm sorry to disturb your *ménage à trois*," said a familiar voice from somewhere near his feet, "but I couldn't wait any longer."

He sat up and rubbed at his eyes, fatigue dulling his reactions. The Reve Guillard was a pale blur crouched at the end of his bed, poised like a ghoul to steal his soul. The elaborate ball-gown, along with her airs and graces of the previous night, was gone; in its place she wore a white one-piece suit folded and draped with sashes to hide her figure. It was hard to tell where the fabric stopped and her deathly pale skin started. Her head, like Xenophou's, was completely bald; the angles of her skull were sharp.

Not a chandelier any more, Martin thought. Rather, a shellfish grown old and crusty beneath its carapace. He wondered whether he could ever come close to the innermost substance of the Reve Guillard, if there was any left at all.

"What are you doing here?" he managed.

"I dismissed the girls so we could be alone," she said, avoiding the question. Her dark, cold eyes regarded the tangle of sheets about his legs. "Their services were adequate for the price I paid, I gather. Certainly their effect on M. Xenophou was worth every cent."

Martin slithered along the mattress until his back was flush with the wall. From that position, he watched his visitor closely. "*You* paid them, then? Why? To make your friend speak?"

"My ward, not my friend," she said, her face closed. Again she avoided the question. "The Change isn't always easy, and it's sometimes very hard. The body is a machine, easily upgraded; the mind, sadly, is not. People either want to be a reve or not, and sometimes the only way to find out is to go through the process: when you stand on the other side and look back, knowing that you can't ever return ... that's when you know for certain."

M. Guillard's potent gaze had drifted across the room as she spoke, and returned to him at that point. "Many choose the fiery path, more than you'll find in the official figures. Self-immolation is not difficult to achieve, if you have the right equipment at hand. All it takes is a nice, clear flame, and plenty of oxygen, and —" she looked sad for a moment "— *gone*. What might have been centuries, ended in a second."

"Perhaps that's what worries him," Martin said, wondering if he was dreaming. "Spyro, I mean. The 'centuries' part. The more I learn about being a reve, the less attractive it seems. The thought of being a..." He swallowed the word *zombie* barely in time. "Being immortal, I mean, does have its drawbacks."

"Yet *you* want it, Martin," she said, her voice forceful. "I feel the desire in you more strongly than I have ever felt it before — even if you yourself aren't yet aware of it, or of what it means."

"I'm not?" he asked, confused. "That is, I do?"

"Of course. And mod Alkis agrees. Having studied the Change in more detail than most reves, his opinion played no small part in my decision to talk with you here and now."

Martin thought this over. She and the mod had discussed him after his departure. She and who else?

"Talk to me, then," he said. "Get it over with. As honoured as I am at warranting such undivided attention from someone as busy as yourself, I object to being rudely wakened when I have company."

"That's fine thanks for the fun I gave you last night, Martin." The reve almost smiled, although the expression was thin. "Fine thanks indeed. But I take your point. I have committed a serious breach of protocol, and should expect brusqueness in return." She turned away for a moment, and laughed once.

Martin waited in silence.

When her attention returned to him, the smile was gone. "The thing I have to say to you is this: there's more at stake here than family pride. Whatever you and your uncle have planned, think carefully before committing yourself to it."

"Plans?" he countered, feigning innocence although his stomach had instantly turned to ice. "What plans?"

"How could there not be one, Martin?" she shot back. "PERIPETY-WEYN, with its heightened attention to detail, has plotted extrapolations of your development given the creative and business acumen of your family's germ line. *Le Comptable Froid* watches human affairs from afar and sees a world ripe for change. Elaine Bennett agrees: that there is something fundamentally exciting about the idea of a new House to which both reves and mortal humans cannot help but respond. Not even Professor Munton himself, the dear old fool, could possibly miss this one." This time the smile was real. "You are in a pivotal position, my boy. And the one in the best place beside you to influence future events is the very person behind your application for revenation: your uncle. Coincidence? I think not. You're up to something, or being forced into something, and it's my job — no, my *responsibility* — to make certain that you know exactly what you are putting at stake before you even begin."

"And what's that, exactly?"

"Why, *you*, of course." She frowned at him as though he had said something stupid. "It still hasn't struck you yet, has it? What it means to be a reve?"

"Well —"

"Consider it now. How do you think it will feel to watch your parents grow old and die? Your sister, her partner and her children? Your aunt and uncle? *Especially* your uncle. What will happen if you balance your long future against his short-term gains and come out the loser in the end? Letting a mortal man pull your strings is the most dangerous thing a reve can do, for the time will inevitably come when the strings fall slack and leave you dangling. Regret is the widow of opportunity, as they say, and eternity is a long time in which to regret your mistakes."

"What mistakes?"

"You'll know if you make them, I promise you that."

"Is that a warning, M. Guillard?"

Again, the abbreviated laugh. "Nothing so crude: just stating a fact. There's every chance we'll still know each other in a thousand years, no matter what happens in the next hundred, and every time I meet you I'll be sure to remind you of the actions you are considering now. Persistence alone can be a very effective form of punishment."

"I'm sure," he agreed, "if you're the one behind it." Then another thought occurred to him: "But that still doesn't explain why you've come to me now. The urge didn't strike you from nowhere. You must have known where my room was in advance in order to send the women here so quickly. Which means you knew who I was all along."

"Yes, yes." She dismissed the allegation with a wave of a hand. "Whether I knew who you were or not is irrelevant. It wasn't until my team had taken a good look at you, and confirmed my impression, that I knew we had to talk. And why not now, when your memory of last night is so strong? Before your uncle has had time to twist your impressions to suit his will."

Martin opened his mouth to protest, but she didn't give him the opportunity.

"He will tell you, no doubt, that we are decadent, fossilised creatures in need of a good shock; that five hundred years of imposed stability has suffocated the Earth and all its living children. But I disagree. It is not change we fear, but *undirected* change. Consider the trends, Martin, and how we embrace them instantly throughout the System. Study how progress *has* been made, in an orderly, rational fashion, without revolution and bloodshed to give it impetus. We acknowledge the need for evolution without allowing chaos to reign supreme, and thereby ground inevitable tensions into constructive endeavours. The short-lived have never had it so good.

"But watch what happens when something takes us by surprise. See how strongly we fight back ... even those of us who may have initially welcomed the change."

"You're reactionary by nature," he broke in, speaking his mind for the first time in her presence. "Nothing I can do will alter that, so I have no choice but to fight it."

"No. Change is inevitable, and House Winterford may yet prove to be the catalyst for something new and exciting — but do let *us* be the judge of that, not your uncle."

The Reve Guillard regarded him with something approaching pity, and rose gracefully to her feet. "That is what I came here to tell you. I have no official role in the Plutocracy, but I am not without influence. Nor am I close-minded. If you choose to confide your plans in me, and I find wisdom within them, then I will support you in every regard. I make just as winning an ally as I do an enemy."

Martin stared at her, stunned by the offer. Discuss his plans with a reve? With *her*? Did she think he was stupid?

His thoughts must have been plainly visible on his face, for she smiled and patted his naked foot. "Do think about it, Martin, at least. I will always be available to talk to you, should you take me up on my offer. But we won't meet again until after you awake from the Change — when, as one reve to another, we can discuss this properly. If we cannot come to an agreement even then, we will have no choice but to go our separate ways."

"And if I choose to forgo the Change?"

She blinked once. "Why ever would you do that?"

He took her point. In her eyes, why *would* he?

"Agreed, then. We will talk afterwards."

"Good," she said, and suddenly the conversation was over. With a curt nod, she turned and headed for the open door.

"Wait," Martin called after her. "What about Spyro? Is he still talking? Has he recovered?"

She stopped in the doorway. "Spyro Xenophou is dead," she stated flatly, her eyes revealing nothing. "*Truly* dead. He killed himself at 06:50 hours this morning."

"How—?" Martin stopped himself with difficulty. That wasn't the right question — he could guess the answer: the fiery path. Through his dismay, he forced himself to think clearly. "*Why?*"

"If you cannot answer that question," she said, "then your understanding of what it means to be a reve is incomplete, and your ability to make an objective decision hopelessly inadequate. *Adieu.*"

The only sound she made as she left the room was the rustle of silk on the carpet, swishing softly like a breeze out of his life.

✳ ✳ ✳

Ten o'clock came slowly, but eventually the ponderous airship docked at *Le Chateau de la Mort Dorée*'s departure platform. Thick cables tethered it to ancient wooden posts as the whining of its electric fans ebbed. The massive, rocking balloon shuddered once as it surrendered itself to earth-bound will, then became still.

Martin, standing in a chill draft blowing straight down from the mountain's snow-capped summit, watched the gondola's ramp unfold towards him with half a mind. The rest was still in his room, catching up on the night's events. It was hard to believe that he was already leaving. The short flight to Jungfrau connected with an orbital shuttle leading half-way around the world where, on his ranch in Texas, Arthur Winterford waited. His uncle would want a detailed report of every event, every word, every insinuation. Martin, as would-be reve, had been in a privileged position to gather information.

What *had* he learned? That the Change was fraught with danger, yes, and that the reves were afraid of what he might do to upset the delicate balance of world affairs, when he emerged from the Change the founder of a new House. Nothing new, in other words, nothing critical. Even in one of their many homes, the reves had been judicious with their secrets.

In a perverse way, that made the Reve Guillard's offer tempting. It almost made sense to consult a reve when plotting their downfall — although his uncle would kill him if he took advantage of it.

The more he thought about it, the more tempted he was to cut ties with everyone and to continue as a free agent, following whatever impulses he felt at the time, or none at all.

But . . . Freedom? As a reve? He doubted it.

"We can't force you to do anything," the blonde had said, and for the first time he truly appreciated what the words meant to him. And to Spyro Xenophou — for whom volition hadn't even entered the equation.

Suddenly, Martin understood.

Reves were dead. The fact that they could still participate in the world of the living was irrelevant: the nanomolecular agents behind the mystery of revenation ripped the life from them as surely as a forty-metre fall would kill a mortal human. All biological needs were left behind in the process, including the need to eat, drink, breathe, sleep and die; to a certain extent, the senses, particularly those of taste and smell, were also muted. In exchange, they received total mastery over their flesh — the ability to produce an erection at will, for instance — and potentially eternal life. But the oldest parts of the psyche sometimes refused to accept the bad things with the good, and compelled them to fight the thought of death being something to accept and to put behind them, rather than something to dread.

Where that fight would lead him, Martin had no way of telling. What he *did* know was what must have gone through Spyro Xenophou's mind mid-coitus with the brunette. Faced with one single, yet fundamental, aspect of his new incarnation, the battle had been won. Or lost, depending on the point of view.

Only then had Xenophou realised what he had done.

Enough, he had said. A farewell, certainly — but to what? The brunette, or life? Or an eternity existing only as a poor facsimile of what he had once been, driven by needs and urges that had risen to fill the ones he had left behind forever?

The conductor whistled from the gondola, and the few passengers began to make their way towards the ramp. Martin picked up his suitcase and did the same, bidding farewell, for now, to the reves of Fool's-Death House.

One month to go. There was so much to see and do before he closed the door on the mortal part of his life. And he didn't want to miss out on anything, while he still had the chance.

It was going to be a long month. He would make certain of that. And a very long afterlife to follow.

AFTERWORD

"Entre les Beaux Morts en Vie" owes much to two writers: Rob Hood, Australia's own "Zombie King" (among other things), and Terry Dowling who, particularly in his Tom Rynosseros stories, is a master at hinting at wonders lying just beyond the frame. I met Rob and Terry for the first time in Sydney in 1995, and was deeply inspired by both encounters. Upon returning home, I immediately set about writing a "non-horror" zombie story.

In the space of a fortnight, egged on by one writer with a penchant for a particular myth and by another who knows how to write his own, two tales came into existence. "Entre les Beaux Morts en Vie" was the first; the second was my story "Passing the Bone". The same personal crises that gave "Bone" its vitality kept this story in a drawer for two years. Until now ...

Even though it has little in common with either Rob or Terry's works (and all the mistakes and inelegances are mine), I'm grateful to both of them for nudging this story into existence. May they continue to inspire me for many years to come.

— *Sean Williams*

STEPHEN DEDMAN

Stephen Dedman is the proverbial writer to watch.

He writes: "I was born in Adelaide in 1959, and have lived most of my life in Perth. I escaped from most of the institutes of higher learning in that city, have held several boring jobs and a few interesting ones (including actor, experimental subject, and manager of an sf bookshop), and enjoy travel as long as it doesn't involve boats, ships, or horses."

His short stories have appeared in *The Magazine of Fantasy & Science Fiction*, *Asimov's*, *Science Fiction Age*, *Aurealis*, and *Eidolon*; and in anthologies such as *Glass Reptile Breakout*, *Alien Shores*, and *Little Deaths*; and his first short fiction collection, *The Lady of Situations*, will be published this year. His first novel, *The Art of Arrow Cutting*, was published in 1997 and shortlisted for the Bram Stoker Award for Best First Novel. His next novel, *Foreign Bodies*, will also be published this year.

Here, Dedman takes on one of the most familiar Greek legends ... but we assure you, *this* story won't be familiar.

A WALK-ON PART IN THE WAR

STEPHEN DEDMAN

Helen stared over the battlements at the Akhaean forces, and sighed. "You're a fool," she repeated. "Why did you have to kill him — and in an ambush, too? This will just make them more determined."

Paris bristled. "He was their strongest fighter —"

"He was a weakling, and our best hope. If you'd let him have the women he wanted, he'd have talked the Akhaeans into going back home. But no, you had to murder him, from behind cover, when he wasn't even armed. And why *Akhilles?* Why not Menelaus, or Odysseus, or even Makhaon? That would have hurt them much more. Instead, Agamemnon's given his armour to Odysseus, who's much more dangerous, and made him even more powerful."

Paris stared at her. After ten years, he rarely noticed her legendary beauty any more, though it hadn't faded. "Odysseus? Odysseus is a nobody with a big mouth, little legs, and the soul of a farmer. Give him a chance and he'll go running back to that duck-faced wife of his."

"Odysseus is the son and grandson of the two greatest thieves ever known," Helen snapped, "and some say he's a great-grandson of Hermes himself. He's a spy, a seer, a skilled liar, a collector of secrets and mysteries, the favoured of Athena, the most clever man in the Akhaean camp, and the reason everyone else is out there." She walked away from the wall, and looked back at Paris, her blue eyes cold. "He was the man who advised my father to sacrifice a horse and have all my suitors swear an oath to Poseidon on its bones to defend my husband against anyone who tried to take me. And they're all there — see them?"

"So he's clever," sneered Paris. "That doesn't make him a seer. And do you know what he was doing when Palamedes went to summon him to the war? Sowing a field with salt! Palamedes had to put his son in his path to stop him!"

Helen said nothing. She had heard the story, of course, but she had also heard that Odysseus had been in a prophetic trance, and the ten furrows sown with salt had been a forecast of ten wasted years. Odysseus was said to have seen strange things in such trances — monstrous beasts; wars vaster than any ever known; cities of glass; great ships with neither sails nor oars, that sailed *under* the sea; men flying like Daedalus in boats with metal wings; magical spears taller than any tower, able to hurl themselves across oceans; and other visions beyond any comprehension.

"Anyway, Odysseus is gone," Paris continued, sullenly. "He and Diomedes have sailed away looking for some weapon that's supposed to win the war for them — the bow and arrows of Herakles, or the shoulder-blade of Agamemnon's grandfather, or something. That'll probably be the last we ever see of either of them."

"No," said Helen, sadly. "If there's a weapon that could give them victory, Odysseus will find it, even if he has to kill the man who found it before him."

* * *

Odysseus, the red-haired King of Ithaka, was dreaming of horses. This was hardly remarkable — the small ship was carrying fresh chariot-horses from the stables of Menelaus, and redolent with the stinks of their sweat and manure. War, Odysseus thought sourly, was a great consumer of horseflesh. None of the Akhaeans had forgotten the oaths they'd sworn on the bones of a horse, or that it had been the Ithakan's idea.

Odysseus woke suddenly, trying to piece together the fragments of his dream — something about horses, and Poseidon Earth-shaker, and the walls of Troy ... a way through the walls. Or over them, or under them ... He shook his head. He'd discovered small gaps suitable for spying excursions, but nothing that would admit an army without quickly becoming a trap.

Unable to sleep, he walked to the railing and stared out over the wine-dark sea, hearing the creaking and splashing of the oars, and the whinnying of the horses in their stall nearby. One of the oarsmen chuckled at his short, twisted legs and small penis; without even a glance in his direction, Odysseus smoothly snatched up a ball of dry horse-dung and threw it at him. There was a muttered curse, and scattered chuckles from other rowers; Odysseus merely dusted off his hands, trying to understand.

He'd disliked horses for as long as he could remember, just as he had the sea. Ithaka was a small and mountainous land, with few plains and fewer roads broad enough for chariots, and though long walks hurt his legs, so did riding horseback. But the dream had been as vivid as any vision Athena had ever sent him, and it was unmistakeably about horses. And wood. And the walls.

Odysseus shook his head and leaned on a railing. He was good at interpreting the dreams of his cohorts, usually to his own advantage, but he was frequently troubled by his own. He tried to rearrange the pieces of the dream into a shape that made more sense. A horse that could jump the city's walls? Not unless the Muses saw fit to lend him Pegasus; even his grandfather Autolykus, an expert at breeding cattle for desirable traits, had never tried to mate horses with birds. Walls of wood? Again, mere wishful thinking. A wooden horse?

He turned his back to the railing, staring at the horses and the ship. What possible use was a wooden horse?

* * *

Sunrise found Odysseus still sitting by the railing, half-awake and staring at the sea as it was tinged with pink, and then with yellow, by the reflection of the sunlight. He looked up warily as Diomedes approached. "Couldn't sleep," he grunted. "Dreams."

The Aetolian nodded. "What about?"

"Horses."

"Probably your guilty conscience," Diomedes replied. "If you hadn't slaughtered that poor horse, we'd all still be at home with our wives." He stretched and yawned, hiding a grin.

"*I* would be," said Odysseus, drily. "Do you miss yours?"

"No, but that's still no reason to butcher a good horse."

"I dreamed about a *wooden* horse. Does that make any sense to you?"

"You wouldn't have to feed it," Diomedes said, after a moment's thought. "Unfortunately, these ones you do, so if you'll excuse me —"

"You're not related to the Thracian Diomedes, are you?"

"No, but I stole some horses from one of his grandsons. Good horses, too, fastest I've ever seen." Legend had it that Diomedes of Thrace had fed his horses on human flesh; the younger Diomedes loved horses as much as his namesake, but considered that this was pampering them unnecessarily. "Now, horses like *his* might do more to win us the war than the bow of Herakles, though I wouldn't want the job of mucking them out. Meat-eaters' dung stinks like — what's wrong?"

"Nothing's wrong," replied Odysseus slowly, after a silence of several seconds. "Just ... something my grandfather taught me, when I was a boy."

"What?"

"I can't remember."

Diomedes stared at him, then chuckled and returned to feeding the horses. Odysseus closed his eyes. He'd only been a boy when his grandfather had died, and the old man had told him a lot that he hadn't been able to understand at the time. He dimly remembered a story of a weapon more powerful than any bow — and Autolykus had known a lot about bows, too; he'd taught him how Daedalus had made Herakles' bow from layers of different wood laminated together, multiplying its power and range. He'd also been an expert on envenoming arrows, and other drugs and poisons. The young Odysseus had been fascinated, and had practised archery until he was able to shoot an arrow through the rings of twelve double-bladed axes set in a row. It was a useful skill for a man with twisted legs barely able to carry the weight of armour and shield —

Odysseus suddenly began shaking, as he realised that it was Autolykus's unknown weapon that had crippled him as a boy, stunting and scarring his legs and leaving him in greater agony than he could recall or imagine. And the only thing he still remembered was that it had happened in the stables.

He staggered back to his bunk, momentarily almost sorry that he'd had Palamedes killed in revenge for involving him in the war. Palamedes had been a military genius, though he was better known as the inventor of dice — popular as a pastime for bored soldiers, but originally designed as a means of divination. The bone dice Odysseus removed from his quiver had been Palamedes' own; he rolled them, and tallied up the score. Six, one, and two. It had to mean something, just as his dream did. He dropped the dice back into his quiver, and brooded.

✳ ✳ ✳

Helen stared over the battlements at the Akhacan forces, and asked, "Who killed him?"

Priam said nothing, but Helen noted that he wasn't weeping as he had when Akhilles had killed Hektor; it was many years since Paris had been the old king's favourite son. "No-one's sure," replied Deiphobus. "He was hit by three arrows. Probably Philoktetes — some are saying it was Odysseus, but he was nearly three hundred paces away at the time ..."

Helen nodded. It didn't really matter; Odysseus had armed Philoktetes and the Akhaeans' other great archers with powerful new bows, so he deserved at least part of the blame. *I should leave*, she thought. *It's the only way to end this war without everyone dying.*

* * *

"You know, I used to like horses once." Odysseus stared at the carpenter as he carved an eye, the size of a discus, out of the fir. Behind him, other slaves were finishing wheels nearly twice their own height, or fetching wood for the fires.

"What changed your mind?" asked Diomedes, lazily.

"An accident," replied Odysseus. "Did you know that Helen tried to escape over the wall last night?"

The Aetolian raised an eyebrow; he had his own sources of information, most of them being Trojan women that he'd seduced, but Odysseus always seemed to hear the enemy's secrets before he did. "No, but I'm not surprised, not with Priam marrying her to Deiphobus. Maybe someone should go in and bring her out."

"Maybe, but Menelaus won't like it. It's not just Helen any more; he's still furious that Paris died before he had a chance to finish him off. He's going to want to kill Deiphobus himself, at the very least."

Diomedes shrugged, and watched the slaves as they laboured. "It's still hard to see *that* as the weapon that's going to bring us victory overnight, after all these years. Nestor is telling Agamemnon that you're insane, that this thing will never work."

"Nestor's an old man, and he's never liked new ideas. Besides, with Makhaon dead, we can't afford to just keep wearing the Trojans down." Reluctantly, Diomedes nodded; the surgeon Makhaon had saved enough lives over the ten years of the war to be counted worth a thousand soldiers. "Too many dead heroes on both sides," Odysseus brooded, "and what have they gained? The survivors have won some pretty slaves and shiny armour, but how can we know what's happening to our kingdoms while we're here? This horse is going to fulfil my oath and take me home; that's honour enough for me."

✳　✳　✳

The Akhaean soldier was thin and ugly, and smelled so foul that Helen took him out onto the roof of the palace and stood upwind before questioning him. "What is Odysseus planning?"

"He's built a great wooden horse," replied the soldier. "It's supposed to be a symbol of the horse the kings swore their oath on — the pieces re-united and the oath forgotten, or something."

"Who told you this? Odysseus?"

The soldier grimaced. "D'you think he'd say anything to me? He's the bastard gave the order for me to spend my days collecting horse-dung."

Helen glanced at her husband, who smiled and shrugged. "Why?"

"For laughing at him," was the sullen reply.

"I mean, what does he want with horse dung?"

"I don't know," replied the soldier, his tone making it clear that he'd never wondered, either.

"Maybe it's for poisoning arrows," suggested Deiphobus; both sides dipped arrows and spears in manure when no other venom was available.

"Might be," said the soldier, after a moment's thought. "He's had a load of some yellow powder brought in from somewhere, too; I don't know whether it's a poison or a medicine, but you'd think it was gold from the way he's hidden it."

Helen studied the Akhaean carefully. He was too tall and far too thin to be Odysseus, though she knew that the Ithakan had learnt the art of disguise from the notorious Autolykus and almost certainly visited the city frequently. And the soldier seemed sincere enough, motivated as much by hatred of Odysseus as by any hope of gain ... but Odysseus was cunning enough to have used just such a man to carry his own lies and poisons into Troy. It occurred to her that that might be what the wooden horse was intended to do; carry poison or pestilence into the city. Or maybe ... "How large is this horse?"

"How large? I don't know; Odysseus wanted it small enough to fit through your gates, so the legs are a bit short, like his ... maybe half as long as a galley, I guess."

How many men could stay hidden inside a space that large, she wondered. Forty, fifty, maybe more, but was that enough to take the city, even given the advantage of surprise? She looked closely at the soldier, wishing for a moment that he *were* Odysseus, or one of his messengers, so she could ask what the Akhaeans had planned for her. Death, or forgiveness? She was sure she could seduce Menelaus into sparing her, given time, but Odysseus might have persuaded Agamemnon to keep her away from her first husband. Or would he have counselled mercy for her, for reasons of his own?

"What else do the Akhaeans have planned?" asked Deiphobus.

"They've told us to be ready to sail by the full of the moon. The horse has to be ready by that time, too."

Seven days, thought Helen. Seven days, and this war may be over, one way or the other. She wondered who her husband would be when the moon began to wane.

✳   ✳   ✳

Troy's best archers watched from the top of the walls, waiting for the order to fire, as Akhaean slaves and soldiers dragged the great wheeled horse towards their city by moonlight. The order never came, even when the soldiers came within a few paces of the western gate; none of the Akhaeans seemed to be armed or armoured, and they fled towards their ships as soon as the horse was in place. It was almost an hour later that the gates opened and a small team of Trojans emerged to examine the figure. Apart from the head and neck, which had been carven with skill and obvious care, it was merely a collection of rough-hewn planks shaped into enormous cylinders. The front left wheel, of soft fir-wood, had broken under its weight. Tapping on the legs and body suggested that they were hollow, but filled with something like sand.

Helen, remembering the soldier's story about the yellow powder, stared curiously at the horse from a tower in the northern wall. Behind her, she heard the unsteady footsteps of Priam; flanking and supporting him were two of his youngest sons, Capys and Thymoetes. "What is it?" asked the king, querulously.

"Some trick of Odysseus's," she replied.

"The word going around the city is that it's full of treasure," Priam grumbled. "A peace offering, reparations, a sacrifice ... some of the people want it brought inside, others want it destroyed. Deiphobus and Laokoon are demanding that it be burnt, and Kassandra is wailing that it'll kill us all. I've ordered the gates shut, only a few soldiers to go outside. What do you think? Do you want to see it?"

She stared at the horse, then nodded, and followed him down to the gates.

*　*　*

Helen walked cautiously around the horse three times, keeping a safe distance and looking, with no success, for a trapdoor. *In thankful anticipation of a safe return to their homes*, read the inscription on the left flank, *the Akhaeans dedicate this offering to the Goddess*. "Maybe we should take it to the temple," suggested Thymoetes, softly.

Capys laughed. "Athena always favoured the Akhaeans anyway, especially Odysseus. I say either we burn it at once, or break it open and see what's inside."

Both ideas were popular, Helen thought, hearing the shouts that were coming from inside the city. Laokoon, another of Priam's sons, hurled his spear at the horse's belly before anyone could stop him. The Trojans gathered around watched, some half-expecting blood to drip from the rent in the wood, but all they saw was a trickle of fine dark powder. Helen rushed forward and caught some, wondering why she was filled with fear by a handful of dust.

"Burning sounds good to me," said Deiphobus. Helen glared at him, then called out to Menelaus, imploring him to come out.

Deiphobus grabbed her from behind, one arm around her chest, the other under her jaw. "What are you —"

"If it *is* full of fighters," she hissed, "wouldn't it be better to get them out alive and ransom them?" She tossed her head, breaking free of his grasp, then called out to Odysseus in a perfect imitation of Penelope's broad, flat accent. Priam stared at them, then nodded.

"Do it," he ordered, then turned to Thymoetes. "Have as many good archers as you can find line up on the walls in case anyone comes out."

"And what if they don't?" demanded Laokoon, as his brother ran for the gates.

"Then we burn it," said Priam, grimly. "Before sunrise, when the wind changes, and let the people see what we think of the Akhaeans' gifts."

*   *   *

Seven hundred paces from the western gates, the Akhaeans' best archers sat around a small fire and played dice for slaves — except for Odysseus, who stared towards the city, his great bow in his right hand, his favourite spear (tipped with the barb of a sting-ray) in his left. Six, one, two, he repeated silently, as though it were a prayer, rather than just the formula Autolykus had taught him. Six parts of saltpetre, the white crystals found under old piles of horse manure, to one of sulphur from the hot springs, to two of charcoal, well mixed together, then wet to form a paste, and dried to a black powder. Autolykus had taught him to use a handful of the dust for creating smoke, bright light and noise to create confusion, but the young Odysseus had wanted to see what an urn filled with it would do. The blast had crippled both of his legs, disembowelled his favourite pony, and set fire to his grandfather's stables. The wooden horse that the Trojans were preparing to burn contained more than a hundred times that amount of powder, plus stones and metal shards. Odysseus saw the flash, and a moment later, a sound like thunder as the horse exploded.

*　*　*

The Akhaeans took the city just before sunrise. The blast had cracked the thin western wall, blown one of the gates from its hinges, and started fires in the city; more importantly, it had killed Priam and most of his family, as well as the city's best archers, and hundreds who had gathered around the horse to watch it burn. Helen had fled when the fire began, and Deiphobus had chased her to her chamber, where she stabbed him with a dagger. Menelaus found them there, put down his sword, and led her back to the Akhaean fleet while the other Akhaeans fought over the spoils. Neoptolemus, son of Akhilles, dragged Priam's body to a peninsula that would later be called Gallipoli, and left it there to rot.

*　*　*

Odysseus stood lashed to the mask while his crew rowed on, their ears stoppered with wax. Determined to be the first man to hear the song of the sirens and tell the story, he scanned the surrounding rocks for the feathered women. There was no sign of them, but the winds carried sweet voices to his ears; come to us, he heard, come to us and we'll tell you the future.

I've already seen the future, Odysseus thought. Weapons that kill warriors and cowards, kings and slaves, all alike. Wars that level entire cities. The age of heroes ended, nothing more than a memory, a story told by the bards and only half-believed.

AFTERWORD

I often tell people that the way to start a short story is to bang two ideas together and see if you get a spark. This one came about because I banged a title I liked against a character who's interested me for most of my life.

I discovered Greek mythology in a big way a few months before the first moonwalk, when my teacher asked me to find out what I could about the god Apollo. I became hooked, and bought myself an illustrated translation of the *Odyssey* for my tenth birthday.

Over the next few decades, I read as much Greek myth as I could find, and learnt some of the history behind it, as well as making several false starts at stories and novels based on the myths.

Odysseus is my sort of hero — clever, devious, arrogant, curious, practical, beloved of the Goddess of Wisdom, descended from the God of Thieves, an actor and tale-spinner and dream-interpreter and spy. Best of all, he's a draftee, who would rather be home than fighting a particularly stupid war. Unfortunately, I wasn't convinced by the idea of the Trojan horse, and I decided there had to be more to the story than that.

Not including twenty-seven years of research, this story took about a week to write. Apart from the *Iliad* and *Odyssey*, Robert Graves's *The Greek Myths* and M.I. Finley's *The World of Odysseus* and *The Ancient Greeks* (all Pelican Books) were invaluable. My thanks to whatever gods there be for good bookshops.

Oh, and it's a science fiction story, too. One of my *other* favourite characters from Greek myth was Daedalus ...

— *Stephen Dedman*

ISOBELLE CARMODY

Isobelle Carmody began her first novel *Obernewtyn* at high school and has been writing ever since. She completed a Bachelor of Arts and a journalism cadetship while she finished the novel. Her award-winning *Obernewtyn Chronicles* have established her at the forefront of fantasy writing for young people. She won Book of the Year for her urban fantasy *The Gathering* and received considerable critical acclaim for this and for her collection of short stories, *Green Monkey Dreams*. The title story of that collection won the 1996 Aurealis Award for the best young adult short story.

Her most recent novel, *Darkfall*, is the first in a trilogy for adults, was shortlisted for the Aurealis Award for Best Fantasy novel in 1997. In the same year her novel *Greyland* won the Aurealis for Best Fantasy novel in the young adult category. Carmody has also won the 3M Talking Book of the Year Award and the Children's Book of the Year Award for Older Readers.

She divides her time between Prague in Eastern Europe and her home on the Great Ocean Road in Victoria. She is currently working on *Darksong*, second in the *Legendsong* trilogy.

In the dark fantasy story that follows, we explore the labyrinthine cobbled streets of Prague in search of … shadows. And discover that everything has its price.

THE MAN WHO LOST HIS SHADOW

ISOBELLE CARMODY

Light floods from all directions, banishing every trace of night. Only a frozen transparency holds back the darkness.

There is a young couple in the booth opposite sitting so that although they appear to be languidly independent of one another, their bodies touch all along one side from shoulder down through the hip and thigh to the heels, their connection far more intimate than if they had been wound together explicitly. They are not foreign as I am, and even in a no man's land like this establishment, whose success depends upon its rejecting utterly any trace of the culture within which it finds itself, they belong in a way that I do not. Part of it may be because they are casually dressed while I am wearing my formal but now somewhat crushed travelling clothes. Or maybe it is that they are young and I am not.

The girl is very tall and slender as women here seem to be — young women, anyway. The older women are as bulky as bears in their winter coats, their expressions forbidding and surly. The stewardesses on Thai Airlines, which I flew for the first part of the trip here, were as small and fragile as tiny blown-glass blossoms, while the German stewardesses on my second flight, were older. Young matrons with thick competent arms and faces. Here the young women have still, remote faces. One can see it is a general type and the girl opposite fits it. The waiter brings them two drinks — orange ade, perhaps, and a plate with two chocolate-coated cakes. A waiter is an anomaly in this sort of place, and yet his presence is a sign of the hybridisation of two cultures, each trying to consume and subdue the other.

The girl takes up the plate and cuts into the cake, her expression unchanged. Inside the coating of chocolate is a pale soft sponge or maybe some sort of creamy filling. She offers the laden fork to the boy, and my stomach spasms dully in what might be hunger. He is sitting bolt upright, although she is now resting her back against the seat, her spine bent into a delicate bow and curled around the long flat belly. She eats the two cakes slowly, licking her lips and talking, but never smiling, never showing any emotion. Her companion nods, and watches her with ravenous attention.

The waiter brings them a tall glass of fruit salad topped with a fat loose whorl of impossibly white cream. The boy's turn, I think, but he gestures at the glass and the girl sets aside the plate she had been holding and takes it up. Again she scoops up cream and fruit and offers it to him, and again he refuses. She eats the whole parfait with the same dreamy absorption. When she sets the glass down, the boy runs his hand over her belly possessively, then slides it around to pull her to him to be kissed. When he releases her, I see that her hands have not moved throughout the embrace and her body retracts automatically to its former languid bow.

The boy has become aware of my regard, and gives me a curious look. I do not glance away, embarrassed. I realise that I feel almost no sense of self consciousness. It is as if the affliction which has brought me to this strange outpost, has left me free of any need to pretend to be normal. The boy calls the waiter and pays the bill and as they leave, the young woman settles her limp, expressionless glance on me. There is no way of knowing what is going on in her mind. Perhaps nothing. Now that they have gone, my exhaustion returns and I begin to think of leaving. I wonder if I am afraid, but my emotions are slightly unfocused so that I am not sure from one moment to the next what I am feeling.

Beyond the sheet of window glass is a utilitarian rank of petrol bowsers flooded with light, and beyond the asphalt surrounding them, lost in shadow, is a road leading back to the highway bounded on either side by a dense pine forest. That road connects to the city and I see it in the glass as I saw it through the frosted window of the taxi upon my arrival: a city street winding away and steeply up, street cobbles shining wetly. On either side of it, unbroken, ornate facades of buildings, art nouveau and gothic details picked out delicately by the buttery gold of the street lamps.

The thousands of tourists who come to see this city must feel they are stepping into the past, yet when the street was new, night would have been an all-consuming darkness so that nothing would have been visible; the brash light which symbolises the modern world thinks naively that it has banished darkness — from the streets, from corners, from the hearts of men and women. But it is eternal and it will find its way, its crack, its vein.

The castle appears beyond the glass now, seeming to be lifted above the snarl of old town streets surrounding it on beams of light, to float in greenish illumination, and I find I am back in the taxi that is not a taxi. Such is the power of the castle, this city.

The driver glances at me in the rearview mirror and tells me in brutish English that the lights are switched off the castle just before midnight. I think how I would like to sit somewhere — in a cafe perhaps — and wait to see it swallowed up by the night.

"You have business?" he asks, a touch of curiosity. Perhaps he senses my affliction, though it is virtually unnoticable at night. He wonders why I am here. I could tell him that the turbulent history of this country, the stony eroded beauty of this city that is its heart, fascinates me.

"Business," I agree. A strange business.

I do not know how I lost my shadow. After the first shock wore off, I told myself it was freak chance. My shadow might not even have known what it was doing when it severed itself from me. I could easily envisage myself walking and hesitating at some slight fork in the streets, my shadow going on sunk in its own thoughts, failing to notice that it did so without me. Seconds later, I would choose the other way. Maybe after a time it realised what had happened and retraced its path, but by then, I had long gone.

That was one of my earliest theories. Hopes you might as well say. One does not like to admit the possibility that one's shadow has left on purpose. I consoled myself with a vision of my shadow, slipping frantically along walls and paths searching for me, wailing as forlornly as a lost child, occasionally plunging into pools of shadow and emerging with difficulty because it lacked a form to pull it from the larger shadow.

But now, I can more imagine its relief at being cut loose. It may have been a fortuitous accident that freed it, or maybe it saw its chance to be free, and took it. Either way, I blame my passivity for our estrangement. Caught within the roaring machinery of the relationship between my parents, I had learned to defend myself with stillness. But having gained the habit of passivity, I could not lose it and so as an adult, I found it almost impossible to engage with life. I was a fringe dweller of the most meek and timid ilk and if someone had accused me of being a shadow in the world, I would have admitted it mildly.

But that was before my shadow was lost, and I understood by the gaping void its absence left, that it is we who need our shadows, not they us. Without it to anchor me to the earth, I became dangerously detached. I dreamed of the reassurance of its company, its small tug at my heels, its soft movement before me, feeling out my path like a blind man's cane. Without it to bind me to the earth, I am like one of those astronauts whose each step on the moon is so buoyant as to suggest that they might any second step into infinity. I am afraid that without my shadow, I will soon make just such a step into oblivion. It has gone far enough for me to understand that I am diminishing without its darkness to balance me.

The taxi swerved violently to avoid another taxi that had tried to pull out from a side street and the driver muttered what sounded like a curse. I noted indifferently that I had not felt the slightest fear at our near collision. That numbness is an unexpected side effect of my affliction.

Of course, I did not know what it meant to have lost my shadow. After an initial response of blank disbelief upon discovering it, followed by a mercifully brief period of doubting my sanity, I sought help. Ironically I went to a doctor first, a general practitioner more accustomed to removing warts and administering antibiotics and tranquillisers than to treating a man with an ailment as sophisticated and mysterious as mine. She offered me the latter and seeing the shape of her thoughts, I said somewhat haughtily that she need not suppose that anything was wrong with my mind. Could she not accept the evidence of her eyes as I had done? I lacked a shadow. What could be more empirically concrete? Yet she simply pretended to be confused by my symptoms.

"What exactly do you want?" she demanded finally.

I asked her coldly to refer me to a specialist in shadows, since her own training seemed to have left her ill equipped for more exotic illnesses. Somewhat maliciously, she sent me to a radiologist, whose view of shadows was shaped entirely by his seeking cancers and tumours in X-rays day after day. I can only say that his judgement was seriously warped by his position.

When I told him of my problem his eyes blazed and he clutched my arm hard enough to leave a bruise, proclaiming that I was the first human to have escaped the curse of shadows. He confided his belief that they were not bestowed by god as was generally supposed, but had been served upon us by some force which he refused to name. His mania was apparent when I questioned him about the purpose of shadows. He gave me an affronted look and asked what sort of man I thought he was, to ask him such a question; exactly as if I had asked the shade of his pubic hair. He examined the X-ray plate he had insisted on taking and developing, suspiciously, then pronounced resentfully that he saw no shadow.

After that, I gave up on the medical profession. I was not really ill, I reasoned. Having lost a shadow I was more like a man whose wife leaves him, clearing out their apartment with mysterious speed and efficiency. With this in mind, I consulted a private investigating firm. The man who ran the agency gave his name as Andrews. Since I could not not feel at ease addressing him in this manner, I contrived not to call him anything.

"I've never been asked to shadow a shadow before," he said when I had laid the matter before him. I can only suppose he meant it as a joke but I did not laugh. I am not good at humour, and I told him this. He squinted his eyes at me and seemed suddenly sobered as if my words had made him take me seriously.

"Perhaps that's it. Think of it from their point of view. Having to endure being dragged about, never having a chance to exert their own mind or will or taste. They're worse than slaves because they can only emulate. Nothing they do is original. There must be millions of them constantly plotting a coup, fed by dreams of freedom. And on top of that, to be faced with living with someone who has no sense of humour.

It must be unendurable." He seemed very sincere, but a certain reticence in my own character prevented me breaking down and confessing my fear of precisely this thing — that some profound lack in me had driven away my shadow. That was a matter to be resolved beween my shadow and I.

"Can you find it?" I asked him, finally, flatly.

He looked through a leather ledger before consulting with his secretary, and after some negotiating, agreed that he should have a modest retainer for a week. If after that time, his enquiries had divulged no promising clues, our contract would end. If he did find a lead, I would pay him $100 a day thereafter, including expenses, until he found my shadow or my money was gone.

I gulped a little at the size of his daily fee, but a modest, hard working life has enabled me to put aside a very good sum, and to comfort myself, I reckoned that ten thousand dollars spent on finding my shadow would still leave ample for my old age, and perhaps would even run to a convalescing trip to the Greek Islands off-season, after it was all over, so that my shadow and I could re-evaluate our relationship.

Unfortunately after a week, the investigator could report nothing. He confessed that my inability to remember when I had lost my shadow was a stumbling block. I blushed when he spoke of this for his words seemed to me to suggest that I had been criminally careless. Though I continued to argue that the loss could only have happened a little before I noticed it, he seemed to doubt me, and made me doubt myself. Mulling it over, I discovered to my horror that I could not remember the last instance I had consciously noticed my shadow. I ran my mind over the day before my retirement, and then the week and months leading up to it. Finally, frantically, I began to run my mind over the years preceding, but still I could not recall seeing my shadow on any specific occasion. I envisaged all of the bright sunny days I had lived through, from forest walks in the autumn to a dip in the blazing summer heat, to no avail.

I could recall seeing my reflection many times, but not my shadow. I told myself at one point that, after all it was only a shadow, and then was chilled, for perhaps it was just such carelessness that had driven it off. If that was so, I avowed remorsefully, I would show how I valued it by the very fervency of my search.

Fortunately my retirement meant I had no appointments or ties to hold me back. In fact the investigator had the gall to suggest my retirement on the very day I had noticed my shadow missing, pointed to a link between the two events. Absurd especially since he could not substantiate his notion with anything aside from the most spurious and simplistic choronological causal link. Was he suggesting my retirement had provoked the departure of my shadow, I demanded? He bridled at my tone and though we parted politely, I did not go back to him.

"Behind there, gardens," the taxi driver said nodding at a high graffitied wall. I wondered why the garden was walled. Perhaps it was a zoological garden and some sort of wildlife dwelt in it, but perhaps not. Already I could see this was a secretive city and in such a place, a garden might be considered to be dangerously wild, and needing to be retrained. I saw the driver watching me.

"Gardens," I said.

But I was thinking of how I had returned at length to my building after recovering from my first horror at the loss of my shadow, having come to the conclusion than I must go away from my own country if I wanted to find it. My compatriots were not interested in shadows, after all. They were creatures of sunlight and brightness for the most part and even their violence was radiant and garish, devoid of true darkness. I needed to find an older world with crannies and corners. I needed a place where I would be irrelevant even if I was to behave in ways that would mark me eccentic or even mad. That meant a city. An old city.

And then, that evening as if in an answer to my soul searching, the person using the control in the communal television room changed channels, and I found myself watching the end of a documentary in which the camera showed a series of views of an ancient city. The last shot showed a cracked wall, where a child's shadow walked along the shadow of another wall, beneath a rolling scroll of names. The documentary ended abruptly and I gave a cry of disappointment.

What is that place? Do you know where it is? I asked the other residents seated about in the mismatched chairs. A flat-faced, sombre-eyed man grunted that he ought to know since it was his own city. He had been a child there. Before the occupation. His parents had escaped and had emigrated. I asked if they understood shadows there. It was a risky question but there was a surreal quality to the light in the room that allowed it.

"There was a time when people had to be shadows there," the man said.

My landlady reproached me for my selfishness when I told her of my intended journey. "What would your grandmother think of such behaviour."

I regretted immediately that I had once spoken to her of my grandmother, but I said that if anyone, she would understand most profoundly what I was doing.

My landlady said sharply that it was probably so, since my grandmother had been as mad as a cut snake. I could see that she was offended in the way only a woman whose mind is so convoluted in its masochism as to regard everything that occurs in the world as being somehow aimed at her. Nothing that happened, not a car crash in another city in which a stranger dies, nor the razing of a park to build a racecourse, nor the swearing of a drunk weaving from a pub, is exempt from being gathered into her aggrieved personal world view. Of course it is a stunningly self-centred, even sociopathic, means of regarding the world.

My grandmother was a woman of incredible wisdom, but it is true that she was insane. Perhaps it was the weight of all that wisdom that cracked her mind open like an egg. When she was very old, not long before the end, she became disorientated physically. She was always imagining she was in the house of her father, no matter where she was; that my home, or the hotel or mental institution or public toilet, were somehow connected to it, if she could just find the right door. She was frequently exclaiming at a picture or vase, saying hadn't that been moved from the mantlepiece in her father's study, or from the hall table, and worrying that it would trouble him.

"It is very vexing when things are moved around," she would sigh and scrub at her forehead fretfully with a tiny clenched fist.

It took some time for me to realise her apparent confusion was in fact an awareness of links which are buried under life, and hidden from reason. Children see these links between things very clearly, I believe. It is why they weep at one stranger and smile at another. So do the elderly, who slough off reason without regret, see these links. Indeed, perhaps with the same gusto as many of them throw off their clothes in public, they welcome back to themselves the Eden-like simplicity and clarity of childhood. Even before my grandmother died, I had begun to realise that her confusion was simply a deeper seeing of the world and the documentary had suggested to me that finding my shadow might take such vision. That frightened me because that manner of seeing cannot be learned or treated as a trick. That which allows one to see such links, of necessity blinds one to other things. Nevertheless, I vowed that at least I would follow this one strange clue without question.

I told myself that bereft of its caster, a shadow must be forced to all sorts of ruses and opportunistic leaps to shift itself about. Chance must rule its progress and I was ready to let go of all the comforting order and planning that had so far hedged my existence, and give myself to the roads of chance. If one would enter the kingdom of heaven, one must come naked like a child. So my grandmother used to say.

The airport had been very crowded, or so it seemed to me. But perhaps it is always like that in the international terminal. I presented my ticket and little bag to the departure desk. Boarding the plane, I felt exhilarated and thought of a quotation I had read on my desk calendar the day I left work. "What does not kill you will make you stronger." It can only have been a warning, for little more than an hour later, walking to the tram stop in bright afternoon sunlight, I noticed that I cast no shadow. I stared down at the ground in front of me, feeling the sun pouring on my shoulders and on the back of my head. I turned and looked up, intrigued and puzzled to find out what second light source had erased my shadow. The shadow of the light pole alongside me fell on a wall. With a feeling of unreality, I held up a hand to the wall, but it cast no shadow.

I have no memory at all of the remainder of the trip home. How had I managed it staggering with terror, yet neither losing my hat nor briefcase heavy with the paraphernalia from my desk?

Another taxi swerved across in front of us, forcing the driver to run over the tram lines. The cobbles made the wheels drum under the seat, and I closed my eyes, remembering intimately the way I had been pressed into my seat as the plane left the earth and launched itself into a long, drawn out vibrating dusk in which the sun seemed to hang for hours half submerged by the horizon. I had declined food, despite my hunger. I dislike the prefabricated nature of airplane food and resolved to treat the long flight as a period of fasting and mental preparation for my search. I did not drink any tea or coffee, but took only water as if I were on a religious pilgrimage. Night fell and twelve hours later, it was still night. I felt on that plane as I feel now; as if

I have entered an endless night that will not be broken until I am reunited with my shadow.

When the plane landed, it was so dark a day outside that it was indistinguishable from night. It seemed an omen to me. People exclaimed over the fog and there was talk of long delays for connecting flights. The woman at the transit station explained reproachfully to a complaining man from my flight that we were lucky to have been permitted to land at all. She looked interested to hear my destination.

"That's becoming very popular. Some say it is the Paris of the 1920s all over again," she approved in round vowels so plump they were like fruit waiting to be picked.

Day passed imperceptibly into night and still there was no call to board. I resisted suggestions to stay overnight. The smell of food made me feel faint and I decided to break my fast and while the hours away with a leisurely meal — perhaps even a light beer. The last meal I had eaten was a dinner of lamb chops and boiled potatoes prepared by my landlady the night before I left. I was so hungry that the thought of even that grudging meal made my stomach rumble. Nevertheless, I was grimy and sweaty after the long hours of travel and I decided I would bathe before eating. I exchanged my last bank notes for English pounds, and managed to locate an attendant to unlock the shower and give me soap and a towel.

In the booth, I undressed slowly and took a very hot shower, enjoying the water on my tired skin. Another effect of the loss of my shadow has been to render my skin dreadfully dry and itchy. After what seemed a very short interlude, the shower attendant hammered on the door and in an indescribable argot, gave what can only have been a command to make haste. I obeyed, surrendering the soiled towel and giving her a pound tip to demonstrate both my disapproval and my high mindedness.

This transaction reminded me that I would now need to change a small travellers cheque if I wanted to eat. Coming out of the restrooms, I patted my pockets searching for my wallet. Unable to find it, I decided I must have left it in the shower cubical. Although I was convinced that I had not taken it out there, I checked. Then it came to me. I had removed my jacket to be hung in the plane, taking out both the wallet and the thick plastic sleeve containing my travel documents, and sliding both into the seat pocket. On arrival, I had taken out the travel agency pouch, but I had no recollection of retrieving the wallet.

I went to the information desk, puzzled by my lack of apprehension. I put the curious deadening of my feelings down to jet-lag.

"If you had realised immediately," the man said regretfully, a touch of Jamaica in his tone. Nevertheless he would make some calls. Can I come back in an hour. Not a question. I sat down for a while near his desk, then it occurred to me to see if I could simply report the cheques stolen and have them replaced. Money, after all, was my most pressing need. My cards and other papers could be replaced at another time.

I spoke to the young woman at the Thomas Cook counter, who assured me the cheques could be replaced quickly, so long as I could provide their numbers which were supposed to be kept separately. I explained that the sheet of numbers was packed into my bag, which had been checked in some hours earlier, and might already have gone on ahead and even now be waiting for me at my destination.

"That is against regulations," she told me with certainty. "The bags must travel with the clients. Always."

I said nothing, knowing as she did that bags sometimes went without their people, just as shadows sometimes travelled alone. It wasn't meant to happen, but it could. The announcement for my flight to board came over the air.

"I will have to get the cheques once I arrive," I said.

"You can't mean to go there without money," she exclaimed. The genuine concern in her tone simultaneously touched me, and reminded me of the mysterious nature of my trip. It came to me that this mishap was a sign that I was failing to understand.

The young woman mistook the question in my eyes and leaned over her smooth counter to explain her words. "In a country like that, you must have money. Everything is for sale. Everything costs and you are safe as long as you can afford the price. Safety has a price, just like comfort or food or coffee."

I sensed that under these words, she was telling me something important, but I could not seem to understand. My mind felt numb. I told her that I had made up my mind to simply go on. Surely this would be the most unreasoned response to what had happened, and therefore the most apposite. Maybe it was even a kind of test. At my request, she wrote the address of their office, saying there was surely a cheap bus to the centre and I could walk from there. Alternatively, I could take a courtesy bus to one of the bigger hotels. The Hilton, for instance, where they would not want money immediately, and would quite likely sort the lost cheques out for me.

She was kind, but I had no desire to spend any of my money on a hotel like the Hilton, which raised in me the same objections as pre-packaged airline food or MacDonalds. I would not find my shadow staying in such a hotel and to go there would signal surrender. I would get a bus to the centre of the city after changing the little remaining cash I had, and walk about until day broke. Then I would get the cheques replaced. I did not try to make any plans beyond that, for even that might be too much.

I checked back with the airline attendant who said no-one had handed in the wallet. I gave him my landlady's number in case it should appear. I disliked doing that, but I had no-one else's name to give other than my employer, who was not the sort to maintain warm connections with former employees. The severance payment was generous enough to make it clear that I was to expect nothing more of him.

Boarding the small plane that would carry me on the last leg of my journey, I wondered what my boss would think if he knew I was on my way to a city full of shadows and danger, where everything had a price, although I had no money, or so little as to be meaningless. Perhaps he would even regret my retirement, and wish he had persuaded me to stay on. The thought should have given me pleasure, but it was tasteless, and I began to feel uneasy about myself.

On the plane I ate the small club sandwich offered, and drank as many cups of coffee as I could fit into the short flight. The food seemed only to make me hungrier and the sense of disorientation increased. It was no longer possible to pretend that I was not sickening.

The face of the customs official at the airport was flat and severe, but his eyes were the same soulful brown as the man in the television room of my apartment house, and absurdly as he took my passport I wondered if they could be related.

"Reason for visit?" he asked. His thick finger tapped a blank space in the form I had filled out. He slid a pen through the small window in the glass separating his official niche from me. I took it up and noticed my fingers were trembling. I tried to focus my thoughts. It was incredibly difficult, for even when I had understood the question I could not seem to think how to answer it. I looked at the official and found him staring and cataloguing my features for a report to be added to a file of suspicious foreigners.

I could feel sweat crawling down my armpits. I forced myself to write.

"Research," he read. "What kind of research?"

I felt I might be about to faint or have some sort of convulsion. All of my glassy calmness seemed to rupture. My heart beat in jerky arhythmic spasms. Then suddenly, with a feeling delirious clarity, I understood that my reaction was a premonition connected to my ailment, and to my arrival in this country. Without thought, I simply told him why I was there. I felt as if I had peeled my skin off in front of him. I felt that having told him my secret, I could not draw a breath without his having permitted it. I felt a drowning, tremulous emotion as if I had put my life in his hands. I had powerful urge to kiss his hands.

"Your shadow." He said this, not as a question, but as a repetition so exact I realised he had not understood the word. His English must be regulation minimum and solely connected to his job. He stamped the passport and slid it to me with the visa folded on top. As I took it up, I felt as if I had shown myself naked to a blind man.

But by the time I walked out into the night carrying my bag, I understood that this had been a necessary encounter, an emotional procedure to be endured, and no less vital for entry to this country than getting an official visa. I felt stronger, though more detached than ever.

From the timetable, it seemed as if I had missed the last bus to the city. A short, swarthy man sidled over and asked if I wanted a taxi.

"Special taxi. Very cheap for you." He had grasped the handle of my bag and was trying to wrest it from me. I held on and he ceased pulling at it. Perhaps he was surprised at my strength.

"It's impossible," I said. "I don't want to take a taxi."

He looked around furtively, and I had a memory of the Thomas Cook woman warning me about taxis in this city. She had claimed the majority were run by a vicious local mafia, and many of the drivers acted as pimps for gypsy prostitutes. She had told me of a taxi driver leaping out of his cab and beating two American tourists with a truncheon because they had crossed the street too slowly in front of him. Such fearless brutality suggested powerful if illicit approval had been bestowed officially. But the man holding onto my bag did not exude any air of power nor even of particular malignity. In fact, he looked more desperate than anything else. His clothes were ill fitting and grubby, the cuffs of his jacket and trousers badly frayed. I wondered if he really had a taxi, or merely sought to lure me to a discreet corner of the carpark and mug me.

"I don't have the money for a taxi," I said. He stared at me in sullen bewilderment and so I made a dumb show of the day's events, reaching for my wallet and discovering its loss.

He let go of the bag. "No crown?" Now it was I who didn't understand. Was it that he now somehow imagined I was like royalty who are reputed never to carry money? "You no want taxi?" This possibility appeared to confound him.

"Later," I said, pointing away from myself as if at some hours distant. Then it occurred to me that the best way out of my dilemma might simply be to ride about in a taxi until morning, when I could visit a Thomas Cook office.

"I don't want a taxi, but I would like to make a tour of the city?"

"Tour? Now?" He gaped at me.

I nodded firmly. "An all night tour. Fixed price. No meter."

"Tour," he said, as if he was sucking the word to decide if he liked the taste of it. He nodded judicially. "Fixed price tour. Cheap. You come."

I made him name a price, then let him take my bag. After all, it contained little other than a change of clothes and several changes of underwear. He ran ahead into the misty darkness, and I tried to calculate how many hours since I had slept last, but was defeated by the time difference between my country and this one, and by daylight saving on top of that. Did they bother saving daylight here, or did they save night instead? I realised at some level that I was becoming dangerously light headed. My nostril hairs seemed to be on the verge of freezing and the air was so cold it hurt to breathe it in.

He was standing by a car. "No taxi," he said.

I took off my jacket and let him bundle me into the car.

He drove quickly and it seemed to me it was uncannily dark outside. There were no lights along the highway, and no moon or stars. I told myself it was overcast, yet I could not help but feel the darkness was thicker here than back home, congealing at the edges. He did not slow as we reached the outskirts of the city. I stared out at the streets which flickered by like a jerky old black and white movie. Everything looked grimy as if the dense blackness were slowly rubbing off onto the city.

"Metronome," the driver said, nodding at a set of dark steps leading up from the roadside, and pointing up. "Up," he said.

"A metronome?" I asked doubtfully, thinking I must have heard wrong.

"Doesn't work," he said. "Bad. Stupid."

Another taxi roared past us so fast the car shuddered. Its red tail lights burned like coals in the misty air. "Taxis very bad here," the driver muttered. "All criminals."

All at once we rounded a sharp bend only to find our way blocked by the taxi that had passed us. Or perhaps it was another taxi. It had parked in such a way as to block the road completely. My driver stood on his brakes and tried to turn without stopping. The car slewed around and mounted the sidewalk with a great thump that at first made me think we had struck someone. Before I could speak, there was the sound of running footsteps and the driver's door was wrenched open.

He gave a thin scream as two huge men dragged him out of the seat and began punching him savagely. He did not fight back. He merely held his hands over his face, and when he fell, he curled into a foetal ball. I could not see properly then, because another of the assailants was blocking my way with his back. I groped for the door to let myself out, but the lock button had been removed. There was a lot of screaming and shouting outside, most of it from the driver. Then there was an ominous silence filled with heavy breathing.

The big man whose back had blocked my view, climbed into the front passenger seat and turned to look at me. His hair was dyed white, but his eyebrows were dark and almost joined over the bridge of his nose. Another thin man with dark greasy-looking hair slid into the driver's seat and turned the key. The big man continued to stare at me expressionlessly as the car backed down from the sidewalk. Then he pointed solemnly through the window. As I turned to look, he hit me on the head hard, and a second, deeper night consumed me.

*　*　*

I woke to find myself lying full length along the back seat of the taxi that was not a taxi. My jacket had been thrown over me. From that position, I could see nothing except that it was still night. Gathering my strength, I sat up. Outside the car windows the darkness sped by. There was no sign of the city nor of any buildings. We were on a straight open highway, driving very fast.

The driver said something and the big man turned and lifted a truncheon. I shook my head.

"There is no need for that," I said.

I don't know if he understood me, but he lowered his arm. He studied me as if my calmness interested him, then he said something in his own language to the driver. The other man shook his head and began to shout. The big man said nothing until he was silent, then he turned back to me and pointed through the front windscreen.

"Karvu. Coff-ee," he said.

Looking down the road, I saw a faint illumination on the horizon. The brightness grew until I could see that it was an all-night petrol station attached to a fast food restaurant. The car pulled off into an access road and curved round to come to a grinding halt in the gravel car park. We were at the farthest point of the light. There were only two other cars parked alongside the restaurant. One was very new and red.

"You come," the big man said. He said something else in his own language that sounded like a warning, and I nodded.

They walked one each side of me as we approached the restaurant. The driver pointed at the bowsers and the big man shrugged, steering me deftly through the shining glass doors. The harsh light hurt my eyes and I was glad of the thick paw on my shoulder. I thought I might vomit because of the light, but could not think how to express this. The big man pushed me into a booth and eyed two men sitting in the opposite booth.

"I just wish you wouldn't bring up the war," one said in an American voice. "It's a sore point with these guys. They think we betrayed them."

"You did," the other man snorted in laconic German-accented English.

The thin driver sat down, and gave the two men a dangerous look, but the big man patted his breast pocket and shook his head.

"All of that is ancient history. It's in the past," the American's tone was irritated. Neither he nor the German seemed to have noticed our arrival.

"Nothing is past here. Haven't you learned enough to know that?"

Silence fell between them, and I wondered what had become of my original driver. Had he been killed? The big man rose and went to a phone. The driver squinted at me through a fug of evil smelling smoke, looking as if he wished I would make an attempt to escape or call for help.

"We could have got coffee closer to the border," the German said.

"Coffee. Sure," the American's voice was ironic. "We've got a deadline, Klaus. Why don't you wait until we get somewhere civilised."

"You don't understand," the German said with friendly contempt. "You don't understand anything but disinfectant and prophylactics. You're afraid of everything, including your own shadow."

The mention of shadow galvanised me. For the first time, it occurred to me that the final step on my journey might be death. I realised I had known that all along, but had feared to look at it squarely. To distract myself from the horrifying realisation that I was not much troubled by the thought of dying, I wondered what border we were to cross. Or perhaps we had crossed it already and were travelling in the opposite direction to the German and the American.

"Aren't you afraid of getting a disease?" The American asked, fastidious but curious too.

The German laughed. "The possibility makes the pleasure more intense. Darker. But this place offers deeper pleasures."

"A stretch of god-forsaken highway where the snow looks like dirty sperm. And those women. The way they just loom up suddenly in the headlights with their black leather skirts and fishnet tights and fake fur coats, their eyes like petrol bombs about to blow up in your face. They scare the hell out of me. How can anyone stop. How can you get aroused by that?"

"They wouldn't be there if no-one stopped," the German said almost coyly. "I've stopped every time I pass this way, since the first time and every time I do, I am afraid. Nothing is more terrifying than to stop and take one of these women into the car. They take me down into the dark so deep I don't know if I'll ever come up. If it's possible."

"But they're just whores. Terrible rough whores with scars and thick thighs. I read in *Time Magazine* that they're the worst, most dangerous prostitutes in the world." The American's voice was lace-edged with hysteria.

"It's true," the German murmured.

"I'm not afraid. It's the disease ..."

The German laughed and called for the bill, and as he paid, the big white-haired man returned from the phone. He nodded at the two men as they left, then slid back into the booth beside me. It came to me that the phone call had been about me. That they had been waiting for it to decide my fate. Would they now kill me or beat me up and leave me for dead? Were they going to try to ransom me? Or use me as a hostage? These thoughts fluttered distantly though my mind, like leaves blown along a tunnel.

The waiter brought three espresso. The white-haired man must have ordered them when my attention was elsewhere. I drank, enjoying the cruel strength of it. I had never tasted such bitter coffee before, like the dregs of the world. The caffeine hit me like a punch to the heart.

An hour passed and the phone rang. The waiter glanced at our table in such a way that I realised he knew my assailants. Probably even knew that I had been abducted. The big man went to take the call. He nodded. He shook his head. He shrugged and said a few words. He nodded again. He put the receiver back on its cradle and came back to the table decisively. He said two words to the driver. Who lit another cigarette. Neither of them spoke to me. Neither of them looked at me.

A strange tension devoid of emotion filled me.

"What will we do?" I asked.

The big man tilted his head. "We? There is not we."

I grasped for something to say, to link us. To hold me to the earth.

"There is the war," I said.

"The war is always going on."

I felt a sense of loneliness, of being finally detached, that overcame a dull surprise at his speaking English so easily.

There was the sound of an engine approaching. Both men looked away through the glass and I felt abandoned. The noise increased until the headlights loomed and fused with the light from the petrol station. The car had tinted windows so it was impossible to see who was inside. There was the sound of a horn and the engine continued to run. The big man rose from the seat beside me and nodded to the driver, who reached into his pocket and threw a set of car keys onto the shining Formica.

"You have your own business, eh?" the big white-haired man said, and he winked solemnly and paid the bill. The two of them sauntered out the glass door and climbed into the waiting car — a taxi, I saw, as the doors slammed behind them, and it sped away sending up a spume of gravel in its wake.

As the car drove out, another car pulled in. A young couple emerged and stretched. They entered and I watched them slide into the booth where the American and German had sat. Their bodies touch all along one side from shoulder, down through the hip and thigh to the heels, their connection far more intimate than if they had been wound together explicitly.

Walking into the freezing night some little while later, I glanced back at the blazing lump of cement and glass. It looked surreal. Like some outstation at the end of the world. It began to snow lightly, white flakes swirling against the blackness. Climbing into the driver's seat of the taxi that was not a taxi, I inserted the key. The car started the first time despite the rapidly dropping temperature. I let the engine idle a moment, then put the car smoothly into gear. I felt no impatience and no fear. My body felt weak, but my hands were steady as I drove out onto the verge of the highway. I had no idea which way was the way back to the city.

I went left, remembering to drive on what was for me the wrong side of the road. It produced a queer feeling of unbalance in me, and as the light of the petrol station fled behind me, I reflected how strange and surreal it was to be driving into the unknown with such a feeling of absolute rightness. I could almost feel the proximity of my shadow in the paradox of it. The snow was still falling, yet blackness pressed against the car so hard I fancied it was slowing it down. After several kilometres, I realised that the car was indeed slowing. The petrol gauge showed the tank was empty.

The car coasted and I steered it, my mind a blank. I felt no need to make a decision. I had gone too far to pretend control over my life now. I had gone out of the blue and into the black. Snow flew like huge moths. I squinted to see the white line through them. The snow thickened and I realised I could no longer discern white from black.

The car was slowing right down, and I directed the wheel a little to the right, and at the same time, the snow ceased to fall, and I saw her, a woman standing beside the road against the vast rising mass of the forested hill behind her. She wore a slick black jacket and long black boots. As far as I could tell, she wore no skirt or stockings. Her long legs shone with the same blue-tinged white as her neck and face. Her hair was so blonde as to seem to give off its own radiance.

The car rolled to a halt a few steps from the woman. She turned slowly and my heart beat slowed. I told myself she could not see me, that it would be impossible to see anything in all of that streaming light; but her eyes seemed to swallow the light, and penetrate to me.

She came towards the car, approaching the passenger door in a sturdy undulating stride. She tapped at the window with nails as long and curved and transparent as a dragonfly's wings.

Aside from her hand splayed against the window, I could see only her torso; the patent leather, a liquiescent black, outlined her round hips and breasts. The passenger door opened and she entered the car as smoothly as a dancer to slide into the car, and with her came an icy blast of air. She was older than she had looked from a distance and more stocky. Her hair shone with such a silvery pallor that it might have been stranded with grey. She might have been close to fifty, and although her skin was like fine velvet, there were intricate webs of wrinkles at the edges of her eyes like the sort of embroidered lace created by wizened nuns in some strict fanatical order of silence. Her mouth was purple-black, as if she had sucked some dark potent fruit whose juice had stained her. Eve's lips might have looked like that, after she bit into the fruit of the tree of knowledge. But her eyes were the bright shining miraculous blue of the skies above my own land, and nothing is more pure or relentless than that.

"You are tired?" she asked in mangled English.

"I have not slept for a long time," I said. The words were difficult to formulate, as if my lips were reluctant to obey me. As if it was too late for that.

"It is long. The road."

She reached out and switched off the headlights. We were plunged into the intimate ghastly green of the dashboard light. The colour made her look as if she were a corpse and her eyes seemed transparent. Her hair was black now as if it had become saturated with the night, or with something seeping out from the heart of all her whiteness. "What do you want?" She spoke English as if through a mouth full of liquid.

"I am looking for my shadow," I whispered. My own voice sounded foreign.

"But it will cost you," she said.

She leaned away from me, and slowly, her eyes on my face, drew aside the slick black edges of the coat like the lips of a wound, to reveal the full smooth curve of her breasts where they were pressed together into a voluptuous cleavage. They were white as milk and downed like a peach. She reached a pale hand between them and scooped one breast out. It was so soft that her fingers sunk in it. Only now, with her hair swept back to bare her throat and bosom fully, did I notice that there was a vein coiling from her neck to her breast. It writhed under her skin as if it had its own life. It was as delicate as the threaded flaw in purest marble and it moved towards the tip of her breast as if to drink, or escape.

I began to shake my head. I wanted to tell her that she was mistaken. I was ill, but not old. Not so old. She reached out her free hand to slide around my neck, and pulled me towards her. She was strong as a peasant and a ripe odour flowed over me as she lifted the breast, offering the thick nub of her nipple.

AFTERWORD

I had just left my home on the Great Ocean Road in Australia when I wrote "The Man Who Lost His Shadow". It was the end of spring, so the days were chilly, but though it lacked heat, the sunlight suffused the sea-mist with gold and the world smelled tantalisingly of salt and the summer to come. As ever, Australia never seemed more beautiful and precious than when I was leaving.

I had met Jack Dann at the Melbourne Writers Festival, and he mentioned that he and Janeen Webb were putting together a collection of science fiction and fantasy stories. I was keen to be involved, but had nothing to hand and can't write to order. However, Jack was not prescriptive at all, and I did have a story floating around in my head which I wanted to write for Nadia Wheatley to thank her for launching *Greylands* for me. I had decided to make this my first project when I returned to Europe. If it didn't come together in a few weeks, I would give it up. Stories are harder for me to write than prose for a novel because they seem to demand something very intense from me.

I didn't reckon on how I would feel coming back to Prague. It is a beautiful ancient city bisected by the bridge spanned Vltava and built where woolly mammoth hunters once roamed. There are labyrinthine cobbled streets and a multitude of churches and lovely buildings, but it was so dark and the stone seemed so hard and heavy. Never before had the grimy film left on this city and its people by decades of totalitarian oppression seem more in evidence to me. The sun didn't shine for three weeks as I wrote. Daylight seemed no more than the brief grey flicker and at three in the afternoon, night closed over the city like a lid. You could almost hear the clunk. I felt like Persephone caught between darkness and light, and of course, this permeated the story as a subtext...

— *Isobelle Carmody*

WYNNE WHITEFORD

Born in 1915, Wynne Whiteford has been an aircraft assembler, reporter, editor, and a prolific writer since the 30s. His first science fiction story was "Beyond the Infinite," which appeared in *Adam and Eve* in 1934, but he seemed to catch fire in the 50s, and his sf stories such as "The Non-Existent Man" were selling to overseas markets such as *Amazing*. In the late 70s he began writing his *Kesrii* series of stories, and from 1980 to 1990 he turned his hand to writing novels, which include *Breathing Space Only*, *Sapphire Road*, *Thor's Hammer*, *The Hyades Contact*, *Lake of the Sun*, and *The Specialist*. He was awarded the Epicurean and Cultural Society Short Story award in 1987, the Ditmar award in 1990, and the A. Bertram Chandler Award for lifetime achievement in Australian science fiction in 1995.

He writes: "As a child, I was stirred by stories my father told me of a six-months expedition through the center of Australia to Darwin and back, when the Government had visions of opening the inland to settlement. Fortunately, it didn't happen, and the unique outback environment has survived, but my father's experiences ignited my imagination, feeding the lure of places over the horizon.

"Eventually, I found my own adventures in far-off lands, returning home to my stringybark forest to weave past, present, and future fiction from fragments of the endless variety of human activity all over our planet."

In the story that follows, Whiteford returns to his native country — and to the outback, where the otherworldly remnants of the Dreamtime can be found in the very rocks themselves.

NIGHT OF THE WANDJINA

WYNNE WHITEFORD

The Director lifted his eyes from the spread-out map and looked at the other three men around the table. "Agreed, then? We make a series of test bores at intervals of two thousand metres along the anticline from here" — he gestured with his pencil — "to here."

There was a perfunctory murmur of assent from the Chief Geologist and the Accountant. Both were older than the Director, but they had given up trying to compete with his inexhaustible energy. He looked intently at the gaunt, sun-mottled man at the left end of the table, noticing the pulse beating almost imperceptibly near his temple.

"Something wrong, Kel?"

Kel seemed to snap back into the present moment with an effort, running a hand through his greying hair. "Not too happy about the area, that's all." As he looked at the Director his eyes, normally steady and controlled, were momentarily wide and haunted.

"But you've worked up that way before."

"Yes. With no luck."

The Director spread out his hands. "So it's a calculated risk."

Kel shrugged resignedly, and the Director closed the meeting. But as the Accountant and the Chief Geologist were preparing to leave he caught Kel's eye and made a hold-on signal with his finger. Kel spent a little time getting his papers together, wishing a good-night to the other two as they went out through the door. As soon as they were out of sight he froze, and both he and the Director stood looking at the closed door as the footsteps faded along the passageway.

"Time for a drink, Kel?" asked the Director as the sound of the elevator door clashed along the passage.

"Thanks, Don." Kel stood staring through the window across the panorama of Melbourne, with its higher towers gilded by the late afternoon sun. He could see the bay to the left through the clefts between the buildings, and away to the right a jet was landing at Tullamarine.

The Director walked across the room and handed him his drink, noticing the unexpected tremor in his hand that sent tiny waves across the glass.

"Kel," he said, "we've been together since we started this game. Something's bugging you. What is it?"

Kel looked at him thoughtfully before answering. The Director was a big man with an easy smile, somehow boyish until you looked at his eyes. They were small, bright eyes, somehow older and harder than the rest of him.

"I'll tell you, Don. But I don't want it on record."

"Sure." The big man shrugged, then turned suddenly and switched off an unobtrusive tape recorder on top of a filing cabinet. Kel stared at it as though he hadn't been aware of its presence, and the Director touched the eject button, extracted the cassette and laid it aside, looking expectantly at Kel.

"You mentioned somewhere there was an Aboriginal site in the area?" said Kel.

"Oh, that? Only the one. Took the trouble to get any sacred sites identified first — otherwise a claim might go in after we'd hit the jackpot."

"Okay, but I don't want to drill anywhere near it. Right?"

The big man looked at him fixedly for a few seconds, his eyes exploring the tanned face. They'd moved a long way apart, he thought, since the old days when they'd gone drilling together.

"Not worried about spirits, Kel? Blackfellows' curses?"

"Hell, no. No reasonable person believes that sort of claptrap today. Although ..."

The pause lengthened out. "How d'you mean, *although*?"

Kel swallowed some of his drink. "I was thinking. We know a lot more today than they knew in the dark ages. Even a lot more than anyone knew twenty years ago. But we don't know it *all*."

The Director had a curiously controllable face, like an actor. He looked at Kel with his lower lip thrust forward slightly, one eye half-closed, the opposite eyebrow lifted high.

Kel gestured with his glass. "When I say I don't believe in ghosts — I mean nothing is ever going to convince me that the spectre of Captain Cook or Ned Kelly still roams about. But look, Don, something bloody odd happened to me years ago when I was doing a geophysical survey down south of the Kimberleys."

"What were you after?"

"Oil — when I was working with the other crowd. That was when they were all carving up the North-

West Shelf, and everyone was looking for oil in the most unlikely places. I had three blokes with me — Gil, the fellow who fired the charges for underground echoes, Pete and Djerri, who were all-rounders. Pete was what you'd call a good instinctive mechanic. Djerri was an Aborigine, who knew the country — there were times when he found things to eat that the rest of us wouldn't have been game to touch."

The Director moved some papers on the table with his left hand so he could glance at his wristwatch. Suddenly he sat down at his desk, lifted his phone and punched out a number. His face seemed to soften for a time.

"Hi, Kit. Been held up a bit ... Right. See you."

Replacing the phone, he pointed to one of the bubble chairs. "Better sit down, Kel. I want to hear this."

* * *

It was about this time in the afternoon (began Kel). We'd been doing a run of test bores along an anticlinal fold that looked a vague possibility, but with no luck. It outcropped in a long, low ridge that had resisted erosion, and at a high point we found four stone slabs set upright, about the height of a man.

The sight of them, from a distance, seemed to upset Djerri, whose people had belonged to one of the coastal tribes that knocked around the Wyndham area. He said the stones had been put up, or looked after, by a tribe called the Ungarinyin, and he was hesitant about staying with us as we drove up along the ridge for a closer look.

The ridge wasn't very high — we were getting well inland where the Kimberleys were starting to flatten out into the Great Sandy Desert — and Gil and I were able to drive along the crest in the Landcruiser, Pete and Djerri following in the heavy truck with the drilling rig.

Very desolate there in the late afternoon. Nothing in any direction except reddish sand sprinkled with saltbush and a bit of spinifex struggling to survive. No birds. You know, you get birds of some kind in every part of inland Australia, but there were none here. Didn't even see any lizards. Only sound was the eerie sighing of the wind.

There was an outcrop of rock near the upright stones, and in a sheltered hollow Pete found paintings on the rock surface — vaguely human figures with round heads, no mouths, and marks around their heads that suggested lightning. They reminded me of something I'd seen, somewhere, but couldn't recall.

"Wandjina!" shouted Djerri, stepping back.

I stood looking at the painted outlines for a long time. They'd been carefully done, with smooth, confident lines that suggested the artist knew what it was all about. But they'd been painted so long ago that centuries of weathering had almost obliterated them in places. It was obviously Aboriginal work, but there was something about the figures that looked alien.

"What's wandjina?" I asked Djerri.

His dark, red-streaked eyes looked startlingly wide. As far as I could determine from what he told me in short, disconnected sentences, all that part of the Kimberleys was aware of the Wandjina cult, a belief held not only by the Ungarinyin, who lived around the immediate area, but by a couple of other tribes called the Worora and the Wonamble, or something, that used to control the area nearer the coast.

"Some of this white paint doesn't look all that old," I said.

"Men of the tribes touch up the figures sometimes," explained Djerri. "Part of rain-making ritual." He began to move away, pointing to the round-headed figures. "The Wandjina were heroes who came from the sky, or some people say, from the sea, back in the time of the *ungud* — what you might call the dreamtime."

When he told me that, I realised where I'd seen something like these paintings before. On a TV program, a fellow called von Daniken had shown rock paintings of non-human figures with what looked like space helmets and flames around their heads. Some had been painted in the Sahara, some in Central Australia, and somewhere else. Of course, there had to be a simpler explanation than the coming of beings from space, but in this empty wilderness the painted figures had a chilling force.

Well, I was in trouble. I wanted to drill right there, because it was the highest point on the anticline and would give us the best chance of striking any oil, if it had been trapped under the upfold. But Djerri didn't want any part of it, and neither did Gil.

Odd guy, Gil. Thin, wiry, with a sun-blistered forehead and peeling nose, and eyes that seemed to stick out when he was excited, as he was now. He was the sort of fellow who'd like to see the National Trust elevated to a totalitarian dictatorship. You know — the status *quo*, period.

Well, we sorted it out in a way. Djerri simply quit. No ill-feeling about it. He borrowed one of the two trail bikes we used for reconnoitering, took some food and a bag of water with him, and strapped them onto the pillion with bungee cords. Sitting astride the machine, he looked up at me.

"Be careful, Kel," he said. "I'll see you back at our last camp." And that was it. We shook hands, and he started the engine and rode off, following our tracks back. He didn't look back at us — just kept riding at the same even speed, holding his shoulders high the way his people do, until his red shirt and battered, wide-brimmed hat dwindled to a speck in the distance, partly obscured by the trail of fine red dust he raised behind him.

"All right," said Gil as we watched him go. "It's okay with me as long as we don't drill right on the site."

"Good!" I said. Although the sun was well down toward the horizon, I decided to begin a test bore straight away, rather than have an argument flare again tomorrow morning.

We manoeuvred the truck into position and put out its stabilisers, and lined up the drilling rig. We began drilling a short distance away from the upright stones.

As the drill ground its way down into the dry red soil, I stood looking around me. The hot wind whispered through gaps in the eroded rocks along the ridge. Below, nothing in sight grew higher than the stunted saltbush and, whichever way I looked, nothing moved between me and the heat-haze that blurred the horizon.

Pete, the mineralogist of the team, was excited about some bits of weathered black glassy rock he'd found near the paintings.

"It shouldn't be here," he said.

"How do you mean?"

"It *is* obsidian, isn't it? Volcanic glass. Form of rhyolite. See?"

"Well, don't worry about it. It could have been brought here from somewhere else."

Pete went on collecting pieces. "I don't get it," he kept muttering to himself. He was a careful type, stocky, solid, almost obsessive. I walked back to the drilling rig, which Gil was now operating in the absence of Djerri, listening to the laborious puttering of the engine and the sound of the bit grinding its way down into the dry red soil.

"Look at this!" called Pete suddenly. His dark eyes looked at me over the tops of his glasses. "These things look as if they're parts of something. Here —" He scrambled to his feet, holding the pieces of dark glassy material in his hands. "They all have a convex surface and a concave one, as if they're parts of a hollow cylinder that's been shattered. Sure, the edges are worn away by the abrasion of windblown sand, and some of the pieces are missing."

"That bit looks like a section of a hollow ball," I pointed out.

"There's another like that. I reckon the original thing was a cylinder with rounded ends."

I studied the pieces for a long time. "Could it be part of a volcanic gas bubble?"

"Out here? Where's the volcano? Anyway, the bubble'd have to blow up to a certain size, and hold stable pressure for a long time while the stuff solidified." He shook his head. "No. This thing's an artifact."

"Cut it out, Pete. Look at the erosion wear on the edges. Looks as if it's been sand-blasted for thousands of years. Artifact? Who d'you think made it? The Wandjina?"

This got a laugh from Gil, and Pete dropped the subject.

There was a noticeable change in the sound of the drilling rig. The engine speeded up, although the amount of red soil coming out of the hole dwindled. Gil swung the bit out of the hole and switched off the motor.

"Hit something," he said. "Couldn't be a different stratum yet."

The slanting light of the reddening sun left the hole completely dark. Gil walked round to the cabin of the truck and returned with the big five-cell torch, directing its beam down the hole.

"What the hell — Say, look at this! It's more of that damned rhyolite, or whatever Pete called it."

I took the torch from him. "Looks like the same stuff, but I think you've cracked it."

"Can't understand why the drill didn't grind it to powder."

"Want to drill beside it?"

"No. Reckon we could dig it out."

We dug it out, while the swollen red sun flattened out into a broad oval on the mists of the skyline. We worked quickly, because the dark really jumps on you that close to the equator.

The thing shook all of us, when we got it out into the light. Against all reason, we had to admit that it *did* look like some kind of artifact.

It was a cylinder about ninety centimetres long and nearly thirty in diameter, with rounded ends. It reminded me of those glass balls the Japanese use as floats on their fishing nets, but it was too thick and heavy to serve that purpose — it would have sunk like a rock in water. One end was marked with a twisting, whorl-like pattern. Pete voiced the thought that was forming in my mind.

"Looks as if it's been sealed off. Heated, spun around, and sealed."

"Wouldn't that have left a pip of glass sticking out, like an old-fashioned light globe?"

"Could have been ground off. Let's take it around to the front of the truck and look at it in the headlights. Careful, though, the drill's cracked it — see?"

The sun was down now and the quick purple dusk of the desert was already sweeping over us. Gil was carrying the cylinder, and Pete went round to the driving side of the cabin to switch on the headlights of the truck. A second before the powerful lights blazed out, Gil tripped over a piece of equipment lying in the shadows and sprawled headlong. The glassy cylinder struck the end of the heavy steel bull-bar across the front of the vehicle and burst with a report like a gun shot.

We were never quite able to agree on what happened next. The way I saw it, at the instant the lights came on the broken shards of the cylinder were still rocking on the ground, and a twisting cloud of whitish vapour seemed to swirl upward from them. It didn't spread out indefinitely, as I expected, but seemed to spin like a whirlwind, although there wasn't enough wind about to generate a vortex.

It spun upright, about the height of a man, then it moved quickly away from us, first travelling down the beam of the headlights, then abruptly veering sideways into the dark.

"What was it?" Gil's voice was an octave higher than I had ever heard it.

"Say," said Pete in a stunned monotone, "you don't suppose..." He let his voice trail away.

"Suppose what?" I broke in sharply.

"You know those corny old Arabian Nights yarns about genies in bottles?"

"Rot! Only a whirlwind. A willy-willy."

Pete looked unconvinced. Gil licked his finger and held it up.

"The wind's coming this way. It went across *that* way."

"All right," I snapped, "so it was an eddy."

"An eddy? Who are you kidding, Kel?"

By now it was almost dark outside of the zone of the headlights. Pete reached in and switched them off. Then, after a few seconds of near blackness, he switched them on again, and no-one commented. The wind stirred fitfully through the clefts in the rocks, and none of us seemed inclined to move away from the bright path of the lights.

"Well," I said at last, "we can't stand here all night."

"Wait," said Gil, and taking the big torch he climbed on to the roof of the Landcruiser. "Switch off the headlights now," he called down to us.

He swung the long beam of the torch in a slow careful arc. Once, the light seemed to pass a drifting wisp of fog-like vapour at an indeterminate distance, and Pete and I both asked "What's that?" in a sharp tense chorus.

Gil whipped the beam back, waving it from side to side in gradually widening sweeps. But now there was nothing.

We didn't sleep much that night. It was bad enough when it was dark, but when the moon came up it was worse. We found ourselves peering out at the pallid landscape until the clumps of saltbush seemed to flit about at the edge of our vision.

"Just thinking," mused Pete in a dreamy voice, "why did they put genies in bottles?"

"Look!" I exploded. "That's enough thinking for tonight. Let's get some sleep."

A few minutes later Gil suddenly sat up. "What was that?"

"What?"

"That sound. Like a sort of whisper."

"Probably a bat."

"No. It was like a voice."

"What'd it say?" I kept my voice hard and derisive.

"It was like a whisper in a different language."

"Abo's language?"

"No. Not like any language I've ever heard."

Angrily, I got up. The embers of the little camp fire were still glowing unevenly in the faltering wind. The landscape was bleached with moonlight. I walked over toward the drilling rig.

Nothing.

I turned. I was not quite sure, but something seemed to move between me and the fire.

You know the way you can look down through clear water to the bottom of the stream, and the bottom seems to shake as a ripple passes over the water? It was an effect like that, as if there had been a visible ripple in the air.

I walked cautiously back to the camp fire and found Gil standing.

"I heard it again," he said.

He bent down and picked up the big torch, then began to walk away from the fire, down the moonlit slope toward the scrubby saltbush, swinging the beam of the flashlight from side to side. Then, when he was about fifty metres away, he screamed.

It was a strange chopped-off scream. It brought Pete to his feet. We both began running toward Gil. He seemed to stagger sideways, as if he were fighting something we couldn't see. The beam of light flailed wildly, and then abruptly he dropped the torch. It lay on the ground, its beam cut short by a clump of saltbush. "Gil!" I shouted as we ran.

Before we could reach him, he fell, then quickly came to his feet again, moving away from us in a lurching run. I picked up the torch and swung its beam onto his staggering figure.

There was something wrong with the way he ran. He ran without swinging his arms in rhythm with the movement of his legs, and the length of his stride kept changing, as if he were experimenting with it. The height he lifted his feet kept changing, too, as though he had never run before. Yet his movements, though badly coordinated, had unbelievable energy.

"Gil! Gil!"

He ran in a wide circle in great, leaping strides, his head on one side, his arms swinging randomly like the arms of a doll, a marionette.

A marionette! That was the effect, exactly. As if something else were operating his body — something able to move it, yet utterly inexperienced in controlling this type of body.

He raced back towards us. I shone the torch beam full in his face, but he gave no indication of noticing it. His eyes were fixed and blank, like the eyes of a dead man.

He lurched past us in that ghastly, leaping run, leaning sideways as he veered in a curve, then straightening up, lengthening his already too-long stride. Once, he crashed through a clump of saltbush, sprawled to the ground, rolled to his feet and raced on.

"Into the Landcruiser, Pete!" I shouted.

As we climbed aboard, he said, "She's low on fuel."

"We'll have to chance it." I started the engine.

"Okay." Pete jerked his thumb over his shoulder. "We've got a full jerrycan in the back, if we're stuck."

With the lights on high beam, I drove after the distant racing figure. He was heading southeast, and we could see his course by the disturbance of saltbush and spinifex.

"Look," said Pete in an awed voice, "how the hell does he keep going so damned *straight*? Like a plane following a beam."

"I was noticing that. It's as if whatever took control of him started by running around learning to make a human body work. Or maybe the way a migrating bird flies around to get its bearings before taking off on a long flight. *Now*, he seems to be heading straight for some definite goal."

"But what? What's out this way? Nothing but desert."

I thought for a moment, then said, "If you go far enough southeast from here, you have Uluru and the Olgas, unmistakable landmarks, and Haast's Bluff, the old meteor crater — but they're hundreds of kilometres away. He'd never get that far."

Pete grunted. "I'm not sure, the way he's moving."

We followed the bounding figure for several kilometres, but although he must have seen our lights throwing his shadow ahead of him he gave no sign of awareness of our presence.

Then, just as I was deciding to drive alongside him, the engine of the Landcruiser spat, stuttered and fell silent. As we rolled to a stop, Gil's figure went leaping on toward the southeast.

Pete clamped the pourer onto the jerrycan, and we tipped the fuel into the tank. "That's enough," I said, "we can put the rest in later."

While Pete was stowing the half-full can back aboard, I tried to start the engine again, but without success. "Damn! We've got a vapour lock. Have to tip some juice into the carby."

I began taking off the air cleaner while Pete returned with the rest of the fuel. A glance ahead showed that Gil's figure was very far away.

With the carburettor bowl filled, the engine started at once. I replaced the air-cleaner, and as I spun down the wingnut holding it Pete replaced the can. I could not see Gil's figure now.

We drove on, sometimes losing the trail where the saltbush was sparse. Eventually, though, we picked it up, following it even where it crossed a shallow, dry water-course by what looked like a single leap. Ultimately, we came on Gil, sprawled on the dusty floor of another erosion gully.

"He's dead," said Pete, shining the beam of the torch on the inert figure. Gil lay like a broken marionette flung aside by a destructive child. His shirt and jeans were spattered with blood from his encounters with the saltbush.

"Let's get him into the Landcruiser," I said. We carefully picked up the lifeless body and carried it to the car. Only after we had placed it in the back seat a chilling thought struck me.

"Let's get the hell out of here, Pete! That thing that took hold of him — it might reach for one of us!"

We sprang aboard, I started the engine and swung the car around. As we headed back, Pete glanced through the back window.

"D'you reckon the *thing's* still out there, somewhere?"

"I'm not going back to look," I said.

We drove through the night and morning, taking the body back to our main base. Heart seizure, the verdict. Well, that would have been right. You couldn't drive a human body at that speed, for that long, without the heart packing up.

Pete and I never mentioned that wisp of vapour we thought we saw. And we never mentioned the strange dry whisper we thought we heard.

Ghosts? Spirits? No, I don't believe in them. Not the classical kind. Unless, maybe, you include the Wandjina from the time of the *ungud*.

But whirlwinds? They put a fright into me even now — even in broad daylight.

* * *

Most of the way down to the parking area under the building, the Director was silent, expressionless.

"I don't know, Kel," he said at length. "It could have been a combination of things. Hallucinations — and there could have been some obscure virus that got into the fellow who died. Something like rabies, say?"

The elevator reached the basement and they walked out into the underground carpark where both their cars were at the far end. As they passed the ramp leading up to the dusk-lit street, a sudden gust of wind whirled a man-sized column of spinning dust around the angle of the wall. The Director leaped sideways with a sharp cry, and when he looked at Kel his face was pale.

"It's all right." Kel's own face had whitened and his voice creaked like a rusty hinge, but he managed a half-smile. "I don't think they come this far south."

For a few seconds they looked at each other. Then they both joined in a shaky laugh, and walked quickly toward their cars.

AFTERWORD

I had been exploring the sparsely settled part of South Australia around the north end of the Flinders Ranges. The track ended at a dry watercourse lined with river gums. I left the car, walked along the silent creek bed. I felt alone on the planet. Then I came to an outcrop of rock with Aboriginal paintings protected by an overhang.

Most resembled others in various parts of the outback — X-ray type pictures of animals — but dominating them were von Danikenesque figures of mouthless, staring-eyed beings from the Dreamtime. They had a disturbingly alien look.

That night, the dark, unpolluted sky of the outback blazed with an uncountable multitude of stars that reached down almost to the deserted horizon. They seemed to make the outside universe more within reach than elsewhere, and I thought of the long-ago artist at the rocks. Did he feel an uncanny sense of something *out there*, centuries before the *X-Files?*

— *Wynne Whiteford*

CHERRY WILDER

Cherry Wilder is a major talent whose work has gained international recognition. To quote the late Roger Zelazny, one of the finest writers ever to work in the science fiction and fantasy genres: "Cherry Wilder does not write anywhere near as many stories as I wish she did. Of course, this makes each new one even more of a treasure and a treat. It is a privilege to visit the landscapes of her imagination and observe the doings there."

She was born and educated in New Zealand, to which she has recently returned after long periods spent in Australia and in West Germany. Her novels include *The Torin Trilogy* and the fantasy trilogy *The Rulers of Hylor*. Her novel *Signs of Life* is a sequel to *Second Nature*, which told of the castaway society on the planet Rhomary. Her short stories have appeared in *Interzone*, *Omni*, *Asimov's Magazine*, and many anthologies, including *Strange Fruit* and *The Year's Best Science Fiction, Fourteenth Annual Collection*. Some of her stories have been collected in *Dealers in Light and Darkness*.

The haunting story that follows depicts the beauty, joy, sadness, and strange poignancy of alien contact . . .

THE DANCING FLOOR

CHERRY WILDER

The dock at Wingard had the monumental proportions associated with Triad North, the company, and with Winthrop A. North IV, the man for whom it was designed. The Archive shuttle hung in the big shadowy facility like a tiny fish in a dark pool: all the passengers were curious, standing at the ports, as they were directed to a slot.

"Cult classic!" said Elliot March, the hotwit of the team. "Been used for trivid locations. Yo, Dayne — they made two runs of COOP VYRAT, SPACE PIRATE here . . ."

"Right here in the dock?" asked Dayne Robbins.

"Aw come on — here and out in the open, on the asteroid."

"Did they shoot on the Dancing Floor?" asked Taya Schwartz.

"No, Doctor." said Elliot. "Not in the episodes I saw. You work on the floor any time, Carl?"

"No, we were in the western valley system," said Carl Curran, "but we had a look at the floor."

Taya Schwartz did not know that the young media assistant had been on the Wingard habitat asteroid before — she must question him about his visit with the trivid team. She was conscious of the fact that her colleagues were all much younger than herself.

The docking was complete; Mahoney, the shuttle

pilot, shot the hatch and they filed out carrying their personal packs. Three android auxiliaries in their service grey uniforms manned the dock; they came bouncing up, full of oxper cheerfulness, saluted Flight-Captain Mahoney, greeted everyone else politely. Taya got their names quickly: Thomas Scott, Philip Grey, Peter Miles.

"Looking forward to your briefing, Doctor!" said Tom Scott, apparently the Leader of the android unit.

"How many auxiliaries on Wingard?" she asked.

"Just us three wishers doing dock duty today and one other, Cliff Watson, out in the green."

A man and a woman from the holding mission stepped out of the elevator; they were the reception committee. The oxper moved away and the Archive party were greeted by Gregor Hansen and Astra Wylie. They were a notably handsome couple, in their thirties, — their bright "colony" clothes had no service markings. The elevator had a smell of earth, of the countryside — the visitors stepped out into bright sunlight and stood amazed by the beauty of Wingard.

The dock was on the ridge that surmounted a deep bowl of green; they looked down into a valley system, earth-green, with earth trees and exotics, stretching into the countryside. Wingard had once supported a population of 1000 mensch, 1000 souls. There were still a few buildings to be seen in the distance. Cottage units and brown habitat huts were clustered in the nearest valley.

"Do the personnel from the mission live down there?" Taya asked the young woman, Astra Wylie.

"Yes, sure," she said. "That's our house — the new unit with the red roof by the tankstand."

The ridge above the valley continued on round and turned into a heavy wall of earth and stone, a miniature mountain range running north from where they stood. It showed the substance of the original asteroid, mined out and brought to this point in space by one of the Triad North companies. Taya Schwartz was able to glimpse a haze of green over the lower portion of the spinal wall: the wilderness area of Wingard, another series of interlocking deep valleys.

The Archive team were accommodated in the Harmony lodge, just beyond the ridge, at the end of the tall white complex that had housed the old Admin, near the dock. Gregor Hansen drove Dr Schwartz, the senior archivist, and Mahoney, the pilot, while Wylie brought the others in a larger electric runabout. Taya Schwartz ran a steady interview all the way checking the known data on the evacuation in 2499, the legal position, the state of the biosphere then and now.

Hansen explained, rather deadpan, that Wingard had gone down because of the life-support crash at Yesod Habitat. A couple of disorders in the water and the air on Wingard were taken out of proportion — the Terran admin panicked, ordered evacuation.

"And the settlers couldn't return," said Taya. "Pretty rough after twenty-five years on Wingard."

"Hard luck for those mensh," said Hansen, with some feeling. "We wouldn't live anywhere else."

"Some habitats have gone down, been evacuated, after more than a hundred years," said Mahoney. "Tough thing here was that it wasn't necessary. Badly handled by Earth admin."

"I remember." Said Taya. "Winthrop North was sick and in deep financial shit ..."

"I heard you knew him, Doctor Schwartz," said Mike Mahoney. "Winthrop North."

Gregor Hansen turned his head to stare at Taya Schwartz, frowning. Winthrop A. North IV tended to polarise opinion; he was the last of his kind as well as the last of his line.

"We studied exo biology at the Pioneer Valley Foundation," she said. "He was an exceptional person but he had more than a touch of mad millionaire even then."

Mahoney gave a guilty chuckle. The last president of Triad North cast a long shadow. The notion of an industrialist who went about in space with his own engineers had always been unreal, reckless; North the Fourth seemed to have worn himself out. He had died ten years ago, in his Canadian retreat; sixty years old and a crotchety recluse, like millionaires of old time.

"Old North cared for this place, for Wingard," said Hansen. "Had his ashes scattered to enrich the soil, like one of the original settlers. I read his plaque in the memorial ground by the Sun Kiln."

"I didn't know that," said Taya.

"How long after the evacuation did Terran Security put in the holding mission?" asked Mahoney. "Was there ever a move to repopulate?"

"I guess there were plans," said Hansen. "Terran Security settled with North, a year or so before he died. There had been annual checks of this place — the problem with the air and the water righted itself with a little help from the bio engineers."

"Archive would like to target the year the Dancing Floor was built," observed Taya, "between one annual survey and the next. A pity nothing was seen by earth personnel."

"Well, Doc," said Hansen. "You said it. *Earth personnel*. The first holding mission arrived in '68, bunch of retired Space Service Joes and their wives or partners. They came in on contract for five years, sort of Recreation Leave. They didn't patrol too much ... they missed the meteorite over in the East Greenwall. They discovered the Floor in 2507, thought it had been there a while."

"And there was no-one out there earlier — hiking, camping, building a holiday hut?" she asked.

"Has someone been talking?" asked Hansen. "Some data was red, at least for a while ..."

"I haven't heard anything," said Taya. "Do I need clearance?"

"Wingard had a bunch of Die-Hards, is all," the young man burst out. "This comes up every time a habitat is evacuated. Some folk will not be shifted ... they run off, hide in the bushes, in a cave ..."

"Don't I know it," said Mahoney. "We had problems at Celestra and Novion."

Taya wanted to hear more about these Die-Hards but she was patient. They had arrived at the Harmony lodge, once the guest house for a beautiful, thriving habitat, which specialised in bio-farming and dendrology. The lodge was a handsome structure in Wright Renaissance style with vistas of dayplex and pillars that resembled dressed wood. There was no-one in the lobby but when Gregor Hansen shouted a young girl and an even younger boy came racing down the staircase.

He introduced them to the visitors: Marla Jenner,

elder child of the other mission family, and his own son Sven Hansen. They had been doing chores in the lodge and minding the systems: Taya understood a lack of personnel, the feeling of rattling around in untenanted buildings on a ghost world.

She was left alone with the children while Hansen and Mahoney went to fetch the baggage. She thought of certain trade goods she had brought along and felt in the pockets of her carrying bag.

"Would you like some of these holovox cards?" she asked. "Birds of Earth? Trivid Heroes?"

Marla, the older girl, nodded to Sven, who wiped his hands on his overall then gravely accepted the two brightly glowing packets. Marla quickly opened her packet and made her card with the Kookaburra utter its laugh. Taya had found the soy-nut health bars which both of them accepted. Marla slipped hers into a pocket but Sven took a big exploratory bite and was chewing heartily when the men came back.

Gregor Hansen dropped Taya's work-pack with an audible crunch and raced to his son, gripping him by the back of the neck.

"What's he got? What you got, boy?" he panted. "Spit it out! Spit it right out!"

As Sven spat his mouthful on to the dusty tiled floor his father wrenched away the rest of the candy bar.

"Marla," he said, tense with disgust and anger. "Take him to the washroom and see that he rinses his mouth out good with the bottled water."

Before the kids were out of sight, heading behind the staircase, Hansen turned angrily upon Taya.

"What was in that candy?" he demanded.

"You can read the ingredients from the label," said Taya. "It is a soy-nut health bar from the World Space Commissary at Armstrong Base. I eat them myself and give them to my grandchildren."

"You hand out any more of this rotgut candy to Sven?"

"No, Mr Hansen," she said. "Is your son not well? Does he have a dietary problem?"

"Soon will have if he takes that kinda junk!" snapped Hansen.

Mahoney looked shocked by the man's outburst.

"The Doctor wasn't to know ..." he said.

"To know what?" said Hansen, looking from one guest to another, red-faced, his eyes narrowed with suspicion.

"To know that you disapproved violently of certain types of food," said Taya. "I'm sorry."

"We live clean here, Mam. That boy has never tasted any sugar or additives ..."

"Well, he still hasn't," she said evenly. "Read the label, Mr Hansen."

"Why should I believe that shit thing, a printed label from some World Space supply outlet?"

"Why indeed," she said. "Where is my room, please?"

"Up one flight," he said. "Mezzanine Number 27. Elevators are non-functioning."

She picked up her work-case and strode off up the handsome staircase, with dark treads of wood substitute and a banister of black metal rods.

"Doc! Doc! I'll carry your bag!" called Mahoney.

"Thanks Captain," she smiled down at him. "I'll be fine!"

She heard Mahoney trying to take the man from the holding mission to task; when she turned her head at the curve of the stairs the children had come back. Sven was sitting emptily on the bottom step while Marla picked up his mouthful of chewed up candy bar. She was not using paper of course or any kind of manufactured wiper but a bunch of big papery leaves.

* * *

Taya Schwartz was stung by memory. The door of room 27 was open to receive her — she staggered into the spacious guest suite. The windows were open and the kids had placed a vase of fresh flowers — yellow daisies and statice — on the desk. She put down her case and sat on the bed, wearily. She thought of soft *amyth* leaves and of the chocolate she had eaten on a far distant world.

The Archive team, all quartered in Harmony, walked over to the Admin diner at 19:00 hours; the briefing was scheduled for 21:00. Taya was not really pleased with this — she liked to relax alone before a briefing, but there was no food outlet in Harmony lodge. The Admin was well-lit, clean and fresh, with a reggae band on the monitors.

"Hey, this is better," said Elliot March, under his breath. "Why can't they have our place like this? What makes the difference."

"The oxper," said Taya. "They take care of this building."

Dayne Robbins, the Medic on the Archive team, was also their commissariat liaison. She was already helping in the canteen along with the oxper Miles and Grey. The food was very good: fresh Wingard vegetables along with the specials they had brought from the Moon. There was a range of tea, fruit boosters and juice. Dayne brought their dessert and settled at the table.

"Problems of interaction," she said. "Experienced anything?"

"The holding mission are hard-line anti-service, against World Space," suggested Taya. "Possibly they're anti-Earth as well: Spaceborn or Never Returns."

"*What?*" said Elliot. "How you make that out, Doc?"

"It's true," said Dayne. "They can barely interact with the android auxiliary teams. The kids aren't allowed to speak to them or enter this building. Groups of service personnel who visit Wingard for any reason — to inspect the dock facility for instance — have a minimum of contact to the Jenners and the Hansens."

"It wasn't like that when you were here with the media team, Carl!" exclaimed Elliot.

"No — but these are new guys," said Carl Curran. "The first holding mission were older folk, veterans from World Space taking it easy on their Recreation Leave. Don't know where they found these two families."

"I know that," said Mahoney. "They came from the planet Arkady. The southern continent — has an official name now —"

"*Oparin*," said Taya Schwartz wistfully.

She left the others in the canteen and sat in a pleasant window bay in the lounge, looking out over the green valleys while she went over her material.

Presently Hal Jenner, the senior member of the holding mission came and introduced himself. He was a well set up man in his forties, with dark eyes and thick dark brown hair clubbed back with a strip of green cloth. His manner was relaxed and genial: compared with his younger colleague, Hansen, he was a diplomat. He explained, first of all, that he had been checking the road into the inland that morning.

"One of the androids reported a fallen tree," he said. "I had to take care of it."

"*You* had to move the tree?" Taya couldn't resist it.

"Well, no, just tidy a little," said Jenner.

"That would be Cliff Watson, out there," she said. "I've worked with auxiliary personnel several times and found them reliable colleagues."

Hal Jenner caught his breath.

"How many people on Wingard, Mr Jenner?"

"Four adults in the holding mission," he said, "Hansen and Wylie, my wife Fern and myself, our two children Marla and Dan, and Sven Hansen, makes seven all told. Then there are the folk at the Old Mill — three souls, former colonists. You're bound to hear of them — our little family of Die-Hards. Those are all the people. Then World Space sends in their units of androids, four at a time, replaced every half earth year, from Armstrong Base."

Taya had already registered in the hard-nosed young Hansen a more friendly attitude to the original settlers. None of these people had been members of World Space — they had been carefully recruited from Earth, from Arkady and from the employees of Triad North.

"You've made contact with the Die-Hards, Ranger Jenner?"

Hal Jenner laughed.

"Yes, sure Doc," he said. "There were reports from the first re-settlers, those World Space veterans. They swore there were a few settlers still out there, old folks like themselves, two women and a man, living in the wilderness. We didn't believe them overmuch —"

It was a slip.

"Why not?" she asked. "Because they were from World Space?"

"Well it turned out they weren't lying," he said. "I seen the old fella first. What you'd expect. Skinny old man with a beard down to here. Name of Gunn, Ben Gunn. Asked for medical supplies, water filters and so on. We took down a good load — food, all kinds of good stuff we thought they might use. There they all were, Old Ben and his two old gals, one called Vona? Other one Kirsten, maybe."

"Would it be possible for me to speak to them?" she asked.

"They are very shy," said Hal Jenner. "They have a deep need to be left alone — and we understand that better than most people. You could send a message on their systems . . ."

He shrugged his shoulders a little hopelessly.

"So your family and the Hansens were recruited on Oparin, in Arkady." Taya pursued, changing the subject.

"We had the wilderness and rough farming experience," he said eagerly. "Gregor and I are both Rangers, Arkady rank. The women are trained Medical Technical Assistants."

"Will you ever consider expanding the numbers of the holding mission — repopulating?"

"No!" he said firmly. "Why should we? Our new specialised projects with the trees and vegetables are flourishing. We're working on a quite different scale from the original Wingard settlers. Besides it's not up to us entirely ... this is a matter for E.A.A. — Earth Asteroid Administration; they have the resettlement rights for all Triad North habitats."

"You are extreme separatists," she said, holding his gaze. "Ranger Jenner, how can you work for an Earth Utility?"

"It's worth it to live on a clean world," he said. "We keep a close watch on the E.A.A. So far we haven't caught 'em cheating on the deal. They don't bother us too much."

"Is it a bother to receive the Archive team?"

"No Mam!" said Jenner with a broad smile. "The Archive facility operates from the Moon and from other manned planets and habitats. Completely separate from World Space and it's a private foundation, not linked to the World Security Organisation or any of its segments."

＊　＊　＊

It was time for the briefing. She followed Jenner into a small conference room which looked pleasantly full — there were the two families from the holding mission, the four members of the Archive team. At the back, separated by tables and chairs, were all four oxper. Cliff Watson had come in from the outback.

Taya spoke last. Eliot March explained the work of Archive — mapping resources throughout the Solar

System and near planets. He was careful to explain what every member of the team did: he himself was responsible for admin and for flora and fauna, wild and cultivated. He would work closely with Ranger Hansen. Carl Curran was the cameraman and media specialist; Dayne Robbins was their medic and commissariat assistant. Dr Taya Schwartz was a specialist in extra-terrestrial artefacts.

Carl gave a very brief rundown on his work and Dayne simply praised the quality of the Wingard vegetables. When Taya took the floor she had a short round of applause from the oxper. The big projection screen worked perfectly: she changed the order of the pictures and hit them with a shot of DanFlor III in full sunlight.

In a meadow filled with bright green grass and ringed with dark scrubby bushes, tall as a hedge, there was a strange construction. Three tall wooden pillars looped with swags of rough green fabric, like fishnet, stood at the edge of a prepared space, 50 metres by a hundred. The space was slightly depressed in the center, a shallow bowl, paved with 80 centimetre slabs of moulded stone, a bright sandy yellow. The paving-stones were closely packed, fitted together; there were no sharp angles or corners; the stones had rounded edges.

"This is the Dancing Floor which Montezuma Antonio Rivez, the great exo-biologist, found upon *Habitat Three*," she announced. "It was the third example to be discovered; this was the year 2465. This type of artefact had already been given the popular name of a Dancing Floor."

The name came from the report on the first artefact to be found — on Europa, the moon of

Jupiter, in 2440. There were two stations of space personnel on Europa at that time, in carefully insulated "cities", Paris II and New Hyatt. The exploration of the underground seas and their biology was highly competitive.

A surface patrol from Paris claimed to have watched the building of a strange artefact by a team of eight aliens rated 5.4 on the RK Index, the Rivez-Klein scale of humanoid visual affinity. The builders had a small vessel, roughly the size and shape of a World Space Class Upsilon Transporter, not clearly visible behind a ridge. They worked behind a highly developed air-dome on the level site of an older Earth station.

When the pavement was completed there was a pause of ten earth-equivalent hours while the moulded paving stones set or were dried. The patrol, comfortably encamped behind their own ridge, held their position and kept watching.

Then as the bulk of the gas giant was at its closest to the moon, Europa, they beheld the construction team dancing, they swore it, on the big paving stones. The builders/dancers looked even weirder, their RK index even greater, without their work clothes. They leaped with uncanny grace from stone to stone, in a certain pattern. The paving stones lit up as the dancers stepped upon them. The watchers believed that this light came from some device within the stones, or possibly from the footwear of the dancers. They put forward the notion that the dancing-floor, as they called it, was some kind of communication device.

The patrol, already overdue, returned to their Paris base and broke the news of their exciting discovery. But a mischievous concatenation of circumstances — bad karma said some — ensured that the dancers and their floor were never confirmed.

"Yes," said Taya, answering a question. "That is correct, Ms Jenner — it was a seismological disturbance, an earthquake. The area could not be searched for a long time. There was no sign of a wrecked space vessel and only a few fragments that might have been paving stones. The men and women from the Paris patrol on Europa were not fully believed. They were partially discredited as witnesses because of inter-station rivalry.

They were accused of "zonking" — drinking alcohol, taking illegal drugs. They were *ranked* — lost service credits — for not calling in. The team explained this by saying that reception was very poor. They suspected that the builders of the Dancing Floor had a strong electronic presence and would have been immediately aware of any other signals, including the use of trivid equipment. They had attempted some holoks when they first arrived but the alien air dome spoiled the prints.

All that remained of this alleged encounter was the name "*Dancing Floor*" which went into use, however, in reports and later in the media. The same way as "flying saucer" entered the world languages long ago.

∗   ∗   ∗

So there was no original footage on the Europa floor but a good simul and some originals of the second artefact, found on Ceres in 2455 by a survey team sent out by Rivez and Klein from their newly formed Archive Foundation at Armstrong Base. They had their own satellite in the asteroid belt and picked up the Dancing Floor on Ceres.

One member of the Paris team from Europa, the retired Lieutenant Cole, C.P.V., was available to accompany this survey team. The structure was confirmed by this officer as another example of the alien artefact as built on Europa.

*   *   *

"This Space Service Lieutenant," said Hansen, "was old, retired, and had been discredited back then on the Jupiter satellite. Could he give good confirmation, Doctor?"

"In my opinion, yes," said Taya. "If we recap we can see the progress of the Rivez-Klein investigation: the destroyed artefact on Europa, Dancing Floor I, 2440, then the Dancing Floor on Ceres, 2455, and the example we have before us on the screen: Dancing Floor III discovered in 2565 by Monty Rivez and Hanna Klein on *Habitat Three*."

She took a question from Tom Scott.

"Yes, Leader Scott, that arrangement of three wooden pillars, looped with green stuff resembling fishnet is unique to Dancing Floor III. It seems to be a copy of a classical ruin on Earth — maybe copied from a holok or photograph of a painting."

"Doctor Schwarz," said Hal Jenner earnestly. "Any idea what was going on? What they were doing this for?"

"No, Ranger Jenner," she said. "There have been many theories — the original idea of a communication device is not borne out by anything in the stones themselves. I go along with a spiritual or religious ritual. We have the general picture of a team or teams from a highly developed space-travelling race moving through the Sol system and building these artefacts on uninhabited asteroids and habitats. There were unconfirmed reports of sightings of some vessel that might be a mother-ship beyond the asteroid belt. Rivez and Klein believed there might be other undiscovered examples. Dating is important, it would help. The last artefact to be discovered is the Dancing Floor here on Wingard."

Taya brought up its picture on the screen and the oxper reacted as humans might or should have done, recognising a local treasure. They clapped and called out, hey that's it, there's our floor. But the holding mission could not react with pleasure because the oxper did, and they were the artefacts of hated World Space.

Taya could not go on without calling the holding mission.

"Ranger Hansen," she asked, "what do you feel about this artefact on your habitat home, this Dancing Floor?"

"What do I *feel* ...?" Hansen was puzzled or pretended to be. "Well, I suppose it's impressive. Alien artefact. Not seen any before."

Jenner saw what she was driving at and rallied the settlers, including the children, with a glance.

"Heavens, we *like* it, don't we guys? Yay-Hay-Hay for our Dancing Floor!"

He clapped and the others echoed the strange Oparin cheer.

"Doctor Schwarz," broke in Elliot March, "has this floor been validated? I mean there were cases on Earth and on Arkady ..."

The question made the mission folk bristle but Taya was amused by Elliot's provocation.

"Yes, there have been attempts to copy these artefacts in several locations, including the planet Arkady," she said. "Sometimes these were crude hoaxes, fakes, but the one near Riverfield, Arkady, was an art-work, part of a festival display. Also, the replica in New Mexico is a careful attempt at a re-creation, using all known data and a new silicon matrix. The Dancing Floor here on Wingard has been sampled by an oxper team three years ago and accepted as genuine by Archive, the Rivez-Klein Foundation."

※　※　※

Taya went into her wind-up and into the Archive team's biggest PR exercise. Yes, she was certainly looking forward to seeing the floor tomorrow. And she had all the help she needed — Cliff Watson would drive the trekker. In two days the team would have completed its program. On behalf of the Archive Foundation she wished to invite all the inhabitants of Wingard, the people here at the meeting, to a picnic in the green on the third day. A viewing of The Dancing Floor, number four, Wingard's own. She understood that the day was Midweek, with a work free afternoon ... Hal Jenner accepted at once, quite heartily enough, on behalf of the holding mission, and the auxiliaries were pleased.

The meeting ended not with supper from the Commissary but with herb tea and home baked cookies brought along by Ms Jenner. The program for the rest of the archive team was settled for the next day.

Taya made sure that the central system outlet in her room at the Harmony Lodge was activated. She combed sleepily through the forests of memory and the endless data banks in search of one called *Weltfic*, a name which made German archivists laugh. She tried her Kamalin special assisted free association test and came up with two words *flint* and *silver* which sent her back to minerals and palaeontology as an association for that elusive name, *Ben Gunn*.

*   *   *

The roads were of packed earth, shot through with pebbles, the substance of the asteroid. It was time for the misty morning rain. They went skimming down from the lodge on the eastern road and drove by a pass through the central divide, something between a ravine and a conduit. There was a sign post which said *Sun Kiln*.

Cliff explained there was another disused pass further north and two closed tunnels on the east wall and the west wall — the settlers had used them to check the outer skin of Wingard. Nowadays the oxper did an occasional fly-past or used their viewers.

They drove on enveloped in green: beech and berioska from Arkady and wild apple trees. The wilderness area of Wingard was beautiful, full of vistas that might have come by chance but might have been designed, like the fake ruins of eighteenth century estates on Earth or the swathed pillars built near the Dancing Floor on *Habitat Three*. There was a stonework bridge over a grassy ravine and a tall building like a silo, covered with vines.

Cliff Watson, who was a boyish oxper, with black hair and brown eyes, kept up a running commentary. She came in with her question:

"You know the settlers, the Die-Hards who still live out here, Cliff?"

"Why sure, Doc," he grinned. "Old Ben and his two friends, Vona and Kirsty. They live in a place called the Old Mill, though it never was a mill I don't believe. Got it done up very comfortable. They even have their own trekker and they've been known to drive about a little. Guess they had the whole place to choose from, when everyone else was lifted out."

"What do they live on?"

"Got a fine garden, couple goats, bunch of bantam-fowls. They don't eat much meat except a little of the turkey jerky and fish we bring them from the Commissary."

"Could I get to meet them?" she asked. "I don't want to intrude on their retreat but they might just have seen some activity in connection with the Dancing Floor."

Cliff looked a little flickery with embarrassment.

"Well, truth is they don't have any regular contact even with us wishers from the auxiliary teams," he said, "but I could ask them."

"Take them some data," she said.

She handed over printouts on the Archive foundation and on herself.

"Now there's something," said Cliff, changing the subject. "Bit of a meteorite came down, side of the hill, over there. You can see where it burnt. The people at the Mill, they saw it come down about four, five years back, gave the auxiliary network a report."

The morning rain had stopped right on time. Taya examined the scarred hillside through her surveyor's goggles.

"I'm anxious to log the time when the Dancing Floor was built, Cliff," she said. "What have we got? A period of nearly fifteen years since evacuation, when Wingard was all but deserted."

"Sure," he replied. "Few clean-up operations, observation trips, from Armstrong, even from Earth. Oh, these Building Team fellows, they had all the time under the sun to fix up their artefact!"

"Is that what you call them? Building Teams?"

"BTAs," he grinned. "Building Team Aliens. Just our name . . ."

He swung the sturdy vehicle round a curve in the road and fell silent. There was the Dancing Floor among its fringe of trees, doubly lit by the sun, for it was lined up with Wingard's eastern row of reflectors on the central ridge to their left.

The road ran at a safe distance from the stones and there was a wooden shelter shed, a viewing place for the floor. Taya was glad when Cliff let her off with her equipment and went on with his routine patrol. He was carrying pig feed, among other things; a family of wild pigs had been introduced illegally years ago and no-one had the heart to cull them out. They had the place to themselves, Cliff pointed out, except for the birds and the pollination insects. The settlers had had a few goats and chickens but there were no other "wild animals".

She found a good place for her little four foot tower which incorporated all the measuring and recording devices she preferred. Her first step, always, was to make trivid footage and some holok stills of the floor and its surroundings.

The Wingard floor was a little more compact than

the one on Habitat Three and she knew, from scrapings taken by the earlier auxiliary team, that the composition of the stones had altered very slightly. More natural white sand, plus a yellow dye, coupled with the matrix gel, a weird semi-organic substance like some of the river-crystals found on Arkady. She took her readings, then walked out on to the floor.

Taya Schwartz had seen the "Giant Steps" on the moon, examined the blue caves on Itys. She had been among structures so weird and ingenious in the Australian desert that she had been loath to admit they were earth-made, in other words, a hoax.

As a young girl she had seen the wonders of Earth for the first time, had wept to see the works of humankind. The ruined cities of America, the temples of Mexico, and, beneath their protective air domes, Stonehenge, the Pyramids, and Abu Simbel saved from the flood waters.

She had flown to the Fire Islands, as a child; she had walked the white streets of the city of Rintoul, the Golden Net of the World. Her childhood friends and teachers had had huge fringed eyes, soft hooting voices, strange hands, with two proto-thumbs in apposition. Nothing alien was alien to her — rather she was an alien herself, born and bred on Torin, in the sign of the Sea Serpent. Now she stood deeply impressed by the beauty and mystery of the dancing floor.

She slid a palm-sized memory card from her tower — although she knew the patterns by now — and walked on to the floor. She stepped on to a stone in the center of the row of double stones which formed the northern border of the floor and began to move through the routine. She always experienced a great feeling of lightness and agility when she performed this exercise. There were longer leaps which she could not accomplish and it was believed, through contact with the Europa witnesses, that the dance had contained twirls and twists and figures for two or more dancers. There had been clear markings upon the stones of Habitat Three for several dance patterns.

Taya completed the simplest routine which brought her right across the shallow bowl of yellow stepping stones to the southern border, with a couple of side trips to east and west. She went slowly and completed the "dance" in eighteen minutes with one rest and a couple of repeats. By this time she was certain that she was being watched by two persons, two humans, standing in the trees not far from the shelter shed.

She walked carefully back to the center stone and looked directly at the watchers. One of the women turned and fled, running off along the road, "into the green". Taya could see her bright shirt flying and the dust raised by her sandals.

The second woman came striding through the trees and the moving leaf shadows. She was as tall as Taya herself, a good-looking fair woman in her fifties. They were both wearing practical zipsuits but the grey of the newcomer seemed a little better kept than Taya's well-worn blue cupro. They met and shook hands in the center of the floor.

"Small system!" said the woman. "Vona Cropper, Dr Schwartz!"

Taya found that she *did* know the woman but where or when they had met eluded her.

"I'm sorry," she said. "I can't quite ..."

"Must have been twenty years ago — You delivered a paper at Humboldt County. I was on earth leave."

"I'm sorry to send your friend running off!" said Taya.

"Kirsty, Kirsty Allen, is very shy."

* * *

They walked back to the tower and Taya found herself handing out trade goods again. A set of all the floor dance routines on palm cards. Then she dug into her satchel and they sat in the shelter shed and drank lemon lift. She felt a certain distrust that she could hardly explain — had the holding mission infected her with their separatist thoughts?

"You live at the Mill, then," she said. "I asked Cliff Watson to request an interview. Any chance of that?"

"Oh we know the archive team are here," said Vona, stalling. "We're cybernauts. Not into face-to-face. Where you staying, Doctor?"

When Taya mentioned the Harmony Lodge the woman handed over a card of her own with lengthy site numbers.

"No need to call. Just leave a channel open."

Taya began to talk about gardening, the range of vegetables they were able to grow down in the eastern valleys. Had they done well at the Old Mill with the new types of water storage crystals? No, they were only hearsay to the cybernauts — Taya opined that she might come up with a bag of the little devils. Worked well on the moon, in the planter domes. She slipped in her question about the meteorite over yonder on the ridge — had Vona or her friends seen it?

Vona laughed and went off into a graphic account of the night the meteorite came down. Put on a real show for them — a clear bright evening, only Ben saw it coming and called them out to the platform. Their whole place shook. Of course they put in a report through the oxper — time rushing on, was it five, six years ago now? And they went down next morning to take a look at the site and to check on the Dancing Floor, see that the impact hadn't moved the stones any. All there was to see was the big burn mark over yonder.

So the Floor had been built some time earlier, persisted Taya gently, any chance of finding out the year? Any chance the Mill dwellers could have missed the building of the floor? Unlikely, said Vona, they often came this far down the valley. But the Die-Hards — she used the term with a grin — only came to settle in the Mill about '68, '69, when the first holding mission came in. Before that they had been living on the western side of the Divide in one of the houses but when the new folks arrived Ben decided to move further away. The Mill was really a tourist lodge from the old days; they had it done up pretty good by now.

"And the Dancing Floor was already there," said Taya.

"Just beautiful!" said Vona. "Of course we knew at once what it was. We didn't put in any report. Just waited until the new oxper units began to patrol. One day they brought some of the Veterans down this way for a drive."

Taya sighed deeply.

"I respect everyone's need for privacy, even for a family life in solitude, here on Wingard. But there's too much separatism. These new young families from Oparin, on Arkady. I feel as if the whole system was polarised, flying off into fragments ... I wish we could come together more."

She felt that it was a feeble plea for togetherness; she was still holding back, out of habit, appeasing people to get her precious information. Vona Cropper looked at her with a kind of pity.

"There's plenty of cybernauts out there. Place buzzes with talk, with ideas."

They parted with a handshake; Vona Cropper went striding off down the dirt road, among the trees. Where Taya must not go. Hell, what would they do to her if she simply followed? Stood outside the phoney "Old Mill" shouting and pleading to speak to an old man and his two old girl-friends.

Taya went on with her measuring but the work had become drudgery. Something about the Die-Hard women, the one who ran off, the one who fronted up and talked to her so blandly, had aroused her mistrust. After a break she took the detector wand and went round the floor: the fragment and debris count was higher than she would have expected.

She walked east, towards the dark scar from the meteorite, and the wand picked up an unusually large piece of metal-coated ceramic. It had been buried almost thirty centimetres down and laid bare, she guessed, laughing, by a pig rooting for wild yams. Part of an electronic grid? She bagged it up carefully, controlling her excitement. Hunches and wishes were part of any research project; this *could* have come from the Dancing Floor team, the BTAs.

The trusty wand picked up the vibration of the trekker coming back along the road; she was glad to drive off with Cliff Watson. Nope, he hadn't seen the two women, Vona and Kirsty; he left the information pinned on their door where they'd be sure to get it.

"What is it with all these mensch, Cliff?" she burst out. "Die-Hards? Separatists? Wingard has a positive ecology! It was designed by Win North and his team to hold a thousand interactive, living, sharing, beings, humans and androids, visitors from other worlds ... I remember he said once ..."

Her voice betrayed her, she began to choke up from pure loneliness and longing for days gone by, but she brought it out: "Taya, I thought of that one as a way-station, a stop-over on the way to Old Earth. Who can you think of from your planet, Torin, who might take the long journey, the way you did, as a young girl?"

"That's great," said Cliff. "I mean with the sharing and the way he included some of us poor wishers and mensch from other worlds. I'm telling you, Doc Schwartz, people think we have no feelings but it's deep-time bad to be shunned the way we are here."

They were nearing the pass which led to the Sun Kiln.

"Have we time to visit the memorial ground by the Kiln?" she asked.

"Why sure!" said Cliff. "We have no time problem, Doc. I can call in."

In fact, she guessed, he had already done so; oxper could communicate head to head. The journey through the pass was another reminder of the fact that they were on an artefact, a constructed habitat. Then they were in the afternoon sun, boosted this time by the reflectors on the western slope. The Sun Kiln was a solid group of ceramic faced cones, smokefree, with high-wide collectors reaching right up above the divide. It was not far from the "homestead" valley where the holding mission families lived.

Trash was burnt in the kiln and it was used as a crematorium. The names of settlers whose ashes had enriched the soil were engraved on stones in a low wall beside a lawn of low-growing grass, the type adapted for earth cemeteries. Only a few persons rated a plaque of hardwood or metal in the grass; there was a special new wall lower down for the veterans from the first holding mission. Right up near the kiln, on the slope, there was a large new plaque of wood substitute and anodised silver duralloy.

WINTHROP ARGENT NORTH IV
2443–2502, Christian Era Dating
His ashes enrich the soil of Wingard.

"How was this done Cliff?" she asked. "Was it a big official ceremony?"

"No, Mam," he said. "Little shuttle flew in via the last company Go-Down on Mars. Couple of old Triad auxiliaries flew the shuttle and left a report in the dock. The habitat was deserted. Small party from Terra scattered the ashes and laid down the plaque."

Taya stood with bowed head in the strange sunset light. She drew out her amulet with a yellow beryl from the mines of Tsagul and remembered when it had been given to her, the Only One, the human child, by Nantgeeb, the Great Diviner, the Maker of Engines, and by Taya Gbir, her daughter and Taya's namesake. She held it, sending out a prayer to all the universe for coming together, for sharing, for all that Winthrop North himself had wished. And truth came, piercing her darkness like a strong beam of light ...

She concealed her excitement, if that was the right word, until she was back at Harmony. She cleaned up and changed and automatically went into the ordering of her research material, the most basic routines, before dinner. When Elliot and Carl beeped she left a message on her own system, deliberately showing her hand:

Wingard is a Way-Station for visitors in the true Pioneer spirit.

Taya walked along with the team, the kids, and it was Carl Curran who gave her another piece of the puzzle.

"Here's the strip I took, back then with the film team, Doc," he said. "The floor and the valley wall where the meteorite hit. I'd say the Dancing Floor had a narrow escape. Y'see that burnt area?"

"All greened over now," said Taya, peering at the excellent clear strip in its viewer. "Can I get a copy of this, Carl?"

"Why, this one is for you, Doc!" he grinned. "I already made you this copy."

The deep, blackened scar on the eastern wall reached down into the valley, seemed to come within fifty meters of the Dancing Floor. Now it had all been greened over.

"See anything of the folk from the Mill, Carl? The Die-Hards? Two women and a man, all older people?"

"Well," he said, "we knew they were there but they were a real no-contact group."

Elliot came in with a report on the Holding Mission projects: absolutely triple A. The Oparin families, Hansen/Wylie and the Jenners, were the best test-gardeners he had ever encountered. Dayne came to eat with them and they were a cheerful work group, winding up their plans, kidding around with the oxper, Phil and Tom, thinking of tomorrow's picnic at the Floor.

Taya felt bad for holding back, for not being able to take them into her confidence at once. They were good kids, she knew it, the fault was in herself; she had a kind of generation loyalty. But there were two parts to her discovery, a coming together of two ideas, in the classic mode of scientific breakthrough. She passed Carl's little film strip to Mike Mahoney.

"We're in for some surprises at this picnic," she said. "Take a look at this film of Carl's, everyone."

"What is it?" asked Mahoney, urgently.

"The Dancing Floor tests out as very new," said Taya. "Suppose it *is* very new? Notice how close the burn marks for the so-called *meteorite* five years ago come in Carl's strip. It has all been greened over now. The scar on the eastern wall is small — maybe it was minimised too. The team built the Dancing Floor and suffered mechanical failure at take off. That was a crash site."

"Shee-it!" said Elliot, taking it up at once. "And you think they coulda done a cover-up that big?"

"Who we talking about here?" asked Dayne.

"The Die-Hards of course!" said Elliot.

"But, Holy Rome," exclaimed Mahoney, keeping his voice down as they were all doing, "where would they put the debris, the — the remains? Could they just *bury* all that?"

Taya chuckled, finding another piece that fitted.

"Oh there's a place right there," she said. "The old tunnel on the eastern outer wall, not a long way from the crash site. The settlers used it when they patrolled the outer surface of Wingard."

"It's crazy," said Dayne. "There are only three of them. Why not report the truth to an oxper team? They must know this would be a great find — for Archive, for all exo-biologists."

"Their privacy is more important to them than anything else in the universe," said Mahoney. "Die-Hards, pardon me, are plagged, insane — I've seen 'em before."

"Or maybe they believe — their leader believes — he owns the whole game," said Taya, sadly. "Wingard belongs to him ..."

Elliot March stared at her, the blood draining from his face.

"*Doc!*" he gave the smart kid's cry of despair. "*Why didn't I think of that!*"

She gave him a slight frown, enough to stop him blurting out her hypothesis.

"We won't move on the tunnel or any other thing," she said. "I'll get them to the picnic."

"How will you do that?" asked Mike Mahoney, who seemed to have figured things out.

"It's called *pressuring* these days," said Taya. "But it has a good old-fashioned name: *blackmail*."

* * *

Back in at the Harmony lodge she found a gift outside her door: passionfruit wine from the Jenner family in a white ceramic bottle. She took a drink and looked out at the eastern valley system, silvered under the augmented light of the moon. There was an alteration in the sound of the systems and a voice said: "*I got your message.*"

It was at last the voice of an old man. She felt a tightness in her chest and thought of the vacation in Maine, the warm nights in New Mexico.

"How are you doing?" she asked. "How is your health? You're seventy years old now."

"Which makes you seventy-three," he said. "They got a shot of you, the girls. Looking good, *dancing,* for Goddess sake. Age is having trouble wearying you or custom staling —"

"Shut up, you old cheat!" she said fondly. "We know what came down and where you hid the remains. I'll have a report or I'll make a report."

"I knew something like this would happen," said Winthrop A. North. "What put you on to me?"

"I recalled your friend Vona a little better. I saw her at Humbolt as part of your PR team." She said. "I make a guess that Kirsty ran off today because she is someone I know really well, maybe one of the secretaries, Christina? The man I knew took no chances and could have remained virile for a long time."

"Lot of educated guessing ..." grumbled the Resurrect.

"The oxper found me that databank, *Weltfic*," she said, laughing, taking another mouthful of the passionfruit wine.

"I knew there was something in that name, *Ben Gunn*. You were leaving clues. Ben Gunn is an ex-pirate marooned on Treasure Island by Captain Flint. The heroic villain of that old-time blue-water romp is Long John *Silver*, a reference to your middle name."

"Oh pirates are always good," he said. "There was that trivid team, few years back — *space pirates* now."

"Oh North," she cried, "have you got any treasure for me, for Archive, for Rivez, truly dead, orbiting Ceres in a Snow White capsule, or for Hanna Klein, one hundred and three years old in a veterans home in Florida-on-Terra?"

"Okay," he said. "The Die-Hards will come to the picnic. Don't blow my cover, Taya, old lover. We have treasure beyond your wildest dreams ..."

* * *

The picnic had wound down a little, after the races and the games. Sprawled groups on the green, among the trees, on the southern edges of the dancing floor in perfectly adjusted weather. A party was seen approaching along the road from the Mill; an old green trekker came on slowly with Vona Cropper striding ahead. She waved cheerily to the assembled company and went at once to the sound system, back of the floor and talked to Cliff Watson and Peter Miles who were working there.

"Greetings to the Archive team and all the inhabitants of Wingard." She was smooth but very serious. "This artefact, the Dancing Floor was built almost six years ago: the vessel that carried the construction team crashed soon after take-off. We were able to give a little assistance — there was a blessing that came out of this sad time. This music was mixed and assembled from many sources by all those at the Old Mill."

The music was slow, oddly melodious, like some of the neo-classical nature-wave concerts Taya had heard in California. The two women, Vona and Kirsty, took their places at the head of the Dancing Floor, on the row of larger stones where the dance began. The central stone was empty. Taya caught her breath and was drawn to her feet, with many of those watching. One of the children uttered a faint cry. The old man, "Ben Gunn", came to the floor leading by the hand the one who would lead the dance.

The Dancer was very thin and slight, giving an impression of frailty. It was swathed in a loose white shirt, hiding, perhaps, the strange shape of the upper body; the strong muscular legs were its most "humanoid" feature. The Dancer, following every cadence of the music, raised a pair of long arms, with fringed extensions on the "hands." It held gently to one side, its small, oval head, decorated with a quiff of pale hair. The Dancer led the dance, and the humans from the Mill followed, with an appropriate humility.

And in all those watching — all, all of them, Taya, was sure of it — there was a response so keen and sweet that it would remain with them forever. Here was a coming together, here was a curious grace, beauty so strange that it could break the heart.

* * *

Taya saw it all with an astonished recognition. There it was at last, the lightness, the agility, the travelling leaps, the patterns upon the stones. Yes, it was a solo performance — the folk from the mill repeated a few of the steps but remained in the background. Perhaps they were there, she guessed, to encourage the Dancer, to give comfort.

Then as the dance was done and as the music faded there was hand-clapping, muted cheers and sounds of praise from all those watching. The Dancer stood still in the centre of the floor and Kirsty, in her yellow shirt, ran out with a package which it held between its two hands. It came lightly across the floor to where Taya stood.

She scanned its shape, the pale mask of the face, the texture of skin and hair, the eyes, like small gemstone clusters. She took the package it offered: a woven kit-bag of trivid cassettes.

"*Tay-ah.*"

The voice was soft, whistling, issuing from a pale lipless mouth.

"Dancer!" she replied softly. "Thank you! We thank you! The Sol system thanks you and your comrades."

The mission families and their children, the auxiliaries, the Archive team all took her tone so readily that she knew the Dancer had worked its magic upon them. They replied softly, with love. The floor and the trees and the distant slope of the eastwall echoed with their sighing "*Thank you — thank you —*"

Then the Dancer backed away, bowing, holding out its hands and it was seen to be tired, drained of energy. The two women from the Mill hurried out, gave it support and led it gently back towards the trekker. Only the old man remained, directly opposite Taya Schwartz. Out of pure devilment she raised her surveyor's goggles and stared closely at the face of Winthrop A. North IV.

Someone had said or written, long ago, that people don't so much *change* as they grow older, they grow more like themselves. Sure, he had aged, perhaps more than she would have expected, with his healthy life, upon Wingard. But the smile he gave her was a familiar smile. He raised a hand in something between a wave and a salute; Taya returned the gesture. The Dancing Floor glowed between them like a map of the years. Then he too turned aside and rejoined his family; the trekker drove away up the dirt road to the Old Mill.

The other inhabitants of Wingard were in a euphoric state, she heard a child, Dan Jenner, crying out: "*We saw him dance! We saw him dance!*" Taya went to the sound system of the oxper vehicle and did something that she hardly needed to do, with these cautious settlers, here upon Wingard.

"The presence of this being, the Dancer," she said, "and the dance we saw belongs to Wingard. It is your secret, perhaps forever. We don't want this precious survivor disturbed. I'll evaluate the trivid cassettes taken by the family at the Old Mill and prepare some for you all to see, Ranger Jenner."

She consulted briefly with the Archive team who were as happy as she had ever seen them. Knowledge, not publicity, was the mark of the good archivist. In time there might be sensational revelations of one kind or another, some things always got out, especially secrets of the Universe.

Taya drove back with the auxiliaries and sensed at once that there was something else, beside their usual cheerfulness and the excitement of the dance. She had asked them to keep a sharp look-out: their senses were keener than human senses.

"I didn't expect this," she said. "I believed that the people from the mill would tell us about the building of the floor and the crashed BTA vessel. I expected, maybe, a chance to examine the crashed vessel, hidden in the tunnel on the east wall."

"We kept a sharp look-out, Doctor," said Tom Scott. "Observed the survivor, the Dancer, you called him."

"What is it, Tom?" she demanded. "What did you find out?"

She looked around and there were smiles on all their faces.

"Surprise for all us poor wishers," said Cliff.

"Matter of the skin texture, the hair, oh everything," said Peter Miles.

"The Dancer is something we don't have a word for," said Philip Grey. "Can't say he's an *android,* 'cause that comes from a word for *man,* for human. Hope this won't upset anyone. This survivor is the auxiliary of another species."

"You're sure of this?"

"We got through to that wisher, head to head, Doc," said Tom Scott. "He has a weird range of data, had to fall back on images some of the time. He gave us names to call him."

"Don't tell me," said Taya Schwartz. "Let this be *your* secret until I've evaluated the trivid material. I'm suffering from overload."

They laughed softly.

"He sure was pleased that we existed," said Cliff Watson. "The Mill folks had told him about oxper, androids, but he found it hard to believe."

AFTERWORD

The stories of Wingard, the empty asteroid Habitat, and Taya Schwartz, the human child born on Torin, found their way together. The craving for isolation comes up against the need for contact and communication. I have, apparently, an undying interest in puzzles and surprises.

— Cherry Wilder

JANE ROUTLEY

Jane Routley was born in Melbourne in 1962. She graduated from Monash University with a Bachelor of Arts (hons) in South East Asian history and studied Librarianship and later professional writing at the Royal Melbourne Institute of Technology.

Her first job as a librarian was running an occult library for the Theosophical Society. She went on to become a cataloguer — or, as she says, "One of those people who work out the little numbers that go on the back of library books". In 1992 she abandoned "this exciting career" to go and live first in Germany, where she wrote the novel *Mage Heart* and then in Denmark where she wrote the novel *Fire Angels* and is currently working on the third book in this trilogy. She still dreams of living in Australia, especially during the European winter.

In the quiet, bucolic story that follows, Routley takes us for a walk into the English countryside ... and into magic.

TO AVALON

JANE ROUTLEY

All the way there in the car, Gina's head was filled with the strains of Brian Ferry's "Avalon" — the haunting sounds of female voices singing in the distance — and with visions of women dancing serenely in eternity in silk dresses with hooded falcons on their wrists.

"And so to Avalon went the four little Aussies," she thought dreamily. She luxuriated in the sense of magic.

But when they got to Glastonbury Tor, the place where Avalon was said to have once been, there was no magic.

Near the stile at the bottom of the Tor a notice board was covered with horrible pictures of sheep that had been worried to death by dogs. The women's voices in Gina's head turned off with a loud click at the gory photographs.

"Please keep your dogs on a lead," the sign said. "This is private property. Please respect the safety of the sheep."

As they followed the long line of people up the path to where St Michael's Tower stood on the top like a finger pointing at the sky, it was clear that the other visitors ignored the sign and let their dogs run at will.

Glastonbury Tor was more a kingdom of sheep than a kingdom of faerie. Sheep were all over the sides of the hill — great woolly bundles like cartoon clouds standing on ridiculous skinny legs. The grass was grey and nibbled to hard stubble, just as it would have been at home in Australia. Narrow paths made by sheep feet spiralled all up the hill side. The sheep ignored the tourists and their dogs unless they got too close, at which time they would skitter away like nervous fat people, to start grazing again a few yards away. Gina couldn't help feeling sorry for them surrounded by annoying people and dangerous dogs and wanting only the peace to grow fat and woolly. And it looked as if someone had been bothering them more seriously too, for many of them had stripes of blue or green paint on their backs. Some vegetarian protest perhaps. There were plenty of New Age types among those climbing the Tor.

It was a remarkably pleasant day for spring in England with golden sun and a mild blue sky and only a hint of chill in the wind that buffeted them as they climbed.

Unfortunately everyone else thought so too. There were so many cars parked at the bottom, so many climbers up the paths and so many people milling round the tower at the top that it was impossible to even take a picture without other people in it, let alone to get some sense of atmosphere. The place reminded Gina of nothing more than the old graffiti and urine-stained tower at home in the Maranoa gardens in Melbourne. She tried to recapture the haunting singing in her mind, but it was blotted out by the intensely ordinary laughter and chattering of those around.

With resignation, the four of them made their best attempts to take people-free pictures of the tower and sat down inside the tower eating Mars Bars and reading the plaque commemorating the Bishop executed there by Henry the Eighth.

But Gary as usual had a plan to chase away mundanity.

"You remember me telling you that Glastonbury Tor is supposed to be an invisible three-dimensional maze that leads to Avalon," he said. "I went on-line a couple of days ago to see if I could find out any more and look what I downloaded."

He pulled some paper out of his bag and passed several sheets each to Meg, Gina and Alan.

"This," he continued, "is from a web site call the Celtic Twilight Travel Zone. Some loony has done a computer-generated list of all known paths up Glastonbury Tor. I thought we could have a go at finding the way to Avalon."

"But there must be hundreds of paths," protested Alan.

Gary grinned. "I thought just one or two. You know . . . in the spirit of random chance. It seemed like the right thing to do here. Kinda symbolic. I mean, you never know . . ."

Gina laughed. "Geez Gazza. What an idea! You're such a dag," she drawled in her broadest Strine.

"Well I think its a great idea," said Meg, squeezing Gary's arm.

Her voice was reproachful as if Gina had insulted Gary which hadn't been Gina's intention at all. It was just that the idea was pure Gary. Weird and kind of dumb but nice as well. He had been planning this trip for weeks. No doubt he would have similar little tasks for them to perform wherever they went.

"Of course it's great," Gina said now to smooth things over. "Let's do it."

"Right!" said Gary, who to her relief didn't seem at all annoyed. He wasn't one to bother with extraneous emotions when he had a project underway. "You take the north side, I'll take the east, Alan can take the west and Meg'll take the south. Just do one or two paths. You see they've recommended the ten most likely ways up each side. And if by any chance you do find Avalon, don't get so carried away with the feasting and dancing that you forget to come back and get the rest of us." He wagged his finger in mock admonishment. "Remember how quickly time passes in these faerie worlds. Right! We meet back here at 4.00 pm.

Then suddenly something black crashed into Meg's back, knocking her to the ground. Meg shrieked in fright and papers scattered everywhere. A small black sheep staggered back from Meg, re-balanced itself and galloped away off round the tower.

"Ah shit!" yowled Meg. "I'm covered in mud. Fucking sheep! I hate sheep. They shouldn't be allowed. Damn."

Meg favoured a kind of Victorian hippie look. Today's burgundy velveteen dress was certain to show the mud badly. Gary flapped around her, picking her up and brushing down her skirt and back. Gina and Alan picked up the dropped papers. Gina was certain this episode would put an end to the whole expedition, but to her surprise Meg was quickly mollified and ready to go on. She and Gary set off together down the hill and Alan and Gina climbed down the other side.

"Pretty strong words for a vegetarian," said Alan once they were out of earshot of the other two.

"Yes," said Gina and left it at that. She wasn't about to get into back-stabbing Meg this early in the trip, though no doubt her resolution would fail soon enough.

No-one could know Meg for five seconds without her vegetarianism smashing its way into their consciousness. Gina's first experience of her had been pretty typical. At the house warming party Gina and Gary had thrown at their shared flat in Palmers Green, Meg had shown up drunk as the proverbial skunk and told Gina she wouldn't shake hands "because I don't shake hands with cannibals". She had then proceeded to persecute a blind workmate of Gina's all evening about the slavery of his guide dog (a cheerful Labrador with the habits of a vacuum cleaner who was only too delighted to be anywhere food was) and to stub out her cigarettes in the pepperoni pizza as a protest. On the other hand, Meg had a striking fragile beauty and Gary had been very taken with her.

Gary and Gina had met a few years before at the Tolkien Society back home at Melbourne University and a shared interest in all things Arthurian caused them to become firm friends. Gina could never understand why such a nice man as Gary had such ghastly girlfriends. Perhaps it was inevitable that you didn't like your male friend's partners. Whatever! She hadn't bargained on Gary's asking Meg along on their Easter tour of Arthurian sites and she wasn't looking forward to sharing a room with her. She had a sinking feeling that Meg was going to be the ghastliest girlfriend of all.

At the bottom of the hill Alan and Gina separated and Gina picked a set of instructions from her sheet.

They were easy to follow as long as you knew the directions of the compass. They were also pretty inexact. They simply described the number of steps you took in a given direction. On the other hand directions in fairy stories always consisted of seven steps here and three steps there. Perhaps vagueness was part of the formula. Following the instructions she climbed up round the hill a couple of times in a satisfyingly anti-clockwise direction. Widdershins. Widdershins was the way you always reached magical kingdoms. These people had at least done that much homework.

To her amusement she discovered that she was following a series of sheep tracks. This really was a kingdom of sheep. Who knew, perhaps the sheep in their wanderings occasionally stumbled upon the maze and into Avalon. The idea tickled her sense of humour and she laughed out loud. Sheep heaven. A dogless, touristless place of juicy grass. Brilliant!

"What's so funny," said a voice. Alan was sitting on a nearby bench.

"What are you doing, you slacker," she cried. "Get back to work there."

"I've finished one path," he said. "I'm having a break. Its a hard climb. Want a drink?"

She marked her place with a rock and went to sit down beside him.

"Quite nice out here, isn't it. The sun's almost warm for England," he said, passing her a bottle of bitter lemon.

"For England," she agreed.

He seemed a nice guy, Alan. He was a workmate of Gary's — a tall skinny guy with curly hair and blue eyes. Quite cute, really. More importantly he was weird enough to understand Gary and Gina's keenness for the matter of Britain, while at the same time exuding a kind of good natured practicality which had already shown itself in his handling of road maps.

"Isn't that the little black sheep that knocked Meg over?" he said now. "Look. That guy's been chasing it."

The black sheep was grazing nonchalantly on the grass. A thickset man in old corduroy trousers and a tweedy coat was moving carefully towards it. Just as he got close enough to make a lunge for it, the sheep jumped forwards and skittered quickly away. There was something unusual about this sheep's skittering, however. It peered back at the man and "baaed" derisively at him; almost as if it were teasing him. As they sat watching, man and sheep continued like this all around the base of the hill. Once the man lost his balance and came down arms flailing with a slow comic slide into a muddy patch. It was like watching something out of the Three Stooges. Gina had to giggle.

"That most dangerous of all things — the clever sheep," quoted Alan.

"Do you think we should tell someone the sheep are being bothered?" asked Gina as the comic duo disappeared round the hill.

That's probably the farmer chasing it. Its a ram, see and he won't want it mating with his ewes. Otherwise he'll wind up with a lot of small spotty lambs next season."

"You know something about sheep then?" asked Gina.

"Ah yes, you're talking to the original farm boy here. I'm from Hamilton. You know — where men are men and sheep outnumber people a thousand to one. I grew up on a sheep farm eating lamb chops with my mother's milk. Don't tell Meg though."

"So why do all those sheep have coloured stripes on their backs? I thought it was some kind of joke but they all seem to have them."

"You civilians may think its a joke but to us farming folk its a very serious and delicate matter. This is a breeding flock and when the farmer puts rams in with these ewes, he wants to know which ewe is likely to be pregnant. So he paints the belly of the ram with this coloured paint and when the sheep mate, it leaves a coloured stripe on the ewes back. Then you can tell which ewes have been mounted. And with the different colours you can find out if each ram is doing his duty. Otherwise they're not much use to keep."

"So if they happen not to be in the mood one season, its off to the slaughterhouse with them?"

"That's right. Enough to give anyone performance anxiety."

"Not much of a life being a sheep."

"Well they don't want much. Though if I were these sheep, I'd be dreaming of a field with nicer grass which didn't have all these tourists tromping through with their dogs."

* * *

Climbing about on the hill all afternoon seemed to have brought Meg and Gary closer then ever. At dinner that evening, the two of them decided to climb the Tor by moonlight when surely there'd be fewer people there.

"Better chance of reaching Avalon by moonlight," joked Gary.

Gina could tell they were reluctant for her and Alan to come with them so the two of them stayed behind in the little vegetarian cafe where they'd eaten dinner. Gina's dread of sharing a room with Meg disappeared under the greater worry that one day soon Gary would invite Meg to move into their comfortable flat with them. She could picture how it would be — a flat strewn with velveteen gowns and antique corsets, with Meg sitting cross-legged in a cloud of cigarette smoke, laying down the law on political correctness like some kind of Buddha of the Bushfire. She had a feeling that Meg's arrival would have to mean Gina's departure.

She did her best to hide her depression from Alan, although the desultory conversation they had about Melbourne and the skinny girl in a black beret who droned out Leonard Cohen songs didn't help at all.

* * *

It had been hard to find a place to stay in Glastonbury. Their B-and-B was run by a little old lady who reminded them all of elderly aunts back in Australia, but the accommodation itself would have shamed any elderly aunt of Gina's. The grimy little room was decorated with little signs saying things like "No showers after breakfast" and "No extra tea bags will be given". Gina stood beside the shower for 10 minutes before deciding it was not going to warm up and performing a quick wash all over with a face cloth and chilly water. The bed, decorated with a mauve counterpane, sagged. To her horror the sheets were made of ancient badly-pilled nylon. Her fine hair cracked and danced as she slid gingerly between the covers. Surely that long dark hair beneath the pillow was not one of hers. It didn't bear thinking about.

She almost wished she was out on the fresh clean hillside with the sheep and Meg and Gary and the full moon rising above the Tor. Almost. But it was cold even here in the room and so she simply lay there feeling grubby and uncomfortable.

When she had been in Australia, Britain had always seemed like a marvelous place full of history and beauty. All young Australians went there at some time in their lives, following some ancestral call. It was part of their natural life-cycle, coming between finishing school and beginning marriage and home buying. When they came back they all said how great it had been. Now Gina suspected they had been lying.

"Perhaps my expectations were too high," thought Gina. She had expected magic, not this cold, grey, grubby country, where the plumbing was bad and the food was often nasty. And there were people everywhere crowding in on you. She lay there feeling the lumpy sheets against her cringing skin and thinking longingly of warm, spacious Australia with its pure, white light and its lean, clean gums. If Gary had come crashing into the room that moment proclaiming that he'd found the path to Avalon, Gina would probably have refused to go, for fear of another disappointment, and opted for a ticket home instead.

* * *

Footsteps creaking past her door roused her from a fitful doze. She saw that the sky was paler outside and gratefully got out of her nasty bed. Outside she found

Alan coming back from the bathroom with his wash bag.

"It's 6.00," he said. "I'm just going up to the Tor to see if I can get some shots without people in them. Want to come?"

She was glad to get out of the B-and-B and into the fresh cold air, but it was not a good morning for photos. The whole town was cloaked in grey mist and you could see nothing but grey cloud from the Tor. Even at that time of morning, a couple was out walking unleashed dogs up the hill.

"Look," said Alan. "There's our friend, the black sheep."

The sheep had got themselves into an enormous line and were filing round the hill, delicately picking along the sheep paths on their spindly legs, zigzagging first uphill, then down. Over thirty of them moved purposefully along as if intent on reaching some special feed. In the lead the little black ram skipped along gaily, every now and then jumping into the air like a new born lamb. The file disappeared and reappeared out of the mist three times during Alan and Gina's climb.

When the two of them reached the top of the Tor, the couple walking their dogs went back down the hill past them, and suddenly they were completely alone.

Gina's feet echoed hollowly on the stone floor of the tower. She leaned against the doorway. Outside the world blurred gently into cold white mist. The blades of grass were silvered with ice. She could almost imagine Arthur's death barge floating out of the mist with the hooded queens in attendance. A fey sense of wonder shivered along her spine. Celtic magic sang its siren song faintly beyond the edges of reality.

"Avalon," she whispered softly, "Isle of apples, Isle of glass, where legend blends to faerie."

Beside her, Alan sighed. She sensed that he too felt the magic.

There was a crunching of grass and suddenly the line of sheep filed out of the mist and across the hilltop before them. The moment of magic shattered under the precise patter of their little cloven feet.

They looked at each other ruefully and Alan laughed.

"Sheep! From the sublime to the ridiculous. Come on. Let's go back. Or we'll be missing our English Breakfast."

He took her hand companionably and they went down the hill together.

"Does anyone know why they file along like that?" she asked. The sheep seemed to have done a complete circle round the hill top and were now coming round the slope towards them. The little black sheep was still gambolling in the lead.

"They say . . . "

Suddenly the two of them stopped stock still with amazement.

The black sheep had given a little jump and disappeared into mid-air like someone going through a door. It had been close and clearly visible. There was no chance of a mistake.

The sheep behind it jumped too and disappeared, and the one after that as well. As the two watched every single sheep in the file completely vanished one by one leaving only the empty hillside and a distant silken susurration of magic behind them.

AFTERWORD

"To Avalon" was written as a direct result of a visit to Glastonbury Tor on Easter Sunday 1996. My preconceptions about the Tor and my actual experiences of it as crowded and sheep filled were very like those I have attributed to Gina in the story. There were even photographs of mauled sheep on the stile. I'm not sure of the exact origin of the legend that Glastonbury Tor is a three-dimensional maze into Paradise/Fairyland, but I know a number of people told me about it before I went. As I wandered about the Tor thinking about this legend and my experiences as an Australian traveller in Britain, this story began to percolate in my brain.

— *Jane Routley*

STEVEN PAULSEN

Steven Paulsen discovered ghost stories and science fiction when he was twelve years old, and since then he has had a fascination with the bizarre, the unexplained, and things that fill him with a sense of wonder. He has been actively involved in Australian science fiction, fantasy, and horror for over ten years, as a reader, bibliographer, writer, reviewer, interviewer, and editor. In recent years he has established a reputation as an authority in the field and has twice won the William Atheling Jr Award for excellence in science fiction criticism.

He was the founder and editor of *The Australian SF Writers' News*, a writers' market guide and news magazine which was published between 1992–1995, and his articles and interviews have appeared in a variety of magazines including *Aurealis*, *Bloodsongs*, *Eidolon*, *Interzone*, *Science Fiction*, *The Scream Factory*, and *Sirius*. He has written essays for *The Encyclopedia of Fantasy* edited by John Clute and John Grant, and the *St James Guide to Horror, Ghost and Gothic Writers*, edited by David Pringle. Most recently he was assistant editor and primary contributor to the Melbourne University Press *Encyclopaedia of Australian Science Fiction and Fantasy*.

Steven Paulsen is also the author of numerous science fiction and horror short-stories which have appeared in various magazines and anthologies such as *Terror Australis — Best Australian Horror*, *Strange Fruit*, *Worlds in Small*, *The Cthulhu Cycle*, and *Fantastic Worlds*. His children's horror novel,

The Stray Cat, published in Australia in 1996 has now been translated into German, French and Bahasia Indonesian editions.

In the next story, Paulsen takes us back to the horrors of Vietnam where those walking point sometimes see more than just the Viet Cong in the heat of battle.

MA RUNG

STEVEN PAULSEN

Take a man and put him alone,
Put him 5000 miles from home,
Empty his heart of all, but blood,
Make him live in sweat and mud.
— Anonymous Vietnam Digger,
"The Boys Up there"

* * *

"Long Green" east of Dat Do, Phuoc Tuy Province,
Vietnam — 12 March, 1968.

Concealed in the jungle on a ridge above the Viet
Cong mortar platoon, Sergeant Steve Lund gave the
SAS patrol its instructions. He sent "Johnno" Johnson
and Evans the medic around to the left of the enemy,
while Papas and Barnes took the right flank. Lund
stayed behind with Hutchinson the signaller to set up
the M–60 bipod machine gun.

Clad in badgeless tiger-stripe uniforms,
camouflage cream smeared on faces and arms, the men
melted without a sound into the sun-dappled
undergrowth. Jungle phantoms.

Taking up position within sight of the enemy,
Johnson slid the water bottle from his belt, careful not
to make a sound, and rinsed the dust from his dry
mouth. Stinging sweat trickled into his eyes. He
replaced the bottle and checked his rifle magazine,

turning the weapon's safety catch to full automatic. Finally, he removed a white phosphorous grenade from his webbing and settled back to wait for the signal.

Insects buzzed and flitted in the hot air.

Suddenly, movement in the gully below the VC caught Johnson's attention. He swore under his breath as he recognised a patrol of hapless Diggers blundering into the enemy's line of sight.

Then there was activity from the VC — they too had seen the Australian infantrymen and were hastily repositioning their mortars.

Johnson levelled his rifle.

"Wait for the signal," hissed Evans as he took one of the white egg-shaped grenades from his own webbing and clicked it into the launcher at the end of his rifle.

There was a short series of hollow thuds from the Viet Cong position as the mortars began. Their first shells fell short, exploding in a clouds of dirt, branches and other debris. But one found its mark, sending the Australian soldiers flying, shrapnel tearing through them.

Johnson gritted his teeth. He squinted with the sun in his eyes. Sweat ran in rivulets down his face, neck and back.

Finally the signal, a burst of M–60 tracer, streamed into the VC camp. The white grenades followed from left and right, exploding with short, sharp cracks, spewing eruptions of deadly white phosphorous.

A screaming VC burst from cover, writhing, limbs flailing, the upper part of his body burning like a roman candle. But his agonised cries were cut short by a compassionate round from the M–60.

Other VC charged through the jungle towards Johnson's and Evans' position. Johnno brought his rifle to bear and spurted the full twenty-eight rounds from the magazine into the moving shrubs. A torrential rain of bullets ripped through the enemy from three points.

Then silence descended over the jungle once again.

Smoke drifted aimlessly amid the shredded foliage, the sickly-sweet smell of burnt flesh pervading the air. A lone bird began to chirp and chatter somewhere high in the trees.

Johnson slammed home a new magazine and moved cautiously forward, his rifle muzzle pointing wherever his eyes looked, his hand motioning Evans to fall in behind. Avoiding the paths and tracks, they moved swiftly and silently through the jungle, down into the gully, leaving the others to mop up any remaining pockets of VC resistance. Cries from the wounded Diggers penetrated the dense greenery and led them towards the fallen patrol.

Parting a fan of jungle fronds, Johnson revealed the clearing in which the Aussies had fallen. They lay scattered near the centre; two black-clad VC guerillas standing over them with bloodied knives drawn.

Outrage and fury welled up and made Johnson's chest go tight. Even as he watched, the closest of the guerillas turned his attention to a wounded Digger desperately trying to squirm to safety. Johnson yanked back hard on the trigger of his rifle and sprayed the VC, his bullets spinning the men around, shredding their chests like butcher's meat.

Entering the clearing, Johnson and Evans hurried to the aid of the two Australians still left alive. Evans knelt by a corporal with most of his lower jaw missing — the man was gasping for breath, red bubbles forming and bursting in the cavity, his face splashed with blood and saliva. Johnson went to the other man, the one who had been trying to squirm away. This soldier had been hit in both legs, but appeared otherwise unharmed.

"It hurts like fuck," the man gasped as his gaze fell on the SAS corporal.

"Easy, mate." Johnson quickly jabbed him with a shot of morphine, tore a field dressing open with his teeth, and began to tend to his legs.

"The bastard was gonna kill me!"

"Take it easy, mate — dustoff choppers'll be here soon. Before you know it, you'll ..."

Johnson's head jerked up, his keen hearing had detected a sound; dry twigs or leaves crunching, the swish of foliage. He motioned the wounded man to silence and raised his rifle.

Suddenly a half-naked, frightened-looking VC guerilla, hardly more than a kid, burst into the clearing, his AK–47 barking and kicking as it spewed tracer.

The soldier Evans was tending bucked and jerked, blood and flesh spraying from him. Evans went down with a scream as his legs were shot out from under him.

Johnson swung his weapon at the gunman, squeezed the trigger, and threw himself to the ground. His rifle squirted a round, which went high, then jammed.

The VC triumphantly turned the muzzle of his gun towards Johnson, but for some reason did not fire.

Instead, the man's mouth fell open and his eyes grew wide in terror.

"*Ma qui!*" the VC yelped, shaking his head, his eyes bulging. He lowered his rifle, and began to back away. "*Ma rung...*" It sounded like a plea for mercy.

Johnson cocked his rifle, checked the chamber with trembling fingers for a jammed case. Clear. But before he could adjust the regulator, two pistol shots rang out and the crazed VC guerilla crumpled to the ground.

Johnson rolled over to see Steve Lund brandishing his automatic pistol, emerge from the jungle. Behind him came Hutchinson and the rest of the patrol.

"Check the VC for papers, diaries, maps," Lund snapped. "Papas, help Evans. Hutchinson, call in a dustoff chopper and get these blokes out of here." He turned to Johnson. "You all right, mate?"

Johnson clambered to his feet and shook his head slowly from side to side. "I thought I was a fuckin' goner." He threw his arm around Lund's shoulder and squeezed him. "Thanks, pal. You saved my life. Perfect timing, you scared the shit out of the nog. He had me, my rifle had a stoppage."

Lund shook his head. "It wasn't me who scared him, mate. I was still drawing my pistol when he stopped shooting. He saw something else, not me."

Johnson looked puzzled. "What'd he see?"

"Dunno. Shadows ... Somethin'." Lund blew his breath out. He lowered his voice. "Shit, Johnno, it looked like there were blokes standing over there."

"Blokes?"

"Those poor bastards behind you," Lund indicated the fallen Diggers. "I saw 'em ... I saw somethin'. *He* saw 'em. That's what scared the little prick, not me."

"Don't be fuckin' stupid," Johnson said. "If the brass hear you talkin' like that you'll be hauled in front of the shrink before you can say Jack Robinson."

Lund studied his friend's face for a moment, then shrugged free of his arm. "C'mon Hutchinson," he yelled, "where's that flamin' chopper?"

* * *

I got a letter from me sheila the other day,
She said "I've found a new bloke while you've
    been away",
So I got pissed with me mates, Darryl and Fred,
Best mates I ever had, but now they're both dead.
— Rob Dawson, "Me Mates"

* * *

SAS Hill, Task Force Headquarters, Nui Dat, Vietnam
— 23 April, 1968.

"What the fuck are ya doin' out there?"

Steve Lund was sitting outside on a folding chair with his back to the tent, his feet soaking in an enamel dish of scarlet-purple water.

"Tryin' to get rid of this bloody tinea," Lund yelled. "Whadda ya reckon?"

"Huh?" Johnno Johnson emerged from the tent, only to shy away from the sunlight. "Jesus it's bright, dunno how ya can stand it. What's that purple shit?"

"I can stand it, mate, because I stuck to Tiger beer when the Fosters ran out last night. You drank nearly a whole bottle of Bundy. That stuff'll kill ya."

"Bullshit, it puts hairs on your chest."

Lund was studying his feet. "This purple shit's Condy's crystals. Reckon it'll do any good?"

Johnson snorted. "Wouldn't count on it." He yawned and stretched, gazing bleary-eyed across the campsite, noticing men hanging around in small groups outside the tents and prefabs erected between the plantation rubber trees. "What's everyone doin' out there?"

"Same as me. Waitin' for Mouth Matthews."

"*Him*? Why bother?"

"'Cause the blokes over in Two Squadron got fed up with the little prick last night. They got him paralytic, walked him out to the urinals, made sure he fell into one of the drums full of piss, fished him out, chucked him in that tent over there and closed it up." Lund chuckled and looked up at the sun. "How hot do you reckon it is? Eighty? Ninety? By the time the dickhead wakes up, he'll be fuckin' ripe. I don't wanna miss it."

"Neither does half the camp," Johnson said, nodding at the men hanging around, smoking, chatting.

"What about you, Johnno? You okay today?"

"Whadda ya mean?"

"About Rhonda, droppin' ya."

"Yeah, bitch. She never could go without it for long."

"You can talk," guffawed Lund. "How many of those bar girls in Saigon and Vung Tau have you screwed?"

"That's different."

"Yeah, I know, you went on and on about it last night. Lucky I'm your mate. Nobody else would've put up with ya."

"Get stuffed." Johnson gave him two fingers. "Look at the shit I have to put up with from you."

"That's what mates are for. You can count on me pal." He chuckled. "How about a beer? I reckon these Condy's crystals make a bloke thirsty."

Johnson disappeared into the tent and returned with two open cans of Tiger beer. "They're warm."

"Who cares as long as it's wet."

Johnson lobbed one to Lund who caught it with practised ease, holding it clear while some of the beer frothed over. "Hey, did ya hear what the nogs are callin' us?"

"Callin' who?"

"Us, the SAS."

"Nuh."

"*Ma Rung. Ma*-bloody-*rung.*"

"What's it mean?"

"Umm ... Forest spirits. Tree men. Phantoms or ghosts of the jungle." Lund snorted. "Something like that. They reckon Ho Chi Minh's put a price on our head. Six thousand piastres."

"Cheap skate. We're worth a darn sight more than that. Ho Chi Minh's a cunt."

Both men laughed. Lund raised his can of beer in a toast. Johnson did the same. They touched cans, and gulped down the warm beer.

"Lundy ...?"

Lund wiped his mouth with the back of his hand. "What?"

"*Ma Rung* ... Isn't that what that crazy VC said? You know, in the clearing after the mortar attack?" Johnson took another gulp of beer. "When you saved my life. When you reckon you saw somethin' ... ?"

"I never saw anythin', mate. Shadows, that's all."

"Sure." Johnson nodded. "Whatever you say. I owe you for that, Lundy."

"Any time, pal. We're mates."

They clinked cans.

"Yeah, mates."

"You gonna hang around for Mouth Matthews?"

"Wouldn't miss it for quids."

* * *

The green banana grove, and the betel palm,
Seas of green rice, and plains of silver water,
All are home to the ghosts of the fallen,
Who tread the paths of lost souls.
    — Tran Thanh, "*Ma Rung*" (translated by
    William Cobb)

* * *

Near Bien Hoa and Phuoc Tuy Province border,
Vietnam — 9 October, 1968.

Johnson was in front on point, Hutchinson was bringing up the rear and the rest of the patrol were strung out in between. They were on a high priority reconnaissance mission into a free fire zone — here anything that moved was fair game.

During the previous half-hour they had spent only ten minutes on the move, olive-drab shadows, and for the other twenty minutes they had remained as motionless as statues; listening, watching, dripping wet with their own perspiration.

It was pack-time — the time when enemy traffic was heaviest — and the SAS patrol was approaching a known North Vietnamese Army route.

Johnson gave the thumbs down signal and the six men sank into the lush undergrowth. Twelve feet from them, a North Vietnamese Army platoon was passing along an intersecting track.

They watched and counted and listened . . .

It was almost an hour later when eventually they moved on.

The SAS avoided tracks, instead they moved like stalking cats through the almost impenetrable walls of the jungle. When it was necessary to cross a track, they waited, listened, watched, then moved across it one by one at short intervals. Now, Johnno Johnson listened, straining hard for any sound unusual to the jungle. Birds twittered and chirped, insects buzzed. He moved . . .

The low pitched bark of a Russian-made AK–47 assault rifle sent the SAS commandos diving for the spongy musty-smelling jungle floor.

Johnson staggered as the first burst of automatic fire ripped through his upper arm. The second shattered his left knee-cap and he suppressed an agonised scream as his leg collapsed and he went down hard.

In reply, another burst of automatic fire tore through the thick jungle foliage, this time the higher trilling of Papas' American-made M–16. Before the last spent cartridge had hit the ground, the splintering crack of breaking branches sounded from the canopy and a khaki-clad North Vietnamese regular plummeted from a nearby tree, his jungle leaf hat following after him.

The confrontation was over as quickly as it had begun.

Sergeant Lund appeared at Johnson's side with Evans the medic. After a cursory examination, they swiftly administered a pain killer, lifted Johnno between them and slipped soundlessly back into the jungle. They travelled quickly and quietly for some distance before finally stopping to attend to his injuries.

"Jeez you're a lucky bastard, Johnno," Lund said in low tones. "Fuckin' hell, you should be dead by rights."

Johnson grimaced as Evans cleaned his shoulder wound. "Thanks for the vote of confidence," he said through gritted teeth.

Lund's tone became serious. "We've got a problem, mate. We're gonna have to push on." The sergeant frowned and rubbed his crew-cut stubble. "We can't take you with us, so we're gonna have to leave you here and pick you up on our way back tomorrow. Okay?"

Johnson nodded, "Yeah, I understand."

"I can leave a bloke with you if —"

"It's all right," interrupted Johnson. "I'll be okay. You need every man for the mission. And like you said, 'I'm bloody lucky'."

They dug Johnson in beneath a tangle of thick undergrowth at the foot of an ancient forest tree. When he was comfortable they whispered farewells and Lund signalled the patrol to move out. But as the sergeant made to follow his men, Johnson grabbed his sleeve, holding him back.

"Listen Lundy," Johnno said. "I want you to do something for me." He fiddled with the thin gold chain around his neck, trying to release the catch. "I want you to take this cross." It came loose and Johnson held it out to Lund, a small gold cross on a thin chain. "If for some reason I don't make it, I want you to make sure my Mum gets this." He gave a humourless chuckle. "She gave it to me for luck."

"There's no need for this, mate. You'll be fine. All you gotta do is sit tight."

"Come on Lundy, humour me. Just in case."

"Okay, Johnno." Lund shook is head. "But you're taking a risk. What if I don't make it?"

"You better, pal. I'm relying on you."

* * *

The afternoon torrential rain started shortly after the others had left, as Johnson had known it would. It beat monotonously upon his jungle hat and drenched him to the skin within minutes. The worst part was, he knew it would fall at the same soaking rate until some time during the night.

He was uncomfortable. Unlike his arm, which Johnno could not even feel, his leg throbbed painfully. The pain-killers Evans had administered were beginning to wear off, and what had started as a dull ache was now becoming difficult to bear. He contemplated the additional syringe the medic had left him, but decided to save it until the last possible moment.

He felt strangely vulnerable in his dugout refuge between the jutting roots of what looked like a giant rubber tree. Unusually so, because not only was he hidden by the roots, but he was also surrounded by thick undergrowth making him virtually invisible to the probing eye.

This exposed feeling nurtured a growing desire to act, to do something. But there was nothing he could do but wait. Wait for rendezvous with the others and, hopefully, safe-extraction ... Or wait, who knew how long, for the inevitable.

He checked his rifle: it was set to full automatic. He listened, straining hard for sounds beyond the relentless patter of large raindrops and the trickle of running water.

Already the jungle floor was underwater, transformed for a time into a shallow swamp. Johnson felt like he was sitting in a tepid bath. But it was not refreshing. He was hot, starting to burn up with a growing fever.

He listened and waited, all the time his fever and pain increasing. He watched large blue-black flies edging their way towards his bloodied bandages. He thought about home, and wondered if he would ever return. Images of Rhonda came unbidden, her curly blond hair, her large pale-nippled breasts. Strangely, he imagined himself standing in the outer at the MCG, watching the cricket. He remembered drinking Tarax creamy soda at the corner milk bar ... It all seemed *so* far away.

The pain intruded and brought him back to the dank-smelling jungle. He wanted to moan, but was too scared someone would hear. He gritted his teeth and thought about Lund and the other blokes on the mission. Would they come back? Or would he be left to die there in the dirt and mulch of the jungle floor like some wounded animal? Lundy wouldn't leave him. Lundy was a mate. Johnno pressed his eyes closed, squeezing out a few tears, breathing heavily. He tried to make plans, think of a way out, until finally he could think of nothing else but his pain. It burned and throbbed through his entire body. Then he administered the morphine Evans had left him.

The agony subsided as the drug took effect and shortly he began to feel drowsy. Night approached and the rain continued monotonously and Johnson fell into an uneasy sleep. A sleep tormented by weird dreams and spasms of pain. Dreams in which Viet Cong soldiers were having sex with Rhonda, where the patrol did not return and Johnno was forced to crawl through the jungle on shattered limbs.

* * *

Johnson awoke with a fright, startled by a ruckus in the trees above him. Clumsily he swung his rifle toward the commotion with his good arm, realising as he did so that it was only a group of tiny monkeys, probably arguing over a piece of fruit.

It was morning. His lips were dry and his throat was parched. He took a drink from his water bottle and allowed himself a moment to reassess his situation while he woke fully.

The jungle was steaming, the rain had stopped now, and the morning sun was reclaiming the moisture. Johnson's shirt and kit had already dried out, but the hole in which he was sitting was still half full of muddy water and his trousers and boots were sodden.

His head was woozy and his wounds throbbed.

Gritting his teeth, Johnson lifted his injured leg from the hole and propped it against one of the tree roots. Despite his care the movement sent jagged shards of pain shooting up his leg and beads of sweat broke out on his forehead. He unsheathed his knife and cut the remains of his olive-drab jungle trousers off at the thigh. As he bent over to examine his leg he cursed.

There were at least half a dozen bloated leeches stuck fast to his leg and there were sure to be others elsewhere. He felt his stomach muscles contract as he thought of the little buggers latching onto his balls. He wanted to take out his waterproof matches and fry the fat grey creatures until they curled up and dropped from his body. But even in his fevered state his training would not allow it. The smell of burning phosphorus might be enough to give him away. Instead, he checked his dressings and settled back to wait, trying to put the blood-suckers out of his mind.

He hoped everything was going according to plan. The others should return some time around midday, depending on enemy concentration. Not so long.

Enemy concentration . . .

Johnson peered out of his hidey-hole, searching the jungle, but he found it hard to focus. He drank some more water. His fevered mind began to conjure up weird paranoid scenarios. He imagined VC moving through the jungle, and at one stage he felt certain there was somebody hiding in the foliage above, watching him. Then he began to think that the VC were waiting to spring a trap for Lundy and the others.

The pain in his leg began to throb in time with his heart-beat. Johnno felt light-headed and knew he was feverish. He removed the magazine from his rifle, examined it, and carefully clicked it home again, terrified the sound would be heard.

He started counting ants to calm himself, get control.

Then he heard movement: branches cracking, the swish of foliage as something brushed past. His first thought was that the others had returned, and only his training stopped him from calling out. Besides, they would not have made so much noise.

Johnno pulled himself with his good arm to a vantage point, but had to steady himself as his head spun and he felt faint. Then he heard voices, Vietnamese voices. Slowly parting the foliage before him, Johnson could see a group of North Vietnamese Army soldiers stopped in conversation on a nearby track.

One of them broke away from the others as he watched, striding purposely towards Johnson's position. Johnson levelled his rifle, breaking out into a cold sweat as the man continued to close the distance between them. Finally, just as Johnson began to tighten his finger on the trigger, the man stopped, barely a couple of yards from the muzzle of Johnno's rifle, and began to kick away a patch of underbrush.

Sweat dripped off the end of Johnson's nose. His heart beat seemed so loud, he felt sure it would give him away. The soldier appeared to be looking straight at him and he found it an effort to resist the urge to fire.

Then the North Vietnamese soldier lowered his khaki trousers and squatted to relieve himself. Johnson silently let out the breath he had been holding, and noticed he was trembling.

But just at that moment when Johnno thought he was safe, the enemy soldier lurched wildly to his feet with his trousers around his ankles, and began yelling as he fumbled with his rifle.

Johnson squeezed the trigger, spraying the man with automatic fire at point blank range, making him dance convulsively and sending pieces of his equipment flying into the air.

Silence followed. The other North Vietnamese soldiers had disappeared. Johnson wriggled back into the cover of his dugout.

Suddenly the jungle exploded as AK–47 shells ripped through the shrubs and tree-tops, shredded foliage falling to the ground all around him. Then it stopped.

Johnson waited, listening; they were unsure of his exact position. He heard a rustle then a clunk over to his left — almost too late he realised it was a grenade and he crouched, crying out in pain, in the bottom of his hole. Nevertheless, the explosion that followed flung him backwards and stunned him.

Johnno shook his head, the only sound he could hear was a ringing inside his skull. Pieces of splintered tree-trunk had punctured his face and arms like darts, and acrid smoke choked his lungs.

He blacked out.

As he began to come around, Johnson experienced a peculiar feeling. A sense of detachment, as though he were observing events rather than a participating. He thought for a moment that he must be dead, then the quiet blackness gradually gave way to bright sunlight and the racket of a frenzied rifle exchange.

His head swam and his vision was blurred. Then he knew he must be alive, because his leg still burned and throbbed exactly as it had before the grenade had gone off. Looking around, half squinting into the morning sun, he could make out the silhouette of someone standing over him, someone madly firing a rifle into the jungle.

Not a moment too soon, Johnno thought. He shielded his eyes trying to focus and see who it was; he felt certain it was his mate Steve Lund standing over him.

But Lund's silhouetted image seemed to fade and waver, like a picture on a poorly tuned TV. Once he thought it was Rhonda, then his Mum. Johnson shook his head and rubbed his eyes. A rush of dizziness and nausea hit him and his vision blurred. Gradually the feeling passed and he looked up again …

He could still see the shadowy figure above him, oblivious to the North Vietnamese fire directed at them.

"Lundy?" Johnson's voice was a feeble croak.

"Keep your head down, mate," a voice came between bursts. It sounded like Lundy. The figure waved and sprayed another round into the jungle.

"Lundy …"

Dizziness again. He broke out in a cold sweat.

Even though he could not make out his friend's face, Johnno felt certain Steve Lund was looking down, smiling. But Johnson sensed it was a sad, longing sort of smile.

"Careful, mate," Johnson managed as darkness overtook him once more. "I'm relying on you."

* * *

Some time later when Johnson next came around, he had the sensation of movement and realised the gunfire had ceased.

"Lundy …" he mumbled. "Lundy …"

"Sleepin' Beauty's awake," a voice said.

The movement stopped and Johnson opened his eyes. He was lying on the ground with Evans, the patrol medic, bent over him. By his feet, Hutchinson was on the radio.

"Safe extraction signal green," Hutchinson said. "Over."

Johnson could see the green smoke signal billowing into the air above them.

"Okay," said a metallic voice on the radio, "I see green. Out."

"Here have a drink." Evans held an uncapped water bottle to Johnno's lips. "You've earned it — looks like you had quite a time with those nogs." Evans lifted Johnson's head so he could slurp groggily at the water. It trickled down his chin and neck. Then Evans lowered his head back to the ground and turned his attention to Johnno's wounds.

Johnson lifted his good hand to wipe away the spilled water, and his fingers came in contact with the gold cross around his neck. He smiled to himself, thinking Sergeant Lund must have replaced it while he had been unconscious.

Evans' voice interrupted Johnson's thoughts. "I can hear the chopper — we'll be out of here before you know it, Johnno." He offered him another drink.

"No," groaned Johnson. "Thanks." He rolled his head to look for Lund. "You guys showed up just in time. Where's the Sarge?"

Evans licked his lips nervously and could not look Johnson in the eye. "I'm afraid Lund didn't make it, Johnno. The poor bastard copped a VC booby-trap last night. Jumpin' Jack. Blew 'im to fuckin' bits."

Johnson shook his head incredulously. It was impossible. Lundy had saved his life. He had *seen* him.

"I know it's a funny thing to say," Evans went on, "but I reckon you're lucky that sniper put you out of action. Otherwise it would have been you on the point."

"No!" Johnson croaked as the extraction helicopter appeared above them in a burst of noise and wind. "It's bullshit," he protested. "Lundy saved me!" But his cries went unheard as the chopper descended noisily into the clearing, the grass around them rippling in the wash of its rotor. The air felt cool against the heat of Johnson's face.

Johnson's searching gaze darted about, confused, as they lifted him into the belly of the chopper. He couldn't see his mate. Lund *was* missing. Johnno clutched for the thin gold chain around his neck, found it and jerked it free. How could it be? He held his hand up in front of his face, but saw only a faint glimmer before his vision blurred and he was forced to close his eyes.

"Easy, Johnno," came Evans' soothing voice close to his ear. Fingers pried the chain from his grasp. "Careful, mate, or you'll lose that. Let me take it."

Johnson tried to speak, to yell his denial, his confusion, but his feeble whisper was drowned by the sound of the helicopter.

Darkness began to close in on him . . .

"I'll have you blokes safely back in a jiffy," Johnson heard the pilot yell as the machine lurched into the air.

Then he passed out.

AFTERWORD

During my teenage years I can remember eating tea while watching the images of Vietnam on the six o'clock news. The war was beamed right into our lounge room. Diggers in jungle greens. Rice paddies. Helicopters. Burning villages. Frightened children. Young men bearing weapons. At first it all seemed remote, foreign, but gradually the reality of the war began to intrude. A mate's older brother was sent off to fight. A girl I was keen on fell in love with a "nasho", and although we had never more than kissed, she was soon pregnant to him. He went AWOL one week before he was due to leave for Vietnam and they ran away together. The kid across the road received his call-up papers. The Vietnam War loomed over all our lives like a storm on the horizon.

Some of my friends joined the peace movement and began to demonstrate against the fighting. I attended a moratorium march once and was amazed to find old ladies, young mothers and scared kids marching alongside the so-called radicals. In my final year at secondary school I pasted John Lennon and Yoko Ono "War is Over" stickers all over the school. Then, thankfully for me, it was "time for a change" and the Whitlam Labor Government abolished conscription, and it wasn't too long before the war was over. But even though I never had to face the horrors of Vietnam, I was touched all the same. Those years, those images, had an indelible effect on my life.

Since that time I have read a lot about Vietnam; the people, the country, the war ... I have talked with men who were part of it. I have grown to respect and admire the grit and stoicism shown by those who went to fight. So this, primarily, is what influenced me to write "Ma Rung". I wanted to reflect all the images in my mind and the emotions in my heart; the tragedy, experience, fear and the courage.

So "Ma Rung" could easily have been a mainstream story. Indeed, some might argue that it is. But during my various readings about the war and the people of Vietnam, I was fascinated to find numerous references to "ma rung" or "ma qui", the "people of the forest". Spirits or ghosts of the jungle. The Vietnamese people, both North and South, tell us about them. Australian and US soldiers speak of them. They are part of the folklore of the jungle.

Shadows … Imagination … Ghosts …? Who knows for certain? The only thing I do know is that with so much emotion, suffering and death it seems more than likely that if there are such things as ghosts — spirits of the dead who have lost their way — then you will find them walking the battlefields of war.

— *Steven Paulsen*

ANDREW ENSTICE

Andrew Enstice grew up in England and was educated at Emmanuel College Cambridge, where he held an open scholarship. After completing his MA at Cambridge, he took his PhD at Exeter University. He came to Australia for a visit in 1980 and what with one thing and another, has been here ever since.

A former scriptwriter-producer with Granada Television in the UK, he has acted as script adviser and writer for a number of film and video productions. He has also written and directed for the theatre. He is twice winner of the Bridport Arts (UK) poetry award, and winner of the St Kilda Short Story Prize. He has written many academic articles and papers for journals, magazines, and conferences in Australia, Europe, Britain, and the USA.

Andrew Enstice is the author of *Thomas Hardy: Landscapes of the Mind*, which critic John Halperin called "a genuinely important book". With Janeen Webb, he has completed an edited collection of essays on myth and fantasy, *The Fantastic Self*, and a controversial study of Australian racism, entitled *Aliens and Savages: Fiction, Politics and Prejudice in Australia*.

He is currently a senior lecturer in literature at the Australian Catholic University in Melbourne.

In the story that follows, Enstice reminds us of the ominous darkness and numinal brightness of dreams ... and the fragments of poems and memories that we carry with us forever. Here then is that very special dream ... the one we will all dream.

DREAM, UNTIL GOD BURNS

ANDREW ENSTICE

The darkness was an old friend. He wrapped it round him, comforting.

There was no way of telling how long he had been unconscious, how long awake. He slipped seamlessly between sleep and waking, the patterns of dream absorbing the other senses: sight was still denied him.

They had not removed the bandages then. But he felt the absence of discomfort where the drip had fed into his arm. He was comfortably cocooned, tucked neatly into position, arms folded, his head cradled in what felt remarkably like satin covers.

He had gradually grown used to the hospital routines of being tested and measured and analysed and X-rayed and then rolled into a convenient corner to await return to his room. There were times when he felt like a parcel, bundled, wrapped, delivered, marked "return to sender". It encouraged patience (he appreciated the pun: one word had led to another, and another, language unfolding into a private universe he could substitute for the shared world of the senses; it gave him something to hold on to, a game to amuse him in the long hours alone and waiting).

Other senses were returning now. He was aware of voices around him, muffled voices. He imagined the partitions that screened him from the busy world. The occasional fragment of speech came through, a louder voice perhaps. Male. Impossible to recognise the speaker: he wondered idly which of the doctors would make himself unpopular by loudly lecturing his colleagues. Farnley? Yes. A man of clear opinions, firmly delivered. Polowski? Loud, certainly, but too explosive. There was a droning quality to the voice, something that hinted at a man who liked his conversations one-sided. Apshaw then. Perhaps.

The trouble was, they were all so damned opinionated. He felt sorry for the nurses, who had to wear it every day. At least he was the patient, the nominal focus of their professional concern. And he could escape at any time, burrowing down into his private world, away from the hectoring, lecturing, tedious voices that pursued for a while but eventually fell silent, petering out in distant volleys of anger and pique, fired randomly at unseen passing nurses.

Then the sound of Sister Jones rose up to memory, brisk hands tucking the sheets, inserting the thermometer, efficient, undeviating, a vocal, yapping terrier who followed him down and down and down. And that specialist — what was her name? — the one who sounded as though she was rapping out orders on parade.

There was some trick of acoustics, some shift in position perhaps, that brought the voice through clearly for a moment.

"...a special kind of man. John was ..."

Not much to go on. But then, he was used to that. A life made up of fragments, broken sentences, phrases littered through the darkness like scraps of paper in the roadway on a wet day. He was used to picking up the scraps, tucking them away in the corners of his consciousness, arranging them to see their effect. In his private universe, reality was a scrapbook.

He opened the book now, at the page marked "John".

What Johns did he know? Uncle John, of course, dead long since. There was a distant memory there, a roar of sound, the swell of ten thousand voices raised in angry unison. Uncle John was the one who had introduced him to football. Uncle John, a vague blur of a face — never much of a memory — but a crystal voice, smiling, warm. Uncle John, who met his end on the terraces, leaping to his feet with the crowd, with one accord, roaring out the challenge of life in the instant of his death.

He smiled at the memory. Turned the page. John. John. A cousin? Someone's child, perhaps? Godsons, from the time when they all did that kind of thing?

There was John Mearson of course: the rich, salt taste of hot buttered toast; late-night arguments punctuated with the voice of Joan Baez singing Yeats' "Inisfree"; or was it "The Man who Dreamed of Faeryland" — how did it go? — "Why should those lovers that no lovers miss/Dream, until God burn Nature with a kiss?" It seemed to make sense when they were young: John Mearson, the best of friends at college until he walked in one day with Evie at his side. The look on his face — that was easy to recall. Though, come to think of it, John's face was also blurring now. But the expression of mingled pride, and awe, and tense suspicion — that remained. He had borne Evie in like a prize, and when she left, she took their friendship with her.

But what would John Mearson be doing in the hospital? Too much coincidence. He turned the page.

And came up with a shock against another faded memory. John. John ... Evans? Again, the face was misted over, as though in the darkness vision lost clarity as it lost its significance. But some details remained sharp. The multiple flecks of colour in hazel eyes; the mouth, with its sheltering black moustache; a mole beside a crooked nose, broken long ago in some childhood football game.

John Evans. He was — had been — John Evans. In another life. In another universe. It had been so long, he had forgotten. So long since he had felt the importance of a name, alone in the darkness. So long since he had needed to look in the mirror to reassure himself that he was real. So long since he had fussed over the minutiae of gradual aging, absorbed the microscopic changes of feature into each day's redrawn map of himself.

All that had ended, that day on the football field. He had no memory of it, but they had told him, early on, how the low tackle had pitched him headlong into the goalpost, fractured his skull, torn the sclera of his eye.

Who knows how long ago.

"... John was an example to others, a shining light in the common darkness of our world. A man dedicated to ..."

It jerked him back again. He banged the book shut on that page. Closed the painful memory. Now, what other Johns did he know? Johns on the ward? It sounded like a eulogy — no-one made speeches like that unless their object was safely dead. Or very old.

Or retiring from politics. There were no politicians in the ward, so far as he knew.

Old John Haskin. Now, there was a possibility. A frail voice, a withered arm resting lightly on his, talking slowly of the distant past, of the woman he still loved, as she was back then, when she wore the flowered print frock and he carried the picnic basket, and the sun shone from a permanently cloudless sky.

The page turned. Old John slipped away, back to the flower-strewn fields of his past. There were other visitors, other hands touching his. Max, and Evie. Max, with his bullfrog voice, the patient, compassionate brother-in-law, solicitous for Evie's anguish at her ruined husband's bedside. And Evie herself, the warm touch of her, lips soft against the small fragment of his cheek that lay bare to the circulating currents of hospital air, the scent of her body, her breath mingling with his, her words whispering in his ear.

"Come on, John. You can do it. You know you can. The doctors say you can talk if you really want to."

Talk. So much talk.

"Remember, John. Remember our first date? New Year's Eve, and no buses or trains, and all the taxis were taken. Remember the queue — there must have been a hundred people, and the heavens opened, and we were drenched, and you gave me your jacket, and we walked in the rain. And then we were outside the Hilton, and I said, what are credit cards for?"

And when the clerk said, "double?", they looked at each other. And she said, yes. He touched the memory gently, smoothing it into place. Turned the page . . .

Something had changed. He was suddenly aware of the silence, deep and velvet. He let the scrapbook slip away, whirling down into darkness.

There was a bump, and he felt himself being rolled forward. No jolts from the trolley wheels catching; no jarring crash as they pushed him through the swing doors. He felt his senses sharpen, tuning to the slightest variation, straining to identify what was happening. He could hear music now. Vivaldi. His favourite.

The movement stopped, and stillness returned, as though a door had closed on the music. The silence was electric, full of some tension he could not identify. He held his breath.

The sound erupted all about him, roaring, wild. For an instant he was stunned by the force of it on unprotected hearing. And then he felt the heat, racing from discomfort to a tearing, clawing agony, and the light crept in on the edges of his darkness, red raw, visceral, and the smell of burning filled his nostrils. His senses were overwhelmed. He opened his mouth to scream, but couldn't remember how. His senses melted, coalesced in white pain, vaporised. Arrowed upward, keening into the light.

* * *

The small group of mourners had begun to disperse. An overweight, ruddy-complexioned man in his late thirties stood with his arm around a younger woman, comforting.

"You mustn't blame yourself, Evie. You did everything you could."

Evie eased herself away from a solicitous arm that seemed to have strayed towards her breast, and looked back at the building they had just left. Her eyes were red from crying.

"I know, Max. But I can't help feeling we should have waited. There were so many times ... It was like he could see everything, hear everything. I'm sure he knew we were there."

Max shook his head sorrowfully.

"Those were just reflexes, you know that. He was dead long before they turned it off. That wasn't really John in the bed."

Max resumed his protective grip on his sister-in-law, and turned her firmly away down the path that led towards the waiting car. The line of vehicles pulled slowly away from the kerb. Behind them, a thin trickle of smoke had begun to rise from the crematorium chimney, staining a brilliant sky.

AFTERWORD

"Dream" was just that: the product of a restless night's sleep.

It was one of those brilliant dreams you absolutely must write down while you're still half asleep — most of which turn out in the morning to be a string of random notes between which the conscious mind can find no logical connection. This time, I seemed to have something (although, admittedly, not a lot — just a sketch of a square, box-like object, surrounded by what might have been garden sprinklers. Not much to go on, but enough to jog the memory.) The substance of the story was there: The rest — all those minor things, like characters, plot and coherent structure — took shape after I had buttonholed Janeen Webb at work and (as we all do from time to time to our long-suffering friends) bored her rigid with my dream. Instead of recalling an urgent appointment, she listened patiently, made some suggestions about ways of turning dream into fiction, and suggested I get on with it (still valiantly resisting the urge to look at her watch).

There's just a possibility that the catatonic central character owed something to childhood memories of Edgar Rice Burroughs' tales of Mars. I can still recall the pleasure of holiday reading on wet August days by the seaside in England. All the books that were absent from home on the grounds of literary suitability suddenly became an acceptable alternative to draughts with the bottle tops standing in for counters, or Scrabble without a dictionary, or jigsaws with the final three pieces missing.

As for the rest, well, some of the characters come straight from my own life (I still haven't made it up with my former college friend), and the sleazy brother-in-law just insinuated himself into the story — it seems to be his style.

— *Andrew Enstice*

SEAN MCMULLEN

Award winning author Sean McMullen has gained a major reputation for his scientifically accurate "hard" science fiction. But he is also well qualified to write fantasy: having studied several units of history alongside his physical science subjects at university, he is also a karate instructor and the winner of several martial arts tournaments. As a result, his magical worlds are rigorously worked out, and his characters have a strong, earthy realism about them. And he writes the action scenes from experience!

Sean was born in Victoria into a Scottish-French-Irish family, and now lives in Melbourne with his wife and daughter. He has a Masters degree from the University of Melbourne, and works as a computer systems analyst. His fiction has won the Ditmar award three times and the Aurealis Award, and his short fiction has appeared in such magazines as *Analog*, *Interzone*, *The Magazine of Fantasy & Science Fiction*, and *Universe* overseas, and *Aurealis* and *Eidolon* in Australia. His novels include *Voices in the Light* (1994), *Mirrorsun Rising* (1995), *The Centurion's Empire* (1998) and *Souls in the Great Machine* (1999). He is an expert in the history of Australian science fiction and has won four William Atheling Jr Awards for excellence in science fiction criticism, and co-authored *Strange Constellations: A History of Australian Science Fiction* (1999) with Russell Blackford and Van Ikin.

Here is the story of the young mage Velander — and the devastating weapon Silverdeath, which operates according to the mathematical rules of . . . magic.

QUEEN OF SOULMATES

SEAN MCMULLEN

Weapon: This artefact, also called the Dragonrings and Silverdeath, is known to have fallen from the sky during a war among the gods in the very distant past. When inactive it assumes the form of metal armour, and while in this form it was stolen from its heavily guarded shrine. Once the thieves learned the true potential of Weapon they were so terrified that they buried it under a massive rockslide in the Seawall Mountains. The Councilium of our Order has inspected the site and is satisfied that even ten thousand men could not dig it out in a decade. Thus Weapon may be considered to be lost forever, and so no longer a threat to our world.

(Extract from the Annals of the Metrologan Order: 10th day of the 8th month, 3127)

* * *

The walled city of Larmentel had withstood the army of Commander Ralzak for five months when his patience finally ran out. Larmentel was rich, beautiful and massive, with a high, crenellated outer wall circling the cisterns, market gardens and storehouses that supplied its citizens. The citadel wall protected the inner city, where temples, palaces and mansions of white stone blocks rose in terraces to look out over the surrounding plain to distant mountains in the northeast. Stone gargoyles poked tongues and bared buttocks at the enemy beyond the outer walls, and nobles sipped wine from glazed pottery goblets shaped to a likeness of the head of Warsovran, the self-styled Emperor of Torea who was Ralzak's master. Ralzak's siege engines and storm climbers had been thrown back from the outer walls in every attack, and those defeats had cost him dearly.

The kingdoms of the southwest had been biding their time to see whether Larmentel would fall to the invaders' onslaught, but now they were beginning to lose their fear of Warsovran and rally. Sitting on the thick Vidarian rug in his tent, Ralzak read the reports of his diplomats and spies while Weapon stood beside the open flap, gleaming with the sheen of quicksilver and seeing through blank eyes. The walls and terraces of Larmentel were plainly visible in the distance, blushing red with the sunrise.

Ralzak looked from the city to Weapon. Weapon had the shape of a man, and was wearing Warsovran's band-plate armour and sword over a black tunic. In the five weeks since he had become Weapon's master and assumed command over Warsovran's forces, Ralzak had been afraid to use Weapon. For three years Warsovran had devoted fifty thousand slaves and ten thousand men-at-arms to digging it from under a rockslide in the Seawall Mountains. Thus whatever it was, it had value — and perhaps power.

When discovered, Weapon had the form of common body armour, but when Warsovran had put it on it had immediately melted and flowed to become a skin of flexible metal that covered him. What remained of him was his shape alone. A hollow, ringing voice declared that its name was Weapon, and that it was ready to do Ralzak's bidding.

Ralzak was totally unprepared for this magical warrior, and feared to use it at first. He merely announced that Warsovran was wearing a new type of armour, and everyone but Ralzak thought Warsovran to be alive and in charge within his fantastic skin of living metal. His famed judgement and acumen were gone, however, and the alliances that had been formed by the brilliant and charismatic man were rapidly weakening. Warsovran was now a figurehead, and he gave no commands. For the past five weeks Ralzak had been discovering that he was not his equal.

"I never asked to become the supreme commander," Ralzak confided to Weapon. "I'm just a soldier. I know my place and it's not here."

"Agreed," replied Weapon in a flat, metallic voice.

"Defeating a few of the homeland's neighbours, expanding our borders to advantage, that was my forte. Conquer a continent? I know neither why nor how. What would you do?"

"I cannot advise. I am to be used. Nothing more."

Ralzak had heard those words before. He considered carefully, looking back to Larmentel. The city had to fall, but he did not need its people or wealth, nor did he want the luxury of its mansions and towers for his own dwelling. In his own way he was a simple man, fond of life in the field with his troops and politically unambitious.

"Destroy my enemies," said Ralzak, gazing over at Larmentel again.

His voice was muted, as if he was just muttering his thoughts out aloud. Weapon regarded him with the blank sheen of its face.

"The feat is at the limit of my powers," Weapon explained in its flat yet ominous voice.

"So, you *can* do it," replied Ralzak.

"Yes."

Ralzak stood up and glared out through the tent flap at the distant walled city.

"Larmentel is the strongest city in all Torea. With Larmentel gone my other enemies are mere cyphers. How quickly could you break Larmentel?"

"In minutes."

Ralzak turned and blinked, his lips parted slightly. Weapon remained impassive. The metallic sheen that enclosed the head of what had once been Ralzak's master had the outline of human form and Ralzak wondered if the man beneath was still aware of what was happening.

"So, ah, when can you strike?" asked Ralzak tentatively when the silence began to lengthen.

"Now," replied Weapon.

"No, no," said Ralzak, with a hurried wave of his hands. "I want my troops positioned, ready to take whatever advantage you can give them."

"Not necessary," Weapon assured him.

Ralzak considered this as he began pacing before the flap of his tent, favouring Larmentel with a scowl at every pass. At last he beckoned to Weapon and they went outside together.

"I still want to be prepared in my own way before you strike," said Ralzak.

"I am yours to command," replied Weapon.

Ralzak's preparations took two hours. Men on active, relief and sleep shifts were all ordered to strap on armour and stand ready. The infantry were deployed at five strategic points to prevent the escape of anyone from the city, while elite lancers were stationed to ride for any breaches that the enemy might make. Storm climbers with ladders and water shields stood in closest of all. It was 8am before Ralzak was ready, wearing his own armour and standing with his sword drawn.

"Do your worst," he commanded, pointing with his sword to the undefeated walls of Larmentel.

Weapon's skin began to shimmer, then crawl as if tiny silver ants were swarming over it. Its head expanded, transforming into a shimmering silver globe. Ralzak noticed that its hands had become white, and even as he watched white skin was exposed at the neck. Warsovran's jaw became visible, and by now the globe had expanded into a sphere the size of a tent. Commander Ralzak shrank back as the mouth, nose and eyes of the emperor were exposed. The globe became bigger than a house, and it grew translucent. As it detached itself from its host Warsovran's body toppled to the ground and lay still. Ever growing and fading, the globe began to drift upwards and over towards the besieged city. Soon it was so insubstantial that it was no longer visible at all. The sky was blue over Larmentel, and all seemed serene and calm. Ralzak began to wonder if Weapon might be playing some humiliating hoax on him.

Without warning a huge rent appeared in the sky above Larmentel, spilling a column of yellow and crimson flames. Fire burst down through roofs and poured out through windows, fire flung heavy tiles about like leaves and turned great wooden beams to ash within moments. Breakers of flame cascaded outwards, sweeping along the streets and out to the citadel walls where they burst like waves on a shore then rose high into the sky. To the amazement of the besieging army the circular wall of fire then curled back upon itself to converge above the very centre of Larmentel. All that was left was smoke. The heat had been so intense that it scalded the faces of the nearest besiegers. Larmentel's heart was burned out. The torus of fire, a third of a mile across, had spilled out from the centre, its edges rolling upwards, then backwards. It was as if the flood of burning had been a spring that had reached its limit.

"Brilliant!" shouted Ralzak. "The greatest of all strongholds, annihilated!"

Suddenly he realised that Warsovran was standing beside him, pale and thin, but again himself. "You did well," the leader who had brought down a dozen kings said hoarsely to Ralzak.

Riders were despatched with a demand that the outer gates of Larmentel be opened to Warsovran's armies, but the surviving defenders were already streaming out of the city. Larmentel had been stabbed through the heart, and citizens were bleeding out through its walls.

"I must return to the capital," said Warsovran, beckoning for a horse. "You will remain here."

"But, but Larmentel has fallen, Emperor, the triumph —"

"Is yours, Commander Ralzak. Stay here, make an example of Larmentel for all others to know and fear. You are Weapon's commander, after all."

"But where is Weapon?"

Warsovran pointed above Larmentel.

"I do not understand," said Ralzak.

"I shall write out a series of incantations for you to make just before the eighth hour on certain days over the months to come. They will invoke Weapon in ever more powerful and frequent fire-circles. You must invoke it again and again until its energies are exhausted, and then it will fall from the sky above the city. When that happens, find it and bring it to me."

Within the hour Warsovran was riding south with a strong escort. Ralzak rode in triumph through the main gates of the outer wall at the head of a squad of heavy lancers. Except for the inner citadel, the city was intact and brimming with wealth and potential slaves. Closer to the centre, he looked down a long, straight avenue to the citadel area. The mighty ironbound gates of oak had been blown out and burned to ash, and beyond was a glowing ruin. He rode as close as he could urge his horse. Nearby houses were ablaze from radiant heat, and the charred corpses of people who had not even been touched by the torus of flames littered the streets.

Upon leaving the city, Ralzak declared his eyes closed for three days, then gave his men the freedom of what was left of Larmentel.

* * *

70 days:

At the western port city of Gironal the lateen-rigged demi-schooner *Arrowflight* crept under full sail past the sleek galleys of Warsovran's navy. The young boatmaster, Feran, stood at the steering oar, enduring jeers from idle marines aboard the galleys while his crew prepared to trim the sails once they passed the breakwater and reached clear winds. It was only when they were well out to sea that a man emerged from below and walked haltingly over the rolling deck to where Feran stood with a bearded man in his mid-twenties.

"You're safe for now," said Feran. "This is Laron, our medician and navigator."

"What shall we call you, Learned Brother?" asked Laron.

"Lenticar is my real name," he replied, blinking with surprise at Laron's perception. He gazed at the receding port with relief. "I've had so many assumed names that I sometimes wonder who I might really be. Let me be Lenticar."

Lenticar was lean, tanned and stooped from years of hard work in the open air and sun. He had the fearful, furtive gaze of one who had been the slave of brutal masters for too long, and he wrung his hands and bowed involuntarily each time that he spoke.

"How long to Zantrias?" he asked, holding onto the wooden rail as the waves rocked them.

"Fifty days would be a fair estimate," replied Laron. "We need to collect and discharge cargo to maintain the guise of a coastal trader."

"Fifty days may be too late."

"Fifty days is all I can offer. Is it about that fire-circle weapon that Warsovran used to break Larmentel?"

"It may be."

"Did you know he used it again?"

Lenticar's eyes widened. "No. Which city was burned?"

"It was only a test over Larmentel's ruins, and apparently no lives were lost. In a circle of over a half-mile across there was not a scrap of wood, cloth or flesh left."

"So it was bigger than the first time?"

"Oh yes."

A steady wind filled the sails and drove them through the waves. The *Arrowflight* was too small to be a warship yet fast enough to escape privateers, and so was well suited to move freely between ports of all alliances. Feran had been at sea since the age of eight, and at eighteen was the youngest boatmaster working the Torean coast.

✳ ✳ ✳

120 days:

In the early afternoon the *Arrowflight* tied up at one of the long stone piers in the port of Zantrias. A large temple was visible in the distance, perched on a verdant hill three miles back from the coast. Feran escorted his passenger through the port to the safety of temple complex, and at the hospitalier's portico they were received by the Elder's assistant. Here Feran was told that his work had been well done, but that he was no longer needed. As he made his way back through the empty Gardens of Contemplation someone hailed him.

"Learned Terikel, how delightful to see you again," he said as a blue-robed priestess approached, attended by a student girl in green. "And Deaconess Velander, I see that your are still ... a deaconess."

"And you are now a boatmaster," Velander observed by the red shoulder tassels of his deck jacket. "Congratulations."

"Will you be in port for long?" Terikel asked.

"About eight days."

"Velander and I need more practice with spoken Diomedan. Are you available?"

"For Terikel and Velander, always. Why not walk back with me now, speaking Diomedan?"

Once through the gates and past the guards Feran softly asked "Have you any more news of Warsovran's weapon?"

"There have been two more tests," Velander replied. "One of them was a week ago, and burned a circle two and one third miles in diameter. The King of Zarlon was invited to see it happen. The other was sixteen days ago and smaller."

"What have you learned?" asked Terikel.

"The first fire-circle was a third of a mile in diameter. I learned that from slaves that the *Arrowflight* carried on commission. As for the second test, we only know that it took place from tavern talk by Warsovran's troops. Maybe he was not sure why it worked the first time, and did not want witnesses if it failed."

All the way to the docks they discussed the figures that encompassed destruction combining the swiftness of lightning with the power of a volcano.

"What can be done to fight it?" asked Velander as they approached the *Arrowflight* along the pier.

"Just what we are doing: learn its workings," Feran replied. "How many days until you are ordained, Velander?"

Velander shrugged. "Eight — but five of those are vigil. I have to fast, drinking only rainwater while I endure ordeals and interrogations alone."

"Hah, it's brave of you. I always have a crew to suffer with me through my ordeals."

"Battles with privateers?"

"Hangovers."

Terikel stifled a giggle, and Velander shook her head.

"I shall not be completely alone," Velander added confidently. "One's soulmate customarily endures a fast nearby to give comfort. Learned Terikel will be fasting in the Chapel of Vigils as I fast in the temple's outer sanctum."

"And then you become a priestess with twelve years of celibacy before you," sighed Feran. "Who could endure such a wait as that?"

"Not you, boatmaster?" asked Terikel.

"Not I, learned, celibate and holy ladies."

They reached the *Arrowflight*, but priestess and deaconess turned back. The schooner was being unloaded, and the air was full of the curses of wharfers.

"So, which do you fancy?" asked the deckswain as Feran stood watching the pair walk back down the pier.

"Me?" asked Feran innocently.

"You," chorused the deckswain and Laron.

"Velander's just a serious puppy, but Terikel! Ah, she's like a queen."

"The little one adores the priestess, while that curly-haired, brunette priestess is as protective as a mother cat," observed the deckswain. "I'd not like to come between them."

"I've been asking around, as like I always do," said Laron. "Just three years ago Velander was in deep trouble. She had killed several people — apparently by accident but I know no details. Terikel's sister brought Velander here and got her into the temple academy. When Terikel's sister was murdered by Warsovran, Terikel made Velander into a sort of foster sister. She became her friend and mentor, and even found sponsors for the girl's years of study. As far as Velander is concerned, Terikel is her friend, sister, saint, and queen. She would die for Terikel, and probably kill for her too."

*　*　*

That same day the Concilium of the Metrologan Order met the agent that Feran had delivered. The man was by now wearing the earth-brown robe of a lay scholar.

"This is Lenticar," said the priestess who was Concilium Elder. "He was captured early in Warsovran's wars of expansion, and worked in slavery for three years. Lenticar, tell the Concilium what you told me."

Lenticar bowed to the Elder, then to each Concilium member in turn.

"The, ah, essence is that I spent three years in an army of slaves, digging out a collapsed ravine in the Seawall Mountains. One day, late last year, there was a great commotion down at the base of the diggings. We had reached the rocks of the old riverbed, you see. The area was sealed, and the six hundred slaves who had been working down there were put to the sword. The other fifty thousand of us were marched out at once to build a fortress on Vidaria's border. I escaped as we travelled, as the guard was by then a lot less strict."

"Did you see what was discovered?" asked a priestess.

"No, but I heard rumours that even the guards of the slaves closest to whatever it was were killed."

The Elder now stood up again.

"We have learned that within a few days of the discovery Warsovran arrived with Commander Ralzak. Just over a month later that fire-circle thing burned Larmentel's heart out. Now Warsovran is testing it on what is left of the city, and has learned how to refresh it more quickly. Word arrived by an auton bird this morning that a fifth test scoured the life from an area four and two third miles across. That is enough to destroy any army, and is probably adequate to conquer this continent."

There was a hurried, alarmed murmur among the members of the Councilium.

"Then why does he just detonate it over Larmentel, over and over?" the Examiner asked.

"Larmentel is a shell, and now worthless. He wants the other cities intact, so he seeks to frighten his enemies with these obscene demonstrations. Sisters, Warsovran has sworn to wipe out our order. For some of us it is time to flee, and time for the rest of us to fade."

* * *

122 days:

Velander sat on a stone bollard and looked down on the deck of the moored *Arrowflight*, slowly combing and re-pinning her brown, wavy hair back from her face with little ornamental combs. Terikel was nearby, bartering for something at a pier stall.

"Deaconess, should you not be keeping a vigil for your ordination?" asked Feran in Diomedan as he emerged through the deck hatch.

"As of noon, yes."

He strode up the gangplank and stood beside her, smelling of sweat, sacking, tar and resins.

"Have you had a good breakfast?" asked Laron. "There's five days of fasting ahead."

"I've gone hungry for longer," she replied enigmatically.

"In your travels?" asked Feran.

"To ... develop self-discipline, to practice for this day. How does my Diomedan sound? Could I pass for a native speaker?"

"You sound like a foreign scholar, but speak confidently. Why do you ask?"

"Oh, just curiosity. Did you know there has been a fifth fire-circle? It was four and two third miles across."

"That's not common knowledge," said Feran slowly, avoiding her eyes.

"So it's true?"

"How did you know about it?"

"I lived three years among common folk, Boatmaster Feran. They have ways of finding out, just as priestesses, nobles and kings do."

"And now you ask about your spoken Diomedan. Could it be that you might go there soon? This morning I noticed crates from the temple being loaded onto a deep water trader bound for Diomeda."

"I know nothing about that," replied Velander uncomfortably.

"Is it because of the fire-circles?"

"It was two years ago that Learned Terikel suggested we learn spoken Diomedan from you. She said I studied too much of mathematics, and that I needed the balance of an exotic language. There were no fire-circles then."

Feran conceded the point. "Well, it's meant two years of charming company whenever we dock here."

"I cannot make out what energies drive the things," Velander said hurriedly, anxious to avoid this subject as well.

"I'm puzzled too," said Laron. "Magic is too limited in terms of raw power, while hellbreath oil must be pumped out of a hose and does not burn hot enough to melt stone."

Druskarl, a senior eunuch of the temple guard, strode down the pier from where the deepwater trader was being loaded. He was wearing the tunic of a pilgrim instead of his usual armour.

"Deaconess, your vigil starting today," Druskarl said in a sharp, expressionless voice.

"I am under the escort of the Learned Terikel," replied Velander in a parody of Druskarl's hard, flat voice, gesturing to where Terikel was holding up a pilgrim's pack and arguing with the stallholder.

"Deaconess! Ordination vigil starting noon," Druskarl insisted.

"Nobody knows that better than me, Druskarl," she replied firmly.

"I note that the temple is shipping books to Acrema with you as escort," Feran interjected.

"Druskarl noting *Arrowflight*'s masts hinge between braces," he countered. "Can lie flat."

"I smelled the scent of old books as your crates were carried past to the trader," Feran pointed out. "I am no stranger to libraries."

"Druskarl no stranger to ships, Boatmaster. *Arrowflight* riding high in water."

"The *Arrowflight* is nearly empty, and our bilges are being pumped and scrubbed," Feran explained with a trace of condescension in his tone. When speaking with the Druskarl, that was a mistake. "So, is your order moving to Acrema before Warsovran turns his fire-circle on Zantrias?"

"What are strange hatch covers below load waterline?" Druskarl asked instead.

"They are for looking through," Feran answered smoothly.

Druskarl frowned, neither believing him nor seeing the joke. "Below waterline?"

"Yes, in an hour there will be more cargo aboard and they will definitely be below the waterline."

"Druskarl say masts of *Arrowflight* easy to lowering. *Arrowflight* easy to sink, also. *Arrowflight* pretend sinking in shallow water when chased. Low tide coming, hatches closed by divers, crew ship pumping out, then ship floating."

"But we are not fishes. We would drown."

"Gigboat bolted upside down to frame on deck."

"It would fill with rain otherwise."

"Gigboat holding air if *Arrowflight* sinking."

Feran's eyes narrowed.

"Some people have minds so sharp they could slice precious parts of themselves off," he said sullenly to the tall, powerfully built eunuch.

"They like to people having sharp noses, yes?" asked Druskarl.

"Well parried, Sir," said Laron, standing back with his arms folded.

"Good Sirs, we need to bid you both farewell," Terikel cut in as she returned with the canvas pack. "Velander has to prepare for her ordination in five days."

Terikel cross-grasped hands with both men in turn, but only Feran felt a scrap of paper slipped between his fingers.

✳   ✳   ✳

At noon Velander was formally summoned to the outer sanctum of the temple by the Elder, and began five days of fasting to prepare for a vigil that would see her emerge as a priestess. In the *Arrowflight*'s master cabin Feran examined the scrap of paper that Velander had given to him.

It was a scroll of tissue, the type used on messenger birds. There was a preamble that was not easy to follow, but it eventually became clear that the authors were two priests of the Metrologan's brother order. They were disguised as peasants who were staying not far from Larmentel, and helping to strip everything of value from the ruins. They had witnessed Warsovran's weapon being used for the fifth time. There were second-hand descriptions of the first four tests and quite accurate figures on the destruction's extent. Each test had been at the 8th hour of the morning, and every time a perfect circle had been blasted and scoured by the most intense fire imaginable. Many stones had partly melted or crumbled, and the fire had penetrated to the deepest cellars and tunnels. Not a scrap of wood, food or even charred bone had survived, but they noted that the bodies of fish in a deep ornamental pond, while boiled alive, were at least whole and uncharred.

"*It is our feeling that Warsovran's Commander Ralzak has a weapon of such potency that no city or army could stand against him,*" the report's minuscule writing concluded. "*Total annihilation in a hopeless cause is far less constructive than surrender in the knowledge that Warsovran's day will pass. Our order can continue to work in secret until more enlightened times return and —*"

There was a short pen-slash, as if the writer had had his arm jolted, then the fine writing commenced again.

"*We have just seen a fifth wall of fire over the city, one reaching right to the outer walls. It burst from the sky at the eighth hour in the form of a torus about a half-mile above the centre of Larmentel, spilling fire down the centre to blast all before it before rolling back into the sky and down its own centre again. It covered the radius from the centre to the outer walls in the time one needs to draw a deep breath, and made a sound like a continuous peal of thunder. The degree of annihilation was the same as before on the ground. Make what you will of this ghastly nightmare, we shall release a bird with this message and send more news as we are able.*

Learned Deremi and Learned Trolandic"

There were figures and dates for the five detonations of Warsovran's weapon going back 120 days. Feran was intrigued by the line about the fish in the pond, because that meant the weapon had limits. Appended in different handwriting was the name of a dockside tavern, *Stormhaven*, and the word *dusk*.

Feran gazed through the cabin window's fretwork at the port. Were the weapon to be used on Zantrias, the *Arrowflight* could be sunk with its crew, and with the air in the gigboat they could last as long as six hours. The only drawback was that the schooner needed several minutes to sink, and the weapon could raze the port in as many seconds.

✳   ✳   ✳

127 days:

Five days of drinking water alone and eating nothing had left Velander unsteady and weak, but feeling strangely self-controlled. At noon she was led into the inner sanctum of the temple by the Examiner, and they meditated together for two hours. The Councilium then entered and subjected her to an intense, aggressive barrage of questions about knowledge theory, verification, and her own personal loyalties. She was run ragged, but did not break. Presently she was left alone to meditate again while the Councilium discussed her candidature.

From the distant harbour Velander could hear the bell at the end of the stone pier ringing the change of tide, followed by code for shipping movements. *Steady Prosper*, *White Wave* and *Bright Leaper* had arrived, but there were no departures. *Arrowflight* was cleared to sail the following afternoon. So, Feran was still there. Perhaps Terikel and she could go down to the docks and wave him off as priestess and priestess after one last hour of Diomedan practice. She felt so weak, though, and three miles was a long, long way.

Late in the afternoon Velander was led out to the plaza before the temple, where brushwood had been piled up in a blackstone grate shaped like a huge, clawed hand. All priestesses and students in the complex had been assembled on the stone steps to watch Velander's last ordeal begin. Everyone except Terikel, of course, who was in the little Chapel of Vigils further down the hill. As the sun touched the horizon, trumpets sounded from the steps of the temple's outer sanctum, and Velander took a firebrand from the temple's eternal flame and plunged it into the brushwood. The blaze symbolised the light of knowledge being ignited against the onset of darkness, and the brushwood fuel was a reminder that knowledge must be tended closely or it would quickly burn out. If she could endure through the night to stoke the flames until dawn, she would automatically become Learned Velander as the sun cleared the horizon. The watchers filed down from the steps, leaving her alone to her task.

Staying awake seemed such a simple thing until one had to do it after five practically sleepless nights and no food at all for as long. The supply of brushwood fuel was cunningly measured so that too much piled on at once would burn out before morning. One had to actually be awake, not to ... nod! Velander caught herself falling forward. The fire was still burning: she had drifted away for only moments. She tossed a bundle onto the flames and sat back, again drowsy with the smoke.

Someone to talk to was all she needed, but Terikel was keeping her own vigil after no more sleep or food than Velander had been allowed. Terikel was suffering too, and her soul-mate's ordeal could not be wasted. Velander cast about in her mind for a problem, and thought of Warsovran's fire-circles.

The tests had begun 64 days apart, halved to 32, then 16, then 8. There should have been a test on the second morning of her fast, then one on the fourth, and one on the fifth. Somewhere in the temple complex a bell rang the 8th hour past noon. Another test would happen at this very moment, then at 2am the next day, 5am, 6.30am, 7.15am, 7.42am ... and soon after that the tests would converge on some time around the ninth minute past 8am. That was it! Nine minutes after 8am tomorrow Warsovran would become able to use the fire-circle at will ... or perhaps it moved back to lengthening intervals after the convergence. Perhaps he had to make his conquests very quickly, or the interval would soon be 64 days again.

She thought to the years ahead. To be ordained in the Metrologan Order one had to do six years of study, then vow to follow ordination with six of travel, six of research and six of teaching. It was not a celibate order, but marriage was not permitted until the teaching years began. She put another bundle of brushwood on the pyre, then circled it slowly to keep herself alert. Terikel had once endured this ordeal, after all, and now she was fasting again for Velander. Don't fail Terikel, Velander told herself as she forced her legs to walk.

* * *

Velander was down to two bundles of brushwood when a brilliant bead of light appeared on the eastern horizon. Her fire was still burning brightly, and in tribute the temple bells began to ring out. Priestesses and students streamed out of the darkness and Velander was swept away to warm broth, a bath, a suit of blue robes, then a lengthy audience with the Elder.

All through the celebrations and ceremonies Velander thought of Terikel, who had endured the same privations yet got nothing more than the satisfaction of supporting her soulmate. A canvas pack with the symbolic contents of dried fruit, water, a writing kit, coins and books was presented to Velander. The Elder signed her ordination scroll, blotted the ink, then rubbed it with beeswax to waterproof it.

"Twice the usual number of subjects in half the time," the venerable priestess said approvingly. "But what is your favourite?"

"Mathematics," Velander replied dreamily. "Oh and languages! Languages, definitely."

She was taken back out to the seamstress to have the straps of her pack fitted properly. Sleep washed over her like waves over a sandbar, and she chattered to stay awake.

"What has been happening for the past five days?" Velander asked.

"In the temple, port or world?" asked the seamstress.

"Start with the world and work back."

"The King of Zarlon has invited Warsovran to send an ambassador. That fire-circle thing of Warsovran's has him as frightened as our own monarch, you know. *I* think it's all a trick. Notice how it is always set off in the same place? I think it's just slaves spreading hellbreath oil. The eunuch guard Druskarl sailed on the evening of the first day of your vigil, and who do you think was waving and weeping on the pier? Why it was Learned —"

"Has Warsovran's weapon been tested again?" Velander interrupted, shaking her head to clear it.

"Twice more, as I've heard."

"Twice more? In five days?" Velander asked slowly, pleased that her convergence theory was holding true.

"I'm sure of it. I have my sources."

"Are they reliable?"

"Oh ... yes and no. If a Councilium meeting is called within a quarter hour of an auton bird arriving, I know that another fire-circle has burned. Pah, the way that Warsovran has been squandering hellbreath oil! Just what is he trying to prove? He's just like a little boy playing with fire, and one day the fire will get out of control."

Suddenly a jumble of figures began to cascade into order in Velander's mind. The Elder's words returned, followed by those of the seamstress: *twice the subjects in half the time, one day the fire will get out of control.*

Velander knew only four fire-circle diameters and even those were approximate, but a trend was there: a third of a mile, no figure, just over a mile, two and a third, four and two thirds ... and what of the latest tests? Six should have been nearly ten miles across, and seven over eighteen.

A deep, cold chasm suddenly opened up within Velander. Twice the diameter in half the time! The fire-circle was doubling with each detonation, but in half the time. It was not being tested, it was out of control! Velander calculated frantically, oblivious of the seamstress chatting to her as she adjusted her pack's straps. Detonation 8, just under 38 miles after one day. Detonation 9, 75 miles after half a day. The 10th would have been at 2am and 150 miles across, followed by one at 5am a staggering 300 miles from rim to rim. It was nearly 7am now, so about half an hour ago a fire-circle must have burned the life from a circle 600 miles wide. The next would stop a mere ten miles short of Zantrias in perhaps twenty minutes, and after that ...

Screaming the single word "Run!" Velander tore away from the seamstresses and ran from the fitting room. She fled down the stone corridor beyond, swaying and stumbling from five days of fasting. It was three miles to the beach, but Terikel had to be warned first. She ran across the plaza of the temple complex where her pyre was now ashes and into the dormitory cells. Terikel's cell was empty, with the bed made up. The refectory! Velander ran down the stone steps and across a courtyard where stone dragons breathed water into a lampfish pool, then burst into the refectory. The first shift of priestesses and novices was eating breakfast in silence while a novice stood at a lectern, reading from an ancient text.

"Terikel!" Velander shouted. Silence and stares answered her. "Run for the beach, the fire is coming!" Velander added by way of explanation, then whirled and dashed out.

There was a last chance: that Terikel had fallen asleep in the Chapel of Vigils when the temple bells had rung out to announce Velander's ordination. The chapel was not far from the main gates to the temple complex, just beyond the Gardens of Contemplation. Velander screamed Terikel's name as she ran, shattering the serenity of those who were there to meditate, then stumbled up the steps to the chapel. The glowing stub of a coil of incence was tagged with Velander's name, but the benches beyond were empty.

Velander hurried past each row, in case her soulmate was asleep on the floor. Outside, the thief-bell was being rung, and people were calling her name.

Soon they would catch her, they would think she was having a fit. Explanations would take time, perhaps hours, but only minutes remained. It was three miles to the docks. The *Arrowflight* could be sunk but still hold air to breathe. It would take long enough to convince Feran of the danger, let alone the Elder. Velander took the stub of incense and extinguished the glowing point in the skin of her left wrist.

"By this mark I'll carry your memory forever," sobbed Velander. "Forgive me for deserting you, Terikel, but I tried my best."

The gates of the temple complex were not yet locked as Velander neared them, but the two guards were alert with their glaves at the ready. Velander stopped and panted a tangle of life force between her hands, then flung it. One guard fell with glowing amber coils wrapped about his ankles, but the other tried to slam the gates shut. Already weak from the first casting, Velander breathed more life force between her hands and flung it, binding the second guard to the heavy oak slats of one side of the gate. The effort of casting so much life force cost Velander greatly in strength, and she shambled through the gate, barely able to hold herself upright. The pursuing priestesses would catch her in moments unless ... the casting binding the first guard suddenly collapsed and streaked to Velander, swirling around her head and quickly dissolving into her skin. As the second casting returned to her, she was able to break into a headlong, unsteady run again.

The Metrologan Order wore light sandals and loose trousers under an outer robe, well suited to running. Velander dodged past a wood cart delivering fuel for a baker's oven then ran through the market square where stall keepers bartered with customers. So much life, but they would all be dead within an hour, she thought. The sky was clear, and there was no wind. It was a perfect, flawless morning. Children were playing knucklebones on the cobbles, and two town constables were making a leisurely patrol. Should warn, must warn, can't warn, Velander thought. She could snatch up one child and try to save it, but the constables would soon catch her and explanations would take hours. Pain lanced at Velander's side and her lungs burned, but still she ran. She cleared the square. Two miles to go, perhaps less.

She ran on more slowly, but still at her body's limit. Down was safe, down was to the sea. She looked up as the port watchouse loomed, then stumbled over a gutter and sprawled. Dragging her self up, she ran again. One mile to go now. Knives plunged into her left knee at every step. The streetside stalls became more nautical in their wares: netting, floats, cordage, sails, tar, ship's biscuit. Suddenly the buildings vanished, and Velander was facing clear sky and masts. The docks! Her legs betrayed her, she fell, crawled a few feet, then got up. She stumbled a few paces further, fell again, then crawled for the pier.

"Learned Sister, are you all right?" asked a docker in alarm.

"Leave me alone, pilgrimage," she wheezed.

With an ever growing crowd behind her Velander forced her aching legs to support her again and shuffled along the flagstones of the stone pier. Five ships along, unless they had sailed already. Five ships to — the *Arrowflight*. She literally fell down the gangplank and flopped to the deck, gasping for Feran. Laron's face filled the blue sky that she lay staring into.

"Velander?" he asked.

"Release hatches," she panted. "Sink. Tell Feran."

"Shush!" he said in alarm, dropping to his knees and bending over her. "There are people on the docks."

"Soon — all dead. Fire-circle, coming."

"Get the boatmaster," Laron said to the deckswain, suddenly comprehending.

"But Sir —"

"I know!" shouted Laron. "Just get him. Velander, the weapon is at Larmentel. How —"

"Out of control. Reach here, only minutes."

Feran arrived, stripped for sleeping and wearing only sailcloth trousers. Laron hastily related what Velander had said. Feran thought for a moment, looked to the crowd gazing down from the stone pier, looked to the upturned gigboat bolted to its frame, then beckoned to the deckswain.

"She knows something," he said softly. "Cast off, use the sweep oars to take us near the deep mooring buoys." He walked across to the carpenter next. "Go below, and at my order release the sink hatches," he said quietly.

The man goggled at him, then gestured to the crowd on the pier. "But Sir, we're within sight of at least five hundred people. They'll know our secret."

The schooner began to move as the crewmen pushed against the stone pier with their sweep oars.

"Soon it won't matter —"

Directly to the north a curtain of flames reaching miles high burst over the Blackstone Hills, then stopped as if it was some god's guard dog at the end of its chain. The flames towered above the little port, boiling high into the air before coiling back upon themselves. Continuous thunder rolled over the port, and heat seared the faces of everyone watching like the blast of an open oven. Then the fire vanished back into a cauldron of smoke that followed in the wake of the huge, blazing torus that had barely spared the port.

Some people began to leap into the water at once, while others rushed for the ships that were still tied up along the pier. Fights broke out with the crews as they tried to cast off, desperate to escape. Feran glanced back at what Velander had spared them, then rushed to where she was trying to sit up.

"How long?" he demanded.

"Less than a half hour, more than twenty minutes," she replied, staring to the north where the sky was a wall of brownish-white smoke. "Why don't you sink the boat?"

"We need to reach deeper water."

The masts and rigging took many precious minutes to bring down and secure. Several ships and boats managed to get under way in the meantime, and one medium sized galley-ram actually cleared the harbour. With the hatch chocks knocked out the *Arrowflight* began to sink quickly and Feran ordered his crewmen under the gigboat. After another minute the *Arrowflight* gave a loud gurgle, then sank on an even keel to thump softly into the sand below. A moment later the water around them blazed a whitish green, brightening until they had to shut their eyes, then a deep, shuddering thunderclap resonated through the water and their bodies. There was a terrible hissing, with a rushing sound as if a huge breath was being drawn by the world itself. Someone near Velander began to pray. Others joined in, not all in the same tongue. As suddenly as it began the light faded and the rumbling became a declining hiss. The water was distinctly warmer around them.

"That wasn't so bad," came the deckswain's voice. "Any number of folk might have survived by diving off the pier."

"Talk sense," panted Feran. "We're at least fifteen feet deep here, yet feel the heat. The air above will be as hot as a smithy's forge for hours."

"You'd char from the lungs outwards by breathing it," added Laron.

Feran freed a sweep oar and managed to push it up vertically. The wood was charred at the end when he pulled it back down. Yielding at last to the torments that her body had endured, Velander passed out.

*　*　*

Hundreds of miles out to sea Warsovran was bailed up with his officers on the quarterdeck of a large caravel-built merchant ship. The crew was in a state of blind terror after seeing an immense wall of fire, water and steam surge out of the east to tower over them, then collapse.

"You can't make us sail into that!" shouted the bosun, pointing to the roiling mass of fog and ragged waves that now lay not a mile to the east. "What if that thing comes back?"

"Then we're dead anyway," Warsovran said in a clear, sharp voice that was firm with authority. "The firecircle that follows is always twice as big." He lowered his sword and let the point rest on the deck. "What you have just seen is a god's weapon turned loose by a fool. Now it is spent, quenched by the sea, and I *must* return to Larmentel and get it back."

"Meaning no disrespect, Emperor Warsovran," said a midshipman, "but if you think we're goin" near what caused *that* you can take a jump and swim."

"The lad's right," agreed the bosun. "We're six hundred miles out to sea and yet it was grand fearsome. What's Torea look like after that's been over it? And what land are you planning to burn next?"

"I am a ruler, I have no interest in annihilation. Until my idiot commander unleashed that infernal weapon from the gods I was uniting Torea's kingdoms under a single empire and bringing them order and discipline." He jabbed his finger to the east. "*That* was an accident. Now the weapon lies spent at the centre of Larmentel for *any* scavenger to pick up. Would you rather it fall into the hands of yet another fool, or be safe in the hands of someone who can control it? You *must* help me! I *do not need* to use the fire-circle weapon, and I want to make sure that it is *never* used again."

They began to argue over his words, which did indeed make sense — provided that one could trust him. Warsovran was adept at swaying crowds, especially when playing them for his life. He had got them wavering over a difficult dilemma, and now it was time to offer an irresistible reward.

"You need only take me to the port of Terrescol,

where I shall take the horses and supplies we carry and ride on to Larmentel. While I am away searching for the weapon, you can amuse yourselves by digging for melted gold in the ruins of the merchant halls, temples, and even the palace."

There was a highly excited mutter from the crewmen this time, and a great number of fingers pointed east amid the gesticulation.

"Wood burns, paper burns, and even people can be turned to ash, but gold merely melts. If you get there first you may well dig out a half ton of gold before I return from Larmentel. We can sail to Acrema, buy a fleet of ships, then sail back and dig out gold from all the other port cities. Imagine: a ton of gold for every man on the deck."

As he paused for breath the crew gave him three cheers and rushed to raise the sea anchors and unfurl the sails. Warsovran remained on the quarterdeck, glancing to the sun and fearfully estimating when the fire might return to sweep over them if he was wrong. He knew that a fire-circle would be quenched if its entire circumference or more than half its area was over water. According to the finest maps available to him, the latest fire-circle should have been the last ... but mapmaking was by no means an exact science.

* * *

When Velander revived again she was being held up by Laron, and everyone under the boat was silent as they shared the bubble of air. They waited. The water remained warm, but did not get any worse. When a second oar was held up it came down undamaged. Next a seaman swam clear of the upturned and submerged gigboat and held his hand just clear of the surface. He swam back to report it had been like plunging his fingers into boiling water.

The air under the boat became increasingly humid and foul. Another hour passed. They kept very still, not even praying now. The tide was on the way out, and when they could hear waves lapping more distinctly another crewman swam up to the surface. He returned and said that the air was hot but breathable. Others swam out to release the four heavy anchor stones, and the schooner slowly rose to the surface.

A blustery, hot wind was whipping the sea into a choppy confusion as Velander emerged from under the gigboat and waded through knee deep water to the rail where Feran, Laron and the deckswain stood. Behind them crewmen were setting up a valve-plunge pump while others dove to re-chock the sink hatches. Parts of the port glowed like the embers of a campfire through a veil of steam and smoke.

"Is the whole of the world like that?" asked the deckswain.

"Hopefully not," Feran ventured.

"Over water the fire-circle may cool and disperse," suggested Laron.

"But how do you know?"

"I don't."

Velander turned to Feran to ask a question, but noticed that a woman had come up beside him. She was wrapped in a blanket, with dripping, disheveled hair. Curly brunette hair. A harlot from the docks, she assumed, then did a double-take so abruptly that the bones of her neck clicked. Her mistake had been natural. She had never before seen Terikel without her blue priestly robes. Feran ducked his head sheepishly, then hurried off after Laron and the deckswain to help unclamp the masts. His back was a landscape of scratches, while his neck sported three lurid bites.

"Thank you for leaving incense to keep soulmate vigil for me," said Velander icily, pushing her own hair back and feeling for her combs.

"Think nothing of it," muttered Terikel, shivering in her blanket.

Terikel left the rail and walked to the aft deck hatch. Looking down, she saw that the pump had not yet removed enough water to let her enter and retrieve her clothes.

"I nearly *died* because I went searching for you!" Velander burst out, her fists raised and her eyes blazing. "You betrayed me!"

"I failed to be *Velander's* Terikel," she said as she stood at the edge of the hatch, "but that's not the end of the world, is it?" She stabbed a finger at the coast. "*That* is!"

Velander did not appreciate the comparison. "Ironic though it may be, you are now the Elder," she pointed out as she began to wring the water from her robes. "Have you any pronouncements?"

"The celibacy rule is hereby annulled," replied Terikel sullenly.

* * *

Feran and Laron went as far as the stone pier in the corrak while the ship was being pumped out, and Laron went ashore and endured the heat long enough to gather some solidified splashes of gold. They were from purses that had been dropped by merchants who had died where they stood. There was much speculation about whether the entire world or just the southern continent of Torea had been devastated by the fire-circles. Seasonal trade winds could take them the five thousand miles to the continent of Acrema, but was there any point to making the journey? Feran decided to take the chance, and they set sail in the early evening. Battling winds that swept in from the ocean to the hot land, the *Arrowflight* tacked away from the coast and by evening was on a heading northeast. Velander stood at the stern, where the deckswain was taking his turn at the steering oar. Laron was nearby, taking sightings from the stars.

"I must thank you for saving us," Laron said to her suddenly.

"I was saving myself," she replied coldly.

He gestured down to the deck, below which was Feran's cabin. "When it comes to choosing lovers, rules must be cut to the cloth."

"So I have noticed."

"Don't blame Learned Terikel loving the young boatmaster," said the deckswain. "She's spoken to me, she . . . she still wants to be your soulmate."

"I have a new soulmate."

The deckswain scratched his head. Velander looked up to the stars that were guiding them on their five thousand mile grasp at survival. The mathematics of progressions had saved her a bare half-day earlier, and now the mathematics of navigation was taking her to safety. The Queen of Philosophies was ever-faithful, and never let her followers down. Shivering, weak, tired, but totally in control, Velander imagined a cold yet comforting arm about her shoulders.

Has the world ended, Velander asked her new soulmate. Was the fourteenth fire-circle the last, the figures asked in turn. Eighteen fire-circles would have been needed to blanket the world in fire, she calculated mentally.

"I fainted after the first fire-circle passed over," said Velander to the deckswain. "Were there four more after that?"

The deckswain gave a short, bitter laugh. "There was but one that passed over us, but that was enough to roast the world."

Velander allowed herself a smirk.

"Not so. Only Torea, the Great Southland, was destroyed."

"Uh — really? How do you know, Learned Sister?"

"My new soulmate told me, the soulmate who kept me awake to tend my pyre, and who warned me to flee this morning."

The deckswain fell silent, unsure of whether or not she was sane. Velander could hear Terikel just below, sobbing in terror of the world's end. She decided not to announce her latest discovery for five days and one night by way of retribution. Again she imagined a cold, firm arm about her shoulders. Lovers, kings, ships' captains, priestesses, and even magicians knelt before the throne of Mathematics, the Queen of Philosophies, and yet out of everyone in Torea she was soulmate to Velander alone.

AFTERWORD

Velander is an important character in a fantasy novel that I am writing, and she is a girl with a cold, sharp, quantitative attitude towards the magical phenomena in her world. How did she get to be that way, I wondered? Was it from being a bright but friendless bookworm as a child, was it from being an awkward teenager with no aptitude for magic in a world where magic is commonplace ... or was it just because mathematics saved her life part-way through this story — which has been adapted from the book? The answers had to be no, no and no. Velander's attitude, founded in mathematics and logic, cried out to have an intensely emotional cause. Weapon's convergent progression was interesting to construct, but not creatively difficult, yet working out a way to get Velander exceedingly upset gave me more trouble than the rest of the story put together. When I found the solution, a very appealing title also fell straight into place, but this is so often the way it is in writing: the best things happen by accident.

— *Sean McMullen*

DIRK STRASSER

Dirk Strasser has had twelve books published by major publishers in Australia since 1993. His adult fantasy novels *Zenith* and *Equinox* have been translated into German and Czech, and *Eclipse*, the third book in the *Books of Ascension* trilogy, has been accepted for publication in Germany. He is the author of *Graffiti*, a children's horror/fantasy novel, and his short stories have appeared in such magazines and anthologies as *Universe Two, Borderlands 4, Metaworlds*, and *Alien Shores*. He is the co-editor and co-publisher of *Aurealis* — *Australian Fantasy and Science Fiction*, and has been the convenor of the Aurealis Awards. Born in Germany in 1959, Strasser has lived most of his life in Australia. He is currently employed as a publisher for Rigby Heinemann and lives in Melbourne with his wife and two children.

In the accomplished and subtle story "The Doppelgänger Effect", Strasser explores the personal, reflective effects of faster than light travel.

THE DOPPELGÄNGER EFFECT

DIRK STRASSER

"I cannot understand the mystery,
but I am always conscious of myself as two."
— Walt Whitman

Blue shift

The grey drizzled down around him, and Christain knew the time had come for them to kill him again. The tram tracks glistened silently in front of him as he walked down the middle of the dimly lit road. How long had it been since the trams had run through the city? It hadn't mattered before, but for some reason, now that he could see the twin shining lines stretching out through the city's nightscape, it was important. *Parallel, always parallel*, he thought. *If they weren't parallel, it just didn't work.*

He twirled his umbrella slightly and thick drops momentarily cascaded around him. He tried a half-hearted whistle — even thought for a moment about a silly dance step — in the vain hope that something frivolous would forestall the inevitable. In the end he didn't have the will for it. He just kept walking and waiting, the blood rushing behind his ears.

And then it came. Not as he had anticipated — it was always impossible, somehow, to anticipate how it was going to happen. He could hear the sound of a car in the distance. So, was he going to be run over this time? Was that how they were going to do it? The pitch increased in frequency as the car approached him... he braced himself. *Please no, not again. Not again.* He closed his eyes.

He heard a sickening screech of brakes and looked up. Through the thin grey veil of rain he could see the car had stopped, straddling the tram tracks ten metres in front of him. The doors opened and two dark figures got out and started to move slowly towards him, a flash of steel in each right hand.

Not knives. They were always the worst.

He started to run. It was instinctive. The rain slanted in on him, soaking his face. He could hear the wet slosh of running feet behind him getting louder. His foot slipped on one of the tram tracks and he fell.

His breaths ragged, he saw a blur of dark and a dull flash before they punctured his lungs. The last words he heard were, "This is justice ..."

"Jess?"

"Do you know what time... it's happened again, hasn't it Chris?"

"Yes, Jess. They told me the echoes should be fading by now, but I'm still getting them every night."

"It must have been bad for you to ring me."

"It was."

"How lucid was it this time?"

"It was as real as this conversation right now."
There was a silence on the other side of the phone.

"Jess?" asked Christain.

"Sorry... "

"Steve wants you to hang up, doesn't he?"
Silence.

Christain felt a wave of anger. "Jess, tell that bastard to —"

"Why don't you tell me yourself," came Steve's voice.

"Look, Steve, I just want to talk to my sister. That's not much to ask, is it?"

"How about taking into account the time difference here in Perth?"

"It's not exactly the cocktail hour here either."

"Just because you're not sleeping doesn't mean —"

"Yeah, okay, I know: why should the innocent suffer? It's just not that simple." Christain suddenly felt incredibly weary. "Sorry, Steve. Tell Jess I'm sorry for bothering her in the middle of the night. Both of you just go back to sleep."

He hung up.

*   *   *

Red shift

Where do you start? What would Columbus have said? Marco Polo? Cook? Armstrong? Of course, it's not the same, is it? This great journey. It's both infinitely more and infinitely less. And none of the great explorers would class themselves as writers. Yet I do.

What words are you expecting of me? My inclination is usually to do the reverse of what I think my readers expect. To surprise, to shock, to keep you guessing. Is that possible with a billion of you? Is it appropriate? This isn't fiction, after all, and I'm not a journalist.

I've actually given up trying to create something with these words. I'll tie myself up in knots if I think about it much longer. All I'm going to do is give you my thoughts and observations as this great journey unfolds. Simple for me. (Perhaps not so simple for you.) What can they do to me after all? Somehow pull me back to Earth from hyperspace? "Sorry, we wanted your reports to be more formal. This isn't what we had in mind when we appointed you scribe."

Not likely.

Who knows when, where or how you're reading this. Maybe it won't get through to Earth at all. Maybe I'm writing this purely for the aliens who built the *Web*. I guess I really don't know who my audience is, so all I can do is tell you what I would want to be told if I were reading these instalments as we approach hyperspace.

You are probably aware of what I'm doing here. The other nineteen here with me are sending off the scientific observations. No doubt you'll get their views filtered through the media analysts, but I'm not a scientist. I'm a writer. A writer with some understanding of the science involved here, but a writer nonetheless — and I'm going to speak to you directly.

All twenty of us are floating in the *Web*. Not the World Wide Web — this has nothing to do with the internet ... well, perhaps it is connected in some way to a Universe Wide Web, but not in the way you may be thinking. The *Web* is this infinitely complex hyperspace vehicle we're now in. Earth Control gave it the name, not for any more profound reason than it looks like a giant spider's web. Of course we don't know the name given to it by its inventors. They still haven't chosen to show themselves. We're all hoping that they are waiting for us at the end of this pre-programmed journey.

What's it like here in the *Web*? Imagine you are so small that you are *inside* the thread of a spider's web. That's the best way to picture it. Gossamer-thin filaments interconnected in a fractal, a repeating pattern within a pattern within a pattern. I'm floating in one of the strands, and I can move at will through the thousands of filaments until they become too small. The width of the strands is the only restriction on our movement in here. Yes, my physical body is still intact. I'm not some incorporeal being, although it feels a little that way sometimes, the way we navigate effortlessly through the filaments, turning 360 degrees at will and pushing off the walls. I breathe, though none of us have any real understanding how that works. I eat. I sleep. I evacuate. When I pinch myself hard enough I feel pain. I could probably make myself bleed, but I can't see the point.

And yet a spider's web is such a poor analogy in a lot of ways. None of us feels trapped in any way. The strands are fifty metres wide in some places. I've been into the ones which barely take a human, and they continue to taper down to a microscopic level — sub-atomic, so they tell me. Even in the most narrow strands, I don't feel confined. The walls are transparent, like the purest of glass.

And outside, all around us, are the stars.

* * *

Blue shift

"Choices. It's all about the choices you make — and you are in control of those choices."

For some reason Christain found he could no longer look at the speaker on stage. It was too painful. Why had he come here? For inspiration? *Ha!* He had known for a long time that there was no such thing, that inspiration was self-delusion.

He studied the faces around him. No-one was like him. They were all focused on the diminutive figure at the front or the huge screen doppelgänger which loomed over him.

The voice registered but somehow didn't register. "Is the glass half full or half empty. What do you *want* to see?"

"I want to see Isobelle again," said Christain out loud.

The man next to him gave him a curious sideways glance and then returned his attention to the speaker.

"Half full or half empty? What do you want to see? What do you see?"

Christain nudged the stranger next to him. "I can't see any water at all from here." He got up. "This is my choice. I'm getting out of here."

He walked out of the hall and into the street outside. His eyes had the grainy sleep-deprived feel that he always lived with now. He knew he would be able to fight the weariness for a while, but what was the point? He had to go to sleep eventually, and then they would come to kill him again.

Later that night he looked at the photo of his wife next to the bed. He felt the tears well up and started shaking.

"Forgive me," he cried. "Please, somehow, forgive me."

* * *

Red shift

Isn't it funny how some misconceptions are hard to shake? Streamlining. All space ships should be streamlined with sleek ice-smooth surfaces. Like in the movies. I've had enough science explained to me to know it's ridiculous, that there's no wind-resistance in space — but still this web structure doesn't seem capable of travelling fast, let alone the FTL we are assuming it was designed to achieve.

Of course, we're all only guessing as to the purpose of the *Web*. It just simply appeared in our galaxy, presumably at the end of some hyper-space jump. Empty. With a series of mathematical instructions which we've interpreted as an invitation to take this journey. We assume this alien craft was designed to take representatives of humanity to some great meeting, but we really have no idea. Are we humanity's emissaries or simply thrill-seekers on an intergalactic carnival ride? Who knows?

Whatever the case, I'm determined to enjoy it.

What I've found really fascinating is the elasticity of the strand walls. The skein stretches out if you push against it, so it's almost as if there are no boundaries at all between me and the stars. All twenty of us are just floating in space like some celestial beings. I don't know how far this elasticity will go. The strand walls seem a little like a balloon, but no-one's been keen to put them to a real test. All I know is the resistance increases the further out you push. It seems like there's a limit but I'm not game to force it.

We've all discarded the clumsy suits that were given to us by Control. Great name, that! Earth Control. They have absolutely no *control* over the *Web*.

All they hope to do is monitor its movement along its preordained path and, hopefully, continue to receive these communications from the twenty of us on board.

Sometimes I get the feeling that this is just some giant remote control car or perhaps a hyperspace transit vehicle. Next stop ...

✳ ✳ ✳

Blue shift

The sky was bruised and swollen as Christain stood in an open field. Stretching out to the horizon was a brown nothingness. In the distance stood a small building. The clouds groaned and a shaft of ochre light flashed above his head. The sky convulsed as if overwhelmed by some monstrous fit, and the bright rain started to fall.

As the first drop hit Christain, he screamed in agony and started to run in the direction of the shelter. The rain drops pierced him, burning through layer after layer of skin.

The rain. This time it was the rain itself which was going to kill him.

He fell to the ground ...

✳ ✳ ✳

"You keep telling me these echoes I'm having are going to end. I'm dying every night. I'm too scared to fall asleep."

"We're dealing with psychology here, Chris. People react differently." Dr Karies clicked an entry into his palmtop.

Christain ran his fingers through his hair and closed his eyes momentarily, feeling the grit on the underside of his eyelids. "And you still call this *remorse* therapy? It's more like torture therapy. I can't keep going like this."

"Your reaction is an extreme case, Chris."

"God, I hate it when you keep calling me by my first name. It's like you think you're a friend of mine, when you're really my gaoler."

"Come on, Chris, that's not fair. You know that's a low blow."

"I wish we still had prisons. What would I have got in the old days? Four or five years? I could have been out in two. I may have even got off altogether."

"The law hasn't changed. You know that. We've been over this many times. It would have been manslaughter even fifty years ago. Intoxication hasn't been much of a defence for a long time. You were drunk, Chris. You killed your wife."

"And I'm being punished for it."

Dr Karies shook his head. "We don't punish any more. How often have we gone over this since the trial? A hundred times?"

"Yes," said Christain, "it's all so humane now, isn't it? A little laser stimulation on just the right part of the hippocampus, and I suffer the most agonising remorse forever."

"Not quite forever, Chris. The intensity fades in time as the synapses in the lateral ventricle of your brain reform."

"Yes, I know, I learn to live with it." Christain started shaking. "But how can I live with these nightmare echoes every night?"

"They *will* end."

"Before or after I die?" Christain buried his face in his hands.

*** * *

Red shift

We're speeding up now — that's what they tell me, anyway. Of course, there's no rushing of wind around our ears, no whistling noise in the vacuum. It's all in the starlight. We're over 35 percent the speed of light now, and the best I can describe it is that the stars in front of us seem to be huddling whereas when I look back behind us they seem to be spreading out. It's like we're flying into a star cluster and we're leaving behind something that's atrophying.

Star maps are useless now. It's something to do with aberration, the way our speed is causing the starlight to slant in on us. I don't really understand it, but the others are calling it a Doppler shift — the same distortion which occurs in the sound of a car as it approaches and then races past you. I'll take their word for it. There's a dark cone ahead and an even larger one behind us. It's like we're in the middle in a giant barrel of stars between the two cones.

*** * *

Blue shift

"Jess?"

"Yes, Chris, is that you?"

"Did you get the reports I emailed you?"

"Yes."

"Have you read them?"

"I scanned them. Are they real? I'm really worrying about you now, Chris."

"Jess, they're real."

"How come you got a pre-publication copy? Did they give it to all the short-listed writers?"

"No. Jess, just to me. No-one outside Control has read them."

"Should you have sent them to me?"

"No... but, look, didn't you notice anything?"

"Well —"

"Do the reports sound like me?"

"Well, yeah, maybe a bit, but, —"

"Read them again, Jess."

"Okay."

There was a few minutes silence on the other end.

"Well, Jess?"

"All right, if it's not you writing them, it's someone who's pretty similar. Or someone copying your style."

"Jess, there's more. The electronic signature that came through with the transmission — it was mine."

"What?"

"It's been verified by Control. And I've run my own checks on the version they sent me."

"This is insane. There must be a mistake."

"You know how foolproof these electronic signatures are. The world economy depends on them."

"But someone somewhere could have developed technology to copy e-signatures... the *Web*, whoever built it, they must be unbelievably advanced. They could have ..."

"Why? And why *my* signature? What purpose would it serve? To torture me? To say, hey, you were nearly out here in the *Web*, but you blew it. You stuffed up. Instead of being the first writer in hyperspace you killed your wife and cracked up."

"No-one would be so cruel, Chris. They would know how you suffered. You've gone through remorse therapy. You're still echoing in the worst possible way. What else would anyone want from you?"

"Well, Jess, if you're right, then the only other conclusion is that the author of these reports from the *Web* is me."

The phone fell silent.

* * *

Red shift

Constellations are disfiguring in front of us, metamorphosing in a grotesque horror show. Stellar insects crowding, ever crowding before us. And shifting red. Always redder, as behind they continue to die into blueness.

We are now within one percent of the speed of light. The barrel of stars around us has thinned to something like a ring. Each star is now sharply etched in its arc of colour. It's like we're inside a rainbow. Not the thin, intangible ones on Earth, but something vast and real. A stellar rainbow. Red. Orange. Yellow. Green. Blue. Violet. And we're here in these transparent strand walls, surrounded by this spectacle.

I can see it now. The Geodesics. The curvature of space. It's there for all of us now. That explains the mystery. I can see it in the arcs of light. We're like a stream running down a mountain, seeking the inevitable path. How could I have not seen it before? It's like one of those trick pictures — we just haven't been looking at it the right way. But it was here. It was always here.

* * *

Blue-red shift

"Are you sure you're right to drive, Chris?"

I twirled the umbrella above her head and the rain drops spun off. "Of course, I am darling."

"You've got that funny look in your eye."

"Wait till I get you home." I winked. "You'll find out what that funny look is all about."

We both laughed.

"Come on, Chris, let's take a taxi."

"I'm fine, Isobelle. Fine."

"Come on, give me the keys."

I skipped out of her reach, pulling the umbrella away from her. "You're going to get wet now. See what you've done."

Isobelle shook her head. "You're infuriating sometimes, Chris."

"But you love it, right?"

"Yes, but —"

"Isobelle, don't spoil the night. We're celebrating. I feel great. We're both shortlisted to go on the greatest journey anyone's ever gone on. We're a certainty."

"I'm a bit more pessimistic."

We both got in the car and I put the key in the ignition. "I keep telling you, Isobelle, I reckon we're as good as on board. A husband and wife team. A writer and an astrophysicist, both with a public profile. Think of the unbelievable marketing potential for all those sponsors. Each one of us on our own would have had no hope, but this way, we're in, Isobelle, we're in."

Isobelle smiled and I leant over and kissed her.

"I wish I could be so sure about things as you, Chris."

"Stick with me, kid, you'll go far."

Isobelle laughed and shook her head softly. "Let's not worry about hyperspace for the moment. Just get me home."

I winked. "Faster than light. Here we come."

I switched on the windscreen wipers, turned the key in the ignition and the car started.

✷   ✷   ✷

Red-blue shift

I made love to Isobelle last night. I don't know why I just wrote "night". Of course, "night" is the most meaningless word in the universe at the moment. I'm confused. I don't even know why I'm writing this. I know billions of people will probably pore over every word back on Earth, but somehow this all seems like a very private act.

Try to picture what it's like to make love, weightless and surrounded by stars. It was like we were part of the cosmic dance. Twirling. Crowding. Looping. And at the height of it all, it was like a new star had been born, and we were emanating light.

I woke of course, because I'm still human, and we can only glimpse the cosmic dance, but it didn't matter because I was holding Isobelle and could hear her breathing.

Then I remembered the strangest dream. The strangest, strangest dream. It had been the night after we both found out we were on the shortlist to go on the *Web*. We'd been celebrating, and she didn't want me to drive because she thought I'd had too much to drink.

It was so real. It was like I was re-living a scene of my life. But then the strangest thing of all occurred.

From the time I started the engine, the dream split in two, and from then on it was as if I was simultaneously experiencing two versions of what happened. One of them is what I remember. I decided I wasn't up to driving, and we got out and called a taxi. The other was that I drove off. The two reels ran simultaneously in my head for a while. I felt a sickening panic for a brief second through the second reel, and then it went black.

I feel something profound has happened, but I don't know exactly what it is.

✳   ✳   ✳

Blue-red shift

Chris gently stroked Isobelle's photo as he sat on his bed. He had a piece of paper containing a printout in his hand and he read the last line out loud once more to his wife:

"*I feel something profound has happened, but I don't know exactly what it is.*"

He took a deep breath. "I'm going to give it a name, Isobelle, and it will be ours forever."

A calmness washed through him.

"I'm going to call it the Doppelgänger effect."

He got up and carried the photo to the window and looked out at the cosmic dance of the night sky.

✳   ✳   ✳

Red-blue shift

Stranger and stranger still. I am conscious of myself as two. So many questions. Can a car be both approaching and driving away at the same time? What quantum phenomenon has happened here at the speed of light? How does the observer affect the observed? Particle or wave? Finite or infinite? I held Isobelle while she slept. Of that I'm certain. Is this the *Web's* destination? Are we here?

* * *

Blue-red shift

Chris stepped out into the cool night air, took a deep breath and began to walk. The tram tracks stretched out in front of him and appeared to merge at the silent horizon. He looked up at the sky and cocked his head as if he could hear something in the distance.

And for the first time in a long time, he smiled.

AFTERWORD

The Doppelgänger has been haunting stories forever, and it seems that the title for this particular story has been haunting me for a long time. It's almost been a case of a title in search of a story. There's been a story file headed "The Doppelgänger Effect" in my filing cabinet for at least four years. I knew I wanted it to be hard(ish) SF, I knew I wanted space travel of an unusual kind in it, I knew it had to be about the Doppler effect as much as it is about the Doppelgänger effect, and I knew I wanted it to be very, very human.

— *Dirk Strasser*

PAUL BRANDON

Paul Brandon was born in Kent, England, but moved to Australia in 1994. He has been writing full-time for about three years, and has dabbled in most fields including commercial copywriting and television. Before that, he worked in the British film industry as an assistant director, and is very willing to exchange anecdotes for a nice pint of "proper" beer. In addition to writing, he also plays Celtic music.

He currently lives in Brisbane with his wife, Julie.

In the disturbing story that follows, Brandon delves into the darkest regions of the human heart where the hot, snapping monsters of retribution, fear, and sin can blind us to the truth.

THE MARSH RUNNERS

PAUL BRANDON

I hate stories.

I fucking *hate* them. Why is it that people, 'specially the doctors, always smile like arseholes then tell me that I can't hate them all?

I do, no shit.

Every last damn one I've ever been told anyway.

For me, stories only loosely caged the monsters; they were told purely to frighten, to terrify, to mentally beat me into submission so that I would obey. Of course, the punching helped too, but the stories were far worse.

You guys, you just have to categorise things, don't you? Stuff them into neat little pigeons' holes or whatever the hell you call them, just so that it all fits in your world.

Well it don't, you know.

I was eighteen when they locked me away in this hospital, barely more than a girl. Seems a long way off now. 1961. I had my twenty-ninth birthday just last week. No-one said nothing, but I remembered it all the same.

I always have been good at counting.

They call it a hospital, but there's bars on all the windows and most of the so-called doctors look more like prison guards. You might've seen them; they carry needles instead of guns.

I suppose they think I'm safer here, protected from myself. There's always an assumption that those that so readily take life will want to finish their own. I don't believe that. For me, life has become so dreadfully sacred.

My lawyer told me I was a hair's-breadth away from real jail. He told them I was insane, claimed it would be better for me if I was institutionalised. I think it was just easier for him. As if I cared. It's all the same anyway. It don't matter where I am.

If I tell *you* the story, do you promise not to interrupt? I don't want no pointless questions, no disbelieving looks. And once I start, you've gotta let me finish, regardless of what you might think.

Deal?

Do you have a cigarette?

Thanks.

That smell, it draws the splinters of memory out so easily. I like the way the blue-grey smoke hangs in the air, as if it's somehow waiting for the breeze to come and pull it apart. There's something very comforting about smoke.

If you're anything like the others, then you'd already know all about the trial, about me and my father, about the farm, the murder.

Like I said before, you don't know shit.

I figure it don't matter if I tell this now. I'm stuck here for at least another couple'a years 'til my next review, and like last time, there ain't no chance of me cutting free. Judge reckons I'll be fifty before I get out. I don't care. It's not like they can lock me away some more for what I say now.

Close your eyes. I don't want you looking at me.

"They hide between the trees, under the black, twisted roots where the green-skinned water is still and stinks like a fresh-turned grave. They're always watching, waiting ... *Waiting*. You know what for, don't you, my dear Hope."

I hesitated, not knowing whether I should reply or not. His flushed, beet-red face was inches from my own. I could see the thin spiderweb of veins across his nose, his dark, dark eyes, and the chapped, sun-sucked lips that parted as the breath hissed in and out of his heavy body. Every detail. A bead of greasy sweat tracked slowly down his cheek before dripping into my eye. I blinked and turned my head sharply, trying to rid myself of the sudden stinging.

A huge, callused hand gripped my chin, turning my head roughly so that I once more looked into his eyes.

"I asked you ... if you knew ... what they waited ... for." His voice was low, calm. Measured by the steady rhythm.

I nodded as best I could in his grip. The hand left my chin and flashed up to slap me across the face. The noise of it hurt more than the pain, though my cheek felt as if a thousand shards of glass were embedded in there.

I began to cry. He didn't like it when I cried unbidden, but I couldn't help it. He'd not hit me like that before.

Between the suppressed sobs, I shuddered, "They're waiting for me".

"Good girl. And you know what they'll do to you if you're not good, don't you."

This time I replied straightaway, fearful, my whole body trembling. "They'll kill me."

"No, Hope," he said quietly, his lips close to my ear now. "First they hang you up from an old tree branch, your arms up over your head so that you're all stretched out, then, ever so slowly, they skin you, slice by slice, sliver by sliver ..."

I began counting again, trying to shut my mind away from the images he was forcing in there. *Two thousand two hundred ... two thousand one hundred and ninety-nine ... two thousand ...*

I always counted backwards from five thousand. It was harder that way, it needed more thought.

"...you feel it all, every cut of their tiny blades, every tug on your delicious flesh. You want to scream but you can't. They don't kill you, not 'til the end, when there's nothing left anyway but muscle and bone ..."

He stopped. I felt him shuddering, climaxing. His eyes were closed, his lips apart. Silence enveloped us both, except for the distant laugh of a kookaburra somewhere off in the trees. His raspy breathing stopped and he fell atop of me, a dead weight, stifling, crushing.

Two thousand one hundred and ninety.

The longest yet. It was getting worse.

I was holding my breath, as always hoping, praying beyond reason that he was dead, offering my own soul to the devil in exchange for his life.

But he'd always start breathing again.

The hand that had so brutally slapped me now caressed my cheek and face as softly as if I had been a baby. He traced the line of my jaw with a single rough finger, pushing back a strand of damp brown hair before brushing my lips. There was moment, a look in his eyes that I thought perhaps was love — but bought at what cost?

He heaved himself off me, standing tall over the bed while he buttoned up his dusty black pants. The room was so hot the still air scorched my lungs. I looked up at the bare ceiling, at the old boards, the cobwebs, the peeling paint. I could still feel him on top of me, inside my body, inside my mind. His stink filled my nose; old tobacco, sweat and the marsh, and the sour, spicy smell that he'd left me with.

He looked down at me for a long time, standing still. For a moment, I thought he meant to say more, but he just smiled that self-satisfied, knowing smile and left my room.

I couldn't stay there. I slowly got off the bed and tugged my skirt back down. Hesitantly, I crossed to the open bay windows and stepped out onto the verandah.

I could see him, striding across to the tiny wooden church, his hands in his pockets. Behind the fragile-looking building, the sun was just beginning to drop below the tangled tree line of the swamp. The early evening shade brought no respite from the humidity, and I could see the waves of watery heat rising from the small road that connected our dry island to the rest of the village.

My feet sounded hollow on the old boards as I walked around the house then off onto the hard-packed dirt of the yard. I moved woodenly, like one of those string-bound puppets. My shadow stretched ahead of me, as if it too sought to leave the wreck my body had become. I lifted my eyes from the dirt. All around me the air was alive with the noise of animals and birds. Only inside the house, or my mind, was it truly quiet.

The red dust was dotted with tufts of scrubby, sickly-brown grass — our garden. I reached the huge, red-sprayed bougainvillea and stopped, one hand smudging my tears away from my eyes. Beyond it, the turned earth of the field reached away, before the trees closed in once again. The bougainvillea was vast, decades, centuries old, perhaps even as ancient and wise as the swamp. Under the green and crimson flesh of the leaves and branches, its skeleton was an old framework of a small building, some long forgotten outhouse that was probably put up by the first settlers here. Nothing remained of it now other than a few rib-like spars and some rust-eaten corrugated sheeting that was gradually being digested by the ground.

This was *my* place, my *secret* place. I walked around until I could no longer see the church, or the house. Without a care for the thorns, I parted the draping, leaf-clad runners and crawled within.

Inside it was dark; safe. A sacred cathedral, a chamber of solace. Nothing but the damp smell of the earth, the swamp song, and me.

Stillness.

I slowly pulled my legs up until my chin rested on my knees. The soil felt cool beneath me, soft with the mulch of the shed leaves and dead flowers. Insects buzzed warmly in my ears, and I wasn't troubled by the mosquitoes.

The terrible images ran rampant through my mind. The hate was so strong. It was a real thing, living, breathing, dancing through the tangled mass of plant like the ghosts he'd put into me.

They were hideous little things, the ghosts; fat, bloated bodies atop stick-thin birds' legs. Their skin was like tree bark, all split and peeling, but grey and glistening, like a corpse spat up from the river, and their eyes were flat and dead. Fish's eyes. What scared me the most about them though was their dry, chuckling laughter, like the juiceless scraping of a dead branch over a rock, or the sorrowful whisper of autumn's leaves.

I called them the Marsh Runners.

I pictured them skinning *him*, willing it, wishing it with all of my heart until I felt wrung dry, empty.

Only then did I cry.

* * *

The cigarette ash falls from the curl of my fingers, silently shattering as it hits the sterile white tiles of the floor. I don't need to look up to feel the waves of disgust emanating from him. The pen has stopped its incessant scratching as he waits for me to continue. I drop the dead butt and rub at the side of my nose, gathering my thoughts before continuing.

I think I was about ten years old when my father started fucking me.

Oh, things started long before that, but they've hazed away into red images that might or might not've been me.

I started the story there 'cause that's when things became worse, and it was also the first time I saw them.

I guess I was about sixteen.

Usually, I was able to shut myself away, to stuff my feelings deep down, then it just became something unpleasant I had to endure. I could live with that. As

I grew, I suppose you could say I became more accustomed to it, but I reckon he began to feel the whole thing was becoming a little one-sided.

So he started hitting me. Before, during, and increasingly, after.

He was always careful never to leave marks. Do you know how much pain you can inflict on a person without actually doing any damage? Any *visible* damage?

There's one thing I need to make clear. I instinctively knew that the sex was wrong, but I didn't understand why. I also knew that sometimes it hurt, and if I didn't do it, he'd hurt me more. How *was* I to know? We lived in a tiny settlement, nothing more than a few run-down houses and a church that sat on the edge of the wetlands. Nearly everyone who lived there was family of some sort. It was named Murray; locals called it Little Louisiana. But despite the similarities, it was just rural Northern Territory, not Southern America. Mostly folks just sat around drinking, talking about the war and farming the little scraps of land the swamp let them have. Everyone watched out for everyone else. He was the minister, he watched out for all.

Preacher, teacher, child molester.

So you see there was no-one I could talk to, no-one at all. He was the most respected of all the men. What was I supposed to do, walk into town, knock on our neighbour's door, who also happened to be his brother, and say, "Excuse me, but is it wrong for him to do this?"

Wha'd'ya suppose would have happened? Who would they have believed?

Exactly.

Mother died having me, so I never knew her. Father did nothing but curse her soul. There were no photographs, no clothes, nothing. He burned it all. He took it hard, as a personal affront — even more so that she'd died bearing a pathetic, weakling daughter and not a strong, workable son.

Sounds predictable, doesn't it?

I don't know why he told me the stories. Perhaps he felt like he needed complete possession of my mind as well as my body. I know they were always an important part for him. I lived in a constant fear that one day he'd take the knife to me himself. Oddly enough, he was a peculiarly gentle man most of the time. I have no hate for him now. I burned it all out of my soul that night eleven years ago. I'm spent. I'm just living my time.

No, don't look at me like that. I don't want your pity, and I'm damn sure he doesn't deserve it. Don't you think I've spent enough time thinking about him, about what happened? I finally sleep at night now, eleven years of peace after eighteen of torment.

Sometimes I wonder if it really *was* me that did it, like the man in the courtroom said. I don't remember.

Someone once told me that everything has a cost. I know what mine is.

*   *   *

It was fully dark by the time I emerged. I had no idea what time it was, it could have been midnight. I didn't really care.

I was nothing more than a husk, bled dry of tears and emotions, an empty shell that would gradually refill, only to be drained once more.

A heavy half-moon hung in the sky, and pin-pricks of light, a billion lost souls, were scattered across the blackness. The bougainvillea was painted a silver-grey in the moonlight, with the once bright flowers now looking bleached, lifeless. My skin looked the same. Perhaps I had died and was nothing more than a spirit.

I rounded the bush, letting out my breath in a relieved rush as I saw there were no lamps lit in the house. Then I remembered it was a Sunday — father would still be up at Uncle Jack's.

I padded slowly across the garden, my bare feet leaving scant impression on the ground. The night was filled with the noises of the land; the gentle sighing of the wind as it sifted through the close-knit trees, the constant chatter of the nightbirds, frogs and crickets, and the

desiccated, reed-thin laughter of the Marsh Runners, seeping out from the darkest of the deep, water-filled hollows.

I stopped stock-still, every nerve-ending in my body alight. My eyes were wide, my hand pressed to my mouth as I searched the darkness.

Could I see eyes, dead fish eyes, glittering back at me from between the mangroves? Was that the scratching of a needle point knife against wood, or just the fragile breath of the night breeze? That dull splashing — the certain tread of stripped, skeletal feet?

The terror I felt was a stunning fist slamming into my insides, then gripping hold and pulling. My throat closed up, and I could feel the hot flush of both pain and embarrassment as my bladder loosened, then drained down my legs. I couldn't move, I couldn't breathe. My sight was fixed somewhere within the impenetrable nothing between the towering, ghost-lit trunks while my mind screeched away with a thousand unseen horrors.

An owl hooted, startling me so much I nearly bolted for the house. My heart pounded in my ears like a drum, rapid, irregular, and I could feel the veins in my temple throbbing in time. My breathing was ragged as I leeched in air.

Despite the sultry heat of the night, I was chilled to my marrow. How long I stood there, staring into the dark, I could not tell you. Eventually though, free from the paralysis, I hurried my way back home, my eyes never leaving the swamp. I was still frightened, so much so that I forewent a bath, and instead just went to bed fully clothed, unmindful of the smell and the wetness.

I curled up into a foetal ball, the rough blanket pulled tight up under my chin. I lay there motionless, staring out through the low window until the arrival of the dawn. Tendrils of mist drifted out from between the trees like the feelers of some vast monster searching for prey, and even the usually bright birdsong sounded muted and forlorn.

The feeling lodged in my heart then, that things would never quite be the same again.

* * *

It must be about six o'clock. Through the glass and the mesh of the windows I can see the dusk settling down over the gardens. My ears don't hear any birdsong, nor the chirp of the crickets, but my mind does. My mind hears everything.

It's always at this time of the day when I start to miss the swamp. Not my father or the village, fuck no, but the land itself. The wetlands were my balm, the soothing lotion that I desperately tried to spread over myself each evening. It was as the sun went down that he would leave the house and walk up the track to the village for several hours — sometimes the whole night. I'd be left on my own, often without light — we had only the one working lamp, and he took that with him. I remember sitting on the verandah, looking up at the stars, the calming voice of the marshes muttering in my ears.

I remember reading, dreaming.

Reading was my one other solace. Not fairy tales or adventure stories like other children, no. My reading was solely factual. I read voraciously, I didn't care what it was about, as long as it took my mind away for a short time. Along with the heavy old religious volumes, father had a small collection of history books, journals and of course all the text and reference books for the school. I read them all, many, many times.

I often wondered about the world. We had a pile of worn, old *National Geographics*, and when I'd grown bored of the book, and there was enough moonlight, I'd sit there, just letting my fingers trail over the faded pictures.

Wondering.

Christ, what am I telling you this for? All you want to hear about is the murder, right? You're looking for some new angle, something that's going to make your fortune in the literary world.

Shit yeah, why not.

*   *   *

Two years passed. People moved into Murray, people moved out. Nothing much changed.

But the abuse became worse.

The beatings increased. He took to hitting me most of the time now. I don't know why. He wasn't drinking any more than most folks did round here, but there was something new in his eyes, something that had not been there before.

Hatred.

Perhaps he could finally see how much I despised him, and was concerned that I might finally leave. He needn't have worried; where was I to go, *how* was I to go? I had nothing other than what I awoke to in the morning.

I sat on the steps, looking out into the night. The moon was swollen, replete as it inextricably made its way across the sky. The garden around the house teemed with dancing shadows, and here and there, I would often see a sudden blink of grey as a bat skipped over the trees. The rain storm that had beaten down on the roof this afternoon had finally passed, and only a few fractured forks of lightning still stabbed down far away to the north.

I dipped the cloth back into the cold water and carried on washing myself.

He'd liked the storm. The fury of the thunder and the pounding of the rain had only served to excite him all the more.

I touched the cloth to my swollen cheek and cried out slightly as the pain bit in. As gently as I could manage, I dabbed at the bruises, then, when the throbbing had dulled, I just sat there with it cool against my face, my eyes closed against the tears that wanted to fall again. I'd learned a long time ago that tears really did little good. But at least they were *something*. The day I stopped feeling the emotion would be the day I died. But now, my anger was tired, temporarily washed away by the continual smarting.

Rinsing the cloth again, I gingerly dabbed it up between my legs, and although there was next to no light, I could see the dark stains of colour that appeared when I removed it.

I cleaned myself as best I could, but still I felt filthy. I don't think I've ever really been clean my whole life. Don't suppose I ever will be.

Perhaps it *was* my fault he was so rough. He always told me if I didn't look the way I did that ...

I threw the rag back into the pail then raked my damp fingers through my lank hair. The humidity was high, and there was scant breeze blowing. The murmurings from the swamp seemed subdued somehow; usually after a rainstorm the night is alive with a thousand calls and cries. But tonight there was just the usual chatter of the crickets and the occasional distant bark of a dog.

Everything seemed normal though.

I searched the darkness, but could see nothing of them. I relaxed slightly, but could not shift the uneasy feeling that I was being watched. It was like seeing something out of the corner of my eye, but when I turned, it was gone. The unease began to settle in my stomach.

In the two years since I had first heard them, I had come to fear the Marsh Runners far more than I ever did my father. They were always there, just verging on the edges of my perceptions, usually just after he'd finished with me. I often awoke at night, the sweat streaming off my body, my ears straining to hear the lifeless scraping sound that had so terribly dragged me from my sleep.

I remember once feeling a sudden compulsion to enter the swamp. It had been around noon, and I was returning to the house after running an errand when the suggestion suddenly occurred to me. I put the book I was carrying down at my feet and began slowly walking toward the tree line where the soft shadows gathered. I was about halfway across the yard, when my father called to me, breaking the spell. For a long moment, I just stood there, my mind away, then, as suddenly as it arose, the feeling left me. I turned around returned to where the book lay in the dust. I had just bent down when a sudden flight of birds erupted from the branches of the mangroves behind me, their wings clapping together loudly as if applauding my courage. I spun, startled, and for the briefest of moments, I thought I could see the wet glimmer of the sunlight on pale flesh, but then father was calling me again and I was running to the house.

From the greater fear to the lesser.

My thoughts returned suddenly to the present: from somewhere in the darkness to my left came the loud clattering of a kicked can, the sound of someone stumbling, then sharp utterance of an oath. I stood up quickly, recognising father's voice. Despite the full moon, all I could see of him was the weak wandering light from the oil lamp as it swayed along the path that ran under the canopy of trees. But I could hear him talking to himself; and his voice sounded slurred and confused. I knew straight away he'd been sharing the still whisky that Uncle Joss makes in his shed. A cold ripple of dread detached itself from my mind, travelling slowly down my back before settling in my gut. It wasn't often that he returned drunk — he *did* have a certain responsibility as minister, after all, but usually, when he did, the night ended in violence.

He was still a little way off, and as quietly as I could, I hurried into the house, into my room and closed the door. Occasionally, if he thought me asleep, he would leave me alone. Not very often mind, but still ...

I quickly shrugged off my clothes and pulled on my night-shirt. I climbed under the old mosquito net and huddled beneath the single sheet, my head facing the moon-washed wall as I waited for the sound of his boots on the steps.

The house trembled as he staggered across the verandah, and I flinched as a door slammed. I mentally followed his footsteps down the hall and into the kitchen. He was still muttering to himself, and my knot of terror was pulled tighter as I heard my name.

There was a metallic clatter, the sound of cutlery being moved, then laughter.

The methodical clump of his heavy boots coming down towards me.

I was holding my breath, my eyes wide in the darkness. I could hear my heart thumping in my ears — surely he would hear it too and know I wasn't asleep.

The handle turned, and the door eased open, the amber light of the lantern leaking across the floor. His breathing was heavy, laboured, as if he had been running, and as he stepped into the room, I screwed my eyes closed, my fists bunching painfully around the thin cotton sheet.

He spoke my name in that dreadfully soft, sing-song voice that belied his intentions, "*Ho-ope . . .?*"

I didn't answer, couldn't. Even across the room, I could smell the bitter, nauseating reek of the spirits, entwined with the tobacco and his own distinctive smell.

"Hope . . . I *know* you're awake. I've got something for you . . ."

I still didn't turn.

Please God, make him leave, make him die, anything.

Stern, commanding: "Turn around. Now!"

I rolled over slow, my whole body trembling. What I saw I knew would remain forever burned within my mind.

He was standing over the foot of the bed, tall, imposing. The lamp was raised, holding back the thin gauze of the netting, and the wan light licked over him, turning his eyes into hidden pools of darkness. I could see every pore in his face, every bristle of grey stubble in such exquisite detail that I thought perhaps none of this was real and that I was just having a nightmare. His grin was wide, lecherous, and expectant. The stuttering light flicked over his body, and I could see that his pants were undone, and that he was already aroused.

It was then that I saw the knife in his other hand.

I recognised it immediately, and as the sheer terror flushed through me, I had a peculiar moment of clarity as I remembered slicing an orange with it only hours ago. The thought fled as quickly as it had come, replaced immediately by the numbing horror as he knelt down on the bed.

"Look what I found," he whispered, raising the knife up between us so that the blade shimmered in the lamplight. I could see its edge, keen, hungry.

The next few moments I remember only as a scattered collage of images. The panic took control completely. I screamed, my voice shattering the silence of the night, and exploded from the bed with a ferocity of movement that tore the mosquito net from the ceiling. I barely managed to put out my arms before I hit the bay windows. Both doors flew back against their hinges, and I heard the shatter of breaking glass.

I remember fleeing across the garden, the white gauze trailing behind me as if I were a ghost. I was still screaming, and my throat was raw from the sheer power of the elemental sound. I heard him calling my name, but I carried on running, my feet slapping on the hard dirt, my eyes blind with tears.

I ran to the only place I knew was safe.

The bougainvillea reared before me, an indistinct dome of light-flecked leaf and shadow. I plunged inside. The thorns bit into my skin, raked through my hair with a hundred needle-points of pain. The net was torn from me, left to hang on the branches like a discarded shroud. I fell to the ground, the dry earth blooming up into my nose and mouth. I dropped my head down, sobbing, my breath puffing in the dust. I could feel the wetness running down my cheek, but whether it was blood or tears, I did not know.

The silence was overwhelming.

My mind swam, saturated with cascading images of the knife, his grinning face, the play of the lamp on the blade ...

I only had a few moments' reprieve.

I could hear his breathing; rapid, harsh. His footfalls were uneven, unhurried as he circled the bush. The lamp moved steadily around me, its frail light failing to penetrate the gloom in which I cowered.

"What? Do you think you can hide from me? Come out now, Hope. I *promise* I won't hurt you ..."

He chuckled, a soft, infinitely menacing sound. I lay there, as still as a corpse, holding my breath, desperately trying to control the spasms of fear that were wracking my body.

Hatred. Pain. Terror.

The leaves rustled. He was looking for a way in.

I prayed with all that I was for this to stop, for an end to the torment.

The lantern light washed over me, and I raised my head to see my father's grinning face.

"Found you ..."

I edged back, deeper into the bush, my hands and feet scraping against the loose soil, but there was nowhere left for me to go. My back was pressed up against the coarse trunk, and I could feel the rough skin of the bark catching my night-shirt.

He was crouched at the entrance of my church, the colour-bled leaves surrounding him like a swart nimbus. He still held the knife.

"So this is where you hide," he muttered, looking around me briefly. "Still, one place is as good as another." And with that, he put down the lantern and began crawling towards me.

I wrapped my arms about my knees, pulling my legs in so tight I could barely breathe. I closed my eyes.

My mind turned in on itself; a wild animal seeking shelter where there's none to be found. I ran down dark corridors, flung open doors to bare rooms, but still he pursued me, relentless, laughing. I ran on until I came to the end, to the final door.

I knew what lay beyond: my deepest fears, my most secret desires, all one and the same. Without pause, I went there, tumbling through and sprawling on the floor.

Silence.

Nothing.

Back in my other world, I felt his hot breath against my neck.

"Open your eyes."

I couldn't move. Something cold, bitter, touched my cheek. There was a sharp nip of pain, and my eyes snapped open. His face was before me, his own eyes wide, mocking. I didn't recognise him any more. I saw the flash of the blade as he removed it, then pressed its edge deliberately against my bare throat.

I could hear them.

Crawling out of the most hidden places, wet crows' feet scratching as they came across the dirt. Laughter echoed, wind-borne, fear fed. The leaves rustled, and I knew they were around us.

I looked at my father, or rather, at what might have once been my father, and I smiled as I saw the twig-thin hand reach up over his head. He saw my expression and frowned, uncomprehending. For a long moment, the hand hovered there, scant inches above his wiry hair, then it descended with suddenly ferocity and he was pulled backwards. The knife blade was snatched away from my throat, leaving only a thin red line of coldness.

His body bucked as he was dragged by the hair through the blanket of thorns, and his cries were a delightful mix of surprise, pain and fright. One flailing arm knocked over the lantern, snuffing out the flame. I jumped to my feet, following as best I could in the sudden darkness.

By the time I had cleared the bush, the Marsh Runners were almost across the garden. In the light of the moon, I could see their stout, pasty bodies, bathed in the sickly moonlight as they ran. There were two of them, each with spindly arms ending in hands that were tangled in my father's hair. They hooted as they ran, monkey sounds, chilling, primal noises that no longer held any fear for me. Without stopping, they plunged into the blackness of the swamp.

I could hear the noise of the water as my father thrashed in their grip, and his shouts of anger and surprise that suddenly turned into shrieks of pain.

I didn't stop when I came to the fringe of the wetland. I was deliriously happy, and wept laughter as I realised two terrors were suddenly no more.

By the time I reached the clearing, I was soaked through with stagnant water. I had followed the screams and demented giggling like a beacon. I needed no light.

I slowed as the trees thinned around me, dropping into a slow walk. An ancient, lightning-blasted trunk rose up in the centre, a king surrounded by its subjects. The marsh grass that grew around it was spread over with the thin silver light. It was like a small island of brightness surrounded by a sea of dim ebon suggestion.

I crossed slowly to the dead tree, to where my father hung suspended by his arms. Of the Marsh

Runners there was no sign, but I no longer feared them.

I stood under him, looking up, a wide, terrible smile on my face.

"Get me down, Hope, get me down! I'm sorry, I ..."

I could smell his fear, feel it, and for a long time, I just stood there while he pleaded with me.

Softly, I said, "They won't kill you, not 'til the very end, when you're nothing more than muscle and bone," my voice was measured, sure, like his had always been. I knew what to tell him, knew it better than my own name. "First they skin you, piece by piece. You'll feel every cut of their little knives as they pare away your life ..."

He heard it too, the rasping scratch of metal on wood. He saw me look beyond him, to where the Marsh Runners were hugging the tree, gently running their silver blades over the bleached wood.

"What? Oh, Lord Jesus ..."

They stepped over to me, gnarled legs sure and steady on the lumpy ground. They came to just below my waist, looking deep into my soul with those liquid, depthless eyes.

My eyes.

I smiled, feeling the pain, the fear of him, them, fade from me.

But not the hate.

Stepping back, I sat down on a damp tussock of grass, my hands on my knees.

Laughter and joy spilled as easily from me as the bright lifeblood did from him. The shrill, wet-sounding screams echoed around the swamp as the Marsh

Runners set to work, but only myself, and perhaps the moon, were listening.

I was still laughing when they found me two days later.

*   *   *

I can tell from your face that you don't believe me.

As I like to say: I don't really care. Maybe I did do it all myself. Whatever happened, the end result is the same.

They took two lives that night, and gave one back.

The reason I can sit here and be so calm about everything is that this existence is far, far better than the one I had. I've got all I could possibly want here — all the books, all the *National Geographic*s I could ever hope to read. Sure, I'm still being abused, but it's a different thing now. I can put up with the interviews, the drugs, the games. They're nothing. I have everything. Well, everything, except freedom, but that's the cost, isn't it?

Could I have one last cigarette?

He withdraws the flame and I pull the hot smoke deep into my lungs, closing my eyes. The images are still strong, even after all this time. It takes little effort to call them up. Nothing scares me any more, I understand that everything has its place. I look over at him, through the grey smoke that wreaths from my fingers, and smile. He is filled with fear, with apprehension. I can read it on his face. He's thinking of the stories they published about me during the trial, all the gruesome details. The image of my father, skinned and swinging slowly in the night will haunt him for some time.

It was my solicitor's idea to plead insanity. I think it was the only way he could deal with what had happened. There was no way in his mind a rational person could have done what I did. I went along with it, not caring two hoots either way. I didn't tell him about the Marsh Runners, though I suppose that would've only advanced my case all the more.

You see, it don't matter if *they* murdered him, or if I did it myself — the end result is the same, and I wished it with all my soul, so for all intents and purposes, it *was* me that held the knife.

He's shifting in his chair, uncomfortable. The spent butt joins the others on the floor. I hold the last of the smoke deep within me. The room is flooded with harsh, unnatural light. There are no shadows here, no solace. Absently, I wonder what I must look like, what he sees when he looks at me.

I release the smoke in a steady plume. It softens the light a little as it hangs in the still air. I'm tired, bone weary.

I think you should go now. Go off and tell your new story to any who'll listen. I hope you have more luck than I did — but then, you're probably a far better storyteller than me.

AFTERWORD

It's never easy to pin down one single source of inspiration for a story, but "The Marsh Runners" was a little different. To begin with, I just had a part of a location — the vast bougainvillia bush that is the central point of the story. It's actually a very real place — it's on my wife's parent's farm in fact — and for quite a time I'd been intrigued by its peculiar atmosphere, the sense of shelter. So in essence, I started with the image of this little girl hiding within from her fears. I also wanted to explore the idea of the power of the mind.

The story pretty much wrote itself around that. It's a dark territory that I'm really not yet comfortable delving into, and in a way, I'm not sure myself what to think of the outcome. Yet it's intriguing all the same. The best metaphor for it I can think of is that like most people, I generally frequent the airy attic room, complete with polished floors and wide bay windows, but once in a while, we *all* have to peek into the "cupboard under the stairs".

— *Paul Brandon*

ROSALEEN LOVE

Rosaleen Love is one of Australia's best short story writers, and her deliciously wry, funny, and ironic stories have recently gained her the international attention she deserves. She has worked as a university lecturer in both the history and philosophy of science and professional writing. Her writing career began in 1983 when she won the Fellowship of Australian Writers, State of Victoria Short Story Award with "The Laws of Life". She has published two brilliant short story collections: *The Total Devotion Machine and Other Stories* and *Evolution Annie*; and her stories are widely anthologised in Australia and overseas.

The late George Turner wrote: "Here is a writer who takes joy in absurdity, laughing not at life but with it. To Rosaleen Love the extraordinary is what we do all the time." Rosaleen says that she has "a deep and abiding interest in the history of wrong ideas".

Now one might say that Rosaleen's story is about real men ... and wrong ideas ... and virtual reality, which it is ... sort of.

REAL MEN

ROSALEEN LOVE

Who spread the diesel fuel on the Grand Prix track?

One side says it was the do-gooder, bleeding-hearted, soft-headed, gut-reacting, dipshit scumbag Greenies who think any swathe of tired dirt with tufts of green stuff sprouting from it is sacred parkland, and never under any circumstances to be appropriated to racing car ends.

The protesters in their turn protest it wasn't them. Their weapon of choice is the yellow ribbon, tied to the trees that must go to make way for the cars, or the fences that are erected to keep the protesters out. They come in soulful peace, bearing yellow-ribboned witness. Sabotage is not their style.

Who did it? The way it looked, someone had driven round the Grand Prix track in the dead of night, fuel tank open, pump and nozzle attached, and sprayed the track. Made a perfect circuit, the way the Formula One cars do. Then the diesel was shut off and the perpetrators departed. They weren't mugs enough to leave the stuff flowing out behind them all the way home.

The Grand Prix officials went into a spin. "It's not a fair go" they said, "Not the Australian way. It's positively un-Australian."

The un-Australians, they're responsible.

I know who spread the diesel on the Grand Prix track, and it's not the story they're telling. You have to look between the cracks in the grass, between the chinks in the trees, through the lines in the pavement in the park, the park they've turned into a Grand Prix race track, only for three days of the year, they say, only three days, then it can be a park again for the rest of the year, and they know it is perfectly reasonable, they say, what could be more reasonable than that? We have it three days, the ducks get it the rest of the time.

Try explaining that to a duck, especially when all the whhrrrmmrmring is on.

The way they see it, the officials, you have to look for where the real men are, and who are their opponents. A real man will squeeze himself into a cockpit and lie encased, bearing with true grit the ferocious itch of his flameproof underwear. When the gun goes bang, he'll whiz around in circles burning up fossil fuel at the rate of yowoweewwweyikes! There goes another ton of unrenewable energy vaporised to aerial pollution.

There was this one driver who said the Melbourne track was not all it was cracked up to be. What a fuss he caused! There had to be something wrong with him, they said. It must be because he's shit-scared. He's not a real man. Real men drive real cars. Deep down, they reckoned, he was a girl.

You're either a real man or you're a girl.

No, that's not the right distinction. That's not where the real difference lies. You have to learn to think of it this way.

If real men drive real cars, what do unreal men drive?

I want to find me a real unreal man. I'll know my unreal man when I find him. He'll hate life in the fast lane.

Sometimes, in the park, I think I can see some unreal men, lurking between the cracks in the trees. There's one guy I can't quite see. I think he's got an unreal duck on a string and it's flying up there in the sky. I think that must be a factor in the unreal man equation. Real men site chemical factories in the wetlands protected by international wading bird agreements. Real men shoot ducks. Unreal men let ducks fly like kites in the wind.

There's a further question. When is a park not a park?

Real men don't want piss-weak, tree-growing, grass-blowing, worms-churning, ducks grubbing out worms versions of parks, but a real park, economically sustainable, with pit stops, and fuel nozzles, and the men machines that change tyres in a flash and the wild dwrrrrhmmmm of the cars, which, when I hear it from miles off, I know it's a man's noise, this noise, it's a real man's noise.

The men in the pits, the crew that inject the fuel, whip off the tyres, they're like a well-oiled machine themselves, they're like robot clones. Imagine if the robots on car assembly lines were to turn towards higher things, and they're crafty, those robots. Welding car forms takes up only part of all their brain up-time. Secretly they've been taking the skin that flakes off the human workers, the specks that fly through the air like aerial human plankton. They've been taking these flakes of skin, and deep under the car factory, late at night, for they know their robot days are numbered, that car manufacture will go off-shore, to the countries where they do it cheaper and dirtier, so late at night when the machinery whirrs more softly, and just one night watchman patrols the shop floor, the car robots manufacture androids, which they send out into the world to man the pits at Grand Prix time.

That's why they wear all that protective gear, the androids in the pits, so we can't see the spot-welded seams down their android backs. They're unreal men, but not the way I want. They're unreal real men. I want something more.

I want a real woman's unreal man.

"To be a leader", says the leader of our country, "You've got to be a man's man." This guy counts himself a member of that mob.

But that's not the way the song goes. "He will be a fisher of men." When you think of it, a fisher of men is some kind of unreal real man, someone casting out a net into the world, and to this net cling all those who are weary and heavy laden, but not the men's men, who are off standing independently, leading the world's financial markets, oiling the world's war machines, sliding deep down into Formula One racing cars. It was one really totally unreal, real man who was this fisher of men. But that was another time and place, and there was Golgotha and all.

They didn't have a Grand Prix in Bethlehem, but I bet they've got one now. They've got a Grand Prix helicopter track over there, hovering over the warring tribes.

It's so unfair. When the unreal men come right out and fight the real men, it's the real men who always win.

There was this Arrows-Ninja driver, Streganzi. It seemed he just ran out of fuel in the Grand Prix, just kept going, taking the 130-R corner absolutely flat and just kept flying, as if fuel was an immaterial entity, as if his Formula One ran on the *quinta-essentia*, the fifth essence of matter, *spiritus mundi,* fuel of light and air. They tried to flag him down, they knew, the robots in the pits, because their machines know everything, wheel speed, throttle position, roll, pitch and yaw rate, and to the very last drop, just how much fuel he had left. Zero, at the stand-still.

Afterwards they said Streganzi was hyped up on the adrenalin rush and didn't see the signs. His team-mates dumped him in their fury.

But listen to it my way. With Streganzi, his eyes saw the gauges. His brain registered the frantic waving from the pits. His highly-toned muscles reacted the way they should, but that was his body. What he was, in himself, his essential being floated detached, for the duration, just above the car, hovered the way they say the soul hovers above, at the moment of death, before it takes flight for the beyond. There was a ghost driver, doppelgänger, and while the body went through the motions, the unreal man within detached from the base matter of his body and floated, controlling from on high, absorbed in wonder.

Streganzi touched the unreal. He'll never drive again, not Grand Prix, but you could say he wasn't driving then either. It was an unreal man's real car, for the duration.

There are Grand Prix everywhere you look. Prizes for concreting parks, and laying down bitumen over gravel, for the machines to get there faster. There is a prize, and there is a price, and no prizes for guessing who pays and who collects.

The cars come here once a year, to this park, and you can see the changes in them. The cars are evolving and we are their servants. We are the robots that come out and pander to their needs. The cars learn how to breathe and grow and drive themselves beyond the here and now. The humans are left behind. The cars are changing us.

The park is not innocent in this deal. The park is shaping itself around the race. Each year you see it, bits of it are lopped off here and reappear over there. The air is bending more slowly and it's growing thicker with the fumes. The sounds of wrrooroomm! travel more sluggishly to human ears. Petrol particles take root in human brains and send their shoots down deep. It seems right and only natural, that the earth should shift under our feet, that there should be outgrowing, upswelling from deep within the earth, of the forces that got Streganzi. The wheel-changing androids, the doppelgänger driver, the elemental forces of the earth, they're all in this together.

Satan now, that's an unreal man for you. He's what you'd call a real man's unreal man.

Then it hit me. The clue lies in the bitumen. They say that someone spread diesel fuel on the Grand Prix track, but they don't know the half of it. Straight from the bituminous pits of hell, that's where it's from. It didn't fall down from above. *It rose from underneath*. Elemental forces seep upwards from beneath, oozing through the track from below, bubbling through the realms of invertebrate microfauna, sizzling the good worms of the earth, converting what's left of them to a layer of sulphur enriched humus.

In the twinkling of an eye.

The road shall be changed, and the dead shall rise up and take over the pits, and Streganzi will drive on and on and on, and not notice his car is out of fuel, his body is out of the chassis.

The dead, the elementals, the ultimately unreal are converging on this place.

Too many real men have got together here. Action and reaction, Newton's third law swings into motion. The earth reacts, the forces of nature take off on a lightning leap to a wholly new point of equilibrium. The skies bow down to the victors. The whole world breathes a soft collective sigh. The earth's fragile equilibrium is punctuated, its *status quo* upset. Unreal men erupt from the earth, and the city sinks into the abyss.

Satan and the legions of hell, now that's a bunch of unreal men all right and I don't want to have dealings with any of them, none whatsoever. The meek shall inherit the earth, what's left of it, and now it looks like a whole bunch of other stuff is going to happen before the meek get their look in.

When I saw that other unreal man that day with his duck on a string, and I saw him slip behind the trees, I saw another part of the problem. The kind of unreal man any real woman might fancy just isn't there. Not a man's man, but a real woman's unreal man. Now you see him, now you don't, and that's the way of it.

This brings me back to where I started, with the question, if real men drive real cars, what do unreal men drive? Answer: now they drive the earth.

I think I've gone off unreal men.

AFTERWORD

"Real Men" was written in response to some events at the 1997 Melbourne Grand Prix. Someone did pour diesel on the Grand Prix track, and a local politician told us that "real men drive real cars". Next comes the obvious question. If real men drive real cars, what do unreal men drive?

— *Rosaleen Love*

TERRY DOWLING

Terry Dowling is one of Australia's most respected and internationally acclaimed writers of science fiction, fantasy and horror. He is author of *Rynosseros, Blue Tyson* and *Twilight Beach* (the Tom Rynosseros saga), *Wormwood, The Man Who Lost Red*, and *An Intimate Knowledge of the Night*, and editor (with Dr Van Ikin) of *Mortal Fire: Best Australian SF*, and senior editor of *The Essential Ellison*.

His stories have appeared locally in such magazines as *Omega Science Digest, Australian Short Stories, Overland, Eidolon*, and *Aurealis* and in anthologies as diverse as *Fabulous at Fifty, Metaworlds, Crosstown Traffic*, and *Australian Ghost Stories*. His overseas publications include *The Magazine of Fantasy & Science Fiction, Interzone*, and *Ténèbres and Ikarie* and appearances in such acclaimed anthologies as *The Year's Best Fantasy & Horror, The Year's Best Horror 1996* and *Destination Unknown*.

Dowling has been called "one of our finest futurists" (*Independent Monthly*) and "one of the finest imaginative minds of the 1990s" (*Canberra Times*). His work has been compared to that of Jack Vance, J. G. Ballard, Cordwainer Smith, Ray Bradbury, Gene Wolfe, James Tiptree Jr, Kate Wilhelm, Frank Herbert, Harlan Ellison, and Peter Straub, and such South American writers as Borges and Cortazar, though his voice is uniquely his own, earning him complimentary entries in *Twentieth Century Science Fiction Writers*, the Clute/Nicholls *Encyclopedia of Science Fiction*, John Clute's *Science Fiction: The Illustrated Encyclopedia* and, most recently, in the "Movers and Shakers" section of David Pringle's *The Ultimate Encyclopedia of Science Fiction*. *Locus*, the multi-award winning genre newspaper, regards his work as placing him "among the masters of the field".

Dowling has won more Ditmar Awards for Science Fiction and Fantasy than any other Australian writer — nine times! He is also the recipient of two Readercon Awards, a Prix Wolkenstein, the 1996 inaugural Aurealis Award for Best Horror Novel, and the 1997 Aurealis Award for Best Horror Short Story.

A Communications lecturer at a large Sydney college, Dowling is also a freelance journalist and award-winning critic. He reviews science fiction, fantasy, and horror for Australia's largest circulation newspaper, *The Australian*, and his essays, articles, and reviews have appeared in *Omega Science Digest*, *Science Fiction: A Review of Speculative Literature*, *The Sydney Morning Herald*, *The National Times*, and *The Australian*. He is also a musician and songwriter, with eight years of appearances on the ABC's *Mr Squiggle & Friends* (which earned him great points with the editors of this volume!).

The next story is perhaps one of the most daring and experimental in this collection; like most of Dowling's work, it will reveal new facets and pleasures with subsequent readings. This tightly crafted, layered story is about the nature of transcendence . . . and how we perceive — and catch — the light.

HE TRIED TO CATCH THE LIGHT

TERRY DOWLING

There was sunmire curling on the rooftop across from the Centre, the dazzle interfering with Ham's concentration and giving him the first signs of a headache.

"Almost ready," Bellinger said, gently, kindly as ever. He knew what these press conferences did to him.

Ham indicated the airy shimmer, immediately moved his hand back to shield his eyes. "Can we do something about that, Ross?"

Bellinger spoke into his coat-mike. "Polarize 21 and 22. Sorry, Ham. We thought we'd leave it clear for the media. Sunmire's more intriguing than ever since your last disclosures."

Ham nodded. *My* disclosures? Lydia found them. In him, yes, but they were hers.

The filters came on. He was still distracted by the patch of sunmire, but now it was easy to study the audience, searching for faces he knew while Bellinger and the techs made final arrangements for the pre-launch briefing.

The press-room was more crowded than he'd ever seen it. As well as the sixty or more media and departmental people allowed places, there were the large Vatican, Panislamic and other religious contingents, and, surprisingly, a much larger turn-out of various world government delegates who had used diplomatic privilege to get inside.

Grouped together in the front rows, in clear view of everyone, were the veterans of previous missions — Public Relations' idea and still a good one after five years, despite the deaths, the missing faces, maintaining the program's useful, top-secret, quasi-military feel.

Ham counted survivors. Two of the Oneiros 3 crew were here, and in the very front row, Frank Sterman, captain of the Psychos 7 probe sat with mission coordinators Salt and Medda, conspicuous diplomacy, unmistakable, drawing the cameras. Lydia Parkes, lone survivor of the Imago 9 disaster, was seated strategically at the other end of their arc with the independent analysts, their hard-won support invaluable now with the funding cuts being reconsidered.

Her discoveries, yes. Drawn out of him, but hers. Of all the people he had let into his dreams to find God, she was the one he ultimately trusted, finally believed.

Movement among the platform party caught his attention, though Ham didn't have to look to know who that would be. Though Ross Bellinger led the program, it was suave, accomplished and highly-telegenic Richard Salt who, as usual, moved forward to address the group. When Salt spoke, the ratings were always good, though using him had become an obvious tactic for many of those present, even the sympathetic ones.

"I'd like to welcome you all here again today on the eve of what promises to be a very exciting and crucial mission for the Donauer Project and possibly the whole world. Most of you are well acquainted with the general objectives for Oneiros 5, but in view of some recent — misunderstandings — I feel it might be useful to review those goals now." His gaze fell genially, ever so briefly, on certain parts of the room. "So we remain clear on what they are — and what they most definitely are not, nor have ever been."

Ham's own gaze wandered back to the windows. The sunmire concentration had been neutralised by the filters, but he knew it was still there — a fine, roiling knot of focused light. He had never made much of the things until two weeks ago; the phenomena had always been just what the media and science commentators had said: a particularly charming by-product of the "smart" building materials introduced into most of the world's cities after the 2026 Expo. The lifeblood of these self-cleaning, temperature adjusting, security aiding laminates was electromagnetic, and gave rise to the distinctive little clouds of refracting ionised vapour that, eight years later, were enjoying all this renewed attention.

Because of what Lydia had said.

It no longer seemed simple coincidence. Ham imagined the vanquished patch and considered her words at the end of the mission trance, cried out unthinking during the momentous Oneiros 4 extraction: "God is just a by-product of our perception of light." That term again. By-product.

There had been a careless desk tech, an audio glitch, something, but an accident, he was sure of it, not some deliberate "slip" to feed him provocative data. Lying there in the mission room, coming out of the trance himself, he had heard the words and they had amazed him. Lydia's voice. Those words.

"God is just a by-product of our perception of light."

Sunmire, rainbows and mist-bows, coronae, aurorae and crepuscular rays, sundogs and *gegenschein*, everything from mock-suns, mock-moons and mirages to glorics, haloes and lofty *fata morganas* beckoning in the sky — all the countless anomalies of light and electromagnetism, the tricks of reflection and refraction that were no longer quite the same. A beam of white light passing through a prism had become profound again.

"First of all," Salt was saying as Ham drew back, "Hampton Donauer does not have stranded personalities wandering around inside him. The brave men and women whose identities were sent into the subject's dream-life and lost to us in the Imago 9, Eidolon 2, Psychos 7 and Oneiros 3 shut-downs are regrettably dead. They knew the chances; they volunteered ..."

And why? Why did they keep volunteering, Ham wondered yet again, even as a voice called from the audience.

"The mind is a relatively closed system, Dr Salt!" It was Kilmer of NFD, predictably enough, as dogged and contentious as ever. "Why, just last week, Caltech's Professor Raglan admitted that those personality sets, those energies of self, those *people*, Dr Salt, *could* be inside Mr Donauer somewhere, for all we know. Professor Raglan suggested that traces of vestigial imprinting ..."

"Mr Kilmer," — Salt was smooth, so reasonable, seeming to lower his voice but actually leaning closer to the lectern mike and using that rather than his coat-mike to drown Kilmer out — "I'll be more than pleased to answer all reasonable questions presently, if you'll just be patient." The emphasis fell so gently on the fourth last word. "The main point of this pre-launch today is to make sure that we are not sidetracked from the real purpose of the Donauer Project, which — I need not remind any sufficiently informed person — is made up completely of legally authorised volunteers well-acquainted with the risks involved."

Mantovani in the headphones, Ham decided there in his place at the long table on the dais. Any moment now. He always accepted the need, but this time Lydia's overheard remark from the Oneiros 4 aftermath — and the sunmire on the roof across from the Centre, the coincidence of that now — would make it something else, a violation, a hated intrusion.

Salt continued, turning the subject away from the lost missions back to the present objectives, which had to include what Lydia had said, whatever it was she had added after that momentous line.

Sure enough, music came. Not Mantovani, of course — Vivaldi, the tiny subcutaneous implants just behind his ears switching in, Ham keenly aware as always that Project staff and accredited independents would be monitoring that fact scrupulously, aware too how this was part of the vital price, sitting there partly occluded and they all knew. The audience got to see him watching the sunmire, musing, reflecting. They couldn't have planned it better.

Patient, charming Richard Salt would be reminding them yet again of the purpose behind the mind-missions. Repeating, reiterating as they always had to, because people *did* forget the details. How twenty-four years ago, Ham's father, the late, eccentric and gifted Henry Donauer, had shut his infant son off from all information about the world's belief systems, all input about formalised religion. How he had allowed full socialisation to occur through controlled tutorials and carefully screened peer groups and media broadcasts, but always with that one key element missing: no conversation, no books, no reference to organised metaphysics. It was Jean Jacque Rousseau's "Noble Savage" idea expressed in a crucially modified form, but instead of the child being raised outside society altogether, it was just one single vital omission from the societal dataflow. To find out what humans knew of such things *a priori*.

Ham knew this now because the experiment had always been implicitly one of diminishing returns. He still had no formal knowledge of the different cultural belief systems that governed so many lives and governments, so many communities on the planet, but he knew what the experiment was in these final stages.

He'd loved his father. At age 11, when a highly respected if self-serving observer, Camille Jaels, had finally leaked details of the Donauer Project to a European scientific journal, she had paradoxically helped guarantee the Project's survival beyond Henry Donauer's untimely death from pneumonia in 2021. Ham had consented to the ongoing controlled deprivation. Sociologically, historically, parents the world over controlled their offsprings' received cultural knowledge whenever they could, biased learning outcomes, the ways subjective reality was in fact made. At the very least, Henry Donauer was doing no more, no less. Yet from another viewpoint, a wholly scientific viewpoint, he was doing so much more.

And Henry Donauer had always been amazingly frank.

"I want to see what you believe, Ham, naturally and intuitively," he had said. "What your dreams show — what universals are passed on through the genes, through any form of a collective unconscious. Are particular neurotransmitters predisposed? Are such dedicated functions possible, vested applications such as the pleasure chemical, dopamine, gives? Are there such things as adulant biasing as Gina Colfax suggests? Or is it just a phosphene spill, susceptible minds responding to entoptic residue?"

And often when Ham asked, "But just what do you mean, what do I believe?", his father would leave it to one of his trusted assistants — one of the three R's — Ross, Richard or Ruth Medda, to take him through it oh so carefully, explain how he was doing humanity a service, that he was a "pure soul" operating without details of one of the key conditionings.

Though Ham had read necessarily edited texts on the nature of social history, how cultural "norms" led to everything from traditions of boys being raised differently from girls, what caste and legal rights were available, how property was disposed of and so on, he'd accepted it. Still accepted it.

Kilmer was on his feet again, Ham saw, the tall sneering man pointing at him and shouting something. Ham immediately averted his gaze, making no attempt to read the famous science journalist's lips. He was used to fighting the curiosity, again his choice. Instead, he turned his attention back to the sunmire, trying to judge its intensity with the filters on, wondering how long it would last. The trick of light had none of its earlier impact; perhaps it would soon dissipate altogether.

The Vivaldi soothed him but he was aware that he was frowning. He caught himself at it, wondered why he had been. He let his thoughts go back to the Oneiros 4 extraction. The overheard words. The iconauts in the staging chamber, one moment in their imposed trances, tracking his own so-called adulant neurotransmissions, scouring his hippocampus, riding, searching, finding, then emerging, and Lydia's voice full of excitement, saying those words. That word.

God.

Their word, not his. Never his. A person. A place. A state. He had had no such word. Not consciously before they'd given it to him afterwards. A name for a goal, a context, a setting. Lost knowledge. But they had something. She did. Had come back with it, all of them so excited. Before the gentle music came. Mantovani in the headphones.

It had caused a furor among the independent observers, an outcry scotched by Henry Donauer's prerecorded stipulation that such a name should be given to him at age 25, a mere two months away. Fate had simply played a hand.

Now, in the world beyond Vivaldi, Richard Salt was doing his careful best. Ham knew many of the standard rebuttals; the speech plans Richard would be following, sampling, blending. Ham had also listened to plenty of Kilmer/Davidson/NFD edits; he could pretty well model what the man would be saying. Such a dangerous man, Sol Kilmer, a media luminary with his own top-rating, widely syndicated net program, *Living Science*, the sort of man who too often seemed at odds with his own vocation, who rather seemed bent on seeing how people jumped, just to make something happen. But Richard would deal with it. Ham watched the sunmire and thought of Lydia and something — a place, a person, a thing — called God.

*   *   *

"We do nothing more than place observing viewpoints into Hampton Donauer's sleeping mind," Richard Salt said. "Coherent, cognisant, slaved viewpoints to share his dreams. The Donauer Glove lets those personalities, all trained eidetics, monitor the iconography of that REM sleep, bring back the precise patterns. We then assemble them with meticulous care as both a literal image array and a symbol system. The imaging room here at the Centre has — thanks to the generosity of so many of you present here today — become the best in modern clinical psychology. We lose very little."

"People are dying, Doctor Salt," someone called, not Kilmer this time, probably his crony at NFD, Davidson.

"Volunteers are taking acceptable and freely chosen risks," Salt answered. "As you all know, sometimes the dream force is intense, very powerful. There are nightmares, trauma dreams ..."

"Remmers!" Kilmer cried, and others did, NFD plants most likely.

Salt let it pass. "Externally, we have to judge when heightened brainwave activity indicates crisis as opposed to maximum image flow of exactly the kind we need, and sometimes we are wrong. We do not read minds; we read images and track image runs. Simply observe and report. Sometimes our observers are too deeply engaged and sometimes they are lost ..."

"Lost, you say! In a relatively closed system, Doctor Salt!" It was Davidson again, probably trying to set off the *yaddist* extremists. It made great viewing when a glowering fundamentalist or even an indignant monsignor was caught reacting. And, yes, so obviously planned. Kilmer, the champion of science as "everyone's entitlement, everyone's proper entertainment", couldn't afford to say some things, so he had others do it for him. "They're sure to impinge on the dreaming consciousness. I hate to say it, but any god-pictures you get could well be eroding personalities as they die."

There, it was said. Ridiculously wrongheaded and naive, yet tabloid headlines for the next month. His mistake for using the word "lost". Salt could only continue.

"Here's where I tell you two things — Mr Davidson, is it? Firstly, contrary to Professor Raglan's colourful theories, we have not "lost" any of our observers *inside* Hampton Donauer, regardless of how much that notion seems to take your fancy. This has been well documented by independent observers, including members of ACAC and FEDEP. Do feel free to interview them again, if you feel you need to verify your facts. It's on the way out of the Donauer Trance that there is danger, in that stage of the extraction process requiring the participation of the iconauts themselves. In a sense, they bring themselves out, via a careful system of neural phase-downs, reintroducing their own wills. It is then, if they are traumatised and distracted by neural surges ..."

"Nightmares!"

Kilmer? Davidson? Salt dared not stop.

"... and adulant residues, that they fail to complete this process. There is something we call attenuation; there is sometimes the equivalent of a major stroke. It is a simple problem right there at the body-mind interface, where chemicals become consciousness. It is quite possibly insurmountable."

Kilmer would never buy it, Salt knew, because he couldn't use it. The idea of "remmers" had caught the popular imagination — helpless mind-sailors pursued and hunted by nightmares as marauding "free radicals", or, as one old revamped phrase had it, by "monsters from the id". Great copy.

Ironically, it had done harm at the moment of greatest public attention. Certainly the public sponsors were worrying, the Vatican, the Eden League, Gaia Spec, the various Islamic nations, the rest, all the countless, global, corporate "medicis" trying for some sort of positive PR flow-on. The mostly anonymous secret sponsors, well, who knew what they thought?

"Secondly?" someone demanded. And not Davidson this time. Not Kilmer. Geridh, the Libyan diplomat.

"Why don't we let Lydia Parkes tell us that," Doctor Salt said. "Someone who's actually been there. Lydia?"

And on cue the short, compact iconaut approached the lectern, her collar mike engaged. She gripped the lectern's sides and gave her wonderful smile.

* * *

Ham watched the short blonde woman move to the front of the stage and step up to the lectern. She looked so different in her dark blue cutaway suit, so different from when she wore her mission fatigues. Her long plain face was the sort that made you think "dependable" and never frightened people off, yet had a full intelligent gaze that made many more people than Ham use the really quite inappropriate yet compelling analogy that her eyes were filled with light. They weren't, of course, in any quantitative sense, but they carried a force, a vitality and charisma that was carried down into her smile and often made people grab at that allusion before any other.

All so fitting now. You noticed Lydia Parkes when she smiled because it changed her face; then you saw the eyes and it changed something else. It bemused men. That truly rare thing, it charmed and eluded women rather than threatened them. It broke categories and strategies. What her smile did to her eyes was inexpressible.

She began speaking, and Ham had to make himself look away. It wasn't anything as simple as being in love with her. Lydia Parkes had nearly died because of him once, *in* him if you listened to the likes of Raglan, Kilmer, NFD and CIRODEC, overwhelmed with the rest of the Imago 9 crew. Only she had been revived this side of brain-death, drawn out of heartstop, kept from flatline, barely in time. When she'd regained consciousness, she had immediately volunteered for the Oneiros 4 probe and this latest Oneiros 5 follow-up, not really a veteran iconaut given active hours in the Donauer Trance, but treated as one by those who were.

She *knew* him, he liked to believe.

Someone knew him.

Dependable and a survivor. Full of light and life. He had liked her when he first saw her, even before she smiled. He loved her when she did. Had fallen in love with her when he looked above the smile to her eyes again, saw the knowing of him, the caring, the simple caring. Now the whole quest reminded him of her. The muted sunmire did. He wanted to watch her speak, read her body, her set of self, see how she mouthed careful, confident words against the surging strains of Vivaldi, but he looked back at where the sunmire coiled about what was left of itself. While he wouldn't understand all the words she said, he knew what the first ten would be.

* * *

"God is just a by-product of our perception of light," Lydia Parkes said. "That's what I remember apprehending — *knowing* — in an evolved sequence-tree probably thirteen minutes into full REM phase. Excuse the jargon, ladies and gentlemen. It's how we try to identify locales and orient POV under trance. If one of us fails to do that then we're one observer down. It's probably the second hardest thing we have to do: remember to be ourselves in there. The hardest, as you already know, is coming back out again. On this insertion, there was a hallway and staircase from the Donauer Clinic as Stage One, a field of standing-stones from Dorset segueing into Easter Island, a group of birds-into-druids all branching into multiples then. A cloister on a shoreline. A forest lawn with spindles of light. All reinforced motifs, all transformation segues of a very high order. Completely unexpected. The frame POV, Ham's master template for us, was affirming a role for light. Obviously we associated as we always do — allowable reification under the circumstances — posited God of Light, Lord of Light, Let there be Light, but I grabbed it as the *key* determining element of our god-perception. I templated that idea in-trance so I had referents, then jettisoned the lot as we're trained to do. I sought confirmation and found it. Ben and Marjory affirmed and confirmed. Excuse the terms, please. It's how we experience it, as affirmations and confirmations inside our heads inside Hampton Donauer's head. Sometimes we can talk to one another in-trance. We don't know how that works exactly so we don't expect it. Ben and Marjory saw what I did and confirmed. We knew we had locked onto something with an A–1 flag, the highest rating we can give.

"These are Big Dreams, ladies and gentlemen, just as our reports show, just as Dr Jung correctly named them all those years ago. Everyone of us has them — the key dreams that recur over months, years, lifetimes and are traditionally regarded as prophetic and highly significant for the dreaming individual. Not just the usual syntheses of daily minutiae, not just the result of associative data saturation. We have never been sure of riding a Big Dream before. These are allegedly the psyche's own messages to itself, after all, to the evolving individual or carrier it is. Not fashionable believing that these days, but never disproven.

"Allowing these Big or Key Dreams and recognising them has always been the problem. There is so much random and associative iconography, so many hundreds and thousands of image referents available, segues, associants, value-sets to evaluate in terms of the individual. Because we can control something of Hampton Donauer's environment — the day to day information horizon available to him, people he meets and so on — we can often identify the associational material surprisingly well; understandable since much of it is our own daily experience also. Inside him there is a dream, mostly circumstantial, incidental material, mostly just a light-show or the psyche carrying out housecleaning duties. We do what nanotech cannot yet do reliably. Nano probes may glean image ghosts but never the *felt* experience, the recognition associated with them. Sometimes we *know* it's essential data we're seeing because the themes are so powerful and so apparently original. So numinous. That's a vital word for what we get. Just data-streams, then exaltation. Recognition *and* rapture suddenly there. We *sense* the dream as being of enormous numinous significance. Allow that the psyche *does* know when it is being replenished, even if we ourselves as conscious individuals do not. Self, not ego, despite the bigotry and narrow-mindedness, the inherent envy of the ego."

She did not give Kilmer, Davidson or even Geridh time to respond to the slight.

"Deprived of god-lore, many of Hampton Donauer's Big Dreams could well have shown such wonderfully promising image arrays. In comparative terms, it's like the Jungian case of the little girl who presented her father with a notebook containing accounts of dreams she'd had, filled with all sorts of symbolic elements she *couldn't* have lived. We allow that there are such dreams. It is faith in a sense, supported by the most dramatic wave-surges in the brain. Something *is* there, more than just images, and we're trying to find out what that is."

It was as if no-one dared speak. Lydia left a four-beat of silence, then continued.

"Let me clarify something. We have already *proven* we are not inside Hampton Donauer as people. We have repeatedly *demonstrated* that we have access to the man's *revemonde*, nothing more. We've never claimed more. Our opticals are slaved to his, that is all. Henry Donauer very wisely published the technical specifics of the Donauer Glove immediately after Camille Jaels made her unofficial disclosures. Medical experts have confirmed that the deaths resulted from a curious and recurring anomaly we call trauma separation, a massive, regenerative release of neurotransmitters that has the same effect as a major stroke. These are volunteers and it's regrettable but, in a sense, *you* have pushed us to it. Even more regrettably, we have let you. We've published all the specifics on this again and again, furnished you all with technicals verified by your own sanctioned observers and investigative bodies and the accredited independents. I want to know why some of you persist in asking such uninformed questions in the first place."

She read the murmurs rippling through the crowd. "Look at you! Look at this turn-out today. Many of you openly ridicule us yet gather like this even for a pre-launch. You fund us yet challenge the very clearly established terms of our search, even list human rights abuses. You wilfully misrepresent the facts. You have scorned and challenged this program every step of the way. Consider yourselves for a change! Ask yourselves why."

It was a terrible, wonderful moment, a silence of steel and glass, coral-fragile with danger.

She had called them selfish, deluded, ignorant. Vatican delegates. Top-level Islamic mullahs. Diplomats, career politicians and mercenary scientists.

She must have calculated every second that silence could stand, because she was there again.

"The funding has been invaluable. It's let the Donauer Institute and the Donauer Project perfect variants on its hardware, all the different approaches we have tried. Those mission names aren't just window-dressing *as you will already know*. The names are different and so highly numbered because they represent entirely different access and insertion methods. You will have *seen* the data." She was merciless now. "Again, why are you continuing to ask these questions? You have not bought us. We would have proceeded without any of you."

It was still so dangerous. In this room were implicit pogroms, jihads and censure, the capacity for disinformation and reprisal, yet it was all on hold, everyone waiting, allowing.

"And if you think Oneiros 4 gave us something, just wait till you see what Oneiros 5 intends to do. We cannot declare too much at this point; that would be prejudicing the observers. Just remember please that what we stand to find usually has very little to do with memory. This is the unknown appearing *amidst* the known. Something new amongst the memories, not just registering as imaginings but as recognitions. We can identify those moments. Even allowing for anomalies of perception and recognition — déjà vu, jamais vu, presque vu — we have discrete and distinctive EEG signatures for these moments of *rapture* and conviction."

Then someone did interrupt. Not Kilmer or Davidson this time. It was Geridh, fiercely conservative, inflammatory. "But ultimately we still only have your word for it, don't we, Ms Parkes? You could have been misleading us all along, feeding Mr Donauer requisite data, fabricating the alleged discoveries."

"Then why are you here, Mr Geridh?" she asked, then forestalled any reply by raising a hand. "But why not let me answer that, since you're certainly not alone in your misgivings. Like most of us, you're judging the moment. You don't want to miss out on such a vital thing, but it has to be the *real* thing, and you are correct in rigorously challenging what we do because of that. So let me tell you just a bit more about Oneiros 5 and its objectives.

"In our last mission we discovered likely causations for a God-perception in response to light. Having monitored a Big Dream at last, we now mean to approach it from the opposite position, to stimulate Ham's optic nerves and vision centres while he is in REM sleep. He does not know we will be doing this."

For a moment, hundreds of people watched Ham watching the sunmire, a calm handsome young man, as serene-looking now as a Christ or a Bodhisattva.

Lydia continued. "We have devised and field-tested a means to do this. While allowing that at one extreme it could be no more than the phosphene display behind a human's closed eyelids predisposing us to recurring symbols such as mandalas and cruciforms, stars and all-seeing eyes, and at the other the existence of adulant neurotransmitters, a specialised visual predisposition in the cortex, we now mean to send light signals into the relevant areas of Hampton Donauer's brain, then track the resulting image runs. Yes, ladies and gentlemen, this time we will attempt to induce such a theophanic experience. Not just a Big Dream. We hope to trigger God."

At some level or other, everyone hated hearing it. There was shouting. Hands were up. People were standing, calling, clamoring.

Ham looked round at the commotion, then turned his attention back to the windows, forced it there.

"Shall I tell you more?" Lydia said, and kept saying it like a mantra until the large gathering settled again. "If we did *not* attempt this, we would *not* be fairly testing our previous observations. You should expect this as the next step; you should insist on it. We personally — the iconauts — do not need to do this. We have been *in* the dream. We have stood in what reads as the light of sublime ideation; we have lived the moment as profoundly as anyone who has ever experienced epiphany and theophany. We probably have enough data already. But seeing if we can trigger the response is a crucial and appropriate final step, not a redundancy. At least we know you will all be here for the next press conference seventy-two hours from now." And she smiled, marvellously, beatifically, wickedly.

There was such danger. People were muttering. There were one or two cries in various languages, no doubt the usual accusations of blasphemy.

Then Kilmer stood, his hand raised as well, uncommon civility, and the audience let him be their voice.

"Mr Kilmer?" Lydia said, ready for him.

"What is in it for you personally, Ms Parkes? You have, well, experienced God, you say. What passes for God — you imply — in the faith convictions of millions. What is in this for you?"

Lydia could have deflected it so easily, but she decided to answer. Her smile changed, mirrored Kilmer's, became sharing and gentle. "The ancient Greeks were at a similar point to the one we're at now. They were maintaining a vigorously rational society, were mistrustful or disbelieving of their countless flawed and brawling gods and goddesses. The best thinkers, the greatest, truly greatest citizens and states*men* — *men*, regrettably, the women didn't leave such a written legacy of what they thought — then knew to pursue excellence, *aristos*, the life of reason but as the work of art too. They sought *aristos*."

"I did say personally, Ms Parkes," Kilmer said. "Personally."

"We do not have that mindset, Mr Kilmer, just as we do not have the mindset of the Elizabethans or even those who lived during the World Wars. But I believe this: the age of reason is done with too. We need more. Societies regulated by reason alone, just like those regulated by their once so useful founding religions, will fail as surely as those founded on our gods and goddesses. We need more now. I need more now. That's what's in it for me personally. Excellence. Quality. Calling out the Eternal Yes, Mr Kilmer, is not a thing of reason. It is an exultation in the act of living.

But is it just an atavistic thing, a throwback to some old triumph over adversary and adversity? Reason can try to explain it but it cannot do so without first reducing it, stripping it of its psychoactive power, its intrinsic reality. As with any epiphany or conviction or hope or inspiration, the inherent motivating, phenomenological force is lost."

"I'm not sure what you mean by Eternal Yes, Ms Parkes."

"Exactly." Her smile became both exquisite indulgence and the gentlest of knives. "So come along with us on Oneiros 5."

"You're not serious."

"You would quite likely see what we see at the very least."

"I'm not sure I'd trust you weren't feeding me false data."

"Ah, but the others would. The independent observers."

Kilmer saw the trap being set, the loss of control in this assembly. More to the point, his studio heads and viewers were. "What would I gain? Scientifically?"

"Why, perhaps a first-hand experience of God!"

"What, a moment of rapture? An Eternal Yes or two?" He was trying to disparage it. Regain control. "I think I'll pass."

"Then remember you were asked." The trap was closed. He was excluded now. She left him no time to comment. "And now Frank Sterman will recount his experiences with similar light templates in his Psychos 5, 6 and 7 insertions."

* * *

They walked on the beach afterwards, Lydia and Ham, avoiding talk of the next morning's Oneiros insertion at first, just meeting the afternoon in all its vital parts, wavefall, windflow, the warming glow of autumn sun. They walked between the security baffles, the outflung walls of one-way shieldglass, watching everything, pointing and remarking, until Ham did mention the press conference, meaning to use it to get rid of the subject, to highlight how people missed moments like this in the rush for greater meaning. It didn't work.

Ham knew Lydia's mike was on, that Salt or Medda would routinely run the conversations then or later, but he had lived with that all his conscious days.

They walked in the glorious sunlight, enjoying the on-shore breeze, held by an intimacy of the most unusual sort. She knew something of his appetites, his hidden drives and desires, what his shadow self did. She had walked his dream-fields, endured his image runs, suspected causations.

Ham felt easy enough considering, though some of the apartment towers were patched with sunmire. He saw them flaring off cornices and balconies, hazing the outlines. They kept the mission more alive than he wanted right then.

"Richard says we won't need many more insertions. He thinks we've got as much as we'll get."

Lydia accepted the inevitability of the apartment towers too, how the lightforms starpointed the ten-storey Donauer Centre and the adjacent Trade Centre.

"Most of it will be for the sponsors after this," she said. "Confirmation runs until they're all happy."

"Then we close it down." He sounded like a child in his simplicity. He could afford to be that.

"What is it, Ham?"

"I worry. I see the empty chairs for Luke, Isabelle and the others, and I want it over, yes. I just wonder what the others need."

"Is it to do with me?" She had always been direct.

"You nearly died. I don't want you in there again and yet I do. I like it and I don't." And he wondered how many secrets she still had to keep. They said they weren't holding back much now, but what else could there be?

About this God. Godding. Godded. Godness. Goddess. Godless. Godlessness. Godling. Goading. Guarding.

He ran the word till it became meaningless again.

"Lydia, the program doesn't warrant this much attention. Media, yes, but those were senior officials there today, political people. It's out of proportion."

"I know. For some I'm sure it's totally, politically opportunistic in that sense, electorates demanding representation ..."

"But I sensed it from the True Science and World Science groups too. Supposedly nonpartisan. They get our stuff, all the data releases. You think they'd stay right out of it, especially with the media and political circus like it is. First they didn't want to be seen to be accrediting us too much, now they're so visible. It doesn't make sense."

"We haven't looked any gift horses in the mouth, Ham. Maybe it's just the phenomenon itself — why this phenomenon now, why the attention? Why the patch of sunmire outside the windows today?"

"Lots of buildings have them."

"But in sociological, philosophical, theological

terms this has to seem like an Event. We can hardly blame them. How many people throughout history have failed to monitor the key events of their age *as* they were happening? We showed you the cover for next month's *True Scientist*. *Light Said Let There Be God!* I wish I could tell you what *Better Science* and *International Science* have as their cover stories, but I can't."

"We should stop."

"We talked about that after the meeting today. Ross and Richard think we've missed our chance."

"I don't follow."

"They wouldn't let us."

"Officially."

"Legally. Everything. They'd pass rulings through WHO, the lot. Appropriate it all. It's gotten too big. Shouldn't have. Should never have, and what does that tell us? And even if we could shut it down, end it, everything, they wouldn't believe us for a minute. They'd say we'd gone into some new closed-door phase. Inner circle. You think it's out of control now! They'd go crazy."

"What do we do?"

"That's up to you as always. But I'd say continue. Phase it down and give more press conferences, more public appearances. Show them it's diminishing returns. Show them there are no new disclosures, just confirmations. Like the NASA Apollo missions last century. The public will lose interest. Suggest human rights angles to the right people so they lobby for your total acclimation."

"Will it work?"

"Our experts think so. You'd be free of it."

"It's hard to imagine it, Lydia. Things happening for so long in response terms I just can't track. Whatever this God is must be very important. It's so — disproportionate."

"For a long time it gave meaning." She had to be so careful. "Now we want more."

"We make our own meaning," Ham said. "But we *need* more." He looked out to sea, saw the autumn sunlight glinting off the waves. "We need the meaning to come from somewhere else."

It was the sort of astute-facile comment that kept astonishing the Project team.

Lydia didn't hesitate. "Exactly. And that's natural. We're predisposed to wanting that. That's why he did it, Ham."

"Henry?"

"Right."

"We need closure on this, don't we? Soon. It's too volatile."

"Yes."

"God has to be a source. A destination. A maker. A state and a vessel. But an object of yearning."

"Oh?"

"A power base too, but an answer to meaningless."

"I'm hearing you." She was referring to her audio link. "We all are."

"So why do we continue?"

"Confirmation. A bit of hope. Knowing. The nature of the age lets us do it."

"No other age would have?"

She was careful. So careful. "Probably not. Not publicly at least." She took his hand as they walked. "Are you worried?"

"No," he lied, because there was a mission tomorrow, so much to do. "Are you?"

"No," she lied as well and squeezed his hand to show that lying was a good thing when faced with so much truth.

❊   ❊   ❊

The mission insertion went according to plan. By 0530 the next morning, Ham lay deeply asleep at the "thumb" of the Glove, the "stem" of the flower, with five iconauts in their sleeves, heads radially aligned to his so from above he was splendid sight, an El Dorado with a radiant crown of living dreamers — or, rather, non-dreamers, literally entranced fellow dreamers. It was a powerful image, and over time had supplanted the Project's original logo, so now there was just the single vertical line with five others radiating from it, a "dreamer's cross", as the media first had it, a "frightened mop", as Davidson had quipped on *Discovery*, a "spider doing a handstand", as Kilmer had called it on *Living Science*.

Fourteen minutes after initiation, the interfacing began, and five POVs were gradually slaved to the one — as close to functional telepathy as humanity had ever gotten. At twenty-three minutes, readings showed distinctive, coterminous synchrony, the deeply affecting sight of the variant EEGs on the six monitors, formerly dancing apart, now drawing closer, becoming virtually one, never completely overlapping, of course, but braided on the master screen as a coherent cable of dedicated mentation. That too was a media image known worldwide, as famous in its own way as the DNA helix or physician's caduceus it resembled. Ham was leading them. Oneiros 5 was underway.

They were at forty-six minutes when Lydia Parkes died in him.

One moment there was the quiet of the staging room, the low lighting, the barely audible hum of engaged tech. Then there were sudden detonations, corridor alarms, voices shouting, doors bursting in, the startling flash of nocto weapons.

Thirteen minutes earlier, Ham's sleeve would have been hit, but one of the dozen modifications to the Oneiros series had been to rotate the Glove platform yet again for aura exclusion, and ascernium baffles separated Ham from the other sleeves.

The raiders had the old Imago series data and couldn't know what they were seeing. Chris, Ram and Kaori died outright in a nocto sweep; immediate flatline in the ops room. James succumbed to a ballistic strike to the side of the skull. Lydia's sleeve was angled away, Ham's concealed altogether. Coincidence. Lucky coincidence.

An explosion on the roof told the three raiders that the Clinic's Quick-Save forces had destroyed their VTO. They went for contingency. But even as one reached to trigger the Landfall pack that would take out the Centre and half the city block, a Quick-Save omni fired from the door and severed head, arm and shoulder. His companions died the same way.

Ham was safe, but Lydia died in extraction. Maybe if the op techs hadn't been distracted, in fear of their lives, they might have reached her in time. There were 3.8 seconds where she was in extremis from the trauma of massive systems damage before the tertiary systems read the secondaries also down and engaged. She died in the dark of his dreaming, alone and unknowing.

✳   ✳   ✳

They answered most of Ham's questions in the infirmary two hours later, then, when he was out of sedation the following day, finally invited him to the briefing room for the emergency session. There were seven of them — Lydia so noticeably missing.

"Who was it?" Ham could now ask.

Ross Bellinger answered. "Riyadh says the Vatican as usual. The Vatican says Panislamic *yaddists*. The League claims a new San Diego-based Christian fundamentalist group. The UN and the Gaiasts say ..."

"Okay." Ham cut him off with uncommon brusqueness. They would never know. And Lydia wasn't there. Would never be there again. He wasn't sure what he felt.

Ross leant forward, clasped his hands on the tabletop. "Ham, there's another thing."

But Ham had already grasped it. "They could have taken out the complex with a distance strike. Used remotes. They wanted me."

"Seems like it, yes. Someone wants to continue the tests under their own control."

"What do we do?" *Lydia wasn't there*.

Richard Salt answered this time. "Close down the Program. Tell no-one initially. Do it so no-one outside this room knows till you've gone."

"Zimbabwe," Ham said, angry and afraid, but making the old joke, needing it, something. During the early years, the intriguing, peaceful, easy years, a common answer to crisis was to joke about running off to Zimbabwe rather than facing whatever it was.

He said it, they smiled; Ross Bellinger passed him a smart card.

"Quick-Save airvac at 1450. You're off to Zurich and a safe-house." Ham went to speak but Ross cut him off. "Before and during the flight, from when we're done here, you get everything on the religions. The lot. We give you dogmas and pantheons, Ham, everything from jinnis and jihads to transubstantiation. And we're letting the agencies know an hour after you've gone: Mossad, Sintio, Crydin, every other top-line interest group there is. Oneiros 5 was it. No more missions."

"Salting the well," Ham said, another Lydia line. He *was* keeping her alive in him. As him. "Spiking the guns." Mixing her metaphors. *Lydia*.

"Right," Ross said. "So 1450. Before then, you use that comp over there. Call up *Godgame*."

"No." *She wasn't there. The referent in so many equations.*

"What's that?"

"Not yet, Ross. Tell them I've been briefed, neutralised, but no. Not yet."

"She's gone, Ham. She isn't..." He paused, didn't say *inside you.*

"I don't want to know yet!" he cried, ambiguously. "Don't you understand? You're all so good at wanting, seeking, finding and giving answers that you've forgotten what *not* knowing does. The advantage of not knowing!"

They all waited, sensing a vehemence beyond grief, a clarity beyond the chaos of the last two days.

"We aren't only governed by logic," he said. "Don't you see that? We're governed by our perceptions, needs, passions, by our very humanism, by our *bias*, don't you see? Our biasing of objective fact. Our need to. Our splendid triumph in doing so. Humanity isn't just logic. Every public gathering has shown me that, every history book, every scientist I've watched or met. Humanity is also intuition, gestalt knowing, conviction. We are evolved to operate *beyond reason!* To *require* more than reason can provide. Our rationalists have always missed it. We operate *beyond*. That's our ultimate specialisation. Whether as inner truth or placebo, as self-delusion or fervent belief, that's our ultimate survival mechanism — knowing when to set reason aside for *irrational* self-nurturing gains. Our enemy isn't a nervous, manipulative Vatican or bigoted *yaddist* sects or wacky New Agers, whatever *Godgame* will confirm those things as! They're just naturally, desperately, dangerously, even gloriously compensating for the rationalists who also fail to read what human is, who give clear objective truth but in their reductive, contemptuous, misperceiving way, fail to see the balance as well."

There was silence. They let him have it, as much attentive, caring, accepting silence as he needed, the silence, too, of tacit agreement. They knew he had had enough training in sociology to have deduced formal belief systems, the simple self-nurturing and self-deceiving need for something more.

"These are your discoveries, Ham?" Ross Bellinger said. The question was a formality for the audiovee record.

Ham nodded, remembered why Ross had actually asked it and said, "Yes. It's where our humanising values come from. Also a cause for harm. Reason alone makes a poor bedfellow for the human spirit. It disallows the human spirit. There can be no such thing."

Again Ross Bellinger improvised. "Then we proceed to make it known that you have been exposed to *Godgame*. Even give you some salient key words. Is that okay?"

Ham hesitated. A vital integer was missing. "So long as you understand why I'm doing this now. And why not let me give you some of your key words, Ross? Communion. Benediction. Atonement. Sacrifice. Love. Charity. Forgiveness. How am I doing?"

Ross smiled, loving the young man, this known yet always unexpected cornerstone of his own life. "You're doing very well. And you have to keep reminding us, just like this, okay? That the words come first."

"But in the beginning there aren't just the words," Ham said, believing it with all his heart. "There are the feelings, the understandings, the perceptions, convictions and recognitions. Then the names." And he sought again for words which encompassed all he had lost. There was only one.

❋　❋　❋

He was on the roof-field at 1440, wearing maintenance coveralls and cap, carrying a duffel, playing the role of a solitary tech being airlifted back to Aluen. He stood in the cool afternoon wind that lifted over the low parapet from the ocean and watched a patch of sunmire hanging on a corner of the adjacent Trade Centre, a hot kernel in the bright sunlight, as detached and unfeeling as a rainbow.

At 1450 exactly, a Rogan *shaukraft* appeared over Clinic's western side, settled in a flurry of air. The long side door opened; a crewman beckoned. Ham ducked, clutched his bag and ran, but instead of climbing aboard, he remained standing at the door.

"Get in, Sir," the crew tech said.

"Who are you with?" Ham asked.

The tech seemed not to hear. "Please, Sir. We're on a time. Please get in."

"I just want to know who you're with." It was suddenly important.

"Quick-Save Airvac," the man said. "Name's Jell."

A second crew-tech appeared at the door. "Hey, we're on a time, Jell," she said. "Mr Donauer, please get in, Sir."

"I don't want you to have Lydia."

"What? What's that, Sir?" she asked.

The first tech reached for him, but Ham stepped back, eluding his grasp.

Figures had appeared at the door onto the roof-field, wondering what was amiss. Ross or Richard, Ham couldn't tell.

"I said I don't want you to have Lydia."

And he saw that they understood, feigned incomprehension a second after, yes, then abandoned it when they saw he knew.

The first tech reached for him again. "You're safe with us, Sir. We're scientists too."

But by then Ham was running, not to his friends. Diminishing returns there anyway, they'd said.

He ran away from the *shaukraft* and the roof building, the Quick-Save imposters running behind but too late, way too late.

We make our own meaning! At the very least. Eternally yes.

There was sunmire ahead, beckoning, blazing, as meaningless and inscrutable as a rainbow, but all there was, and right then everything there was. He had her with him. He ran. He jumped. He tried to catch the light.

AFTERWORD

I began the story in 1993, and wrote seven or so longhand pages before setting it aside because I kept resisting the ending. When *Dreaming Down-Under* came along, with its wonderful coincidence of title and theme, I went back and re-read what I had and saw how neatly it all matched. When I re-met the story's central character, I saw what it needed to be for him. That was the way it had to go, of course.

Narrative mainsprings? I guess it mainly came out of accepting that there used to be important cultural mysteries in our societies for very good reasons. Equally important, there used to be languages for explaining such mysteries or, rather, dealing with them — of representing while avoiding them, in short, "languages of accommodation" for confronting, skirting, but at least *allowing for* a prevailing and incommunicable gestalt of human spirit in each of us.

While many excellent science fiction writers were challenging the prevailing paradigms so well, making us gasp and marvel at demonstrable truths and possibilities in the universe, many seemed too coolly detached, too off-handed and reductive, even curiously bleak and dystopian, not only in their delivery but in their approach to their task. Exploring truths and possibilities can demand rigorous and unswerving measures, true, but this contradiction fascinated me. For all their smarts, their exciting "What ifs" and careful scientific facts and methods, some genuinely invigorating storytellers seemed either unwilling or unable to incorporate the *lived* knowledge of self and spirit inherent in each of us and in human society, and so effectively disregarded it. They were, in a sense, misreading the age. Powerful stories seemed incomplete and beside the point somehow, even dated, not because the ideas were weak or the content too formidable, but because often a clinical scientific method is still not equal to the task of grasping what it examines.

Regrettably, inevitably, many of our languages of accommodation are either gone or no longer adequate to the task of representing what they once glossed and skirted. Here's where the storyteller, the balladeer, the dancer, the artist, the polymath explainer, can serve: not only reminding us of what we have surrendered, showing what those languages were for and helping to fill the gap left in societal need, but quite possibly helping to keep us linked with all that we are.

The task of the futurist may be much much harder than we thought.

— *Terry Dowling*

DAMIEN BRODERICK

Damien Broderick is one of Australia's most important and well-known science fiction writers. He is the recipient of four Australian Literature Board/Fund writing fellowships, four Ditmar Awards, and one Aurealis Award. His radio play *Schrödinger's Dog* was Australia's entry for the 1995 Prix Italia international radio drama award. He holds a PhD from Deakin University and is an Associate in the Department of English and Cultural Studies at the University of Melbourne. Broderick was a science fiction reviewer for *The Age* during the 1980s and now regularly reviews science books for the *Weekend Australian*.

His novels include *The Dreaming Dragons*, *The Judas Mandala*, *Transmitters*, *The Black Grail*, *Striped Holes*, *The Sea's Furthest End*, *Valencies*, *The White Abacus*, and *Zones* co-authored with Rory Barnes. Some of his stories can be found in the collections *A Man Returned* and *The Dark Between the Stars*. His non-fiction titles include *The Architecture of Babel: Discourses of Literature and Science*, *Reading by Starlight: Postmodern Science Fiction*, *Theory and Its Discontents*, *The Lotto Effect*, *The Spike*, and *The Last Mortal Generation*. He has also edited a number of anthologies, which include *The Zeitgeist Machine: A New Anthology of Science Fiction*, *Strange Attractors: Original Australian Speculative Fiction*, *Matilda at the Speed of Light: A New Anthology of Australian Science Fiction*, and *Not the Only Planet: SF Stories About Travel*.

In the brilliant and disquietingly archetypal story that follows, Damien Broderick reaches back into his past (see his fascinating afterword) to recapture the yearnings of childhood and investigate our culture's disordered fantasies.

THE WOMB

DAMIEN BRODERICK

I

> Twice have I stood a beggar
> Before the door of God!
> Angels, twice descending,
> Reimbursed my store.
> Burglar, banker, father,
> I am poor once more!
> — *Emily Dickinson, 1858*

My father despised biographies, but even more (or so he told his followers) he detested movies and novels and invented stories of every kind. "Fiction is the gossip of those who don't get out much, Rosa," he told me once, with a smile. No doubt I was curled up with a book at the time. "Purveyed," he added, sarcastically, "by those who don't get out at all." So here I am writing a story, his story, perhaps my story as well, possibly the chronicle of us all. No doubt my father would laugh heartily at this. Will laugh. I don't know.

My father, after all, is the Rev. Daimon Keith who revealed to us, in the years prior to his second disappearance, that as a youth he had been abducted from the vicinity of a Clayton school playground by small grey aliens. Indeed, Daimon had been taken up into UFOs not just that once, in Australia, at the age of twenty, but from infancy, and over and again. No doubt it was this germinal and outlandish experience that caused him to devote his middle years to the establishment of the Church of Jesus Christ, Time Traveller (or, as the American chapters have it, "Traveler"), and later Scionetics. At last, as his madness grew deeper and more hilarious, its equivocal memory fetched him to the belief that it was his own Nazarene face which the black-eyed aliens had sculpted from a eroded mesa on the surface of Mars, memorialised so ambiguously in the famous 1976 NASA photographs and twenty-two years later so conclusively unmasked, despite his angry blustering, as my father's fame neared its zenith.

To exist in the shadow — the dark aura, perhaps — of such a father is, you might suppose, inevitably to grow up as a wretch obliged to launch the tale of her own life with details of her father's name and lunatic obsessions. Do not think to find me out so readily. My life has not been so straightforward, nor is Daimon's notoriety altogether just. I am a student of narrative, as are we all in these early days of the millennium, fully up to the mark with anxieties of influence. I have every intention of constructing and revising my father's testament, if only I can find my way to the bottom of it. For now perhaps a sketch must suffice, or a series of arbitrary laminations.

You should know at once that for a long time I understood that he tried to force my mother to have an abortion (or so I was told frequently) and, when she refused in horror, attempted to give me up for adoption three days after my birth, which he would inform his followers had occurred on July 20, 1969, a little after midday, Eastern Australian Time. This, the elderly among you might recall, was the moment Neil Armstrong set his foot upon the Moon, during the first landing by the Apollo astronauts. In fact, I was not born until the middle of 1975, and the gap serves my father's purposes admirably, for people are always taken by how young I seem. It is a subtly tacit endorsement of his esoteric teachings.

His own birthdate is hardly less notable, for Daimon entered the world — by his own account — on August 6, 1945, within hours of that other Little Boy who squalled into heat and light over Hiroshima.

One last prefatory point: although his family and friends call my father "Deems", a childhood nickname, his proper given name is not pronounced "Demon", as the ignoramuses of the mass media assume, but "Die-moan", in the way of its Greek source. If that vulgar error was an occasion of chagrin for a man of the cloth, even cloth so self-elected and flamboyant as my father's, he never allowed his family to perceive it. His name had been gifted to him from his Scottish grandfather, a classicist of minor note in the Ballarat gold fields, and it means, as you may know already, a kind of indwelling spirit or force of nature. Certainly he became that for his daughter, even as Daimon became convinced that he himself was now infested by illuminations from beyond the present: from beyond the world itself.

For all that, I am not Rosa Keith but Rosa Rosch, named fore and aft by my mother Margaret, the strong-willed woman who stole me away me from his clutches when I was five years old.

II

Aboard the Zetan craft

In his dreaming confusion, he knew that it had started again. The musty stench reminded him of mice, the piles and heaps of mouse droppings they'd found in his uncle's empty weekender when they'd gone to Queenscliff for a cheap winter holiday. The bench he lay on was not quite hard, and the long, lighted oblong above his head burned like a pink musk-stick sucked to a piercing sweetness in the vacant eternities of geometry and geography classes. His dry tongue searched his mouth for the absent taste. The brothers would snatch the sweet from his mouth if they found him enjoying it during a lesson. Once, Brother Ronald had literally seized his jaw in one handball-roughened fist and pinched the nerves, forcing the nub of musk-stick out from between his teeth, made him spit it on to the scratched school desk. In the pink darkness, as his heart accelerated with the fright of being here once again, he felt a quirky grin move his lips, at that memory within a dream, because at least Brother Ronald isn't around to torment him.

Something was standing at his side. Something like a doll formed hastily from putty and not left long enough in the sun, moist and pliant, curvy and dirty white. He could not bring himself to turn and look at it. Yet the disgust he felt seemed, somehow, to come from the creature itself. There was another of them at the foot of the slab, with its blobby head and wraparound eyes, doing something to his left foot. That was hard to understand, because normally he was very ticklish. If one of the guys grabbed his bare foot, he'd go into a girlish paroxysm of giggles and flailing around. The thing down there was fooling with his foot, and it wasn't making him giggle one little bit. Quite the contrary. He felt sick with anxiety, and numb, and heavy in the limbs.

He screamed, then, a hard sharp yelp, as a needle went into the flesh between his big toe and the next toe along.

"Hey! Cut it out!"

In the funny atmosphere, his words hung in his ears like underwater echoes. Had he even spoken?

"Fuck!" The bastard was shoving the fucking needle deeper into his god-damned foot! "Jesus!"

This was unbelievable. Every time he came here they did something like this. And every time he told them how much it hurt, how vehemently he detested their invasion of his private places, but it never made the slightest bit of difference. Never did the faintest bit of good. But they were not cruel, he knew that. The one at his side touched his forehead with a cool tube, it felt like, something glimmery and pale, not metal and not plastic, and it soothed him at once. It took away the pain. No, the pain was still there, but it didn't hurt any more. Did that make any sense? It was like shoving with your tongue at a dead tooth. That baby tooth he'd pried at with his fingers and his tongue for a week and half, deciduous tooth they call it, when he was seven years old. He'd even tried that old trick they tell you about, loads of laughs, cheaper than a visit to the dentist, and you got your lucrative visit from the tooth fairy that much sooner. You tied a piece of string around the loose tooth and attached the end to a door knob, and another kid jerked the door open and out popped your floppy baby tooth. It hadn't worked. It had hurt like blazes, and the string tightened and cut into his gum, and he got his backside tanned when Mum came in from the back yard, drawn by his yelping and howling, and found him with this bloody string hanging out of his god-damned bleeding gum like he'd been gargling with a tampon or something.

Deliberately, he turned his head and stared at the putty-grey creature at his side.

Look away! the grey thing told him in his mind. Stop staring at me! You know we don't like you looking at us!

He averted his gaze, feeling horribly guilty, as if he'd been caught staring through a crack in the wall into some girl's bathroom while she was taking a pee or something. Which he had done, now that he thought about it, back in that old dairy they'd had in Olive St, Jesus, how incredible, he'd been 11 or 12 and they still ladelled out fresh creamy milk into washed bottles you brought from home there to the dairy, right in the middle of the suburbs, well, okay, out on the edge of the metropolitan area, but still. And there were milkman's delivery horses, was that right? Hairy hoofed big bastards, sweet natured and much given to shitting placidly and copiously right there in the street. His father made him rush out after they'd been past, carrying a flat-bladed spade and a hessian sack, and scoop up the steaming, heavy-smelling horse crap and bag it for the garden, God, he'd been so embarrassed, none of the neighbours did that, they probably thought his father was a perv of some kind, a manure fancier, maybe they thought we ate it with our milk and white sugar and Weeties.

Get up, the alien told him. We have to go now.

He seemed to float in an amazingly heavy way. They went across the curved brushed-aluminium floor toward the huge curving windows full of stars, and there was a door in the wall but it wasn't actually a door, it wasn't even marked as a door, they went through it without it opening, holy shit! He had just passed through the fucking wall like smoke. No, as if the wall was smoke. Curdled for a moment. Floating. There was that strange stink again. What do these guys eat? With mouths like that, how could they eat anything? Maybe they sucked blood through a straw. And here was that room again, that hallway, full of green-gold tubes in serried ranks. Each was twice the height of a tall man, and inside each there hung a human body, male and female alike, naked, long-haired. Their eyes were closed as if they slept, or were dead. In the green medium they floated, as he floated down the corridor in their midst, and their long hair streamed out from their scalps.

It was too awful to be borne. He squeezed his eyes shut tightly, and looked away.

Good boy, he thought he heard. Do not look. They are just dolls. But he secretly turned his head again and squinted at the ranks of drowned people and his heart squeezed hard and bumped. The tubes were not as large as he'd supposed, not by a long chalk. They were much closer than he had imagined, and they were smaller than the grey dwarfs leading him in their midst. They were hardly larger than test tubes, if the truth be known, and the creatures floating in them — pale, stringy haired, barely sexed — were like foetuses, limbs slightly curved, bobbing in the liquid that preserved them. The horrid little things were less alien than the grey bastards, but certainly less human than anyone he'd ever seen. In fact they looked like some kind of unholy hybrid, some vile intermixing of the two species. He wanted to scream or vomit or reach out and tear things apart in his rage, but he could not move, and the wall parted without opening and he was in his bed again.

He lay staring at the familiar ceiling for a moment, while the pounding of his heart subsided, and waited for sound to resume. A car went by in the street, throwing the edges of its headlights through the closed louvres, and he looked fearfully around the room through slitted eyes without opening them properly. The putty-grey creature stood there still, on the other side of the bed.

As always, something prevented him from screaming blue murder and waking his parents. Anyway, they had to know about this. Jesus, it had been going on as long as he could remember. Two years old, three? Up in the sky, in the blue gushing light beam, drawn toward the clouds and the shining disk, and his parents sitting frozen on the grass in the back yard, beer glasses in their hands, smiling at each other. They hadn't helped. Or was that when he was six, just back from the hospital after getting his tonsils out? There'd been a polio scare that year, and they'd kept him in the private hospital to see he was okay, and during the night the grey Harvesters had come and lifted him and three of the other kids out of the ward. Nobody ever did anything to stop them, not your parents and not your teachers, nor even the brisk nurses or the doctors, the human doctors, that is. Adults were useless, really. They'd let you get fucked up the arse in front of their very eyes and they wouldn't lift a finger to help.

III

20 July 1999, San Diego

My father, Commodore the Reverend Daimon Keith of the spacetime cruiser *Zygote*, sits at ease behind a desk of audiovisual controls. Scionetics devotees face him, cross-legged on cushions. A Saint-Saëns symphony, rendered soft and luminous for New Age sensibilities, fills the room's acoustic background like an odour of cinnamon. At the back of my balding, silver-haired father, on a huge bank of high definition TV screens, a ceaseless montage lifts the hearts of his followers, placing Deems in his proper context: sweet pale Australian sky with little white merino sheep clouds, rust-red outback dunes, the soaring, ancient curve of Uluru like a stone fallen from heaven, the Moon's cratered surface seen from the window of Armstrong's plummeting Lunar Excursion Module thirty years ago to the day, deep heaven itself captured by the Hubble telescope, black as eternity, roaring with a violence of stars and quasar plumes a hundred or a thousand light years in extent. Deems is clad appropriately in his commodore's uniform, silver jump suit cinched at the waist, emblazoned on shoulder and breast with the curiously aching symbols he and his fellow abductees have seen etched into the curved walls of UFO operating theatres. When he speaks to his followers, though, there is no hint of grandiosity or vainglory. This is a man among men and women, a seeker after truth, a witness to the incredible among us.

"Friends," he says quietly, and his relaxed words are captured and borne lightly by hidden speakers to every ear, "let's talk today about one of the oldest questions of philosophy: the meaning of life. You'll be relieved to learn that I have an answer to this question," he says with a smile, to a ripple of quiet amusement, "although it would not please the philosophers who first sought its resolution, or the dreary men and women of today's academies who lack the wisdom or even the curiosity to ask it. I can give you a complete and provable four-word answer to that question, What is the meaning of human life? But my concise reply might merely shock and disturb you, friends, unless we first go carefully through the reasoning that leads us to this revelation — the revelation of the grey harvesters who brought me to its understanding."

"Tell us anyway," cries a fervent voice.

"We're up for it, man," cries another.

Deems gazes at them sardonically. "Really? You actually think you can handle this revelation?"

"Sure."

A little voice pipes, "You'll help us understand it," and everyone laughs, friendly and enthusiastic.

"I will indeed, Sandra," Daimon says with a smile. He leans forward, putting his silver elbows on the desk. "Very well, let's take a chance here. What is the meaning of life? The philosophers and theologians and shamans and public relations flacks struggled with this one for thousands of years. I'm here to tell you, friends, that their answers aren't worth a pinch of shit. We can forget them. The speculations of Plato and Aquinas and Kant about the meaning of human life were exactly as informed and interesting as their speculations about nuclear physics. It's not just that they were wrong about everything that science has since revealed to us. It's not just that their guesses were childishly primitive. No, friends, they weren't even asking the right questions. Which is why the answer to that big question, that ultimate question, seems so hard for us to accept. Until we see through it, and through the question. Here's the answer, friends."

He pauses. They crane forward. Surely they have heard this before, know it as their catechism, but the thrill never leaves them, the burst of creepy shock, that exultant shock of freedom and transgression and sheer good humour in Daimon's UFO revelation.

"What is the meaning of human life? It is the same answer the wise scientist gives if asked, What is the meaning of the sun? What is the meaning of a tidal wave that smashes a hundred thousand suffering people caught in its path? What is the meaning of the sky's darkness at night? What is the meaning of a joyful orgasm that begins a new life?"

He stands up abruptly, and the great screen at his back goes scarlet, a shocking explosion of blood or sunset, and then to total black. In the centre of the void, a tiny flower of piercing light opens. Its petals unfold. It is the universe in the first moments of creation, the Big Bang itself, the universe uttered into existence. Organ chords carry the numinous message. Daimon stands before them, his silvery suit catching light from the screen. He is exultant, and he stares at them with absolute conviction.

"What is the meaning of human life?"

"There is no meaning."

IV

July, 2005, Los Angeles

After my mother was slaughtered, butchered and eaten by Valentine the guru and his followers, I spent the next ten years submitting at night to physical and sexual abuse by members of Harmonic Resonance and studying tensely at a cult school during the day. This is hardly the place to dilate upon that atrocious decade, which I blocked from conscious memory until my chance encounter with Benjamin Thompson, Daimon's adopted son.

By 2003, my step-brother was an established therapist in the USA specialising in deep recovery techniques, having broken some years earlier with the Church of Jesus Christ, Time Traveler (as it was known on the West Coast) after my father denounced his earlier claims and slid the movement's substantial holdings into a Malaysian account for the newly announced Scionetics organisation.

My own powers of recall were in terrible shape, of course, for I had developed a barrage of dissociative personality disorders to permit me to cope, however inadequately, with my rough handling by the

Harmonic Resonance cultists. It was my belief, until Ben opened up the hideous can of worms under my skull, that Margaret Rosch had died in an automobile accident six months after our arrival in the United States, and that I had been adopted by her ditzy friend Katie, whom I called "Mom" from that day hence.

The most curious aspect of this hidden life is that Benjamin had no slightest inkling of our relationship, or of the type of banal horror he would unmask when the hypnotic probing began in his comfortable Los Angeles office. From all the indicator instruments I filled out tediously, a barrage of Minnesota Multiphasic Personality Inventories, Hopkins Image Recognition Test cards, Barber Suggestibility Indices and so on, he had expected that I was a prime candidate for alien abductee of the year.

It was not true; to the best of my knowledge I have never been visited by the grey gynaecologists, never gone into their high laboratories for probing and ovary pillage. I'm sure that's true. When I came out of trance, Benjamin sat looking at me with a very pale and bemused expression. His obese black nurse busied herself with the Mac voice-activated transcriber, a machine prone to lexical ambiguity unless watched closely, and her matronly presence protected both of us from any possible subsequent forensic disputes.

I could remember little of my hypnotic testimony. "Was I abducted by a UFO?" I asked my new therapist hopefully. Anything was better than this awful *not knowing*.

He coughed, and coughed again. Something seemed to be stuck in his throat, and I doubt that it was an alien implant.

"Your name is not Angel," he told me, evading my question, "it's Rosa. Rosa Rosch."

No, my lost life did not instantly flood back into my conscious awareness like a dam bursting. I looked at him as if he were the one with the mental problem.

"What?"

Benjamin sat where he was and extended his beautiful hand to within 20 centimetres of my own. "May I hold your hand?"

I gave my permission. His grip was warm and firm, if, I thought, a trifle damp. He was anxious. His eyes darted about my face.

"Rosa, you are my step-sister."

I withdrew my hand and got smartly off the couch. "Send me your bill," I said coldly, making for the door. The nurse somehow got in my way, and Benjamin reached past her and took my hand again, increasing his grip.

"They did terrible things to you, Angel," he said. "They took away your mother, and your name, and your history, and your peace of mind. But at least they were not able to harm the rest of your family. We thought you were gone for good, Rosa." There were genuine tears in his eyes. "If you wish to see your father, I can arrange a meeting."

I was thunderstruck.

"My father? Don't be silly, Dr Thompson, my father died many years ago."

"No," Benjamin told me, with a smile, "your father is alive and kicking."

"Who is he?" I forced myself to ask, through lips anaesthetised with fear and hope. This man was clearly out of his tree. Dr Ben placed credence, after all, in the routine abduction and pillage of a tenth of the population of these United States, so he was patently unhinged. But then I was slowly remembering, through a numb, shaking haze, the details of the regression: that my mother had been hacked up and stir-fried by sweet-natured people, my own extended mystical family, who claimed to be vegetarians.

"Your father is quite a famous fellow," Benjamin told me, with a certain ambiguous satisfaction. It is hard to dislike Deems, after all. "The Reverend Daimon Keith, founder of Scionetics."

We had not been permitted to read the *National Enquirer* at Harmony, or indeed watch vulgar television programs, and after my escape I had never gotten into the habit. I didn't have a clue what he was talking about.

V

August 1970, inside the UFO

He opened his eyes, and it was happening again. Were they under the bed, hiding beneath the fall of the blankets? Were they peeking at him from the crack of the closet's open door? Were they lurking behind the door? No. The door was closed, it was deep in the middle of the night. Everyone else in the house was asleep. He wanted to huddle into the comforting warmth of body-heated sheets and covers, but somehow they had been pulled away. It was cold. He felt so cold that he was sure he must be shivering, but his legs and arms were so heavy that he could not even shiver. They were standing there next to his bed, looking at him with their huge dark eyes.

"Go away," he said, wanting to scream.

They were just out of view, at the edges of his vision. Were there four of them, or five? The grey doctor was one of them, he could tell that much. They would do things to him again. Within his chilled, heavy flesh, his heart thudded. One thin hand came up over the edge of the bed and touched his own bare hand with a metal rod. He yelped, once, and then his heart slowed, calmed.

"What?" he asked sluggishly. "What?"

He was to go with them once more. They meant to put him on their ship and invade his body again. Despite the effects of the rod, his blood seemed to cool even further. His stomach contracted in fear. Light poured suddenly from the wall between his bedroom and the backyard. The small grey people, dirty-white people, big-eyed bugs without mouths or noses passed into the light with jerky, spasmodic steps. Like frames of a badly-edited old film. Jump cuts. Merging into each other like some sort of overlap. He was in the air and moving into the blue light.

It was so cold. The light was gone. He lay tilted on his side somehow, the blood draining into the left side of his face and body. The slab was hard, unyielding. Yes, they had brought him into the round room again. He recognised the heavy stink of the place. What do they eat? he thought blurrily. What kind of awful crap do they suck up through those lipless little mouths? The grey doctor touched his forehead with a needle. It was sharp, long, glinting in the dimness. The doctor pushed it hard into his skull, like a drill, and it hurt. It was agonising! He could not believe that they were doing this to him again. The sadistic bastards. Don't they know anything about pain? He told himself that he would teach them about pain if they let him loose, if they withdrew this sickening heaviness from his arms and legs. Tears flooded his closed eyes.

"Why are you resisting?" asked the one he called Klar–2.

"It hurts so much," he whimpered. The needle came out of his cranium now and, without cleaning it, the grey doctor put it up into his left nostril. A blob of blood and grey goo clung to the needle as it went deep into his nose. He wished he could faint, or just die. The pain was excruciating, and they would not let him scream or turn away. The needle drilled and drilled, and a stench of burning entered the whole of his head like a ponderous cloud. Out came the needle, the drill, and one of the others handed Klar–2 a long flexible tube with a three-clawed grip at its snout. The grey doctor pushed the new thing up into his nostril. Light burst through his head, and for a moment he did lose consciousness. Despite the torpor they had induced in him, he convulsed in agony as the device came out of his nose. Blearily, he saw that its tiny claw now held a small burred sphere. Klar–2 held it up for general inspection. A drop of blood fell from the device. The grey doctor's eyes were huge and dark, a brown almost black. Throbbing, burning pain hung in his head.

Two of the small aliens took him by the hand, one on each side. The slab rotated until it stood vertical, and then, to his horror and disbelief, it swivelled forward another thirty or forty degrees. He dangled above them, unsupported. This was not free-fall, not a region of the ship without gravity. From time-lapsed moment to moment he felt dizzily that he might fall and smash his nose — his tender, brutalised nose! — on the segmented metal deck. Instead he somehow remained stuck to the hard surface while they inspected him with their gadgets, their stupid toys. He realised suddenly that he was so cold because they had stripped him naked. At the same moment, one of them touched his penis with its machine. To his horror, he instantly got an erection. His rage increased.

"You bastards! Leave me alone, you shits."

They stepped aside into shadows, and the slab whirled back to the horizontal. He lay, heavy, immobile, with his ridiculous hard-on sticking straight up at the lens or light or whatever it was on the ceiling. Out of the corner of his eye he saw a seamless doorway open in the wall to his left, close again. A woman in a silvery cloak and long stringy pale hair came into the chamber, and the aliens did their jump-cut retreat as she approached the slab.

His humiliation was complete. The woman was not quite human, but there was no telling his fucking mindless dick that. It quivered, a randy jolt that was not quite an ejaculation. He remembered that they had done this before. They had brought some kind of tube over and connected it to his penis as if he were a prize bull, and he'd spurted his jism into it even as he had roared his furious rejection of them. Everything blurred. Cliché or not, this had to be a nightmare, a dream, the sort of fantasy you get when you've gone over the edge, cracked up; a stupid, unbelievable image dredged from horror movies.

Something light and cool touched his right eyelid, and he realised that he had been lying hunched with his eyes tightly clamped shut. The pale-haired woman regarded him without expression. She touched her own garment twice, at throat and groin, and it fell from her. Somehow, crumpled, it flew across the room and stuck to the side of the chamber.

She pushed him off the slab.

The metal floor struck his shoulder, and his left ankle clipped the hard edge of the slab as he fell. Emotions collided inside him: outrage and hilarity. He lay on the slick floor, rubbing his ankle, and started to laugh. He pushed himself to a standing position, conscious of his absurd hard-on, and looked over his stinging shoulder at the woman.

She had got herself on to the slab and lay there looking expressionlessly at the ceiling lens. Naked and unpleasant as a fish, she was stretched out like someone expecting a disagreeable medical examination. The grey doctor touched his arm, and he jumped. Where had that bastard come from?

You will give her a baby, Klar–2 instructed him in the weird way they had, without opening his slitty mouth.

"Fuck you!"

There was perhaps the faintest tinge of ironic amusement in the alien's gaze.

He looked back at the woman. At least she was human. Sort of. Her hair was long and unappealing, Alice in Wonderland grown up a bit. On the face of it she should have been attractive, but something about her rigid presence repelled him. Her breasts were small, but sagged a little. Her public hair was thick, untrimmed. She saw him looking at her and opened her legs, lifting her knees. The grey doctor gave him a push in the back.

"Forget it!"

But a kind of sexual pulse passed through him, a perverse pleasure at this insanely obscene spectacle. What, they abduct you into a fucking flying saucer and stick needles up your nose and drill your brain, and then they expect you to root some hybrid alien? Jesus! His erection could not make up its mind. Klar–2 struck him more firmly in the small of his back, and the lights on the control patches around the walls began to fizz and flicker. He had not noticed any lights earlier, or any control surfaces.

The slab was now twice its previous width, a narrow double bed for a celestial wedding. Christ! He approached the woman hesitantly, and let his hand fall on her ribcage. His erection was sagging. Her flesh had never seen sunlight and seemed slightly moist. With a sigh, he clambered on to the slab and lay next to her. There was no response. He played for a moment with her stringy hair, touched one small nipple briefly, sent his fingers down between her legs. She failed to react to his caresses. He licked his fingers and tried again. A sour, faintly rank odour rose from her body as her cunt moistened. He hoisted himself dutifully over her supine body and tried to enter her, but his erection had subsided.

To his amazement, he found himself muttering, "I'm sorry."

The woman looked at him, looked away.

"Just a moment."

He tried to kiss her, and her mouth remained closed and unresponsive. Humiliated, he lay like a log on her.

"It might help if I knew your name," he said.

Cinder, she told him. Had he heard her correctly? A cold demon from hell? The Cinderella of the flying saucers? Was he the prince, then, trying to fit his foot into her glass slipper? Foot: ha! Inch was more like it. But her name fired something in him. His hard-on half returned. He touched her, touched himself, forced himself somehow into her. The grey doctor was watching them with his awful black owl's eyes, and nudged him at the base of the spine with a device. Whimpering, he came in a thin trickle.

He lay exhausted and sick at heart on the slab as she got carefully to her feet and dressed again in the silver garment. "Why won't you tell me anything about yourselves?" he asked bitterly. "Who the hell are you people? How dare you use us like this?"

We have transferred our souls, bodies and minds into computer implementation and moved millions of light-years back into your time dimension, the Cinder creature told him coldly. Our command centre is in another dimension beyond the supposed god you call the sun. We are millions of light-years backwards. The voice you are hearing has been sent billions of light-years ahead.

"I don't understand," he said, sitting up and hugging himself. He felt sticky and abused. "What is this bullshit? 'Light-years' isn't time, it's a distance. A schoolchild could tell you that."

In the singularity metric, the grey doctor informed him, time and space are unitary.

"You mean a black hole?"

One little point collapses all dimensions, the woman told him. Powers gather through that point. It is the main channel for tuning into worlds with greater probability.

"Dimensions? Like, time and space? You mean time and space vanish when you go through a black hole? Is that how you get here?"

The accumulation of time does not vanish. You must understand that space with an infinite rotational energy tensor excludes time. We gather it in and put it to work. Our devices are using up time.

He did not understand. He sat there on the slab, downcast and tired and sad, and waited for them to send him back in their beams of light.

VI

FILM MAKER SNATCHED BY LITTLE GREY MEN
By JUDITH FRIPP (Melbourne, Tuesday)

In 1952, Californian guru and café handy man George Adamski snapped a flying saucer and met the ski instructor from Venus who drove it. In 1975, timber worker Travis Walton was "abducted" by aliens for five days. Two years ago, Australian pilot Frederick Valentich vanished at sea after his plane was buzzed by a UFO, and hasn't been seen since. Now it's the turn of slick ad man and director Damon Keith, 35 (photo at right), to vacation on Venus.

Anyway, that's the explanation from his step-son, Ben Thompson, who watched them take Damon in a blue beam of light. Ben's real father is the famous cinematographer Vic Thompson, now working in Europe and the US with Peter Weir and Fred Schepisi among other ex-pat luminaries of local cinema. His worried mother Zelda, the former Mrs Thompson, is now married to Damon. Confused?

The vanished Mr Keith is known in Melbourne's bohemian arts circles for some entertaining pranks played when he was a comic turn and anti-Vietnam activist at Carlton's La Mama and Pram Factory theatres.

St Kilda police were not commenting on the bizarre abduction claim, although they stated that Mr Keith had been listed routinely as a missing person. By a strange coincidence, Mr Keith recently returned from California, after an unsuccessful search for his daughter. Five-year-old Rosa was allegedly taken to the USA without his permission by her unmarried mother, Ramona M. Roach.

An officer warned that anybody making a false statement to police could be charged and prosecuted. No UFOs were booked in the bayside suburb for exceeding the speed of light on the rainy Saturday night.

Some late night disco revellers made independent reports of a "bright disc" hovering below the clouds near Luna Park. A local astronomer said this was "almost certainly" a shooting star, or meteor.

Ben Thompson, 18, admits he has been a "flying saucer nut" since childhood, when he believes he himself was contacted by creatures from outer space. He can even tell you where they come from — a planet called Zeeta Reticule!

Asked when he expects his step-father to return from his Spielberg adventure (remember Close Encounters of the Third Kind?), the second-year psychology student said he feared for Mr Keith's life.

"They killed Captain Mandell," he said, *referring to a famous jet pilot who crashed while chasing what US authorities say was a weather balloon.*

And who are these little grey men? Aren't they meant to be green? A common error, says Ben. The UFO guys (and sexy gals!) come in plenty of shapes and colours, but strangely enough hardly any of them are green.

Anyone sighting Mr Keith on the ground is asked to contact St Kilda police, who will notify his concerned family.

VII

4 January 2000, Langley interrogation unit 8
Despite the clamour and frenzy caused by my father's second disappearance, he had not been abducted yet again by the Zetans. On the contrary, he seethed in a massively secure apartment (call it a cell and you would not be far wrong) in Maryland, USA. Every night he was fed well, given access to a superior choice of cable first release movies, permitted to swim or exercise in a compact but comprehensive gymnasium, all in the company of one pert young woman or another, each of whom made it clear that as part of her duties she was happy to stay the night in his king-size bed. Every morning he was fed an ample breakfast and then taken to a stark white room and attached to myographs and other stress-indicator devices, and asked by a fresh team his opinions about UFOs, world politics, and the meaning of life.

"I'm writing a new book," he told his fourth pair of interrogators peevishly. "Look in my notebook, there's a directory called *The Zygote Paradigm*."

A red-headed CIA scientist with a kindly expression flicked through his notebook menu and accessed a file. "I have it here, Mr Keith. Do you actually expect us to believe this?"

"I couldn't give a flying fuck. Believe what you like."

Nobody slapped him heavily about the chops. The monitoring equipment did not fry his nerves with an overdose of amps. Spiegle, a fat psychiatrist who hardly spoke during the first couple of hours of their interview, sat back in his easy chair, scratched his well-tailored belly, sighed. Tanner, the red-haired man, said, "Mr Keith, if what you claim is true, this is the most momentous news since the discovery of the wheel."

My father stared at him, and then away, drolly, to an imaginary or perhaps a hidden camera. He knew that much already.

"Tell us about their propulsion system."

"Do you know how a bicycle derailleur gear system works?"

"What?"

"Have you ever ridden a bike?"

"Is this one of your cracker-barrel parables, Mr Keith?"

"I'm an Australian, Dr Tanner," my father told him. "If you're going to insult me, you might at least use an Australian epithet. Ask me if I'm pissing in your pocket, for example. Ask me if I'm bullshitting you. Don't bother, I'm not. It's true, every word, and if you don't believe me you can check with Sir Lindsay Taggard."

Incredibly, they had it on file. "The public servant you hoaxed back in April, 1972? I don't think he'd give you a sterling reference, Mr Keith."

"Call me Daimon, for Christ's sake. Call me Deems. We're old pals by now, aren't we?" He had never seen them before this morning, nor had the previous pairs of interrogators shown their faces once they'd left the room.

"What *about* bike gears?"

"Have you ridden one lately? A trail bike, say, with a lovely little set of ten or twelve gears to get you up the side of the mountain."

"Not lately, but yes. So?"

"How do the derailleurs work?"

"Why, they — There's a sprocket, and the chain — I don't know. Is that what you're saying? That we leave that kind of detail to the mechanic in the store?"

"That's what I'm saying. It's metric defects, and beyond that they send it back under warranty."

The psychiatrist eased forward, lit a cigarette, blew its smoke carefully away from Daimon. "Sorry, I know you hate this, but I get stressed, okay? And we're paying for this place, Daimon. Why do you called them 'Zetans' when you know they couldn't possibly be from Zeta Reticuli?"

Deems smiled at him with admiration. "I thought you were the strong silent type. Are you telling me that Betty Hill invented her star map?"

This was an old, old story in UFO lore. When Barney Hill and his wife were kidnapped by the grey gynaecologists, Betty was shown a holographic map of linked stars. Several years later a school teacher named Marjory Fish painstakingly built a scale model of the sun-like stars within 65 light years of Earth, and peered at it until she found a configuration closely matching Betty's hypnotic reproduction of the alien map.

The red-haired physicist snapped down the screen of his notebook. "You dealt with this Zeta crap yourself in that dumb Jesus book of yours, Deems. Fish would have done just as well if she'd turned Hill's dots upside down and hooked the lines together that way. Besides, the Zeta Reticuli binaries are too young and gravitationally destabilising to have habitable planets."

My father said happily, "I love it when I see you buggers bite. 'Zetan' is a coinage of my own. It has nothing to do with the Fish map. See, the stuff the UFO aliens are built out of is cosmological dark matter, 'Zed-nought' weakly interacting particles. I suppose you illiterate Americans would say 'Zee-zero'. That's why they live near the core of the Earth where the gravity is nice and cosy. So they're Zed-Terrans — Zetans, okay?"

While the physicist had no ready reply to this, the psychiatrist was clearly disappointed; he had expected better of a man of my father's evident intelligence. "I *see*. So you subscribe to the Hollow Earth theory?"

Daimon was disappointed in return.

"Jesus, Spiegle, use your fucking ears. If the Earth was hollow, why would gravity-eaters choose to live there?"

The physicist winked at his colleague. "He's right, Leo. If his aliens are made of WIMPs or even WILPs, they'd sink straight down to the middle of the earth. Or the sun, for that matter. Do they live on the sun, Daimon?"

"*In* the sun, Tanner. Why else do you think every culture in history has worshipped the sun and the stars?"

"Well, light and warmth might have something to do with it, don't you think?"

"Uh huh, sure." My father got up and went to the nice little kitchen, where an espresso machine burbled quietly. He pulled the handle and steamy coffee spurted. "Anyone else while I'm up?"

Tanner raised his arm. "And some cookies."

"What are WILPs?" murmured the psychiatrist.

"WIMPS are weakly interacting massive particles," the physicist muttered back, "and WILPs are weakly interacting light particles. Not to be confused with photons, which are just light particles." He smirked, obscurely pleased with himself.

"The Zetans are the closest thing we can conceive to spirits," Deems told them, carrying his coffee back into the bleak room, a tall pile of biscuits balanced precariously. "So you see, Heaven turns out to be there in both directions — down below, where the priests told us Hell was, and up above, in the stars."

"You think these aliens are sort of like ghosts?" Spiegle asked grudgingly, "discarnate human souls?"

Daimon laughed out loud, a trifle hysterically.

"No, you don't have a soul, Spiegle," he said, sputtering his coffee. "Neither do you, Tanner. Sorry."

"Oh, I see, only you gifted UFO abductees have souls, right?"

"No, you fuck-wit. Did they lock your brains up when they gave you this damned jailer's job? Of course I don't have a soul, I'm an adult. Do I look like a first trimester foetus to you?"

The psychiatrist seemed taken aback. He opened his mouth, thought better of it, mused in silence. My father ate his chocolate cookie. Spiegle said slowly, "And that's why the occupants look like pre-term humans? They're neotenised, is that it? They remain somehow in the human foetal stage, but develop into a different kind of adulthood. Maybe sexless, even."

"Exactly. They are our children. Without us, there wouldn't be any of them."

"Our children grow up and become us," the physicist pointed out uneasily.

"Not all of them," Deems said. "Not those that miscarry in the womb. Not the abortions. Not the ones the Zetans engender and pilfer from the uterus of an abducted woman. And there's a lot of it going around, trust me. Put your wife under hypnosis and ask her. Or your daughters."

Both interrogators looked back at him without noticeable emotion, although there was the faintest tinge of abhorrence in the physicist's voice. "So. UFO aliens are the souls of the aborted."

"To be precise, they're the WILP complexity-correlates of the human foetal central nervous system," Daimon told them, as he had told the others like them during the past week. Nobody listened. Nothing he said seemed to get cross-indexed from one interrogation team to the next. Someone further up the chain of command was insulating this knowledge. And who could wonder at it? This was appalling news, after all. This was diabolical news. This, clearly, was why the truth about UFOs had never been made public, and never would, not by the political and spiritual princes of the world. The Zetans, in one grotesque and illuminating revelation, had snatched away the foundations of human self-esteem, aspiration, had snatched away meaning itself.

"This is insane," the physicist said angrily. "You're telling us that another kind of evolution is going on, parallel to the universe of quarks and leptons and photons and gravitons. And you want us to accept that the sorry accidents of reproduction, the genetic waste, the biological excess, the mutations, the discards — that these are the heirs of the Kingdom of God?"

"That's what your favourite scriptures tell you," Deems said flatly. He really did not care any longer if they believed him, if they listened, if they paid attention. The grey proctologists would find him, even here under fifteen floors of subterranean steel and concrete, and lift him away to their gassy white operation rooms. The little shits were probably here right now, he thought, sitting in the middle of their air which was the heavy crust of the visible earth, listening in their puzzled way to this dreary exchange between three animals without souls.

"How could an ecology like that evolve before humans invented abortion?" Tanner said, still angry, getting angrier. "Is spiritual progress so swift that they developed their nifty starships in the ten thousand years since the invention of the ... what, Leo? What did the Palaeolithic sluts use to scrape themselves out? Gnawed twigs?"

Unexpectedly, the psychiatrist spoke to him sharply. "Control yourself, Professor Tanner." Spiegle met Daimon's gaze steadily. "They taught us in medical school that spontaneous human abortions account for up to eighty percent of all conceptions. I've always wondered why a replicating system shaped by evolutionary pressures would be so wasteful of metabolic energy and ecological resources."

"Well." Deems shrugged. "The *real* question is, why do so many of us go to term and live our pointless lives? But remnant life does have its useful side, you see. We're their parents, and they have to keep us on our toes. Darwin was right in his limited way. The cockroaches haven't beaten us yet in the Red Queen's Race. Or the retroviruses. All those other creepy little fuckers at the top of the food chain."

"What Red Queen?"

"He means the evolutionary arms race. One species gets smarter or quicker or more wired, and then all the others have to hustle to keep up in the same spot. My God. Abortions. Negative reincarnation. This is, this is …" The government's man looked at him with detestation. "This is techno-gnosticism."

Deems gave a yell of laughter. "I like that! Techno-gnosticism! I'll use it in my next book." Suddenly he hurled his empty coffee cup violently across the room, where it smashed on a white wall. The fragments lay curled on the tan carpet like thin ceramic fingers. "If you sons of bitches ever let me out of here."

VIII

From Rev. Daimon Keith, The Scionetic Paradigm, *Chapter 13, "The Meaning of Life", Los Angeles: Jerome Tarcher, 2002.*

Perhaps by this point some of you will have a few doubts about the truth of what I have written, or even about my sanity! Despite widespread reports of UFO abductions, despite the eerily common elements recorded in hundreds of cases world-wide, many people continue to attribute this testimony to fraud, hysteria, substance abuse or mental breakdown. Some psychiatric specialists believe the experience is caused by a brain disorder known as "transient temporal lobe dysfunction".

I have no argument with these sceptics, for I spent several years examining such explanations myself. Certainly I was not eager to believe in the truth of my dreams of UFO abduction, or even to take literally the dozens of hours of careful hypnotic retrieval of those terrible ordeals. Even when I came to understand that these memories were largely accurate, were not fantasies or confabulations, or masks for childhood sexual abuse, I resisted the message of the Harvesters. Who wants to face the dismal fact that human life is meaningless? What kind of stoical stalwart can deal, day after bleak day, with the awful news that we all — child and adult, felon and saint — have no more significance in the darkly radiant scheme of spiritual evolution than ... what? A snake's discarded husk? A male spider chomped by his female mate after his small spasm has inseminated her?

Worse: than the severed placenta thrown carelessly into a hospital bucket after the bloody labours of birth?

But it is so. I must not hide the truth from you, or from myself.

We are of no more significance in the real universe, the invisible, impalpable immensity of dark matter that comprises the true cosmos, than a lump of bloody afterbirth.

But of course, that is only true from the narrow perspective of our puffed human pretensions. A placenta, after all, however lowly and disposable, is not without meaning to the child it nourishes for nine months in the womb. The growing snake's skin has protected it for a season, before it splits into tatters and is left by the side of the road. A baby's first teeth loosen and fall out within a very few years, and for a day we treasure them whimsically, placing them beneath the child's pillow and promising that a fairy will bear them away to some finer land. We pay our gappy infants in good coin for the privilege. As we tuck a dollar bill beneath the pillow, and whisk the milk tooth into the trash, we do not despise that small fragment of organic detritus. But we do not believe our fairytale, either.

The meaning of the lost tooth is not salvation in a heaven of tooth fairies, it is the adult dentition that springs up to fill its gap. And the meaning of terrestrial life is not a transcendental afterlife for the dying human — starving child or withered sage, automobile accident victim or cancer patient, AIDs patient or his selfless helper. The meaning of human life is not afterlife but afterbirth: we are a disposable stage in the production of the Children of Heaven, our Scions, the first casts, the happy miscarriages, the uncorrupted abortions. Those who perish in the flesh before crude matter has infected, corrupted and swiftly corroded their potentially immortal souls. Little wonder that all the false religions of pomp and human glory, intellectual and fundamentalist alike, denounce abortion as the vilest sin. No. Far from being a sin, a crime, an atrocity, it is the release of our Scions into eternity, and so, even as the churchmen pretend to squabble among themselves, they conspire wickedly to prevent this sacrament, this single good deed of human flesh, this midwifery of heaven.

IX

Three days after his outrageous revelation, on a gorgeous Californian summer's day, Benjamin picked me up in his black retro-fitted Porche 944 Turbo and drove me to my father's West Coast home in Malibu.

I was all of a dither, as you will understand, but I did what I could to hide my emotions. This was easily enough done, given my childhood conditioning, but I also wished to avoid slipping into some disabling multiple personality confusion, so I gave vent to my mixed feelings by squeezing my wide brimmed ozone hat in my hands until its sturdy genetically engineered cotton was crushed into a shapeless lump. Benjamin certainly noticed these small convulsions but, adroit therapist that he was (and is), he refrained from comment.

"Did you get the book I sent over?"

I had been studying the yellowed pages of *The Dying Breed* all morning. None of the photos was labelled, so I could not even be sure if Margaret was included. One woman poised on top of an old automobile, haughty and proud, bore a certain resemblance to the face I saw in the mirror, when I could bear to look in the mirror. Still, it had given me a curious and visceral thrill to see her name on the dedication page, placed there by the man who was allegedly my father. And there was a suite of portraits of babies viewed through glass, rows and ranks of the tiny wrinkled things, big pink heads and squinty eyes, and a wry nurse standing to one side of a complex bit of machinery sustaining a tiny little creature barely alive by the look of it. I had a terrible feeling that one was me.

"Yes, thank you. The courier service is quite reliable now they've started travelling in pairs." Things had calmed down quite a lot since the Year 2000 End of Millennium riots, and the even more explosive Year 2001 True End of Millennium riots, but services were still bumpy.

"Have a look at these," Benjamin said, and passed me a folio. He was a handsome man of 45, more boyish than distinguished, and I trusted him implicitly, which is more than I'd been able to do with anyone else since the day I'd escaped from the cult. The photographs were in a variety of styles and voices. I peered out, two or three years old, in big eyed fascination from some of them, or painted colourful daubs with my fingers, or stuffed food into my mouth, laughing and happy. This time I recognised myself at once, and my adult eyes burned with misery and loss. I turned the sheets slowly, examining each hungrily. The first convincing shot of Margaret caused me to utter a soft cry, a hand squeezed at my diaphragm, for it was me staring back at myself: an offbeat beauty, if one made allowances for her awful seventies' haircut and make-up and clothes: defended, waspishly amused. They had burned all her photos at Harmony, of course. Restrained by my seat belt, I leaned forward in the urban racing seat to hug the picture to me, eyes prickling, breathing in little gasps.

X

The Reverend Daimon Keith lived in ecologically responsible luxury. Behind a high fence laced with sensors and lethal devices, his marvellous house, designed according to principles allegedly revealed by UFO architects but thought to resemble certain embargoed ideas from blockaded Saudi, sucked at the sun and polluted air like a flower, and turned them into a cool, faintly rose-scented breeze, gentle indirect lighting, and full-surround musical background. I walked into a round white room carpeted in pale green, with startling art works suspended on the walls: thick slabs of wood in bright gold and purple and crimson, curves and arcs above and radiating bars below, Samuel Barber's exquisite Violin Concerto entering its second movement and tearing my heart out as it did so, and my father, clad for the occasion in normal business suit, having forsaken his silver flying saucer garment or rainbow robes, standing up to greet me from a sunken pit in the centre of the room. His throat worked visibly, and he swayed, and to my astonishment and immense gratification he burst into tears.

"Jesus," he blurted. "Margaret!" Then he shook his head, squeezed his eyes shut, came toward me like a man dazed. "I'm sorry, Flake. Oh God."

We went into each other's arms as if we had never been separated, and everything went very runny and snotty for a while.

XI

Daimon flew me to Sydney, where his wife Zelda preferred to live, and we walked along Bondi Beach while a pair of inconspicuous Scionetics heavies paced us for our own protection. Somehow the Australians had managed to clean up the foreshore with its wonderful white sand, and depollute the blue and white surf, which had been turning into a sewer, Deems told me, last time I'd been here with my murdered mother. We rolled up our trouser legs and splashed at the edge of the mild winter sea.

"I don't understand any of it," I told him, holding his hand. By rights, according to the symptomatology of my condition, I should not have been able to bear his touch, or anyone's. Alternatively, I should have been hard at the task of seducing him with glancing laughing eyes and hints of cleavage, all that. Somehow, though, wonderfully, this was, for the moment at least, simply homecoming. I was all wept out by that point, and my heart was torn two ways at once: by uncomplex happiness and by a more profound dull emptiness that made mockery of the happiness. "What does it mean?" I asked my father, who had made hundreds of millions of dollars and bought the huge old building up on the top of the bluff by telling hundreds of thousands of desperate people his awful answer to that question.

"Come on," he said, "let's get some fish and chips."

We bought piping hot fried shark in batter — it is called "flake" in Australia, which made us both laugh — and french fries, and a six-pack of light beer to wash it down with. One of the heavies fetched a thick woven blanket so we could sit on the sand without getting piles, my father said, wincing at some memory, and a pair of light, insulated capes to keep the breeze at bay. Daimon tore open the paper bag of french fries — "chips" — and inhaled the dietetically dubious odour of salt and vinegar.

"The meaning of it all? Darling, let me tell you what I've learned, what the greys have taught me. You won't enjoy hearing this, but it will," he said seriously, "set you free."

I was apprehensive.

"You're going to say that human life has no meaning," I told him. I knew already that this was his scandalous doctrine, because I had gobbled up a couple of potted and scathing magazine exposes of Scionetics in the previous days, and I wasn't buying it.

He popped the top on a stubby and sucked froth into his mouth. The sun, burning down from the north of the sky, caught his UVA-machine-tanned forehead, slipped down the laugh lines beside his eyes. He should have been wearing a hat, of course, as I was, because the ozone hole was straight overhead in Sydney, but he was protected against cancer, he said, by the painful ministrations of the Harvesters.

"No meaning? Not exactly," he said. "Look, Flake — hey, you don't mind me calling you that, do you?"

I smiled primly. "Not so long as you share *that* flake with me."

He tore me off a hot fat piece of fish, wrapped one end in a double thickness of paper to save my fingers, and passed it over.

"All right, Flake, can you sit still for my two minute lecture on the meaning of meaning?"

I shrugged, nibbling shark. It was sweet and delicious.

"Okay, the starting point is that everyone gets everything arse backwards because they're always facing the wrong way. I mean the philosophers, the theologians, the anthropocists, the fucking quantum holists, everyone except for a handful of old-fashioned semioticians. And even they squibbed when it came to the jump."

"Oh dear." I pushed back the brim of my hat and gazed across the Pacific ocean. Sea gulls circled, trying to snatch our fries. "Sorry, this reminds me of Valentine and the great truth of Harmonic Resonance." The comparison, risen unbidden, made me shudder. Deems watched me. He did not put his arm around me, which was wise at that moment.

"Yes," he said, "we all think we're the first and only ones to understand the secret of the universe. I was always suspicious of people who thought they knew it all. I loved to take the mickey out of the bastards." He sighed. "I'd still be running about like a perpetual adolescent if the Harvesters hadn't told me what's what."

"And what is what?"

A lolloping dog ran past, spraying us with sand. I threw him a cooling chip, and he missed it. What was his notion of the good life? This, surely. And what did his doggy mind imagine was the meaning of the world? But we were not doggies. We made our own chips and beer and polluted our own beaches and cleaned them up if we felt like it.

"Look at the words we use when we ask the most poignant questions, Flake," my father said. "When your mother abducted you and ran off to the States, I raved and flailed and ranted. *Why?* I screamed. Why did this happen to me? I flew to America and tried to find you, and nobody would tell me, and then the fucking guru went to ground with all his witless devotees, taking you and your mother with him, and I had to come back to Australia, and then I was snatched for three weeks by the Harvesters — Christ, it sounds like a bloody soap opera! Well, I ranted and flailed, when they brought me back, and spent a lot of time screaming, *Why?* And when your mother was killed and they told you she'd died in a car crash, you probably ran about asking Why, why, why?"

"I was five years old," I told Deems. "Of course I did."

"Okay, what's the common element here? Three different strokes of ill fortune, and we keeping asking Why? But that's a question that is only appropriately addressed to an intention. Do you see what I mean? Why had Margaret stolen you to America? I've thought about this a lot, Angel —"

"Rosa," I said.

He gulped, and his eyes misted.

"Rosa, I was a typical male of my era. Well, not typical, but even so. And your mother was a confused but strong woman, and she wasn't going to put up with my bullshit. Of course she had to go away. It wasn't me, precisely — it was all of us, our stupid culture, the way we find meaning in attachment to our kids ... She thought Zelda and I were stealing you away from her, and she was probably right."

"I don't even remember Zelda," I said in a grainy tone.

"You'll meet her tonight, she's looking forward enormously to seeing you. But the point is, I wasn't asking for those sorts of answers. I wanted to know Why is the universe doing this to me? Why has the plan of my life — the central plan of the universe, after all — why has it gone so unfairly off the rails? I'm the hero of this fucking movie, right? How dare the extras screw with my happy ending?"

"I suppose we all put ourself in the main role," I conceded, because that's what he wanted me to agree to. But I didn't, not really. My response to disappointment and pain and, indeed, intolerable torment had been to shrink myself, to split my soul into the colours of the rainbow and hide most of the hues in darkness. That's why I've been able to construct this history of my father and my mother and myself, don't you see? I'm the perfect biographer. I have no self. I'm anyone's. I'm anyone.

"Actors spend a lot of time obsessing about Why questions," Deems said. "Motivation. 'What's my character's motivation?' They're looking for a few simple codes, cues to the impulses and behavioural channels of the personality they're about to impersonate. And it's not so strange or hard to do that, because evolution built our brains to perform exactly that function. It's why people love stories."

"We've evolved to be actors?" I stared at him. "I think you've been living in Los Angeles too long."

Deems laughed gustily. "You're Margaret's daughter all right." We both stared at the horizon for a time. "If you're a horse," he said then, patiently, "your DNA built you to graze in a herd, and avoid lions. If you're a lion, your DNA built you to hunt horses in the company of a small squadron of other lions. In both cases, you need an internal model of social life — your own, and your prey's or predator's. When a horse sees the grass sway, it's a considerable benefit if she asks herself horsily, Why did that happen? What's its meaning? Lion or wind? Sniff sniff. Freak, shit, Lion! Lion! Meaning starts by interpreting as deliberate codes the lumpy happenstances of the world."

I mused on this. "It's the other way round, isn't it? We interpret the meaning that's there. I mean, if a Chinese translator interprets my words from English, she's got to start by understanding my meaning and sort of ... carry it over to the other language?"

"Okay, both processes entail each other. The grass means food to our horsie, and its motion might mean danger, because our horsie means food to the lions. So the nutritive values and the possibility of lions are both there in the grass, I guess, before any act of interpretation takes place. But you can't say they have any meaning, in that exact sense, unless the horse is there to start with."

Some Aussie bravos were taking to the frothy water in gaudy wetsuits, clambering on to windsurfers. We watched their antics. Their play was as meaningless, as arbitrary, as open to an inpouring of significance as a whale sounding, as the Budd Hopkins Guardians on my father's Los Angeles' walls. For the surfers, its meaning was the joy of sinew and muscle and eye doing their stuff, the body's balance sustained against the chaotic turbulence of the sea. I sighed.

"I mentioned two other cases," Deems said. "My three-week abduction, and your mother's death. Why did they happen? What was the meaning?"

I sent him a sidelong glance. "Well, I don't even know if it did happen. Your disappearance. Sorry."

He gazed back without expression. "It doesn't matter, you see. Call it a metaphor, if you like."

I was relieved. "All right."

"The answer is, there is no meaning to either event — in the usual, human-centred sense. Something happens, okay. A tree falls over in the forest. All sorts of factors led up to that event — the rain has weakened the soil, the tree's DNA program has closed down its growth cycle so it's gone rotten inside, the wind has picked up because of the accidental arrangement of snow and cloud halfway around the world. So it's all explicable, down to the level of atoms if you had time enough to track it all. But it's not part of any plan. And if you happen to be walking under the tree at that moment and it squashes you flat, all we can say is — 'shit happens'."

"Or: don't walk under trees. That might be one meaning."

"A meaning we read into the sad event, sure. We don't draw it out, we put it in. That's what our brains are good at — making up stories, scripts, schemata. The cognitive scientists have a whole batch of words for this stuff. All of it boils down to one hard fact: we love to write the universe into a text, and then to interpret it as if someone else had written it. That's okay. Horses do it, lions do it, the birds and bees do it." He grinned wickedly. "It's only when we start to fetishise our little knack that it goes crazy and cancerous and eats us up from the inside. We start *looking* for meaning everywhere, forgetting that *we're* the ones who *put* it there."

It was getting chilly, and I felt sorry for those guys out there on their windsurfers. But then nobody was forcing them to do it. We stood up and stretched, shook sand off the blanket by holding one corner of it each, handed the folded bundle to one of Daimon's patient bodyguards who took it back to the car. In the froth at the edge of the sea I noticed two or three limp, diaphanous jellyfish. I bent down to stir them with my finger, and drew back in disgust. They were condoms, washing about in the sandy foam.

"Daimon, this sounds like the crappy New Age solipsism I grew up with. 'You create your own universe.' I'm sorry, but that's the worst kind of hypocrisy."

"No, no," my father said placidly, placing his big-toed feet carefully in someone else's line of footsteps in the sand. He had to hop a little. "All we create is our own meaning. The world, other people, our own inaccessible inward systems — all of that provides the building materials, and the landscape for the architect to work in. But the meaning we end up with is a construct of our minds. It has no necessary connection to the actual priorities of the universe."

"Which are?"

He laughed softly. "Which have nothing to do with us, I'm sorry to say."

"With us human beings? Benjamin said you don't believe people have souls. Is that what he meant?"

"We *produce* souls," my father said. "Cows produce methane when they fart, and destroy the ozone layer. Radioactive decay deep inside the Earth produces thermal plumes that cause volcanoes. We produce foetuses with souls. If they're lucky, they die in time. Or the grey doctors come down and harvest them."

I heard all this with the greatest disquiet, understanding none of it yet. It was too soon, and luckily Deems changed the topic to my own life, the confused and miserable tale of my tragical history with and without my mother.

XII

Later we drove up to the great house when Zelda lived, and I met the rest of my family. My step-mother looked pretty good for a woman nearing seventy. They gave me a fine guest room overlooking the sea, and I slept with the window open for the first time in years. Waves hushed at the foot of the cliff. I dreamed of condoms, and small things squirming, and woke screaming in the strange space of the room.

XIII

A month later, Deems had vanished again. He hasn't come back. His devotees assure me that he has been taken to some finer realm — Mars, perhaps, where he thought his visage had been shaped like an icon gazing at the stars, or the centre of the Earth, or to some alternative dimension. How can I know what to believe? Does it matter? There is no text of the universe outside our inscription of its glyphs, and no meaning beyond our free interpretation. My father, true to his own analysis, or perhaps flying in its face, affected to despise biographies, to detest movies and novels and stories of every kind. "Fiction is the gossip of those who don't get out much, Rosa," he told me, a week before he disappeared, "purveyed by those who don't get out at all." Whether or not we have souls and an afterlife is the kind of question, perhaps the kind of fiction, one should abandon at the departure lounge into adulthood, I now see. I live a quiet life of satisfactory despair. Sometimes I dream of my mother, but just as often I confuse her with Katie, recalling only my Mom's heavy Southern drawl. Zelda and I run the household, hardly an arduous duty, waiting for Daimon's return, and the Scionetics heavies grow more bizarre with each year but dutifully top up our swollen bank accounts. Benjamin and I have two healthy babies. Neither of them, to the best of our knowledge, has been abducted by the Harvesters. I float in the huge tub, scrubbing at my pale flesh, and dream of great dark eyes in pale swollen skulls, and tell myself again and again the story of Deems and Margaret and my beloved Benjamin and all the sweet burdens of time.

XIV

The Starseed Signals received by Dr Leary and Wayne Benner in Folsom Prison, in July-August, 1973, tell us that it is time for "life on Earth to leave the planetary womb and learn to walk through the stars". Life on this planet is now at the halfway point, having produced "nervous systems capable of communicating with and returning to the Galactic Network" where our Interstellar Parents await us. Mankind is about to discover "the key to immortality in the chemical structure of the genetic code ... the scripture of life".

At this time, the signals invite us, the "voyage home is possible ... Mutate! Come home in glory".

— Brad Steiger, *The Gods of Aquarius: UFOs and the Transformation of Man*, 1976.

He hovers, curled in upon himself like a great balding, wrinkled foetus. It's the usual hazy nowhere under pale ribbed metal. Cupped by buoyancy, rocking airborne above dull convexity, he dreams his lucid dreams. All the cycles of metabolism flow as before, his chest expands and contracts in the mechanical bellows of breath. At the edge of awareness, hiding or at least refusing to disclose themselves there in the shadows, the grey Harvesters peer with their unblinking gaze. All about and through him is the humming rapid motion of a billion molecular probes at his trillion synapses. Without waking, without sleeping, he is aware of this prosaic violation.

"Take me back," he tells them through lips too heavy to open. His voice is blurred and hopelessly distorted, lost in the anechoic void, but he knows that they hear him by other than vocal means.

Klar–2 speaks to him through dark wraparound eyes. You must stay with us this time. We will take you to a city all of gold, where the leaves of the tree are for the healing of all nations.

"Horseshit," my father says, forcing his lips to shape the syllables.

Behold, a pale horse, the grey doctor tells him without the slightest trace of humour: and his name that sat on him was Death.

Deems is shown the customary storm of visions. The world is consumed in nuclear fire. Great chasms open in its soft, ripened skin, and all the numbers of humankind tumble into the burning depths. Air sours, foully poisoned, an acid-rain storm that blights every flowering plant and tree and crop in the world. Maggots eat at lambs and babies. Transparent demons move like wraiths at the centre of the earth among the last of the living, tormenting them eternally. It is a terrifying spectacle, disturbing as a nightmare one cannot awaken from. But Deems has been this way before. He is too frightened to laugh, but it is preposterous. This has to be the unadulterated noise of the unconscious, the cheese sandwich he ate before turning in, a mask or screen for something else.

"Pull the other one," he croaks, "it has bells on it."

A little girl comes forward, thin as a Bosnian refugee, pale and gaunt, limbs like a foal's. Her hair is thin and straggly, and she looks at him without fear or expectation.

Take her in your arms, Klar–2 tells him. Give her your human warmth. Kindle her into life. This is your daughter.

"Why do you have doorways and ramps if you can take us through walls and fly us in the air," sceptical Deems insists, exhausted and scratchy. "Why must you torment us with crude surgery when a painless scraping of cells from the inside of the mouth could give you more genetic material than you'd ever need? After all this time, Christ, two thousand years, ten thousand, why are you still tampering with our poor bodies? If you can calm us and heal our hurt, why do you continue to bring such torment to your victims? If we have no souls, why do you terrify simple village children with visions of eternal damnation?"

His throat is dry, hoarse, and the mouse dropping stench is making him feel sick. He tries to turn his head, to look Klar–2 and the others straight in the eye, and they stir uneasily and shift like shadows, like candle smoke in the candle flame's heat.

The little hybrid child gazes at him, arms hanging desolate at her sides. She wears a kind of white shift, and her limbs are painfully thin.

He struggles in the air, struggles for purchase on nothingness, with immense effort brings his heavy feet over the edge of the operating table and down to the tepid warmth of the floor. They rustle and move aside, withdrawing into the shadows, into the light. The girl child stands dumbly, fatherless, motherless, aching, alien, human.

Daimon Keith, my father, reaches out his own arms, then, at last, and enfolds me within them.

AFTERWORD

When I was 13, 15, I was besotted by flying saucers. On dark crisp nights I would creep out from my bed — my "room" was a bunk next to our laundry/toilet, a back verandah fixed up with louvred windows, a little draughty but it allowed me to read forbidden magazines without anyone catching me at it — creep out and lie on my back to stare up with my heart all swollen, gazing at the hard little bright lights and dustings of the stars, waiting for the UFOs to loom overhead. And not just waiting patiently — *impelling* their attention, soliciting with the force of my desire, calling on the same telepathic wavelengths that young Peter Reich was using around the same time, beyond the curve of the earth and across the world's largest ocean, in his doomed attempts to fetch back his mad father Wilhelm, former favourite of Freud, master of the therapeutic orgasm and the pale blue force-field of orgone energy, captain, poor little Peter believed, of flying saucers, crying out to the good aliens (or were they the bad ones after all?) to fetch back his daddy. But it was the FBI who'd nabbed his old man and flung him in jail. Mine had been grabbed by anti-communists, conscripted to their cause in the decades before Vietnam, giving meaning and backbone to his toolmaker's life, plugging the downward thrust of the Red Menace from Asia and points north, wasting his family's, like, you know, *quality time* in endless caucuses and late night plots of unionists against unionists, right against left, informant against spy ... mindboggling self-denying stuff, the very contrary, one might suppose, of Reich's orgasmic raptures. Catholics were not permitted contraceptives in those dark days and nights, as I gather they still are not, although these days the rules are less rigorously attended. So my parents brought six living children into the swelling population, and a dead foetus or two, but without, one might also suppose, a great deal of additional whoopee. So there was a penumbra of anxiety in our household, of shouting hysteria, of stress and strain to go with the poverty. So I went looking in the dark of my early adolescent nights for the aliens. I knew that when they came for me it would be a little better. Perhaps — who knew — perhaps it would even be glorious?

As soon as I was permitted to enter the adults' section of the municipal library I had found mysterious hidden truths lying all about me on the shelves, declaring themselves to me if to few others — a book, in particular, by an upperclass Englishman (although I didn't know that then, didn't know about Honourables and their kind, thank God, being an Australian) named Desmond Leslie, and by an American working-class stiff and scamster named George Adamski, "Professor" Adamski, a handyman for a small cafe below Mount Palomar where, according to my astronomy texts, they had the largest refracting telescope in the world, 200 inches, the very thing to see UFOs with, it seemed to me, because I was given to understand that Prof. Adamski worked there under the big dome snapping plates of the heavens and its zippy inhabitants and on occasion speaking to them in the desert. This odd double book was *Flying Saucers Have Landed*, and along with its richly loony tales of *vimanas* from Sanskrit legend, and Colonel Churchwood's occult lore of drowned Mu, and the devious metals of lost Atlantis, it was illustrated with those famous shots of the tilted, nuts and bolts craft with its three balls — landing gear, perhaps, or something to do with the power supply — and shots of long cigar-shaped "motherships" waiting to carry the small scoutships into hyperspace at speeds greater than light, to Venus and other wonderfully hospitable worlds beyond our atmosphere ... an atmosphere which, as Peter Reich's daddy knew only too well, was even then being remorselessly brutalised by filthy nuclear weapons tests, lethal and mutagenic radionuclides scattered into the high winds and falling into the upturned, trusting faces of children gazing at the stars in search of redemptive aliens in flying saucers.

Then I grew up and understood how extremely unlikely it all was (the Catholicism, the anti-communist obsession, the sexual prohibitions, the UFOs). When flying saucer contactees like Adamski morphed into abductees, snatched in blue beams of missing time and elevated into disks for a spot of anal probing and nasal implanting, my interest revived. This kind of urban myth is so charming, so weirdisimo, so *sci-fi* in the single acceptable sense of that vile term. I gobbled down the revelations of Dr John Mack, Harvard psychiatrist. I seized up Dr David Jacobs, historian at Temple University. I ploughed through C.D.B. Bryan, upmarket journalist. I wallowed in Whitley Strieber and his profitable concoctions. And I laughed my head off at Jim Schnabel's splendid travelogue among the beamed-up, *Dark White*. Somewhere in there, a curious prickle ran down my spine. I started making lists, drawn from these books, of the Signs & Symptoms of Alien Abduction. I recalled the primary school near Monash University, where a whole class and their teacher witnessed a close encounter of the third kind, just a kilometer or two from where I was studying in April, 1966. I glanced back through my own science fiction novels and out popped, one after another, virtually the entire checklist: the investigation and probing on the floating slab, the wafted transition through a wall in a bubble, the mysterious mutant foetus, the transferred embryo, the creatures suspended in tubes, the occlusions of memory, the great-eyed animals with cold voices, the prophecies of doom or transformation . . .

Calm down. I'm not about to spring any unseemly revelations upon you, leap from the UFO closet. But it did focus my amazed attention on the ubiquity of these narrative elements, the odd way in which they seem to have seeped into our dreams and our unconscious (or out of it), long before they were written up in fat lurid paperbacks or dramatised for network television and Spielberg movies. I don't know their source, and nobody else does either. Carl Jung had some confused thoughts on the matter, and experts in millennial delusion figure there's something going on in the cultural depths. Me, I wondered what would happen to someone a little like me who really *did* fall into the trap of hardening these wisps and vapors into concrete. From there, it's a short step for an sf writer to ask: what if it *is* true, after all? Or what, at any rate, if you talked yourself into believing it? What would it be like, living curved and suffocating inside the womb of a culture's disordered fantasies?

"The Womb" has become the spine of a book by Rory Barnes and me, called *The Book of Revelation*. It tells, in much greater detail than I have space for here, the tale of Daimon Keith and his odd trajectory, and of his luckless daughter Rosa, and all the rest of his family intimate and extended, in heaven as on earth. The novel will be published by HarperCollins Publishers Australia, in 1999.

— *Damien Broderick*

TESS WILLIAMS

Abandoning an adolescent passion for science fiction when she went to university to study literature, Tess Williams returned to the genre for her second degree. In 1996, she published her first novel *Map of Power* as part of an MA in Creative Writing, and one of her short stories, "And She was the Word", was shortlisted in 1997 for the James Tiptree Jr award. She is currently working on her PhD, completing a second novel, which is about interspecies communication, and editing a collection of feminist writings.

In "The Body Politic", Williams reveals a brutal, frightening world of the haves and the have nots, of the hungry . . . and the very hungry.

THE BODY POLITIC

TESS WILLIAMS

The Self-tow rocked as Lilly stepped aboard, muffled in a chill cape of shadow. She took her seat opposite the Joe and caught her breath. Chairs of plush green velvet sat either side of a small table. Soft lighting picked up the glistening pink of salmon slices, blue veined cheese cubes, variegated leaves speckled with dark herbs and food morsels of a dozen other colours and textures arranged in tiny china bowls on the table.

The Joe gestured to the Navcom on the back wall. We're locked on to the Bordertown ring road, he said. Take your wrap off and place any protective devices you have with you in the chute. You'll get them back when we're finished. He offered himself for a search, opening his grey tunic wide, lifting his pant legs above his ankles.

Lilly dropped her kill-can into a wall socket. As it sealed itself with a gasp she declined the Joe's offer with a shake of her head. He sat down again, his soft flesh filling the spaces in the chair like putty.

The buses had stopped months ago and Lilly had walked in from Blacktown. With trembling hands she removed the worn blanket wrap and stared at the food. There seemed so much and it was so exquisite. It could be payment enough. The Joe stared back at her, assessing her. Her brown skin was roughened and held a grey tint, but the bones of her face were still good.

If anything, they were more pronounced and exotic with the hunger. The shadows of deprivation coloured her eyes better than powder, and the sudden warmth of the cabin had flushed her cheeks.

The Joe leaned forward slightly and scooped aromatic paste onto paper thin bread that was a mosaic of crushed grain and nuts. He chewed carefully, then took another mouthful. A bowl of saffron rice in front of Lilly exuded a Jasmine scent that nearly made her faint.

Now the dress, he said.

She wriggled out of the black sheath and slipped off her shoes. It was warm. The sights and smells from the table caused her eyelids to flutter. She was naked.

I'm very hungry, she whispered.

Soon, said the Joe, soon. A stick of carrot disappeared into the Joe's mouth and was followed by a satin black olive.

You're from a Nest, he said. I know training when I see it.

His plump white fingers folded a slice of yellow cheese around a strip of smoked fish scattered with capers. After two more pieces, that bowl was empty.

He reached over and ran his hands up the tight skin of her side. As he bent his head towards her, she caught the sharp smell of ginger on his breath.

Lost two ribs, poor girl, he murmured. They often do that in a Nest, don't they? Contradicting the sympathy of the words, his hard, greedy gaze followed the steep dip of her waist.

A thick finger traced the iridescent line above her sex. They took out your womb too?

The Navcom beeped quietly behind him as Lilly nodded.

They did you a favour, he said.

Lilly was torn between his words and the vision next to her hand of a tiny bowl of wet, grey oysters wrapped in pink bacon. She stared at the dish.

Our Maman always protected us, she whispered.

The Nest had been home. Lilly missed The Nest: the confusions of Maman's moods; Doc Savage's scalpel and his soothing pharmacopoeia; the suffering, delirium and ecstasy; the well dressed Joes from Whitetown and the not so well-dressed Joes from Bordertown. She even missed the cage. She sorely missed the Nest.

This Joe smiled without humour. His hand now traced the perfect breast standing out from the harsh corrugations of the woman's ribs.

Implants, he said.

The implants still looked full and desirable, even with Lilly shadow thin and dark. Her heart beat visibly through the soft skin below her sternum.

That's part of the protection, Lilly's voice was a bare whisper.

The Joe cleaned the oyster bowl with another slice of the patterned bread. When he whispered back to her, his voice was plump with contempt.

That's an illusion, he said. There is no protection. There never was protection.

There was a strange light in his eye, a little like battle, a little like lust and Lilly glanced at the airless orifice of the self-tow where the kill-can was sealed. The Joe continued, I could educate you, you know. Their work was shoddy. I would have given you much better if you were in my care. For example, I would teach you not to paint your nails silver.

Lilly looked back to the bowls on the table. He had continued eating all the time that they were talking and so much had gone.

I don't paint my nails, she said. There's no way to buy nail paint. I haven't even any food. A shudder jerked her bones suddenly, then passed through her again, a violent quaking of flesh. She put her hand over her mouth as she gagged.

The Joe's eyes narrowed, You're on something.

Lilly nodded, yes. On the carpet his feet sat pale and soft as maggot flesh.

You're all on something. You know, I've been to Blacktown, the Joe said. And I see what the problem is with you people. There's so much dirt and you people there just sit and wait for someone to help you. He laughed softly and his eyes grew strange again. Don't your people know how to do anything for themselves? Why don't they clean themselves up. Find work.

Raw memories of her late afternoon seared Lilly's nerves: the sudden silence of the perpetually whimpering baby across the hall, the dirty smell of roasting cat from downstairs.

It's not that easy, she hissed, and her curled lip gave another glint of silver which the Joe failed to notice.

He seemed amused at her anger and ate faster. Tiny fish eggs crowded onto a small spoon and disappeared into his mouth. He went back for more until the bowl was empty and streaked with red sauce. The sauce was wet and bright as fresh blood.

You were a Babypro?

Lilly nodded.

Tell me.

The Joe pressed a button. A section of the wall near Lilly's head slid back and revealed a rack of bottles. He extracted one and filled the single glass on the table with honeyed liquid, then he drained it. Lilly's mouth dried out watching him. More than half of the food was now gone from the table.

I'm hungry, she said more loudly this time. I'm starving.

The Joe was dismissive, Yes, yes. I'll pay. Tell me.

The Nest had been famous as far as Whitetown for Maman's Babypros and Fancies, and the Nest was all Lilly remembered. There was no time before The Nest, before Maman and Doc Savage. They had taught her everything. Given her everything. Protected her.

First I was a Babypro. Later I was a Fancy.

A Fancy? The Joe used a green linen serviette to dab at the corners of his mouth in case the pastry just consumed had left an unsightly crumb. Tell me about the Fancies.

Lilly shrugged, this was titillation for the Joe but she answered him anyway. We had different Fancies in our Nest. Lots of them. There was a young boy with breasts and his partner, a eunuch. There was a woman with no breasts and no eyes. There was a strange one, a hermaphrodite and amputee. Couldn't speak. That one was always busy. There was a toothless old woman and her grandaughter, a sucking baby, who earned well for a while. Doc Savage had a belly implant in one of the Fancies, with a concealed drain. For the Joes who liked them pregnant. But the drain became infected and she died. And then there was Eve . . .

Lilly paused.

Don't stop, said the Joe, sensing a reluctance. Tell me about Eve.

She was my partner.

The Joe picked up a pair of tiny cream chopsticks and lifted one of the bowls. Kelp strands marinated in dark sauce and dusted with small, white seeds were rapidly funnelled into his mouth. As the bowl returned to the table, he poured more wine and drank it. When he spoke his lips were wet and repellent, his breath sour as he leaned close to Lilly.

So you did it with her, did you?

Lilly counted the bowls left with food. Only four. She looked at the Joe. They were my Nest. We had to work together. We all did whatever had to be done.

So, this Eve? The Joe pushed.

She was a Pain Fancy. Lilly's eyes seemed too bright and she didn't whisper any more. Someone in the Nest had to do it. Doc tried to make it easier. He deadened her nerves with locals and epis, but she could never be right out of it. Pain Joes don't like that, they want some feeling. And then there was nerve damage.

Nerve damage? The Joe licked wet, thick lips. What was that?

Lilly had a faraway look about her. Oh, you know. At first there was pleasure *and* pain for her. But then she became so sensitive, there was only ever pain. Doc said any sensation was translated as pain by her mind. Near the end, he'd load her with euphorics just so she could walk down the street. And she'd still start screaming if she saw a Whitetown man. In the end she needed looking after all the time, couldn't stand on her own feet, trembled a lot and cried like a baby.

The Joe pushed a whole pickled egg into his mouth and dabbed again with the serviette.

She died, he said bluntly.

Maybe, said Lilly. I went out on a job one day and never saw her again. Doc and Maman said she just slipped out for a moment. They said someone must have got her.

They lied. They killed her. She wasn't useful any more.

The Joe was inspecting the table and had selected the Jasmine scented rice and a bowl of vegetables in a pungent sauce. Expertly he lifted rice and sauced vegetables with the tiny chopsticks to his bowed head. He couldn't see Lilly's face, which had withdrawn deeper into the shadow and was barely visible except for another glint of silver.

You've eaten everything!

Lilly's voice was flat but strong. The Joe's head came up with a slight smile twisting the corners of his mouth and a faint arch of surprise in his eyebrows. He looked across the empty bowls on the table.

Why, so I have, he said. There was a faint note of apology in his voice.

I know what you're doing, said Lilly. I wasn't Eve's partner for nothing. There was a clear challenge in her voice.

The Joe's face became suddenly bored and his manner became brusque. He glanced at the Navcom, We'll be back to your stop soon. We'd better get down to business. He undid his pants.

Why bother? You've already had the pleasure.

Lilly moved forward on the chair. Her fine-boned, waif face that had appeared exquisite and defeated before now seemed sharp and somehow dangerous. Her shadowed eyes glittered in their darkened sockets.

I'm sure I don't know what you mean, he snapped. The silk tunic slid slowly to the floor, followed by the linen serviette.

You do, said Lilly. You're a Pain Joe. You cruise the strip looking for someone who's hungry enough to risk leaving Blacktown. Someone who hasn't the protection of a Nest any more and you play with their need until it becomes an agony for them.

The plump hand threw a bundle of notes on the table.

I'm a man of honour! shouted the Joe, I don't cheat your kind, or any other! Take that and get out!

Lilly scratched the money out of the way, knocking bowls aside and leaving deep gouges in the wood of the table. The Joe stared at the marks in horror. Stared at her hard silver nails.

You know your money's no good in Blacktown, Lilly hissed. We don't use Whitetown currency.

What is it you want? The Joe's fingers shook slightly as they rested on the chair arm.

Lilly switched to a conversational tone, I was Eve's partner. I'm a Pain Fancy too. A brief flicker of relief ran over the Joe's face and Lilly laughed. For the first time her teeth were completely bared. Long silver incisors gleamed on both top and bottom jaws. The Joe paled.

Fool! she hissed. You should have realised! Eve was trained to endure pain and I was her partner!

She stretched her fingers and gently drew the nails down the Joe's thigh, their dull metal sheen caught the light, the rips left in the fabric revealed his pale leg skin.

These nails are metal grafted on to bone, said Lilly. Doc Savage was good to us, in his way. The teeth are metal grafted on to bone too. I'll never lose them. They're hell in winter, but they're my protection. Together with a lifetime supply of Burners the Doc left behind. Rage drug. Gives us bodyquakes, but makes the weak surprisingly strong. All this was Eve's protection too ... until she went out without me.

The Joe's voice had become hoarse, and his eyes were wide. I'm offering you money. More than you're worth! What is it you want?

Slowly his hand crept up toward the Navcom.

Lilly reached forward and took firm hold of his wrist. Her eyes were cess-pool dark as she spoke: emergency switch? Check response sub-routines? Don't bother. I can disconnect one in three seconds.

The Joe was white with terror as her hand encircled his other wrist and she leaned over him. Tiny sweat beads appeared on his forehead as the soft skin of one of her nipples brushed his bare chest.

Tell me what you want, he pleaded.

Lilly laughed bitterly. I told you more times than you deserved to hear, she said. I'm starving. I have to feed.

Then she drew back her lips and contained his final struggle with her Rage fuelled body. Her teeth sank deep into his throat and, as the blood welled, dark and crimson, Lilly drank, tasting and savouring the thick fluid as if it were a fine red wine.

AFTERWORD

This story is a piece which reflects my emerging style — strong awareness of socio-political issues — particularly race, class, and gender coupled with a need to contextualise that information in the existing myths of the culture and a determination to play with genre boundaries. That's why the two women, "Lilly" and "Eve", are very special to me in "Body Politic". They are ambiguous, archetypal figures that persist, even after centuries of usage, in offering fresh and complex readings of the feminine as we understand it today. Their ancient pedigrees offer countenance to the many ideas this story contains, reminding us of barely conscious histories, meanings and relationships that can guide readings of the story and enrich its more modern constructions.

As a writer, I have a particular interest in ancient tales of women who hold some form of power — women who have often been viewed through the patriarchal lens as repugnant and/or violent. "Lilly" is one of these. Based on Lillith, Adam's first mate, she is the "shadow" woman, a creature of the night who has not been allowed to nourish herself in the culture of the story and has been sculpted into a false model of beauty and dependancy. Excluded and invalidated, she becomes far more dangerous than she was when she was working, when she had a "job" to do and belonged somewhere. In a tale of boundaries and boundary transgressions, Lilly exists in violated territory. It is, therefore, only a small step for her to move from mutilated to monstrous.

Some contemporary writers view the use of mythic figures and patterns as something undesirable, a restriction on their capacity to create and a possible slur on their originality. They think that myths can't account for modern pluralistic perspectives on the world. I don't see it like that. My understandings are that these stories that have created our culture stay with us whether we are aware of them or not and they often work themselves out in our institutions and our families, as well as in our literature. They are not, however, ultimately prescriptive because they present in an infinite number of combinations, and offer infinite opportunities for both reinterpretation and a change of focus.

— *Tess Williams*

SIMON BROWN

Simon Brown is the author of the novels *Privateer* (1996) and *Winter* (1997). His short stories have appeared in *Aurealis, Eidolon, Omega Science Digest, Alien Shores,* and *Glass Reptile Breakout*. Some of his stories can be found in the collection *Cannibals of the Fine Light* (1998). He lives in Camden (not New Jersey!) with his wife and two children.

We have not seen the likes of this evocative and sensitive story about the private lives and relationships of the undead since Lucius Shepard's brilliant novel *The Golden*. Here is a glimpse into people who might be our neighbours ... and who must feed their urgent need.

WITH CLOUDS AT OUR FEET

SIMON BROWN

The sun was still a half hour from rising when Leon brought the cows in for their first milking. The beasts were shuffling, snuffling shapes against a paling sky, smelling of grass and damp soil. Leon came up behind them, stroking their flanks, shooing them softly.

As they ambled into the milking shed I led them one by one to the bail and locked them in, then waited for Leon to tell me to get on with it, as always. He paused at the gate and looked at the sky, turning pink now. He sniffed the air cautiously, like a nervous fox.

"There's a change, Andrew. Summer's come early."

"Summer always starts about now," I told him, smiling. "I've got a memory."

Leon glanced at me almost slyly. "I still smell a change." He nodded at the bucket and stool at my feet. "You waiting for a starting gun?"

I went to the first cow and tied back her milking leg. As I made myself comfortable on the stool I warmed my hands against my jeans. Leon sidled up to the cow and patted her nose. The cow licked his hand, tasting for salt.

"There you go, Nancy," he murmured. He had names for all the beasts, but I never bothered. I couldn't tell Nancy from Maria from Betty from Jenny.

The milk came easy, warm and thick, frothing in the bucket. "Bet that's sweet," I said to Leon.

He stood by Nancy's flank, grinning lazily at me, and scratched a scab from a small patch of skin over the cow's spine. "Not as sweet as this," he said, and bent his head so he could lick at the seeping blood, shiny and almost orange under the shed's wan electric light.

Nancy didn't flinch. She was content to be milked, to have her head in the bail trough, to quench Leon's thirst.

I was patient, as the second brother, content like Nancy. When Leon was done we moved to the next beast and swapped places.

We took our time that morning, feeding casually, enjoying the routine more than usual. It made me wonder if perhaps Leon was right after all and a change was in the air, but less to do with the season than something closer to home, something as yet undefined. I felt a sense of anticipation, that something was on its way, but I did not dwell on it.

After the milking we followed the cows to the east paddock and stayed there as the sun rose, watching its light measure itself against gently rolling hills, picking out solitary snow gums and the startling yellow clumps of flowers hanging from green wattles. A mist drifted up from the earth and curled around our feet for a few minutes before being burned away by the sun.

Around us shimmered the purple rim of the world, our little valley surrounded by the low mountains of the Southern Highlands. Eucalyptus oil, suspended in the air after yesterday's heavy rain, made the morning smell clean and new.

"Warm day coming," Leon said.

"Whatever you say, Leon." That made him laugh.

✳ ✳ ✳

We knew we had a visitor before we reached the house. There was a Ford parked in the driveway, a new model, which neither of us recognised as belonging to anyone we knew. Then we saw a pair of expensive black shoes left outside the front door, and we had an inkling. He was waiting for us in the kitchen, pouring water from a kettle into a teapot.

"Christ, you boys get up early," he said by way of greeting. He studied us both for a moment, then added: "You are both looking fine."

"Hello, Father," I said.

Leon said nothing, but Father pretended not to notice.

"I thought you might like some breakfast. I've put a few rashers of bacon under the grill."

"We've already fed," Leon told him.

"I'm still hungry," I said quickly, throwing a warning look at my brother. I did not want any unpleasantness.

"What you get from those cows of yours you can't call food," Father said authoritatively. I watched Leon bite his lip, and Father saw it too. "But, of course, you're only half-blood. You don't really understand the ... need. Perhaps cows fill you, after all."

He was trying to be conciliatory, for Leon's sake rather than mine; he and I had never been sour with each other. Somehow, though, his words sounded patronising and made Leon flush.

Father checked the bacon, turned the rashers over. I started making conversation, retrieving cups and saucers from the dish rack, but Leon refused to join in and I could tell Father was starting to wish he'd never left the city.

But I kept on, anyway, more to fill the silence than anything else, and gradually wore them both down. By the time the bacon had gone crispy and the rind crinkled black, all three of us were sharing small talk. Father had seen enough farming to ask us some sensible questions about the property, and we knew barely enough about his own life in the city to seem interested in return.

By the time we had eaten and drunk our fill, the sun had warmed up the kitchen and Father was beginning to sweat; he was so much a part of the city he hardly ever had proper white sunlight touching his skin. In a few minutes he would have to retreat to a darker room or start to pass out. A couple of times I opened my mouth to suggest we move into the lounge room, but Leon always got in first, asking Father about this or that. It occurred to me after the fourth occasion that Leon was deliberately trying to keep Father in the kitchen, and by then it was getting too warm for us as well.

Father's face was starting to blotch, around the jaws first and then slowly up and around his cheeks and forehead. His pupils contracted to the smallest dark points. I could tell he was not far from fainting and I stood up to go to him. Sudden nausea almost made me double over. Father shook his head, trying to smile, and waved me away, but the action was so feeble it was almost comical.

I grabbed him by one arm and dragged him to his feet. When Leon saw I was determined, he came to my assistance, taking Father's other arm. Between us we managed to get him into the lounge room. As soon as we entered the cool and the dark our strength returned, though more slowly for Father. He and Leon regarded each other for a moment, the look passing between them a strange mixture of resentment and respect, which confused me a little.

Father and Leon sat in chairs while I took the lounge, stretching my feet over the edge. Conversation was scattered and stilted again, as though we were just starting out. Eventually, Father slapped his knees with his palms, which was usually his first preparation for standing up before leaving, a kind of visual sigh. This time, though, he stayed seated and leaned forward, his elbows sticking out at angles so his arms looked like a dog's hind legs.

"I want you both to come back with me to the city," he said, forcing the words into a rush. Then, more slowly: "Just for a visit; I know you don't want to leave your farm, but I want you to see for yourselves how I live."

"Mother told us how you lived," Leon said coldly. "And I remember some."

Father shook his head, his expression genuinely sad. "Your mother wasn't one of us, Leon. She didn't understand. You and Andrew might. I want you to see my home."

* * *

Father left us late in the afternoon, and without an answer. I was willing to take him up on his offer, partly out of curiosity and partly out of a sense of family duty, but Leon was not at all interested in the idea. I saw Father out to his car and told him I'd work on Leon, and he smiled resignedly, not really believing Leon could be swayed.

"He was old enough to know both his mother and me," he said, "and so had to make a choice between us. When you're a child, you can't believe both sides of a story."

But I kept my word, and over the next few days raised the subject every now and then, and gradually Leon came around. I think he knew as well as I that it was only through our father that we would learn about the need that filled us as much as it filled him, even if in a diluted form. Leon and I pretended it was not the single most important thing in our lives; we tried to hide it under the layer of routine necessary in running even a small property like our own, but we both understood our lives revolved around our need for blood to survive — warm blood, the blood of mammals.

On Thursday we went into Warramanga to do the banking and to talk with Jo Liddel, who looked after the local dairy cooperative; then, during the hottest part of the day, we spent a couple of hours in the pub drinking beer and catching up with all the latest town gossip. As we were leaving, Leon said I should phone Father and let him know we were coming.

"When?" I asked, acting surprised.

"Well, this weekend, I guess. Get it over and done with. We can go back to see Jo and ask her to send someone out to milk the ladies. But only for a couple of days, Andrew. We don't owe him anything."

So he went to ask Jo for the favour, and I went to the post office to phone Father. He wasn't home, but I left a message on his answering machine and told him we'd be up tomorrow night, on the Friday.

* * *

The next morning, later than usual, we brought the cows in together. It was a cool start; not cool enough for a frost, but a mist dressed the hills and higher paddocks, swirling as we walked through it. We found the cows on top of White Ridge, where an old wire fence stopped them from falling into the Murrumbidgee River. We stood there for a while, watching the brown water idly wearing away the limestone walls of the shallow valley, watching as the sun slowly took over the sky, feeling time pass by as though we were outside of it.

The cows started lowing. We walked them back to the shed, relieved them of their milk as we relieved ourselves of our nagging hunger. We let them loose nearby so we could gather them quickly in the afternoon for the next milking, then went inside to wait out the day so we could conserve our strength for the drive that night to Sydney.

Leon wrote out instructions for whoever Jo sent to cover us for the weekend, spending some effort over it because he didn't want anything to go wrong with his beloved beasts. I packed our bags, then pored over an old Sydney street directory so I could navigate us to Father's place once we hit the city. Leon said Sydney was the hardest city in the world to drive around, and I believed him. I told him we could drive to Goulburn then catch a train into Sydney, but he shook his head and said we needed the car because it gave us independence. I guess he meant independence from Father, but Leon didn't elaborate.

We did the second milking around 4.00 in the afternoon, then penned up the cows and stuck Leon's instructions to the front door.

"I hope whoever Jo sends can read your writing," I joked, but he just looked sour at me and I felt stupid for trying to make light of it.

As we left the farm and got onto the dirt road, Leon driving, we looked back for a moment, already homesick. Then Leon gunned it and we sped off too quickly for my liking, leaving behind a great cloud of dust that hid the farm behind us.

✳　✳　✳

It should have been a six hour trip, but we did it in seven, not including stopovers at Goulburn and Mittagong so Leon could relieve his bladder, which I told him must have been smaller than a twenty-cent piece. The problems started once we hit Sydney — the street directory I was using was about ten years out of date. Some streets had become one-way, others had disappeared entirely. Once we ended up on a highway that ended up taking us back out of the city.

Eventually, we found the right street, which turned out to be no wider than a country lane with cars parked up on the curb between stunted plane trees. The street was lined with terrace houses, originally made for stevedores and other dock labourers, but now fashionable and expensive, painted in pastels and decorated with iron lace and lead-glass windows. Father's place was bigger than most, comprising two semi-detached joined together, and done up as well as any other on the street. Before we had gotten out of the car the front door opened and he was there, backlit by a hall light, balancing on one foot and then the other as he slipped on his loafers.

Leon pretended to be busy with our bags when Father came down to greet us, but I shook his hand, something we never did on his visits to the farm. I could tell he was happy to see us.

"I got your message this morning," he said, grinning. "Your room is ready, and I've got some dinner cooking." He took the bags from Leon and led us into the house. "I told all my friends you were coming," he added excitedly. I was embarrassed by his eagerness, and Leon seemed surprised.

The entrance hall was Victorian, forest-green wallpaper with a gold design, oak side table and hatstand, an ancient elephant's foot umbrella stand so old it did not look out of place, a staircase at the back with a polished mahogany balustrade, and Father, of course. He was dressed in dark pants, a white shirt under a smoking jacket the same colour as the wallpaper, leather loafers. His face narrow, pinched, looking calm and speculative at the same time.

"Your room is upstairs," he said. "We'll drop your bags off and then get something to eat."

Our room was, thankfully, plain, with two single beds separated by a table with a lamp on it. A small window looked out over a succession of peaked tin roofs, shining like frozen waves in the bright moonlight.

Father showed us his room, and my first impression was that it looked like the hallway writ large. He looked apologetically at us. "My time, you see," he said softly, and ushered us downstairs into the kitchen.

We sat around an old wooden table scarred like the skin of a whale, and ate a lamb stew with thick gravy we sopped up with fresh white bread. Leon and I wolfed down the food, we were hungrier than we knew, but Father barely touched his meal. He seemed on edge, and the conversation we shared was perfunctory.

At the end of the meal Father said: "I expect you'll want to see something of the city tomorrow; do some shopping, maybe."

"We lived here, once," Leon said shortly.

"It's only that I tend to hide away during the day, so I'll leave you to yourselves. But tomorrow night, I promise you a good time. I want you to meet some people ..."

His voice faded when he saw Leon's expression.

"In fact, I have to go out now," he continued. "I wanted to wait until you arrived, but I can't ..."

Again, he seemed lost for words, and Leon and I both understood then he was edgy because he needed to feed properly.

"We'll be all right," I said quickly, and he nodded his thanks.

* * *

After the meal, Leon and I went to our room. Leon was very tired after all the driving, and he fell asleep almost the moment he lay down. I took off my shoes and socks and waited on the edge of my bed until I heard Father leave the house by the front door. I was surprised, somehow expecting him to disappear across the roof tops instead of going on to the street like a normal human being.

I left the room to explore the house properly; driven by curiosity and a kind of nervous anxiety I knew would not let me sleep. My night vision is excellent, and I did not need to turn on any lights. Colours were subdued, but details sharp.

I first went to my father's bedroom, and found on his dresser photographs of Leon and me as children, and a photograph of our mother. Father had never spoken much about her to us. The photograph suggested feelings I'd never suspected in him. She was very young in the picture, no older than 20 or so, and it crossed my mind that Father may have thought of her as two women, the one in the photograph whom he had loved and with whom he had shared his life for so many years; and the other whom had taken his children away from him, the human who had betrayed his trust. It seemed to me ironic that it was the second woman I knew and loved as my mother, and it made me wonder if perhaps that was the basis of the gulf that existed between him and his children, rather than the fact that we were half-bloods: not entirely human, neither predator nor prey.

The next room I visited was the study. A roll-top desk took up one corner, its cover half-open. I slid it all the way back, found a stack of bills in a letter holder, an old fashioned fountain pen, a bottle of blue ink, and blotting pad. Sitting on a second desk, beneath the room's only window, was a small computer, with a writing pad and scribbled sums beside it. There was a painting on the wall, a bush scene in the Heidelberg style, and on closer inspection I discovered it was an original Streeton.

There was little of interest in any of the other upstairs rooms, all bedrooms, nor in most of those on the ground floor until I reached the living room, occupying the whole length of one side of the house.

A shallow bay window gave a view of the lane out front, and on the opposite wall large French windows looked out over the back garden. A leather lounge and two plush seats occupied the centre of the room, facing an open fireplace that appeared as though it hadn't been used in years. The walls were lined floor-to-ceiling with bookcases made from oak and glass fronted. Most of the books were old, covering a range of subjects as diverse as English history and biography, science and, it seemed strange to me, theology. There was a large section devoted to medicine and anatomy. The bookcase nearest the entrance was filled mostly with more recent editions, even a few paperbacks with the spines so cracked it wasn't possible to read the titles. The top shelf was reserved for a group of photographs. My father appeared in each one, always accompanied by a woman. The photographs spanned decades, the oldest looking, judging from the clothing, probably taken in the 1880s; Father looked younger there, but not by much. The most recent photograph showed him with a small woman with a beautiful face and dark hair falling in rings down to her shoulders.

I don't know how long I spent in that room, but I eventually started feeling tired enough to sleep. Before returning upstairs, though, I wanted to see the garden. I left the house through the French windows, leaving them open behind me. The back of the house was bordered by paving and a dry stone wall that supported terraces. The garden was filled with ferns and palms, a cycad or two. It contained no flowering plants that I could see. The lush, semi-tropical vegetation, so different from that on the farm, drew me in, its appearance and smell as strange to me as the city itself. As I followed a series of slate steps to the top tier, cool, wet leaves slapped against my skin. At the end of the steps I walked along the length of the tier, rich humus feeling like a moist carpet beneath my feet. A drip line wound between the plants, and the air was humid, heavy.

I looked up into the sky, found Orion just above the horizon, but the city's lights were so strong that I could only barely make out his form. I took a step sideways, and felt the ground start to give way beneath my feet. I scrabbled for purchase, but it was too late, and I slid downslope for nearly two metres before catching a broad cycad leaf with one hand and steadying myself. Several metres of topsoil cascaded over my legs and feet, flooded like a dark stream down the whole width of the terrace.

Something hard and unyielding scratched between my toes. I knelt down to see if I had unlinked a section of the drip line. The tip of a finger bone was sticking up out of the partly collapsed tier, pointing at me accusingly. Without thinking, I pulled it out. I held three joints, still connected by tegument, creamy white where the soil had dropped off.

Feeling numb, I stood up. Still holding the remains, I started moving back to the house. I took two steps before a terrible curiosity overtook me. Kneeling down again, I scrabbled away at the dirt. I found more bones, most loose, and all belonging to what had once been a human hand, and quite a big one judging by the size of the pieces I had uncovered.

My own hands were shaking now; I balled them into fists. I didn't have the courage to continue digging. I looked back at the house, seeing it differently now, wondering again about the women in the photographs.

But no, I told myself, the hand had been unusually large, and its owner had died not so long ago.

Father had always told us, had even convinced our mother, that he had never killed anyone while feeding. Yet no-one else would have buried the remains in his garden.

I heard someone enter the kitchen, then saw my father illuminated by the fridge light. He brought out a bottle of mineral water, closed the fridge and shut himself in darkness again. I froze, not knowing what to do next. The problem was solved for me when Father opened the kitchen window and called out to me. I had forgotten how good was his night vision; vastly superior to my own.

"I thought you were in bed. Didn't know you were a stargazer."

"You get used to it in the country," I replied, trying to keep my voice casual. "The city makes the sky too light."

"Then come inside and have a beer."

I nodded, attempted a smile. My heart was racing, and I absently wondered if his hearing was as good as his eyesight. When I got to the kitchen he had already poured two glasses of stout. He handed me one of the glasses and raised the other to his own lips, hesitated when he saw me staring at him.

"What is it, Andrew?"

"There's some blood around your mouth," I told him, motioning around my own mouth to show him where.

"I should have cleaned that up," he said levelly. He went to the kitchen sink and slapped water over his face. It ran down his hands, rust coloured.

"Whose was it?" I asked.

He shrugged. "I don't know his name. To be safe, I never feed off the same person twice. That's why it's important full-bloods like myself live in large cities."

"Like you? How many are there like you in Sydney?"

"A dozen or so. Quite a large colony, actually. Melbourne would have a similar number. There are smaller colonies in the other capital cities."

"How many like me?"

"I don't know, Andrew. I'd heard stories of half-bloods, but until Leon was born never knew any. As far as I know, you and your brother are the only ones of your kind in Australia. Nearly all die in childbirth." He looked away from me then. "Or are aborted."

Quickly then, he drank his beer as if it was no thicker than water.

I showed him the finger bones still in my hand.

"I thought I'd been more careful than that," he said.

"You told me you never killed."

He looked surprised. "I have *never* killed to satisfy my need." He pointed to the bones, said more quietly: "This is something else, entirely."

"Something else?" I closed my fist around the bones, hiding them from him. I felt completely hollow inside, as if all emotion had been drained from me.

"Andrew, in my long life I have killed four men. The one planted in the back garden was the first in nearly eighty years. When I was ... younger ... my temper was considerably shorter. I was less forgiving of personal slight or physical threat."

"Why?"

"I returned one night and surprised him. He attacked me with a jemmy."

"Did you drink his blood?"

"Of course. I wasn't going to let it go to waste. Then I cut him up into manageable pieces and buried him in the garden."

I handed him the remains. "You should have buried him deeper."

He nodded. "Will you tell Leon? I don't think he'd understand."

"What makes you think I do?"

* * *

The next morning Leon and I woke early and made ourselves a simple breakfast. I talked little while we ate, but Leon didn't probe. I had decided to tell Leon about last night; I didn't like keeping secrets from him. But in the clean light of a new day, it somehow seemed not so important. It wasn't a secret, I tried to convince myself, it was a confidence. I decided not to tell Leon, but didn't like myself much because of it.

Leon suggested we catch a train into the city centre and spend the day there. I could see he didn't want to stay in the house. I agreed, wrote a note for Father telling him where we were going, and then we walked to the local station. The ride to the city took us twenty minutes; it was strangely uncomfortable travelling in such close proximity with so many people. I hadn't expected it, and couldn't quite put my finger on what made me uneasy. The feeling grew when we left the subway and were swept up by the human tide rushing along George Street.

Perhaps it was just that it had been a long time since I had been in the midst of so many people, since

I was an infant, and it was a shock to my system. I could see that Leon was feeling the same way, so we took refuge in a coffee shop and, in something of a daze, watched the crowds as we sipped on cappuccinos.

"I find it hard to believe they all have a destination," Leon said after a while.

"Maybe it was a mistake coming in today," I mumbled.

"We're too used to the slow and quiet country life." His expression changed. "No. It's something else, isn't it?'

"What do you mean?"

"It's all the warm bodies. So many of them. So much..." He swallowed the next word, then coughed it out like a curse. "So much ... blood."

I knew immediately that he was right. It felt as if we were in a city of animals, a city of cattle, and the realisation made me suddenly nauseous. I hastily drank some cappuccino, but the milky taste made the nausea worse. The nagging feeling in the pit of my stomach reminded me that we hadn't tasted blood since the previous afternoon. It was possible for us to forgo blood for several days, but here and now, surrounded by so many people, the nagging was quickly becoming an urgent need. "Let's go back to Father's," I said.

Leon shook his head. "No, not yet. We can stick it out a while longer. We're not like him."

I was in no state to argue, and weakly followed him as he left the coffee shop. We stumbled across an arcade, old and neglected, with only a few disinterested shoppers milling around under its shabby skylights. We found a second-hand book and music store, and recovered our equilibrium while pretending to sort through the bins of old paperbacks and racks of ancient CDs. We were there for nearly half an hour, and in the end bought a handful of books we didn't really want but felt compelled to buy to give ourselves some excuse for lingering so long, for not facing what had confronted us so unexpectedly. *Our own heritage,* I told myself, *and it makes us feel unclean.*

Outside, we found that the day had warmed up considerably, and the sun's glare bouncing off building and pavement would soon be intolerable. We retreated to a large cinema complex and watched two films in a row. When we reappeared on the street hours later it was not much cooler, but the light had dimmed. The crowds had diminished, too, and we decided to leave before we were caught in the five o'clock rush of homeward bound commuters. At that moment, I think even Leon looked forward to returning to Father's place.

I avoided looking at my fellow passengers, and instead gazed intently out the carriage window. The landscape was cluttered with overhead power lines, rail cuttings and warehouses. It was a drab and dispiriting journey, made worse by the effects of the day. I could sense Leon's own tenseness; we seemed to be feeding each other's anxiety.

I tried to push it to the back of my mind, and found myself remembering our mother. From birth, both Leon and I had needed blood; when we were still with Father, he had satisfied that need, taking it from his own veins. Mother could cope with that; she gave us milk, and he gave us blood, there was a symmetry about it that seemed both ironic and necessary to her.

As we got older, however, our need for blood increased beyond what our father could provide himself. I was too young to remember, but Leon told me Father's solution had included overfeeding himself and then regurgitating the excess. I could only begin to imagine what effect this had on mother, but in the end what drove her to leave Father was the source of the extra blood. It had been possible for her to ignore his needs when it had been closed away from her, a part of his life but not of theirs; that changed when her children became a part of it, and she could no longer consciously ignore that normal humans were being used as prey to keep Leon and me alive.

She fled, away from the city and the darkness, to the small farm left her by her parents. She bought a few head of cattle to supply us with the blood we needed, and tried to live as normal a life as possible, raising us to think and behave like her own people; taking blood from the cattle had been no more cruel, no more inhuman, than taking their milk.

And now I was aware, as I had never been before, of the difference between my nature and my nurturing. I was both human and vampire, and on that train could find no way to reconcile the two sides.

✳   ✳   ✳

And then, shortly after, a second journey.

Father was waiting for us when we returned home, impatient. He waited while Leon and I changed clothes, freshened up, then bundled us into his car.

Leon asked him where we were going.

"To see some friends of mine," Father answered, but didn't elaborate.

We drove out of the city, towards Parramatta. Sydney slid by us, the night revealing a place of neon signs and street lights; the sky drizzled for us, making everything appear brighter, somehow, and less real.

Father didn't talk. Leon and I were tired from the day's events, each of us wishing we were back home on our farm.

Sydney made me feel like an orphan.

* * *

We parked behind a hotel, and father led us into one of its bars. It was a crowded, smoky place, dimly lit; comfortable lounges and chairs divided the space, and a dozen conversations drifted in the background. Father headed for a lounge surrounding a low table at the back of the bar, already occupied by two women and a man. They looked up as we approached, smiled a welcome.

"These are my sons," Father said to his friends, and I heard the pride in his voice. I latched on to that, felt less adrift.

"Leon, Andrew, I would like you to meet Kathryn Goodall, Rosmarie Eckert and Gustave Cosserat."

Each of the three nodded in turn, still smiling, then moved closer together to make room for us. Father and the two women exchanged kisses. For an awkward moment, no-one said anything, then Cosserat nodded to a half-empty whisky glass on the table in front of him.

"I will get some drinks. Cognac, of course, for Edward. And Leon and Andrew?"

Edward? My father's name, I remembered, surprised. I had never before heard anyone call him by his first name.

Leon and I asked for beers, and Cosserat left. I watched him move away, and recognised the kind of effortless grace my father possessed. When I looked back, I saw the two women staring at me. Again, something in the way I was being studied reminded me of my father.

Predators, I thought, and almost immediately realised I was wrong. It was an intense curiosity I felt from them, not hunger.

"I can see you in both of them," the one called Eckert said to my father. Leon tensed. Eckert laughed, the sound like music. "I can see something of all of us in both of them."

Goodall laughed then, too; in relief, I thought.

"We are not like you," Leon said levelly.

Eckert surprised him by nodding. "You are right, of course, you are not like us, not exactly."

"Not exactly," echoed Goodall, smiling to herself.

Cosserat returned, carrying a tray loaded with drinks. He handed father two glasses of cognac. Father threw one down, sighed in relief, then started more slowly on the second.

"Not quite a substitute," Cosserat said to Leon and me in a confiding tone. "But the drink has the ability to take your breath away, to slow you down a little. And it is as smooth as skin on the palate."

Leon and I must have blanched at his words; Goodall and Eckert laughed again, and I could not help blushing. I felt like a virgin at an orgy, both offended and left out.

"But you don't all drink cognac," I said.

"Oh, no," Cosserat answered. "None of us is as

old as your father. He is steeped in his hunger; we are, in comparison, novices."

"What is old, exactly?" Leon asked.

Cosserat shrugged. "I doubt your father could even answer that question. Who can remember before photographs? I have known so many times, so many countries, so many friends, that much of it is a blur for me now. It must be far worse for Edward. I know that when I was young, which is many centuries ago, your father looked then pretty much as he looks now."

"But sometimes our first memories are among the most resilient," Eckert said. "I clearly remember my childhood in Prague. I remember smoke in the winter sky from all the fires, the sun hanging red over the city at dusk. I remember the smell of horse-shit in all the streets, stronger than any other smell. I remember the sound of bells from sleighs on the frozen river."

Goodall glanced enviously at Eckert. "My time is this century," she told us. "My childhood was spent in India, just before it won its independence."

"So you are at least fifty," Leon said ungraciously, but Goodall didn't seem offended.

"Unless there was a previous life," she said simply. "Maybe we are never born. Maybe we simply fill up with life, then burst into flame and are reborn, childlike and empty. Each of us is a phoenix."

"I was born," Leon said then.

Cosserat looked at us sadly. "Yes, we know. Your kind is very rare among us."

"Father told me most of us are stillborn," I said. *Or aborted.*

"We all share a curiosity about our origins," Father said then.

"We are all human, to one degree or another," Cosserat added.

"Do half-bloods die?" Leon asked.

"I don't know," Father said.

"You two are the first half-bloods in your father's experience," Eckert said. "I have known only one, a man. I last saw him over a century ago, when he was already one or two hundred years old. He may be dead now ... or not."

"My sons and I have not discussed such matters in any detail," Father said, apologetically, to his friends. "There are things which all three of us have left unmentioned. I thought it time to correct some of that."

Leon blinked, but said nothing. Like me, I sensed his growing curiosity. I wondered if it would've been the same if we had not visited the city that day and felt overwhelmed by our own natures.

Eckert nodded. "Do you deny your heritage?" she asked Leon and me.

"Not deny, exactly," I said. "We have found another way."

"They feed off cattle," Father said.

His three friends looked aghast.

"They satisfy us," Leon said quickly.

"I'm sure," Cosserat said placatingly. "Have you ever tasted human blood?"

"Not since we were children."

Again, there was a pause in the conversation. It occurred to me then that the whole evening had been leading to this point, and I suddenly felt a terrible anger towards my father. He had set it up so that this very topic *would* arise. I looked at him, and for the first time saw how nervous he was. He met my glance for the briefest of moments, then turned away. *He wants us to submit. He wants us to join him and his friends tonight. He wants us to feed off a human* ...

I saw Leon open his mouth to say something, and I knew instinctively it would be the wrong thing; Leon had not yet realised where the conversation was leading us. It was a confrontation — a choice — I wanted to avoid.

"And what do you all do in this city?" I asked clumsily. Leon shut his mouth, looked at me, frowning.

The others all appeared vaguely disappointed.

Cosserat seemed befuddled for an instant. "Umm, the same as your father," he said eventually. "We have all lived long enough to make sizeable fortunes. We tend to rest during the day, going out only when necessary to advance our business interests. The advent of the computer and advanced telecommunications has made that task much easier."

"You must all have had a trade once upon a time," I persisted.

"Not Rosmarie or me," Goodall said, slightly bemused. "In our day, women were kept."

I looked at Cosserat, who seemed embarrassed. "I was a priest."

"A priest!" Leon spurted.

"A Catholic priest. I have always been drawn to the spiritual life."

"As are all our kind," Father said quietly.

"In my case the pull was a little stronger. I thought the hunger in me was nothing more than the manifestation of my devotion to God."

"You believe in God?" I asked, surprised.

"How else do you explain our existence?" Cosserat asked, genuinely mystified by my question. "How else can we put in perspective the desire that drives us to become predators amongst what once must have been our own kind?

"I was a good priest. I looked after my flock with great love and attention. But the Church could not long keep a blind eye to my agelessness. I had to leave its service; I arranged for an accident. The Church believed I had died at last, and I was free." His expression became sad. "Well, free to wander, to leave behind my home, my friends."

"Then officially you are still a priest?"

Cosserat nodded. "Yes. I still have all the authority vested in me by the Church, but I no longer practice, of course. It wouldn't be ... right."

* * *

There was another round of drinks, this one bought by father, and the conversation drifted a little before Goodall suggested it was time to move on. Leon and I were instantly alert.

"Maybe Leon and I should leave you to it," I said.

"We've had a very long day," Leon said in support.

"Good heavens," Eckert said primly. "By the tone in your voices you'd think we were going out to rob a bank."

"Not exactly ..."

"Or to *dinner*," she added quickly, a smile playing at the corner of her lips.

"I feel like Italian," Cosserat said playfully. "Or maybe Thai."

"Enough," Father said quietly. He turned to Leon and me. "Dinner as in a restaurant, you two. I'm sure you're as hungry as we are. Why don't you join us? If you want to go home after that, I'll drive you back and meet up with my friends later."

Leon and I glanced at one another, and both of us nodded.

"We are hungry," Leon admitted. "We didn't eat much today."

"Missing your cows?" Eckert asked, her smile still teasing.

* * *

Neither Italian nor Thai, but a steak house. I was embarrassed to see that only Leon and I ordered our steaks rare. The watery blood leaking from the edge of our meals actually made the others slightly nauseous.

"Not real blood at all, you see," Cosserat explained. "It reminds me of artificial cream."

"Or soy milk," Goodall added, her face wrinkling.

We ate our meals slowly, talking about books we'd read, films we'd seen; Father's friends even spent some time asking us questions about our farm, about what crops we'd planted, how we made a living, about the recent drought and the even more recent floods. Despite our earlier misgivings, Leon and I started to relax, to enjoy the company we were keeping.

As the night wore on the place became busier and busier; when someone put some coins in a jukebox, we had to raise our voices to be heard by each other.

Eckert complained about the selection of music, mostly country and western, but both Goodall and Cosserat announced they preferred it to rock or pop.

There followed an argument about music, Leon and I contributing as much as the others.

When the meal finished, no-one felt like leaving the table. Several rounds of drinks were bought, but only Leon and I seemed to be affected by the alcohol, our speech slowing and our thoughts becoming increasingly confused. At one point, Leon even got up to dance with Goodall, his usual timidness worn away by then.

Soon after I found myself talking with Eckert and Leon about our father. She had known him almost as long as Cosserat. I got the impression she was being guarded in her replies, but it was obvious she respected and liked him a great deal. Leon, hesitantly, asked her if she and Father had ever had an affair. Eckert smiled sadly, and did not reply at first. Leon mumbled an apology about being too familiar, but she waved it aside.

"Your father and I did have an affair; but it was so long ago that I cannot remember as much about it as I would like. You have to understand, our capacity to recall emotions is as subject to selective memory as normal humans. We remember the good times and the bad times, but not always the events, the causes, behind these emotions."

Leon asked more questions, then, but I found myself wondering about my father's relationship with my mother. How much of their affair did he remember? It hurt to think that, however clear the memories he had of her may be now, in time he would forget most of it. The realisation saddened me, and made me also wonder if a time would come when he would forget about Leon and me.

I excused myself from the table and made my way to the toilets, a sign above a narrow doorway indicating the way. Behind the door was a whitewashed corridor with the men's and women's toilets on either side; at the end of the corridor was an exit. Somebody was standing in the exit, their back to me. I heard a commotion on the other side, then a faint moan that sounded like someone in pain. Without thinking I went to the exit. The person there turned around, and I recognised Cosserat. He looked at me blankly for a moment, then smiled and frowned at the same time.

"Is someone hurt?" I asked, about to edge past him.

"No-one is hurt..." he began, and moved to block my way.

What made me push past him, I'll never know. It wasn't a conscious decision, my brain was too befuddled with drink by then to think so clearly. I think now that it was inevitable, as if the events of the last few days since Father's visit to the farm had all the time been leading to this moment.

The shock of cold rain splashing onto my face startled me. I stood in an alley, my eyes slowly adjusting to the darkness. Then I heard the moaning again. I looked around, saw two bodies against one of the alley walls. I blinked, brushed water from my eyes, and recognised my father. With one hand he was holding a man I had not seen before against the wall; the man was barely conscious, his eyes rolled back in their sockets showing only the whites. My father's mouth was on his neck, sucking furiously. There was no blood, only the sound of air and liquid.

I don't know how long it went on for. I was aware of Cosserat moving behind me, of his own hands gently falling on my shoulders. When my father had finished feeding, he gently let the stranger slump to the ground, then turned around and saw me there for the first time.

Blood smeared his lips, whirled on his chin. The rain quickly drained the blood away.

"This is what it is like for us," he said eventually. "We are parasites, not predators, you see, and must take what we can, where we can, from whom we can."

"What ... what will happen to him?"

"He will wake a few hours from now with a headache. He will be light-headed for a few days. He will remember nothing of tonight, nothing of me."

Father looked up into the sky, let the rain fall into his open mouth. He swallowed the water in great gulps, washing away the taste of blood. When he looked at me again I could see infinite sorrow in his eyes.

"Your mother was right, you know, to take you and your brother away from me. The life I lead is filled with the blood of other people, and my past is nothing more than the story of my hunger. I would not wish it upon you."

"That hasn't always been the way," I said.

"True. I thought it would be fine to share my life with my two sons. But you are not like us; I hoped you might be, for selfish reasons."

I turned on my heel, went back inside. I didn't want to be near my father. At that moment, he repulsed me, made me feel sick to my stomach. When I got back to the table Leon was gone. Goodall was there, and told me that he and Eckert had gone for a walk.

"A walk?"

Goodall frowned, as if she realised she may already have said too much. I ran out of the steakhouse before she could say anything more. I scanned the street for a glimpse of Leon, but didn't see him. I was starting to panic, and didn't know which way to go. I forced myself to calm down, and headed north. I checked at every alley or side street, but still saw no sign of the pair. After a few minutes I crossed the road, made my way south, past the steak house. Eventually I came to a side street that was darker than any of the others, many of the overhead lights having been broken. I ran down, went past an alleyway before I realised it was there. I went back, peered in, but it was so dark I could see nothing.

And then that sound again, the helpless moaning.

"Leon?" My voice was small, barely above a whisper.

No reply. I entered the alley, took a few steps forward. Now I could make out shapes not more than ten metres from me. I forced myself to walk towards them. I recognised Eckert, standing side on to me. She was pinning a woman against the alley wall. Leon's mouth was attached to the crook of one of the victim's arms. Eckert's face was raptured, her eyes staring at the blood that pooled around Leon's mouth, dribbled to the ground.

"*No!*" I screamed, and rushed forward. I knocked Eckert aside, and as the victim collapsed I spun Leon around to face me. His face twisted in sudden rage, and he lashed out at me, his hand slamming into the side of my head. I fell back, lost my balance, and Leon was on top of me, beating at my face with his fists.

I heard Eckert scream, then saw her pull Leon off me and force him against the wall. She was tremendously strong.

"*Stop it!*" she cried. "Leon, stop it, *now!*" He stopped struggling, seemed to fall in on himself.

I picked myself up, stood there in a daze. My head felt as if it was ready to fall off my shoulders. There were running footsteps behind me. Father and Cosserat. Cosserat took one look at the scene, nodded as if agreeing with some thought he'd just had, and picked up the victim, carrying her further into the alley. He laid her down carefully, placing her arms across her body, straightening her legs.

Eckert looked at me, then at my father. "It's all right, Kathryn," he said, and she let Leon go. My brother was breathing in ragged gasps; even in the poor light I could see how white his face had become, and how bloody his teeth. Father went to him, put his hands around Leon's face and gently kissed him on the forehead.

"I'm sorry. I should never have brought you here." He looked at me, then. "I should never have brought either of you here."

* * *

Leon and I stood atop White Ridge, looking across at the curving, blue line of the Southern Highlands. The hills folded in on themselves, shadow and light making them soft as skin. It was morning, near the end of summer. Last night's rain had passed slowly over the land, leaving the grass and rocks glistening.

Our small herd of cows were milling around us, beginning to nudge at our palms. They needed milking, and soon we would need feeding. Leon and I said nothing to each other, for the moment content to be in each other's company, searching in the landscape to find something we had lost, knowing even as we did so that we would never find it.

Below us, in the steep valley of the Murrumbidgee, a mist was starting to rise. We stood there with clouds at our feet, afraid of our past, and even more afraid of our future.

AFTERWORD

"With Clouds at our Feet" is a story about pity, possibly the most destructive of emotions. It is also about fathers and sons, and how the love between them can, with distance and time, express itself as a kind of pity.

The story did not start out that way. Originally, I had intended it to be more straightforward, and quite explicitly horrific and graphically violent, but as is so often the case, the story's characters refused to follow the path I had planned for them. And they were right.

— *Simon Brown*

ABOUT THE EDITORS

JACK DANN

Jack Dann is a multiple award-winning author who has written or edited over fifty books, including the groundbreaking novels *Junction*, *Starhiker*, *The Man Who Melted*, *The Memory Cathedral* — which is an international bestseller — and the recently published Civil War novel *The Silent*.

Dann's work has been compared to Jorge Luis Borges, Roald Dahl, Lewis Carroll, Castaneda, J.G. Ballard, and Philip K. Dick. Philip K. Dick, author of the stories from which the films *Blade Runner* and *Total Recall* were made, wrote that, "*Junction* is where Ursula Le Guin's *Lathe of Heaven* and Tony Boucher's "The Quest for Saint Aquin" meet ... and yet it's an entirely new novel ... I may very well be basing some of my future work on *Junction*". Best selling author Marion Zimmer Bradley called *Starhiker* "a superb book ... it will not give up all its delights, all its perfections, on one reading".

Library Journal has called Dann: "... a true poet who can create pictures with a few perfect words". Roger Zelazny thought he was a reality magician and *Best Sellers* has said that "Jack Dann is a mind-warlock whose magicks will confound, disorient, shock, and delight". *The Washington Post Book World* compared his novel *The Man Who Melted* (published in Australia by HarperCollins in 1998) with Ingmar Bergman's film *The Seventh Seal*.

His short stories have appeared in *Omni* and *Playboy* and other major magazines and anthologies. He is the editor of the anthology *Wandering Stars*, one of the most acclaimed American anthologies of the 1970s, and several other well-known anthologies, such as *More Wandering Stars*. *Wandering Stars* has just been reprinted in the US. Dann also edits the multi-volume *Magic Tales* series with Gardner Dozois, the White Wolf *Rediscovery* series with Pamela Sargent and George Zebrowski, and is a consulting editor for TOR Books.

He is a recipient of the Nebula Award, the Aurealis Award (twice), the Ditmar Award, and the *Premios Gilgamés de Narrativa Fantastica* award. Dann has also been honoured by the Mark Twain Society (Esteemed Knight).

High Steel, a novel co-authored with Jack C. Haldeman II, was published in 1993 by TOR Books. British critic John Clute called it "a predator … a cat with blazing eyes gorging on the good meat of genre. It is most highly recommended". A sequel entitled *Ghost Dance* is in progress.

Dann's *major* historical novel about Leonardo da Vinci — entitled *The Memory Cathedral* — was first published by Bantam Books in December 1995, to rave reviews. It is has been translated into seven languages to date. It won the Australian *Aurealis Award* in 1997, was Number One on *The Age* bestseller list, and a story based on the novel was awarded the Nebula Award. *The Memory Cathedral* was also shortlisted for the *Audio Book of the Year*, which was part of the 1998 *Braille & Talking Book Library Awards*.

Morgan Llwelyn called *The Memory Cathedral* "a book to cherish, a validation of the novelist's art and fully worthy of its extraordinary subject", Lucius Shepard thought it was "an absolute triumph", and the *San Francisco Chronicle* called it "A grand accomplishment".

Dann's new novel about the American Civil War, *The Silent*, is being published by Bantam in the US, Lübbe in Germany, and HarperCollins in Australia. *Library Journal* chose it as one of their "Hot Picks" and wrote: "This is narrative storytelling at its best — so highly charged emotionally as to constitute a kind of poetry from hell. Most emphatically recommended." Peter Straub said "This tale of America's greatest trauma is full of mystery, wonder, and the kind of narrative inventiveness that makes other novelists want to hide under the bed". And *Kirkus Reviews* called it "A ferocious portrait of the Civil War's human toll".

Other scheduled books include *Counting Coup*, a contemporary road novel.

Dann's latest novel-in-progress is about James Dean.

As part of its *Bibliographies of Modern Authors Series*, The Borgo Press has published an annotated bibliography and guide entitled *The Work of Jack Dann*. A second edition is in the works. Dann is also listed in *Contemporary Authors* and the *Contemporary Authors Autobiography Series*; *The International Authors and Writers Who's Who*; *Personalities of America*; *Men of Achievement*; *Who's Who in Writers, Editors, and Poets, United States and Canada*;

Dictionary of International Biography; and the *Directory of Distinguished Americans.*

Dann lives in Melbourne, Australia and "commutes" back and forth to New York and Los Angeles.

JANEEN WEBB

Janeen Webb lectures in literature at the Australian Catholic University in Melbourne, and is internationally recognised for her critical work in speculative fiction, Australian literature and children's literature. She holds a PhD in literature from the University of Newcastle.

Her criticism has appeared in such diverse publications as *Omni*, *Foundation*, *The New York Review of Science Fiction*, *The Age*, and *Magpies*; in standard reference works such as *The Encyclopedia of Science Fiction*, the *St James Guide to Science Fiction Writers*, and *Magill's Guide to Science Fiction & Fantasy Literature*; as well as in several collections of critical articles published in Australia, the US and Europe.

Janeen was co-editor of the *Australian Science Fiction Review: Second Series*, from 1987 to 1991. This bi-monthly journal was the premier science fiction forum in Australia and had a world-wide influence on the genre: it won a Ditmar Award in 1991. She has also been Reviews Editor for *Eidolon: The Journal of Australian Science Fiction and Fantasy* and a judge for the World Fantasy Award.

Janeen's controversial book on racism in Australian fiction, *Aliens & Savages: Fiction, Politics and Prejudice in Australia*, co-authored with with Andrew Enstice, is published by HarperCollins Australia (1998). Janeen has also collaborated as editor with Andrew Enstice on *The Fantastic Self*, a collection of critical essays on fantasy and science fiction (1999). She is currently working on critical bibliographies of William Gibson and Thomas Keneally for the Borgo Press Modern Authors series (US).

Janeen has recently turned to writing fiction: her short story "Niagara Falling", co-authored with Jack Dann, won both the Aurealis Award and the Ditmar Award. Her story "Death at the Blue Elephant" was shortlisted for the *HQ Short Story Prize* and the Aurealis Award in the fantasy category. Both stories are included in *The Year's Best Australian Science Fiction & Fantasy* (Vol. 2), Jonathan Strahan and Jeremy Byrne (eds), published by HarperCollins (1998).

She is listed in such reference works as *The Who's Who of Academics in Australia; The World Who's Who of Women; International Who's Who of Intellectuals; The Dictionary of International Biography*, and *The Melbourne University Press Encyclopedia of Science Fiction and Fantasy*.

ABOUT THE ARTIST
NICK STATHOPOULOS

Nick Stathopoulos holds a BA and an LLB and is one of Australia's premier artist/illustrators. He is the winner of a mainstream Penguin television award and seven Ditmar awards for art. He has produced extensive box art and games graphics for Strategic Studies Group and worked for Hanna Barbera and Disney Australia as an artist. He has also written short fiction and is currently working on an original screenplay and concept album.

About his cover painting for *Dreaming Down-Under*, Nick writes: "The consensus brief: Depict a radically different future Australia to the sweeping desert vistas that have long become cliché. Create a cover reflecting the rich, diverse, fertile contents.

"And so I present a regenerating rainforest, ensnaring a tragic robot from an antique future. Motor functions long dead. Shiny metallic skin dull and pitted. Tiny vines snaking their way through the interstices. Separating joints. Splitting casings. Suspending entire segments in their tendrils.

"A disembodied head still sentient. An atomic brain with a half-life hundreds of generations distant from its creators, still functional. Cybernetic synapses still sparking. Lights — indicating neural function — still glowing.

"Thinking. Remembering. Dreaming.

"Dreaming Down-Under."

If you have enjoyed *Dreaming Down-Under Book One*, look out for *Dreaming Down-Under Book Two* which features more cutting edge stories from leading Australian writers of speculative fiction:

Sara Douglass
Russell Blackford
Lucy Sussex
Chris Lawson
Norman Talbot
David Lake
Rosaleen Love
Paul Collins
Cecily Scutt
Robert Hood
Kerry Greenwood
Rowena Cory Lindquist
Aaron Sterns
Ian Nichols

and a novella by the late George Turner that was unpublished at the time of his death.

Dreaming Down-Under Book Two
ISBN 073226412 X